DOVE IN THE WINDOW
Nominated for an Agatha Award for Best Novel

"Excellent . . . While the characters are perhaps the most vivid feature, setting nearly edges them out. Best of all is Benni's sharp, sassy voice."

—*Booknews*

"Fowler writes beautifully about the picturesque Central Coast, ranching, and local cuisine."

—*Booklist*

GOOSE IN THE POND
Nominated for an Agatha Award for Best Novel

"Engaging."

—*Booklist*

"Brilliantly crafted romantic suspense . . . waiting to be devoured by the reader."

—*The Mystery Zone*

"A fast, fun read that jumps into the action right from the get-go."

—*Telegram-Tribune*, San Luis Obispo, California

continued . . .

KANSAS TROUBLES
Nominated for an Agatha Award for Best Novel

"Mayhem, murder, chaos and romance . . . well-paced mystery . . . fun reading."

—*Daily Reporter*, Kansas

"Fowler's story about a sassy ex-cowgirl and quilter who loves to solve crimes . . . is a lot of fun to read. Fowler has a deft touch . . ."

—*Wichita Eagle*

IRISH CHAIN

"A TERRIFIC WHODUNIT! The dialogue is intelligent and witty, the characters intensely human, and the tantalizing puzzle keeps the pages turning."

—Jean Hager, author of *The Redbird's Cry* and *Blooming Murder*

"A BLUE-RIBBON COZY . . . This well-textured sequel to *Fool's Puzzle* . . . intricately blends social history and modern mystery."

—*Publishers Weekly*

"CHARMING, BEGUILING, AND ENTRANCING . . . *Irish Chain* is a total joy."

—*Clarion-Ledger*, Jackson, Mississippi

"A DELIGHTFUL AND WITTY MYSTERY full of endearing characters. It offers insights into quilts . . . folk art, and historical events that add depth to its multi-layered story."

—*Gothic Journal*

FOOL'S PUZZLE

Nominated for an Agatha Award for Best First Mystery

Berkley Prime Crime Books by Earlene Fowler

DOVE IN THE WINDOW

EARLENE FOWLER

BERKLEY PRIME CRIME, NEW YORK

DOVE IN THE WINDOW

A Berkley Prime Crime Book / published by arrangement with
the author

PRINTING HISTORY
Berkley Prime Crime hardcover edition / May 1998
Berkley Prime Crime mass-market edition / May 1999

The Penguin Putnam Inc. World Wide Web site address is
http://www.penguinputnam.com

ISBN: 0-425-16894-8

Berkley Prime Crime Books are published
by The Berkley Publishing Group,
a division of Penguin Putnam Inc.,
375 Hudson Street, New York, New York 10014.
The name BERKLEY PRIME CRIME and the BERKLEY PRIME CRIME
design are trademarks belonging to Penguin Putnam Inc.

PRINTED IN THE UNITED STATES OF AMERICA

10 9 8 7 6 5 4

To girlfriends
past, present and future
for the laughter and the tears

and

To Juanita
wherever you are
for what might have been

ACKNOWLEDGMENTS

No writer writes in a vacuum. Here are those to whom I owe a multitude of thanks:

For every day, for every word—thank you, Lord Jesus

For their wonderful support—booksellers and librarians everywhere

For courage and stamina on the literary battlefield—my editor, Judith Palais, and my agent, Deborah Schneider

For specialized help and/or comfort—Mary Atkinson, Bonnie Barrett-Wolf, Ginny Debolt, Justine and Jim Dunn, Joy Fitzhugh, Jim and Elaine Gardiner, Karen Gray, Christine Hill, Debra Jackson, Ann Lee, Jo-Ann Mapson, Charlene Marie, Leslie and Joe Patronik

For long and loyal friendship—Jan Annigoni, Kandi Bradley, Juli Scherer

And to my husband, Allen, for always being there. It's been an old-fashioned love song from the moment we met.

DOVE IN THE WINDOW

Dove in the Window is an intricate star pattern made of primarily diamond shapes that give it a sharp, exacting look. Probably of East Coast origin, the early nineteenth-century pattern in one of its many forms presents a picture suggestive of birds resting beak to beak. The design is said to have derived its name from the days when everyone had barns with dovecotes—round holes cut in the gable and a tiny platform beneath—all for the accommodation of pet pigeons. Each square can contain as many as fifty-six pieces, making it a time-consuming pattern not suggested for the impatient quilter. Some other names for the pattern are: Flying Star, Four Doves, Bluebirds for Happiness, Bird of Paradise, Mother's Choice, Flying Fish, Crow's Foot, and Crossroads.

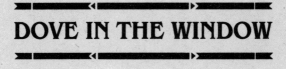

DOVE IN THE WINDOW

1

"YOU SOLD ME?" Elvia shrieked. She slapped her tea cup down into the saucer. "Like one of your cows?"

I swear one of my kitchen windows rattled.

My ever-supportive husband's deep and melodious laugh reverberated from the living room of our tiny Spanish-style bungalow. No doubt a smug "I-told-you-so" from a certain chief of police resided in my immediate future.

I held my hands palms out in entreaty to my best friend since second grade. "Try and think of it as a short-term lease." Then I darted out of her reach, placing my sturdy pine kitchen table between us.

"Benni Harper, I'm going to kill you," she said. Her black eyes flashed, and it occurred to me that repressed in her genetic memory might lurk some incredibly painful means to accomplish that task. Was it the Spanish Conquistadors or Native Americans who smeared their enemies' naked bodies with honey and tied them to ant hills? Well, what she didn't recall genetically, she'd make up for with torture techniques she'd learned being the only female sibling among six males.

"It's just one night," I said, contemplating the distance to the knife drawer. I ran faster than she did in grade school.

Could my thirty-five-year-old legs still beat her? "A few hours. You'll like him." I gave an encouraging smile. "Besides, as your own dear mama has often said, you're getting kinda old. You really should consider Emory. He's very handsome. You'd make beautiful babies."

She glared at me. "He's a geek."

"Geek? No one uses that word anymore, and besides, the last time you saw him he was eleven years old. He's thirty-four now—all grown up. Elvia, I had to offer him something. It was for a good cause. The information he found for me helped solve two murders."

She sipped her Earl Grey tea and continued giving me the evil eye. I considered telling her how attractive she looks when she's angry, then decided that was pushing my luck. My best friend, Elvia Aragon, really is a breathtakingly beautiful woman. A combination of Armani elegance and Latina sensuality wrapped up in a perfect size three. She's smart, too. And law abiding. I was hoping that last trait would not be compromised by my small but audacious act.

Because I had indeed sold her lock, stock, and Charles Jourdan pumps to one Emory Delano Littleton of Sugartree, Arkansas. Well, at least her services for one night. A date. That's all. Kiss not included, unless Emory could weasel one out of her, which I wouldn't put past him. He's got a real way about him, ole Emory does.

Emory is my cousin. Sort of. In that weird, meandering way only Southerners truly understand. His grandfather and my dad's grandfather were first cousins by marriage. And, to make the connection even more complex, Emory's father, Boone Emory Littleton (famous all over northeastern Arkansas for his smoked chicken company—Boone's Good Eatin' Chicken), married my mother's third cousin, Ervalean, after they met at my mother and father's wedding. Cousin Ervalean died when Emory was eleven, and Emory stayed that summer at our ranch outside San Celina on the Central Coast of California while his father closed every bar in Little Rock. After three months of trying to drown his sorrow in innumerable bottles of expensive Kentucky bourbon, Boone was saved at a tent revival and called Emory back home.

I'd seen my cousin since on my occasional trips back to Arkansas with my gramma Dove to visit her sister, Garnet, but he's never returned to California mostly because he's afraid to fly. That's why I felt safe offering Elvia's services when I needed Emory to use his extensive and often suspiciously gained journalistic contacts throughout the South to help me with a couple of murder investigations I'd stumbled into. He'd had a crush on Elvia since he first set his green Southern eyes on her that summer twenty-three years ago. Even at twelve Elvia was turning men's brains to mush.

"Emory's changed a lot since he was eleven," I said, setting a plate of her favorite almond scones from Stern's Bakery in front of her. "And he really did help me. Think of it as a public service." I'd been rehearsing this talk for two weeks, ever since getting the phone call from Emory informing me he was joining the Ramsey clan for Thanksgiving at the ranch this year. His train would arrive at six P.M. on Wednesday. Which was today.

"Nevertheless, I'm going to kill you," she said, her voice determined. Only someone who knew her as well as me would hear the tinge of resignation in her tone. I released my held breath, knowing I'd won. But I'd owe her big for this favor, and she wouldn't hesitate calling it in when it was to her greatest advantage. Knowing when to fight and when to temporarily concede was one of the traits that had turned her bookstore and coffeehouse, Blind Harry's, into one of the most powerful independent bookstores in California.

"Is it safe to reenter the arena?" Gabe stuck his head around the corner of the kitchen door, his deep-set gray-blue eyes inquiring behind round, gold-rimmed glasses. You'd think someone who'd been a cocky Marine grunt in Vietnam, a fearless undercover narcotics cop in East L.A., and was currently San Celina's chief of police would behave a little less like the Wizard of Oz's cowardly lion. That conveys a bit of the power of Elvia's personality.

He said something to Elvia in Spanish that made her red lips part into a tiny reluctant smile.

"No fair," I said. "Speak English."

"Don't worry," Elvia told him. "I'll wait until you leave before murdering her. Then you can send one of your underlings to investigate."

He entered the kitchen, tying his conservative gray-and-blue silk tie. "Good. I've got enough to worry about with all the San Celina Heritage Days security. Try and make it neat. I don't have time to mop the floor this week." He leaned over and kissed me, then rubbed his five-day growth of black-and-silver beard across my cheek. Combined with his gray Brooks Brothers suit and white dress shirt, the beard looked incongruous and a bit sexy. Just a slight deviation from what I call his Sergeant Friday look.

"Ouch," I said, pushing him away. "You're packing a lethal weapon there."

"You're the one who talked me into entering this ridiculous beard-growing contest, so you'll have to suffer, too." He scratched his face vigorously with his knuckles. "So, when does the big date ensue?"

Elvia and I spoke at the same time.

"Never," she said.

"This week," I said.

Gabe laughed out loud.

"Please," I begged her. "I'll hand wash and wax your precious Austin-Healy. I'll work at the bookstore during the next five Christmas seasons. I'll pick every flea out of Sweet William's coat with tweezers." Sweet William was her newly inherited championship Persian cat.

She stood up and picked up her leather briefcase. "Sweet William has never had a flea in his life. You owe me *mucho grande, gringa loca.* Grand Canyon big. Pavarotti big. A bigness of global proportions."

I scooted around the table and hugged her. "Thank you, thank you, thank you. You are the queen of best friends. He'll behave himself, I promise." *I hope* was what I was actually thinking. "Are you coming to the barbecue on Friday afternoon?"

Every year since I can remember, my dad, the oldest of the six Ramsey kids, and his mother, my gramma Dove, have hosted a barbecue at the Ramsey Ranch the day after Thanksgiving for all our friends and family. It coincided with our four-day, no-holds-barred-kick-em-in-the-nuts-when-they're-down poker tournament and semiannual calf roundup. California's Central Coast, having the mildest weather around, didn't have to adhere to the traditional spring roundup common in colder states, and besides, Daddy always liked to get a head start on castrating our calves before they grew too big. To keep his young ranch hands happy, though, he always saved some for the spring so we could have an old-fashioned roundup complete with roping and riding and Rocky Mountain Oysters. But every November, my uncles and aunts left their ranches and came from all over the West to participate in this Thanksgiving ritual of food, cards, and cattle. For four days the ranch looked like a cross between a scout camp, small-town rodeo, and a two-star RV park. I didn't attend last year because I couldn't endure the family crowd after losing my husband, Jack, the February before in an auto accident. But it had been almost two years since Jack was killed, and this year I was attending with Gabriel Ortiz, my new husband, a complex and wonderful gift that God, with more than a little amusement, I imagine, dropped into my life when I least expected it.

Elvia pushed me away, straightening her cinnamon-colored Armani knit suit. "Don't try to make up to me. And, yes, the whole Aragon clan will be there. We haven't missed one in twenty-eight years, have we?" She patted her black hair, arranged this morning in an elegant French twist. "Just keep Emory away from me. I'll agree to a short dinner on the day of *my* choosing. That's it. I don't want him pawing all over me at the barbecue." She pointed at the scones. "I've got things to do. Wrap mine up to go."

"Yes, ma'am," I said, pulling a plastic bag from the drawer. "I promise to keep him occupied. You might be surprised, though. He's quite a personable man now." I held out the wrapped scones, giving her a wide smile.

"He's from Arkansas," she said with a disdainful sniff. She grabbed the bag and stuck it in her briefcase. "Tell Dove happy Thanksgiving for me. See you Friday. Mama's bringing tamales."

"Bless her," Gabe said with a sigh.

She scowled at him. "You know, I actually thought you might be able to control her."

"Better people than me have tried and failed," he said, unperturbed.

"Boy," I said, pouring myself another cup of coffee after she left. "That was close. I thought she was going to leave me flapping in the breeze."

"She should have," he said, reaching into the Stern's Bakery bag and pulling out a cranberry scone. "It really was presumptuous of you."

"So you've told me a few hundred times. But it worked. A female general I saw interviewed on television one time said it's easier sometimes to ask forgiveness than permission . . . or something like that."

"That could be your motto," he said, his voice not a little ironic.

"Ah, take your scones and go to work, Chief Ortiz," I said, kissing him good-bye. "Before crime overtakes the fair streets of San Celina."

After he left, I pulled on my boots and grabbed my worn sheepskin jacket. San Celina had been going through an early cold snap, unusual for the Central Coast, and the days had not gotten much above sixty degrees. When I called and informed my Aunt Kate of that fact, she just laughed. She and my Uncle Rex live in Rock Springs, Wyoming, where sixty degrees in winter is short-sleeve, get-out-your-barbecue kind of weather. They, as well as the rest of my gramma Dove's kids, were due at the ranch tonight. But I had a million things to do before then and only about eight hours to get them done.

I climbed into my old red Harper's Herefords Chevy pickup that I'd finally reclaimed from Gabe's son, Sam, since he had, with the help of his father, bought a 1965 Chevy Malibu. Now that Sam was living at my dad's ranch rather than with us and had a new job at Elvia's bookstore, he and Gabe managed to go for as long as two or three days without sniping at each other. With Sam's plans to attend Cal Poly in the spring, it appeared my stepson was going to be a permanent fixture in my life, for a while anyway. As is not uncommon with nineteen-year-olds, he got along fine with everyone except his parents, and he and I had become friends in the way that two people who share a common passion do. We were both intensely committed to figuring out that person who was his father and my husband, and we loved Gabe deeply, though it was often easier for me to admit it.

This was going to be a busy week and a half for Gabe and me. As curator of our local folk art museum, the Josiah Sinclair Folk Art Museum and Artists Co-op, I was smack-dab in the middle of the San Celina Heritage Days celebration. The co-op had aligned with the women in the Fine Arts Guild to run concurrently a women's western art show. We'd been given a grant from the city as well as from our local NOW chapter and were committed to educating the public about the contributions that women had made and were continuing to make in the western art field. The official start of Heritage Days and the art show was the Monday after the Thanksgiving weekend and culminated with a parade, fiesta, and western dance a week from Saturday.

The museum was presenting a special exhibit on loan from a sister folk art museum in Eugene, Oregon, of nineteenth-century pioneer quilts, most women's only means of artistic expression during the long trek across the West. Our smaller, upstairs gallery spotlighted some of our co-op's own western artists and an antique cloth doll exhibit. Though the exhibits were finished, there were always last minute details that needed to be ironed out before an opening, and as usual our artists would be selling their wares at the Thursday night farmer's market as well as at the fiesta on Saturday. That meant I had to make sure that everyone knew their booth assignments and that the booths and canopies were in good shape and that all the artists were at peace. Well, as much at peace as forty very different, and often temperamental, artists could be. My job was, I had discovered after long, lazy Sunday-morning-in-bed talks with Gabe, very similar to his. We both spent a good deal of our time trying to keep divergent groups of people happy. There were days when I wholeheartedly missed full-time ranch life. Cattle were at least fairly predictable, possessing only a limited number of tricks up their bovine sleeves. Humans were an entirely different creature to figure out and never ceased to amaze me with their creative ways of driving each other crazy. And now that I was the police chief's wife, there was a whole other aspect to my life I'd never anticipated. One that included cocktail parties, charity balls, endless social chitchat, and the wearing of fancy clothes. None of those things had ever been on my list of favorite activities, but I was trying my best to at least not be a liability to Gabe's career, having long abandoned the idea that I'd be an asset.

The museum was already bustling with activity when I pulled into the parking lot. The old two-story Sinclair Hacienda, donated by our local patroness of the arts, Constance Sinclair, had become as familiar to me now as the old truck

I was driving and almost as well loved. If someone had told me three years ago that at thirty-five I'd be living in town, running a folk art museum while trying to juggle a marriage to San Celina's chief of police, I'd have informed them the state mental hospital was thirty miles up the road and that maybe they'd better check in for a little testing. But here I was, and though at odd moments when my late husband Jack's smiling face popped into my mind and sadness froze a section of my heart, I was amazed and grateful at where I'd ended up.

"Four more days," a young potter named Julio commented. We passed each other on the ivy-covered arbored walkway between the museum and the old adobe stables that now comprised the co-op's studios and my cramped but comfortable office. Pale November sunlight dappled his wavy black hair.

"We'll be ready," I answered with a smile. Exhibits didn't tie my stomach into knots the way they did my first few months as curator, though a jittery edge of pre-event anticipation still lingered. I was ready for the crowds this time and looking forward to the week-long celebration of our county's heritage and the Mission Santa Celine's two-hundred-twentieth anniversary.

Spread across my desk was today's *San Celina Tribune*, placed there as it was every morning by my sixty-eight-year-old assistant D-Daddy Boudreaux—the only person who'd managed to keep the part-time job longer than a few months. On the front page was a story about the most controversial subject since a local well-known grower of marijuana ran for mayor two years ago.

San Celina or Santa Celine? Is Historical Correctness More Important than the Homeless?

Apparently a group of people affiliated with the Historical Society had decided that our town's name, the improperly monikered San Celina, should be returned to the proper Santa Celine to match the mission's and honor the French saint the mission was named after. Most people in the town, myself included, never gave much thought about why the names didn't match, figuring it was one of those government snafus that just happened. Research conducted by a local historian revealed that back in the early 1900s the town was renamed by a Texas millionaire who wanted to honor his hometown of Celina, Texas. Seeing as he owned most of downtown and all the city council, that change was accomplished without much argument. Obviously nobody involved was adept at proper masculine/feminine grammar in the Spanish language. But the Texan was long dead and his relatives scattered, so one faction of the Historical Society was determined to set things right. Local Latino groups also strongly supported the change back to grammatical and historical correctness. On the opposite side was a socially conscious group that didn't believe in spending money that could be better used to help finance and run the new homeless shelter or fix potholes in the streets. The measure hadn't garnered enough signatures to be included on the ballot in early November, so a new assault was obviously being launched for a special election.

I was finishing the article when the door to my office flew open.

"Look at these," Shelby Johnson said, shoving a stack of black-and-white photographs in front of me. "I'm so stoked I could dance on your desk. They're going to get published in a major magazine, I just know it. Especially after the photos I'll take at the barbecue this weekend." She nervously pulled on the long dark braid draped over her shoulder and flashed a smile that probably cost her parents what some of our county's migrant workers made in two years. "What do you think?"

I picked up the eight-by-ten of me bottle feeding an orphan calf while another calf poked its head through the slats of the stall to stare at us hungrily. To be honest, she'd managed to capture an expression of vulnerability on my face that slightly embarrassed me. It felt as if she had uncovered a part of me I usually kept hidden. Which was why she was such a talented photographer. A senior at Cal Poly, she'd spent countless days these last few months at the ranch recording her images of me—a typical western ranch woman, if there is such an animal. In essence, I was her senior project.

Born and bred in the wealthy suburbs of Chicago, Shelby grew up in love with the romantic cowgirl images of Calamity Jane, Annie Oakley, and Dale Evans. As soon as she graduated from high school, she applied to colleges all over the West and finally settled on Cal Poly because of San Celina's western flavor as well as the university's excellent photography department. She had confided in me during our days at the ranch that her parents, both successful heart surgeons, were disappointed in her choice of career and university.

"But I'm their only daughter, so I get away with murder," she'd said, her brown eyes sparkling with mischief. She had three older brothers, all studying to be doctors. "I'm the family's greatest unspoken disappointment," she told me cheerfully. "That's okay because they need something to complain about. My brothers are all so perfect." Then she'd lift her expensive Leica camera and snap another picture of me. In time, I became so accustomed to her camera, I didn't react with my customary frozen smile.

"Getting your subject to forget you're there is a very important part of being a photographer," she'd told me once. "I think it's where most photographers fail, and their photographs look stiff and rehearsed."

"I look like crap in most of yours," I'd complained.

"No, you don't," she replied. "You look just like what you are, a ranch woman who loves her animals and her land."

I spread the eight-by-ten prints across my desk. They were good, I had to admit. Really good. She was having her first show in a gallery downtown this week, sharing the featured artist status with another of our local artists, Greer Shannon, whose family had owned ranch land here in San Celina County since the Spanish land grant days. Shelby was hoping not only to make some sales, but also to catch the eye of some of the San Francisco and Los Angeles art critics and dealers coming into town for our much publicized women's western art show.

"Roland's putting this one in the window," she said, her voice squeaking with excitement. She pointed to the photograph of me and the calves. Roland Bennett, a recent immigrant from San Francisco, had opened his gallery—Bennett's Gallery of Western Art—two years ago. He claimed to be a distant relative of Buffalo Bill and loved wearing chamois-colored fringed jackets in honor of his flashy ancestor. Though I found him to be a bit pretentious and too Hollywood-kiss-kiss familiar with anyone he suspected of any social or economic importance, to his credit he had wholeheartedly supported women artists and was showing only women's art in his gallery this month. I suspected his interest was more monetary than a deep concern for equal rights, but as Dove would say, when someone's offering you free manure for your garden, don't complain about the odor.

"That's great," I said. "I hope you sell some of these, even though the thought of me in my dirty jeans as a centerfold in a national magazine is not exactly my lifelong dream."

"It would be nice to get a small pat on the head from the AMA," she said, flopping down in one of my black vinyl visitor chairs. She referred to her family collectively as the American Medical Association and said the only artistic genes they possessed were the Ralph Laurens they wore on weekends. Her dark-lashed eyes skimmed over mine, then looked back down at the buckskin-covered photograph album she held, but not before I caught the glimpse of hurt. She only talked about her family in the lightest, most teasing terms, making jokes about what a source of mortification she was to her parents and brothers. Her unconcerned act didn't fool me one bit, and my heart went out to her. When you're twenty, whether you like it or not, your family's opinions still form a big part of your self-image. But after getting to know her over the last couple of months, I guessed that she'd eventually discover who she was and learn to live with an acceptance of both herself and her family. For a split second, I didn't envy Shelby's flawless young complexion and was thankful to be halfway on the other side of thirty.

"They'll come around," I said. "In the meantime, you just follow your heart. You have real talent, Shelby. There's not a person in the world who can look at your photographs and not know that."

Her moist-eyed, grateful look was heartbreaking. "Somehow I feel like if I could get them in a magazine, maybe the AMA will take me seriously."

I looked back down at her photograph of me leaning against a fence post after shoeing a horse. I was wearing my stained leather chaps and a thin white tank top and held a dripping bottle of Coca-Cola against my neck. In the dim background, Gabe stood half hidden in the barn's shadows, watching me with an expression of desire that caused my neck to warm slightly from the intimacy. My neck warmed slightly from the intimacy she captured in that one second.

"Your work is always so surprising," I said, quickly turning the photograph over. "*And* you're a little sneak."

An impish smile appeared. "In all my photos I like to have a little unexpected surprise for the viewer." She placed the leather-covered photo album she held on my desk. "I made this for you. They're copies of my best shots. I even made the album myself. Copied one I saw in a fancy pants western catalog. I'm not through with you yet, but I wanted to say thanks for letting me tag along for the last couple of months and for inviting me to the barbecue on Friday.''

I took the album and ran my fingers across the smooth leather. She'd painted my brand on the front and decorated the leather with bits of bone and feathers.

"Oh, Shelby, it's beautiful," I said. "I'll treasure it always. Thank you. You know, you're going to have a ball. My family's a bunch of hams, so you'd better bring along lots of film.''

"Great! I can't wait. I know I'll get some good stuff.''

"We'll do our best to look interesting," I said, laughing. "We're tagging, vaccinating, and castrating. Ought to be some intriguing situations there somewhere." I looked at her curiously. "What are you doing for Thanksgiving?" I assumed she wasn't flying home if she was going to be here on Friday. "You're more than welcome to come on tomorrow, too. We're cooking four twenty-pound turkeys.''

"Thanks, but Kip and I are splurging and spending the night at the San Celina Inn. Breakfast in a canopied bed and a fancy Thanksgiving dinner with someone else doing the dishes. Then we're going up to the hills near Lake Santa Flora to take pictures of condors or whatever wildlife surfaces. I'm trying to teach him how to shoot something besides a gun.''

"You and Kip are still an item, huh?" Kip was one of my dad's ranch hands, a young man from Montana who had worked for Daddy about six months now. His family owned a ranch north of Billings, but he'd grown tired of the cold weather and was hoping to buy a small spread in California eventually. According to Daddy, he was a young man of few words, but a darn hard worker. There was no higher praise from my dad.

"Front page and in color," she said, gathering up the photographs in front of me. "He's such a babe. And he thinks I'm smart. I can't tell you how great it is not to be afraid that everything that comes out of my mouth is considered stupid and inane.''

I studied her for a moment, trying to imagine coming from a family where you didn't feel like you fit. No one could blame her for picking a college as far away from them as possible in a place they wouldn't even consider visiting.

''Gotta go,'' she said, jumping up with the never-ending energy and exuberance of youth. ''See you Friday. Should I bring anything?''

''Just your appetite.''

Five minutes later, I was still flipping through the album, admiring her craftsmanship and artistry while lamenting the unglamorous shots she caught of me when my door swung open again. This was the reason I rarely attempted paperwork in my office anymore. When I was here I felt a great deal like Lucy in the Peanuts comic strip sitting in her five-cent psychiatric booth with the sign stating ''The Doctor is In.'' I stuck the album in my large bottom drawer and turned to my visitor.

''Hey, Madam Curator, how're they hanging?'' she asked. Greer Shannon, her fifty-four-year-old face a road map of sun-created wrinkles, grinned at me with strong ivory teeth. Her luxurious, pearl-white hair made me envy the other side of the age line for a moment. If I just had Shelby's complexion and Greer's hair . . .

''They ain't,'' I said. ''And I thank the Lord for that.''

''Amen and hallelujah.'' She stuck her hands deep into her tight sapphire-blue Wranglers. A fancy silver and gold belt buckle winked under the bright florescent lights. ''Did you see those pictures Shelby took of you? Gorgeous. I mean the scenery, of course. That little gal is a real, honest-to-goodness talent.''

''I agree.''

Greer sighed. ''Oh, to be that young and on the cusp of a brilliant career.''

I pointed over at the chair Shelby just vacated. ''Plant

your old bones down and quit your belly-aching. You're no slouch in the artistic area yourself.''

"These bones are tired," she said, sitting down. "I painted until two A.M.''

Though she'd grown up on the Central Coast, Greer had only been a part of San Celina's local art scene for the last three years. Her family, the Montoya-Shannons, were some of the old time settlers in San Celina. The family ranch, off Highway 46, was some of the richest and most accessible ranch and crop land in the county. At ten thousand acres, it was also one of the largest ranches. Like me, she'd spent her childhood on the ranch, leaving in her twenties to marry an oil executive in San Francisco. She lived in the city for the last thirty years where she'd taught and studied art, coming home three years ago after a messy divorce involving her husband and a nineteen-year-old file clerk. But Greer never spoke of her life in San Francisco, except in the most casual and general way. Though from one of what I call the "A" families in the ranching community, she never held airs like some others in that group and was well liked in the co-op. She pitched in without complaining whenever there was a cleanup day or someone needed a ride home or ten bucks for groceries.

She lived in a large, airy cabin about ten miles north of San Celina near the small town of Frio, whose only claim to fame besides the post office was a rowdy, rustic bar that attracted tourists and locals alike. She painted large, beautiful oils depicting ranch life, her specialty showing women and their often mystical and inexplicable relationship with their horses. Her paintings were exquisite in their detail, showing horses rolling, scratching, fighting, running, mating, and giving birth—always with a woman's presence in the background. The details were so striking, so real, it made you ache to run your hand down the flanks of her horses or jump on one and ride forever. She'd recently started making a name for herself, and only a week ago she'd burst into my office to tell me about being interviewed by a new but prestigious western art magazine called *Rosettes*, named for the flower-shaped, decorative pieces of leather found on a saddle or bridle. A gallery in Scottsdale, Arizona, had also inquired about showing her paintings—a real feather in her artistic cap.

"Are you ready for next week?" I asked, leaning back in my chair.

She sighed and leaned over to smooth down the curling fringe on the toe of her deerskin ropers. "As ready as I'll ever be. I don't think an artist is ever *really* ready to expose her work to the public. Roland's done a fine job with the exhibit, though. Shelby's work looks great. You are coming to the reception Sunday night, aren't you?" Greer was Roland's featured fine artist for the show, and he had promised an abundance of wealthy collectors would be there to view her latest works.

"Do I have to wear a dress?"

She grinned. "I'm not going to, but then I'm the temperamental artist. *You're* the prominent society wife. Ask your husband."

I shot her a loud raspberry. "I'll wash the cow crap off my boots. That's as much as I can promise."

"Why, Ms. Harper, I'm touched. I truly am."

"You're touched, all right. But then, insanity is a requirement for brilliant artists, isn't it?"

"If you're not crazy to begin with, you'll get that way after dealing with critics and patrons and gallery owners. I swear, they're worse than cattle people, and we know how temperamental *they* can be." She stood up and slapped her hand down on my desk. "What time's the fun start on Friday?"

"If you want breakfast you'd better show up around six. The actual work will start about seven. We're not doing too many calves—about fifty or so. It's more so Daddy can play cowboy with his brothers rather than actually get any work done. The barbecue will probably start about two, and we're expecting about two hundred people this year. My relatives are a rowdy bunch of characters, so you should be able to take a few good pictures.'' Like many painters, Greer took hundreds of photographs, using them as points of departure for her paintings. I found the contrast between her colorful, sometimes lovingly idealized view of ranch life and Shelby's stark black-and-white realism fascinating. And ironic, considering their backgrounds. Roland combining them in an exhibit was brilliant.

''Good. I need inspiration for a new series I'm contem-plating on the working ranch horse.'' She pointed a finger pistol at me and headed for the door. ''Save me some of Dove's Louisiana hot sausage.''

I held up both hands. ''Can't make any promises when it comes to Dove's sausage. I'd set my alarm if I were you.''

''These days I'm an artist first, rancher second. I don't do alarms.'' She stepped through the doorway, her hearty laugh echoing down the hall.

I typed up a few letters that couldn't wait, then made a tour of the pioneer quilt exhibit. We'd taken out extra in-surance this time, an additional expense that had stretched our working funds until they squealed, so this was the first time we were charging admission—a mere three dollars—but admission nevertheless. It was a big step for us, but in the last year our city grants had slowly dwindled away as other, equally worthy projects were given a financial hand. Just staying even had been our goal for the year I'd been curating, but now we needed to start showing a profit to make up for the government funds that would eventually dry up. I straightened up a pile of brochures, then locked the double Spanish doors behind me. The studios would be closed by whichever co-op member was overseer of the week.

After a quick call on the new cellular phone that Gabe had finally convinced me to carry to verify with Maggie, his secretary, that as of that moment—two P.M.—he had not, as I'd suspected, had lunch, I swung by Baja Willie's and bought three shrimp tacos, a grilled chicken burrito, and an order of beef taquitos with extra guacamole.

When Rod, the civilian receptionist at the police department, buzzed me through the door, I almost tripped over the thirty-pound doorstop on the other side. I caught the bag of food before it hit the gray linoleum floor. Harry's head slowly came up, rotated from side to side, sniffed, then eased back down when he realized that no actual food products had hit the ground.

"Harry," I scolded the huge, black-and-white tuxedo cat who resembled a sluggish cop car more than an elegantly dressed man. "You need to seriously consider Weight Watchers."

His tail flicked once, then he closed his eyes, giving my statement the importance he deemed it deserved. He'd been a stray found at a drug bust by one of the detectives who had a soft spot for cats. Such a soft spot he had seven, and his wife put her foot down about adopting number eight. So he brought the skinny, almost feral cat down to the station, and everyone in the police department immediately fell in love with his I-don't-give-a-shit-about-any-needs-but-my-own attitude.

"A real cop's cat," more than one of the office clerks had commented. In less than a year Harry had become the Nero Wolfe of cats, thanks to the tidbits fed to him by everyone. It was rumored his favorite foods were gin-soaked olives (though only the green ones), peanuts, and donuts with rainbow sprinkles. Though Rod, a serious animal lover, desperately tried to get people to understand that a cat needs a regular, balanced diet of veterinarian-approved cat chow, Harry's size pretty much showed how much stock people put into that information.

Gabe called him "Gato Gordo" and basically ignored the rules that stated no animals except seeing-eye dogs were allowed on city property during business hours. He had, in the last few months, become much more relaxed as a police chief, which vastly improved the morale of his employees.

The door to his office was open, so I called a quick hello to Maggie, the only woman on earth who could order Gabe around without any back talk from him, and then I headed into his office. He sat behind his large oak desk, fingers locked behind his head, laughing at a comment made in Spanish by Jim Cleary, one of his two captains and his next-in-command. Jim was a slow-talking, handsome black man in his middle fifties who, as a result of his years with the LAPD Gang Detail, spoke Spanish as fluently as Gabe. His wife, Oneeda, was a good friend and quilting partner of mine.

They both smiled mischievously at me.

"Speak of the devil," Gabe said.

"I thought I felt my ears burning," I said, setting the white bag down on his desk next to the miniature blue Corvette with SCPD painted on the side of it. His officers had given it to him for his forty-third birthday this year. "This is how our hard-earned tax dollars are spent. Paying city employees to sit around and malign the good names of upstanding citizens."

Jim stood up and slipped his arm around my shoulder, giving me an affectionate hug. "Your husband was just telling me of your near-death experience this morning with your friend Elvia."

I smiled up at his grizzled face. Apparently he'd been talked into entering the beard-growing contest also. "*No problema.* I've been handling her since second grade."

He raised his eyebrows.

"Well," I admitted, "if you do find my body in the bulrushes somewhere, just make sure she gets punished. Making her move down from a platinum American Express card to a gold one should be severe enough. By the way, are you and Oneeda coming Friday?"

He shook his head. "She's had a bad week, so we're just staying in this long weekend. I'm going to get a bunch of movies and a case of microwave popcorn." Oneeda had multiple sclerosis, and her condition was about as predictable as a renegade cow. Jim handled the mercurial aspects of their life with a patience and good humor that seemed almost miraculous to me at times.

"Sounds fun," I said. "It'll certainly be more relaxed than our weekend. I love our family gatherings, but they are not without their speed bumps."

"How well I know that," he replied. He was the father of four children, all grown now and scattered about the country.

"Give her a hug and kiss for me and tell her I'll have a truckload of family gossip for her next Friday."

"Will do," he said. He nodded at Gabe. "I'll get that game plan on your desk by five." I heard him pause at Maggie's desk on his way out and tease her about her latest love—a Black Angus-Hereford cross bull named Maxwell. She and her sister leased a small ranch up north around Frio, and Maxwell was their first large investment. Maggie, fresh from Cal Poly with a degree in Agricultural Management, hoped to ranch full time someday.

"This looks great," Gabe said, tearing open the bags. "I'm starved."

"You shouldn't go so long without eating," I nagged like a good wife.

He sprinkled salsa over one shrimp taco and took a big bite. "We're swamped. I completely forgot."

"What game plan was Jim talking about?"

"The security for the parade and Heritage Days celebrations. There are so many things going on at so many different times and places, our officers are going to be stretched to the limit. Even with the reserves on duty." He stuck a tortilla chip in his mouth. "I still wish the city council hadn't approved that women's western art show to coincide with the Heritage Days. Things will be twice as crowded.''

I pointed a chip at him. ''That's the whole idea. We're hoping to give the women artists as much exposure as possible. You wouldn't believe how much prejudice there is against them in the western art field. We're hoping that shows like this catch on and that women gain more acceptance in the general western art marketplace.''

''I know,'' he said, chewing thoughtfully. ''It just makes my job that much harder.''

''You are a wonderful, wonderful man and a top-notch chief of police. I and all women in the western art world will be forever in your debt.''

His expression turned hopeful. ''I like the sound of you being in my debt. I'll keep that in mind for later on tonight.''

''Not tonight, my oh-so-eager Latin lover. I'm due at the train station to pick up Emory at six o'clock, then it's on to the ranch. Your bag is packed and waiting for you at home. I'll see you there.''

''The bed in your room at the ranch is fine with me even if it is only a queen.''

''Guess again, buddy. I guess I forgot to tell you the rules of the Ramsey Family Hoedown and Roundup.''

''Rules?''

''For the four-day holiday, the women claim the ranch house, and the men bunk wherever they can manage to spread their bedroll. I bought you a new sleeping bag for the occasion. It's supposed to keep you warm as a fresh baked muffin for temperatures down to forty degrees below zero.''

''Sleeping bag?'' he said, sitting forward in his black chair, alarm widening his gray-blue eyes.

''There's only six beds in the bunkhouse, so I'd get there early if I were you and claim one. Believe me, they go fast. Maybe you could call Sam and bribe him to throw his hat over one and save it for you.''

''You never told me we'd be separated for four days.''

"Not the days, only the nights," I said cheerfully. "We discovered a long time ago it was too complicated trying to arrange sleeping accommodations for couples, so we made this a gender-separate weekend. The house is off limits to menfolks over the age of six from ten P.M. to seven A.M."

"Why do the women get the warm, comfortable house?"

I bit an end off my taquito, rolled my eyes, and didn't answer.

"I haven't slept *en masse* since Vietnam," he complained.

"It'll do you good. Make you appreciate me more."

He took a bite of his burrito. "I think this tradition of yours stinks, but I guess I won't be the only man howling at the moon for the next four days."

"I guarantee it. Actually, we've found this weekend works wonders for ailing marriages. There's something about kissing your girl goodnight on the ranch house porch and having to go back to a group of equally horny men that makes you all reconsider the word Thanksgiving."

"How's your cousin Emory going to fit into this weekend warrior mix? He doesn't sound like the type of guy who'll blend in with the macho posturing of the traditional western male."

"Don't you worry about Emory. He can hold his own with you guys. The things I could tell you . . ."

He finished his burrito, then crumpled the wrapper and tossed it in the open bag. "But not right now. I've got a ton of paperwork to do before I take off for the ranch. And you, *querida*, are a distraction."

"And the day I stop being one to you, Friday, is the day I really gotta worry." I picked up my purse and blew him a kiss.

After a few minutes at Maggie's desk admiring pictures of Maxwell in all his 1,896-pound glory, I headed out the front door, taking a giant step over Harry, who appeared to have not twitched a whisker since I came in.

"I worry about you," I told him. "I truly do."

Don't bother, his reclining posture replied.

I drove home and finished up my packing, throwing my duffel bag in the back of my truck and informing my next-door neighbor, Mr. Treton, where Gabe and I would be the next four days.

"I'll keep a lookout," he said, giving me a crisp salute. Seventy-eight-year-old Mr. Treton fancied himself the unofficial guard of our small, tree-lined street. A career Army man, I'd never seen him anything but spit-shined and polished. "I'm in the parade next week," he said with a bit of uncustomary pride.

"Cool," I said. "On which float?"

"The VFW," he said. "We've been working on it for a month. I'm their featured rider since I'm the oldest veteran. I'll be in full dress uniform."

"You can still fit in it?" I said, impressed.

"Of course, my dear girl," he said, his bayonet-sharp features looking somewhat insulted. "I'm *Army.*"

That was a poke at Gabe, who argued good-naturedly with Mr. Treton over our common hedge about the superiority of the Marines over the Army.

"Well," I said, lowering my voice into a confidential tone, "don't tell Gabe I told you, but he can't fit into his anymore." I didn't mention that Gabe had weighed a sinewy 150 pounds when he was eighteen—not nearly enough for his six-foot frame. He looked much better now at 180 solid, masculine pounds. His fanatical jogging and three-times-weekly weight lifting at the police gym gave him a healthier body now than I'm sure he had at eighteen. Still, this gave Mr. Treton something to razz Gabe about.

I put the Yankee Cake I'd baked last night on the truck's front seat and wrapped a towel around the Tupperware cake carrier to keep it from shifting. It was past five o'clock now and though it was only a ten-minute drive to the Amtrak station, the trains sometimes arrived early. If there was one thing Emory hated, it was being kept waiting.

The train station adhered to San Celina's unspoken code of early mission architecture with the requisite red-tiled roof; adobe-white walls; and high, airy ceilings. The station was more crowded than usual with families doing the same thing I was, waiting for relatives who preferred this more land-loving method of transportation. Sitting on the mahogany wood benches in the chilly waiting room observing the tearful reunions of families and smelling the mixed bouquet of diesel fuel, sweat, floor wax, and pine-scented cleaner brought back memories of Dove and I taking long train trips back to Sugartree, Arkansas, to visit her only sister, Garnet. Emory had lived just two doors down from Aunt Garnet in an old Victorian house on tree-shaded Palmer Street in Sugartree. As kids, we'd spent hours up in his musty attic dressing up in stiff World War II uniforms and Evening-in-Paris scented organza formals, the fabric as sheer in spots as onion skin paper. When I was thirteen, he arranged for me to experience my first real adolescent kiss with his friend Duncan Robert "Duck" Wakefield, in back of the Sugartree Dairy Queen one hot, humid Arkansas night. Emory paid his friend, the best looking boy in town, two dollars to kiss his tomboy cousin from California. He still nags me about paying him back with accumulated interest.

The train was on time, but not to my surprise, Emory was one of the last people to disembark. I'd almost decided he'd missed his train when my cousin stepped off, deep in conversation with the porter who was carrying his two Cordovan leather suitcases and a huge, tissue-wrapped package.

There was no doubt to anyone who'd known him from childhood that Emory Littleton had grown from a gawky, bespectacled boy into one fine-looking specimen of elegant southern manhood. Dressed in a pale, slightly rumpled linen suit and wearing fashionable rimless eyeglasses, his clear green eyes brightened when they spotted me.

"Sweetcakes," he exclaimed. "What a sight you are for these sore ole southun' eyes."

Unabashed, I ran across the concrete platform and grabbed him up in a fierce hug. He'd only grown more handsome in the five years since I'd last seen him, and had he not been my cousin, his liquidy southern accent and slow, confident way of moving might have melted even my cynical western heart. I didn't see how Elvia could resist him.

"Emory, you dumb turkey," I said, linking my arm through his. "I thought you'd missed the train. Why are you always so pokey?"

"I was helping a young lady gather together her possessions," he said. "You know Aunt Garnet always said we should lend a helpin' hand to our fellow man . . . or woman, as the case may be. Me and Annemarie became quite the cozy pair on our trip across this fair country of ours. Sweet young thing has people in Paso Robles."

"Emory, you scoundrel. She'd better be of legal age," I scolded. "There are some things even Gabe can't fix."

Emory gave his molasses-slow smile to the porter as he tipped him a twenty-dollar bill.

"Thank you, sir," the porter said, touching his hat brim and winking at me. He turned back to help another passenger off the train.

"Geez, Emory," I said. "I should have known it was dangerous to let you go across the country by your—" My words were interrupted by a high, excited female voice.

"Emory Littleton, you'd better not leave without saying good-bye."

Using her ebony cane, a lady well into her eighties, dressed in a pink lace dress, picked her way across the platform toward us.

"Benni," Emory said, grinning, "I'd like you to meet Miz Annemarie Burchard, of the Atlanta and Paso Robles Burchards. Known far and wide for her wicked game of Hearts."

I pulled my arm out of his and smacked him across the chest. "You never change, you jerk."

"And God is in His Heaven," Emory replied.

After his affectionate good-bye to Annemarie, we walked out to the truck. I carried one of his suitcases since he refused to let me have the tissue-wrapped box.

"Still the consummate cowgirl, I see," Emory commented, settling his expensive luggage carefully in the rusty bed of my truck. "Now that you've caught yourself a man with a regular paycheck, maybe you should think about acquiring yourself a vehicle more appropriate to your social level."

"Which is?"

"Wife of one of the county's higher officials. Rumor has it in the family grapevine that you've actually had to wear a dress for more than weddings and funerals."

"That is pure Yankee propaganda. Sometimes I wear a dress to church on Sunday." I looked at him and grimaced. "But the stories aren't completely inaccurate. I've had to attend more society functions in the last nine months than I have in my whole life. Kicking and screaming the whole way."

Emory's thick blond eyebrows arched in question.

"Okay, more like whining. Being the police chief's wife is different than I thought it would be."

"Most things are. But isn't Señor Ortiz worth the effort?"

I growled deep in my throat. "Most of the time. Gosh, I'm so glad to see you. It's been way too long."

Emory held out the wrapped box. "Likewise, dear cousin. This is for you. And please make note that only my deep and abiding love and affection for you could impel me to lug these tawdry tidbits clean across the country."

I grabbed the box and tore the tissue off, hoping it would be what I thought it was.

"Oh, Emory." I squealed when I saw the case of chocolate Moonpies. I tore open the box, opened a cellophane wrapped pie and took a huge bite. "I haven't had one of these in years. I could just kiss you."

He curled his lip in disgust. "Please, not until you gargle. I have no idea what you see in that white-trash snack food."

"I love you with all my white-trash heart," I said, taking another bite.

"Spill the beans," he said, after settling down in the front seat. "Clue me in on all the gossip from the western end of the clan."

As we drove through the parched, golden November hills toward the ranch, I caught him up on all the birthings, graduations, loves, and breakups of the family. Then I told him about what was going on at the museum and the women's western art show I was helping to coordinate.

"So you *are* becoming quite the little society wife," he said, his voice smug. "And to think I knew you when the only thing you organized was an unruly conglomeration of cattle."

"Don't worry. I'll be back to my old self this weekend. I do like my job and I do love Gabe to distraction, but I can't tell you how much I miss living out at the ranch."

"I know, sweetcakes." He squeezed my shoulder with his long-fingered hand. And I knew he did understand. Though we didn't see each other often, Emory and I wrote long letters to each other and had ever since that summer he stayed at the ranch. Sometimes I think Emory knew me better than anyone else alive.

We chattered like two excited teenagers for the rest of the drive. When we turned down the long driveway to the ranch and passed under the Double Rocking R wrought iron gates, he rolled down the window of the truck and inhaled a dramatic, deep breath.

"Never thought I'd be sayin' this, but I have had the occasional nostalgic longing to smell eucalyptus—even if it does stink like cat piss."

I laughed. "You sentimental guy, you."

The lawn and area around the house was already crowded with RVs, horse and people trailers, and mud-splattered trucks. Emory and I parked behind my uncle Luke's new brown Ford crew cab. From over near the barn, the heavy roar of men's laughter filtered across the yard. Emory and I went into the house first so he could say hey to Dove and the rest of the women.

A wave of women's high-pitched voices rolled over us when we entered the crowded kitchen. Almost everyone was occupied with some chore: rolling pie dough, cutting up vegetables, frying chicken, or folding napkins at the counter. Huge plastic glasses of iced tea and lipstick-imprinted coffee cups rested elbow close to each woman. The steamy room smelled of hot oil, cinnamon, smoky butter, apples, and women's perfume.

"Emory Delano Littleton, you come over here and hug my neck," Dove cried. She put down the hot pie she was pulling out of the oven, wiped her hands on her red calico apron, and held out her plump arms.

I poured myself a glass of tea and sat down next to my aunt Kate, Dove's oldest daughter, at the long breakfast counter while a genial Emory answered all of Dove's questions about the Arkansas clan as well as allowed himself to be poked and inspected as if he were still eleven years old.

"You're too skinny," Dove declared after making him turn around for her. "We'll take care of that these next few days."

"Dove, I have no doubt about that," Emory said, giving her another hug. Her eyes glowed as bright as a Coleman lantern. Emory had wormed his way into Dove's heart that summer he stayed with us after his mom died. He'd arrived at the ranch an angry, hurt, and confused little boy. Under Dove's firm but loving care and the friendship he and I forged because I'd also lost my mother at a young age, he'd gone home after three months healed enough to grow up into a wonderful and compassionate man.

We gabbed with the aunts and cousins for the next hour, and when he found out that the sleeping arrangements inside the house were strictly feminine, we headed toward the bunkhouse to secure him a bed. Luckily there was still one free, so he threw his leather suitcase on the upper bunk, then cautiously inspected his accommodations.

"You didn't tell me it was to be a cowboy campout," he said, his voice accusing.

"Aw, you're tough," I replied. "You can handle it."

Just then, Sam, my nineteen-year-old stepson, walked out of the bathroom wearing a pair of faded Wranglers, his black hair wet from a shower. Just as he did, the bunkhouse door opened and my dad's two ranch hands sauntered in.

"Hey, Sam, did Gabe get a hold of you?" I asked.

"Yep," he said, rubbing a white towel over his hair. His coppery skin was two-toned now with a rancher's tan that ended at his neck and upper arms. "I saved him a bunk. He's not happy about it, though." He grinned at me—a brilliant, white, kiss-me-quick smile that Elvia said sold more books at Blind Harry's than her thirty-percent-off specials.

"A man of obviously superior intelligence," Emory said, trying not to look too disdainful of his rustic accommodations.

Sam looked Emory up and down, then glanced at the two hands who'd stood quietly next to the door. Bobby Sanchez had worked for my father for three years, ever since graduating from San Celina High. A native of San Celina, he'd never wanted to do anything but cowboy. He was a short, wiry young man with black shaggy hair and long sparse sideburns. Next to him was Kip Waterman, Shelby's boyfriend. He was as blond as Bobby was dark and husky with a thick chest and the short, sturdy legs of a bullrider. With a complexion burnt shiny red-brown from working outdoors, he'd be spending a lot of time in the dermatologist's office in a few years if he didn't learn how to use sunscreen.

Being the most self-possessed man I've ever known, Emory calmly ignored their obvious expressions of amusement. Sam's brown eyes gave me a questioning look.

I slipped my arm through Emory's. "Sam, this is my cousin Emory from Arkansas. He's a journalist." I glanced up at Emory. "Sam lives and occasionally works here at the ranch."

After shaking hands with Sam and his cohorts, Emory excused himself to use the restroom.

"Your cousin, huh?" Sam said, trying unsuccessfully to keep the laughter out of his voice. He draped the towel around his shoulders, reached into the large built-in closet, and pulled out a blue chambray work shirt. In his worn Wranglers and scuffed roper boots, he looked every inch the consummate western male down to the superiority he showed toward men who didn't appear to share his overt masculine image. It wasn't the first time I wondered if it had been a good idea for him to move out to the ranch when he was still so impressionable. On the other hand, he was the product of a half-Latino cop father so the machismo roots ran deep—only the clothing was different.

"Don't you be turning your nose up at Emory," I scolded him lightly. "He can hold his own around you macho men, linen suit or not."

The expression on Sam's face doubted me, but he didn't know Emory the way I did. Like most men who first meet Emory, Sam and his buddies vastly underestimated him.

"Cute tan," I said, changing the subject.

He blew out an irritated breath. "It's so embarrassing when I go surfing. Not that I have time for that anymore. But I learned how to shoe horses last week. Thought my back was going to kill me." Sam, a Southern California suburb-raised boy, was learning ranching from the cowpie up. He was a quick and enthusiastic learner, but still green in many areas.

"Wuss," Bobby said. Kip gave a sharp laugh. Sam tossed his wet towel at them. It hit the floor, and Kip kicked it into a corner.

"Then you can appreciate what farriers do for a living," I said. "Your dad said he'd be here right after he got off work, providing there's no horrendous crime wave between now and then." I glanced at the black-and-white schoolhouse clock on the paneled wall. "Actually, he should be getting here any time. Tell Emory I'll see him later. And Sam . . ."

"Yeah?"

"You"—I turned and shook my finger at the other two young men—"and the terrible twins here better be nice to my cousin, or I'll make sure you're all dead last in the chow line."

"Yes, ma'am," Sam drawled in a feeble attempt at a southern accent. "Why, I'm right upset you'd even *thank* we'd all show anything except our deepest respect and best southern hospitality to your bee-loved cousin Emory."

I rolled my eyes and picked up the discarded towel, tossing it on Sam's bed. "And you know what a neatnick your dad is so you all better put the slob routine on hold for a few days."

"*Mi casa no es su casa,*" he said.

"Darlin'," I countered, "this here will always be *my* house, so you'd best toe that line or expect to send out for pizza."

Their throaty male laughter followed me out the door, but I wasn't irritated. Sam was actually a good kid at heart and only got a bit annoying when he was around Bobby and Kip for too long. I was used to that type of rooster strutting, having been surrounded by it my whole life. There's something about men, especially western men, that turned them into a bunch of adolescents whenever they congregated.

Strength in numbers, I suppose. But that was one thing western women learned early . . . how to keep western men in line. Sometimes all that was required was a look. Sometimes it took a bullwhip. Dove trained me early in both.

I was walking back toward the truck to take the Yankee Cake and Moonpies into the house when a voice behind me called out my name. For a moment, it was as if I'd stepped back in time, and my heart jumped in my chest like a hooked fish.

"Hey, blondie," the deep, raspy voice called again. I turned around with deliberate slowness, not certain I wanted to ride down the trail this voice would no doubt open up.

"Wade," I said, feeling my right knee quiver. "*Wade*."

"That's my name. Don't wear it out." His lips twisted into that cocky Harper smirk he'd shared with my late husband, Jack.

He strode across the few feet that separated us and enveloped me in his tanned, corded arms. The familiar smell of Clove gum reopened an almost healed tear in my heart. Jack and Wade had both chewed that brand of gum incessantly. Only sold in San Celina County by a small liquor store in Atascadero, they would buy it by the box when possible since it was so hard to find. A bright red unopened package was in Jack's pocket when they found his body in his wrecked Jeep almost two years ago. Wade held me out from him, his hands gently gripping my shoulders.

"You look great, blondie. Surprised to see me? As Ma would say, I just took a notion to drop by and see you. I flew in and hitched a ride out here. Showed up on Dove's doorstep ten minutes ago hoping she wouldn't turn me away."

I nodded, staring at him, still trying to regain my composure. He'd lost weight since he'd left San Celina a year ago when the ranch he and Jack owned had gone bankrupt. He'd moved to Texas to manage his uncle's cow-calf operation, and the last I'd heard from Sandra, his wife, things were going okay. Living together on the ranch like we did, she and I had once been almost as close as sisters, but our correspondence had dwindled to nothing in the last six months, probably because we'd all moved on to other lives. They weren't technically my relatives anymore, a situation I had difficulty accepting for a long time. But I'd finally let them go. I'd thought. Now Wade was back, and, knowing Wade, it wasn't just a pleasure visit.

"What's wrong?" I demanded. Then, ashamed at my tone, I qualified my abrupt question. "Are Sandra and the kids okay? Your mom?"

"They're fine," he said, adjusting his sand-colored Stetson downward. It shaded his brown eyes from my scrutiny. "Everything's fine and everyone's fine."

I studied him silently. Wade and I had tangled constantly when we all lived and worked together on the Harper ranch. Being the older of the two Harper men, he'd used that position often to influence his mom to vote for decisions that weren't always best for the ranch. Though their love for each other ran deep, he and Jack had fought at least once a week over the running of the ranch. Jack always gave in and usually convinced me to do likewise, often when I didn't think we should. Wade losing the ranch was proof I'd been right, but for me the issue became irrelevant after Jack's death.

"Why are you here, then?" I asked. "I know you, Wade. This isn't just a pleasure visit."

For a split second, his face hardened, then he grinned. "Never could bullshit you, could I, blondie?"

I touched my temple with my fingertips and inhaled deeply, wishing he'd stop using Jack's nickname for me. "Wade, is it you and Sandra again?" He and my former sister-in-law had never enjoyed a marriage that ran smoothly. During the investigation surrounding Jack's death last year when I'd first met Gabe, Sandra and Wade had

almost broken up over his affair with one of the artists at
the co-op.

He squinted his eyes against the setting November sun.
"I think it's really over this time, Benni. She and her mama
took the kids and moved to Dallas. She got a job at an
insurance company there and she's filed for a divorce."

I reached out and touched his forearm, sorry for my in-
itial rudeness. "Wade, I'm so sorry. Is there any chance you
two can work it out?"

He pushed his hat back, and I could see his eyes clearly
for the first time. "Doesn't appear so. Uncle Bob's ranch
was so far from town, and she got so lonely. And . . ." He
let his sentence drift away. I suspected there was more to
their breakup than just the ranch's isolation—Wade had
been known to like booze and the ladies a little too much.

"What are you going to do?" I asked.

He shrugged. "I told Uncle Bob and Mom I needed to
get away for a while. Thought I'd fly out and see some old
friends. And you."

"It's good to see you," I said, though I wasn't exactly
sure of those sentiments. But it was obvious he was in real
pain and, as is not uncommon to human beings, he'd come
back to the place where he'd once been happy and whole.
My irritation at him cooled because I understood his desire
for the idealized past.

"I won't hang around long," he said. "Be on my way
in a few days."

"I'm sure there's lots of people who'll be glad to see
you again. And you're in luck—I baked a Yankee Cake for
tomorrow. Your favorite."

"Guess your second sense told you I was coming," he
said, laughing. My heart cracked again at the familiar sound.
He and Jack were so much alike. But it had been almost
two years since Jack died, and I'd since fallen in love with
another man and started a new life. How could these feelings
of loss suddenly feel so fresh?

"Let's go back to the house and see what's for supper. Guess who came out for Thanksgiving, too? My cousin Emory."

"That right? That nerdy little kid from Arkansas?"

"Not so nerdy anymore. Or little. I do believe he's an inch taller than you."

When we entered the house through the kitchen door, the first sound I heard was Gabe's rich baritone voice begging Dove for a piece of sweet potato pie. All my aunts and girl cousins were staring at him with the cow-eyed adoring looks I was learning to accept when it came to my husband. When Gabe put his mind to it, he could out charm Mel Gibson.

He stopped when I entered the room and looked down at me, his eyes crinkling with pleasure. Then his eyes snapped up to Wade standing behind me. Their smoky blueness faded to a dark gray, and his face became still.

"Wade Harper." In those two words he managed to convey all his feelings of contempt and distrust.

Wade dipped his head in an almost imperceptible nod. "Ortiz."

I said to Gabe, keeping my voice light, "Wade's visiting for a few days, seeing old friends and such. Isn't that nice?"

Gabe's face didn't budge an inch. "Nice," he repeated.

Wade glanced around the room at the now silent women, his tanned face coloring at the cheekbones. "Guess supper's not ready yet. Think I'll go out and say hey to Ben. Reckon he's in the barn."

"We'll be setting the food on the picnic tables out back in about a half hour," Dove said. "Fried chicken, fried okra, corn-on-the-cob, and potato salad. Tell the men while you're out there."

"Yes, ma'am," he said, swinging around and heading out the back door.

When the women resumed their kitchen chores and conversation, Gabe walked across the kitchen to me. He grabbed my hand and pulled me through the back door.

"Mrs. Ortiz," he said firmly, though I'd never actually become an official Ortiz, a point that still occasionally rankled his overabundant supply of testosterone. "We need to talk."

2

"I DIDN'T KNOW he was going to be here," I said before he spoke. We stood facing each other underneath a seventy-five-year-old oak tree that had witnessed a good many of the important events of my life. The sun, a half orange on the horizon, filtered through the bare branches and etched black line shadows across Gabe's cheekbones.

"How long is he going to stay?" he asked.

"I don't know," I said, leaning against the broad trunk. "We didn't talk long. He showed up unannounced about fifteen minutes ago on Dove's doorstep, and she said he could stay awhile. He and Sandra broke up."

"What's he doing here?"

"I have no idea, but I imagine it has something to do with the fact that he lived here for so long, was happy here, had friends here." I picked at the rough tree bark, avoiding his eyes. "I would think you would be a bit more understanding. You know how hard it is when people split up." Gabe had himself gone through a divorce years before we'd met. I glanced up at his cynical face. It held no sympathy for my former brother-in-law.

"He's a flake," he said. He folded his arms across his chest and spread his legs in that stubborn, macho way that always tempted me to whack him upside the head. "I don't like it."

"That's obvious, but there's not much you can do about the situation, so I suggest you calm your raised hackles and live with it."

He glared at me. I smiled back in an attempt to soften my words. Gabe's assessment of Wade was right. He did have problems with hanging out with the wrong people and getting into trouble. After Jack's death, before we'd lost the Harper ranch, Wade had foolishly made a short career of delivering drugs in an effort to make some extra cash. He quit before he was caught, though his actions proved good judgment was not his strong suit. Gabe and I had never discussed the incident since it took place before we were actually together, though I'm sure he knew about it. But Wade and I had a history. He'd known me since I was a girl and I had loved his brother with the powerful, all-encompassing love that people experience as teenagers. Though I loved Gabe and respected his feelings, I couldn't turn away Jack's brother any more than I could one of my own relatives.

I cupped my palms around the elbows of his crossed arms. "C'mon, Friday, it'll just be for a week or so. And I won't even see him that much. He'll be visiting old friends, and I've got a million things to do with the Heritage Days celebration and the art show. I'll probably only visit with him for a few hours at the most, and then he'll head back to Texas." I tugged at his elbows. "Quit being such a hard ass."

Just for effect, he scowled a moment longer before relenting and pulling me into a hug. "I'm going to tell Dove that you're talking like a truck driver again," he said, rubbing his lips across the top of my head. I could feel my hair catch on his prickly beard sprouts. "She'll take you out to the back of the barn with a switch."

I laughed, knowing that, at least for the moment, I'd

talked him out of his irritation. Tilting my head back, I kissed the bottom of his chin. The whiskers felt like little needles on my lips. "If you don't tell her, I promise I'll make it worth your while when we get home Sunday night."

He bent down and whispered something in my ear. I leaned back in his arms and poked him in the chest. "Chief, it'll take more than you not ratting on my bad language to get *that*."

He laughed and rubbed his stubble up and down my neck.

"Stop it," I said, pushing him away. "Geez Louise, I'll have to buy calamine lotion by the gallon if this keeps up."

"I promise I'll keep my thoughts and feelings to myself. All I have to say is, ex-relative or not, he'd better keep himself squeaky clean while he's in my city."

At ten o'clock curfew that first night, the men gathered at the front porch and sang "Good Night, Ladies" as they had at every Thanksgiving gathering as far back as I could remember. It was hokey, but it brought a lump to my throat to see my new husband and his son in the back row, struggling with the words.

After the men retired to their respective bunkhouses, trailers, and tents, I proceeded to give my aunts and girl cousins the details about the meeting between Gabe and my former brother-in-law. I knew better than to try to hold back with this nosy crowd. They'd beat it out of me with their spatulas and knitting needles.

"He is definitely trouble looking for a place to set itself down," Dove said about Wade. "But I couldn't turn the boy away on Thanksgiving. You'd best stay away from him as much as possible."

"Now what fun is that?" said my Aunt Ruby, Uncle Luke's wife. He was the ex-rodeo clown and the craziest of my dad's brothers. And even at forty-nine Ruby was as rabble-rousing as Uncle Luke. They were the ones we kids had loved tagging after because they were always cooking up some zany game or treasure hunt to keep us occupied.

Gabe kept his promise and maintained a watchful distance from Wade through the family Thanksgiving dinner the next day. Wade followed Gabe's lead and stayed as far from him as possible.

Early Friday morning, when I was out in the backyard putting plastic tablecloths over the picnic tables in preparation for the barbecue that afternoon, Sam walked up. He was dressed in faded sweatpants and a tee shirt that showed a cowboy on horseback gripping a surfboard. The words read, "You Can Lead a Horse to Water but You Can't Make Him Surf."

"You're looking more like the old Sam this morning," I commented, smoothing out the blue-checkered tablecloth.

He took another tablecloth from the pile on a metal lawn chair and started unfolding it. "Yeah, I haven't gone completely country. I like working on the ranch, and the guys are all right, but sometimes . . ." He let his words drift off as he shook out the cloth over a weathered table.

"They're just too red-necked and bigoted," I finished for him.

He grinned at me as he ran his hand across the wrinkled cloth. "I made them shut up last night when they wouldn't stop making stupid cracks about your cousin. They're kinda pissed at me right now."

My heart softened as I looked at my stepson's flushed, handsome face. He was so much like his father, and though Gabe felt guilty about he and Lydia breaking up before Sam had turned twelve, they'd managed between the two of them to raise a fine boy. I hadn't yet met Gabe's ex-wife, a successful attorney down in Orange County, but I had to admit, when I observed snippets of Sam's good and kind character, I was very curious about her.

"They're going to start looking for calves in about an hour," he said after we'd finished covering the last of the twelve picnic tables we'd hauled out from the barn a few days ago. "You gonna ride with us or are you staying in the kitchen with the womenfolk?"

"I'll pretend I didn't hear you use that western male condescending tone you've picked up so rapidly," I said.

"I guess that means you're riding," he said, shooting me his drop-the-women-in-their-tracks smile.

"Save the smile, I'm immune. And by the way, Badger's mine today."

"Man, that's tweeked. I'll probably get stuck with Rebel. He's so slow. The only time he hurries is when he's heading back to the barn to eat."

"There's a Southerner for you," Emory said, walking up. He was dressed in his loose definition of ranchwear— perfectly pressed two-hundred-dollar khakis, a Ralph Lauren chambray work shirt, and Lucchese deerskin boots. He looked like an ad in *GQ* magazine. "We do like our vittles."

"Hey, Emory," I said. "How'd you sleep?"

"Fine." He nodded at Sam. "Your daddy's awful proud of you, Sam. He has a right to be."

Embarrassed, Sam ducked his head, murmuring some inaudible answer. "I'll see you in a few minutes," he said to me.

"If you saddle up Badger for me, I'll hide you a piece of Dove's devil's food cake," I called after him.

"Deal," he said.

Emory and I watched him walk toward the barn. "He is a good kid," I said. "There's been a lot of changes in his life these last few months. He's still trying to find out where he fits in and to sort out his relationship with his dad."

"Speaking of his dad, I noticed a bit of tension between him and that brother-in-law of yours."

"Former brother-in-law. Technically, we're not related anymore."

His green eyes crinkled at the corners.

I pointed a finger at him. "You just keep quiet." Emory

did know me better than anyone else. "Yes, he does still feel related to me and yes, I think of Jack every time I look at him. I'm confused enough without your nonverbal comments, thank you very much."

"Just enjoying the show. Better than *General Hospital*."

"There will be no show. Gabe has agreed to keep his distance, and I'll try to see Wade as little as possible. Things will be fine."

Emory just nodded and smiled that irritating, superior smile.

I showed him a fist.

"Oh, go play, cowgirl." He shooed me away with his hand. "I myself have no need to prove my masculinity by emasculating young bovines, so I'll visit the kitchen ladies and offer my superlative taste-testing abilities."

I headed out to the barn where all the men and a few of my girl cousins were congregated. Most of my relatives had brought their own horses, and for a little while there was a flurry of activity while everyone tacked up and received their assignments from Daddy. With this many people riding, gathering fifty or so calves would be a cinch—finding them in a couple of hours instead of all day as it would have taken three or four riders. Plenty of time to play cowboy without getting too dirty for the barbecue at two o'clock.

Gabe was talking to my uncle Clarence and Sam, discussing the price of some Black Angus yearlings Clarence had just sold at auction. That showed how hard Gabe was trying to get along with my relatives, because he hadn't eaten beef for years and found my family's obsession with it a bit tedious at times.

"Hi," I said, going up and giving him a kiss. "Going to ride with us?" He knew I was just teasing. Gabe was an excellent horseman, a talent that had surprised me when I found out about it, but he disliked riding and, like Emory, didn't care for any ranch work that involved cattle.

"Think I will," he said.

My eyes widened in surprise.

"I'll take the Honda ATV, then," Sam said. "You can have Rebel."

"Thanks a lot," Gabe said. "Does he come with AAA coverage and a cellular phone in case we need a tow truck?"

"I see you've heard about him," Sam said, laughing.

Wade rode up on Gigi, Dove's quarterhorse, then quickly moved into a group of my relatives when Gabe gave him a hard look.

"That was rude," I told Gabe as we adjusted our saddles and found out our assigned area, the old hunter's cabin and barn at the back of my dad's two-thousand-acre ranch. A creek ran across the back of the cabin where certain mama cows liked to hide among the overgrown brush. Gullies and washes were Badger's specialty. An eight-year-old, quick-footed paint gelding I'd bought six years ago and trained myself, he loved to climb up and down hills so much that I'd threatened to rename him Jeep.

"What?" Gabe asked innocently and smiled his devastating smile.

"You wouldn't get away with near what you do if you weren't so good looking," I grumbled, tightening Badger's girth.

Before we could argue further, a brand-new shiny black Ford half-ton pickup pulled up beside us with Bobby Sanchez driving. His two female passengers were members of the artist's co-op. They slid out of the front seat and walked over to us.

"Hey, Parker, Olivia," I said. "Isn't this a little early for you guys? Nice truck."

"Hey, cow-woman, where's the beef?" Parker twisted a piece of her straight brown hair around one long finger. Cut in a shoulder-length pageboy with thick, even bangs, her hair was as nondescript as she was. From the first time we met, she reminded me of that girl in everyone's school who was always the teacher's pet because she was so obedient and quiet. But anyone who got to know Parker Leona Williams (so named because her mother loved Parker House rolls) came to realize that all her creativity was focused on her art. Known to her rapidly growing and fanatically loyal cache of collectors as P.L. Williams, she was a recent addition to our artist's co-op. Her specialties were meticulous pencil renderings and autumn-toned watercolors of various aspects of western life. She worked part time at Roland Bennett's gallery downtown, barely subsisting on her meager salary and on the money from the occasional sale of her work. A native of Bakersfield, she often used migrant farm workers as subjects in her paintings because she herself was only one generation removed from the Okie migrant workers who had settled the Central Valley in the thirties.

"You'll see plenty of beef today," I assured her. "Bovine and otherwise." I grinned at Olivia, who gave me a thumbs up. She wore a bright red flannel shirt, tight Levi's, and an electric blue down vest. A dark sketching pencil was tucked inside the thick knot of black hair piled haphazardly on her head.

Olivia Contreras specialized in western Latino life with a personal affinity for the Latino cowboy. Her acrylic paintings were bright, bold, and big—just like Olivia herself. She'd recently made a sale to a small museum in Santa Fe, which was an important addition to her portfolio. She'd also won the very sought-after commission for the Heritage Days poster. Her colorful painting depicted the Mission Santa Celine, the Sinclair Hacienda, the Chumash Indian petroglyphs at Painted Rock, the old Sam Lee store in what was once San Celina's bustling Chinatown district, and the Ruiz-Simon Victorian house in downtown San Celina. The poster hung in every business downtown and would be on sale all next week. Both artists were here at my invitation—to view the roundup and to experience a real ranch barbecue.

I gestured at the glossy truck that, if my estimation was

right, cost at least twenty-five thousand dollars. "Who'd you steal the truck from?"

"It's mine," Olivia said, leaning against it. "I couldn't resist."

I nodded but couldn't help wondering where she got the money to buy the truck. She was one of the more vocal complainers of poverty at the co-op. I scanned the large group of people milling around.

"Have you seen Shelby?" I asked. "We talked earlier this morning, but she's disappeared. She's supposed to be riding with us today."

"I saw her and Kip at the bunkhouse about fifteen minutes ago," Parker said. Her voice lowered. "They were having one horrendous fight."

"She ought to tell that red-necked *cretino* to take a hike," Olivia said. "I just hope if she's putting out that she's protecting herself 'cause I'd bet fifty bucks he's screwing around on her."

Parker shrugged. "I think she's a pretty sharp lady."

I didn't comment. I'd been, with great determination and only a modicum of success, trying not to get involved in the gossip that flew like swift little sparrows around the co-op and museum.

"Anything in particular either of you are looking to observe today?" I asked, trying to change the subject. Ignoring their tempting tidbit of gossip was almost physically painful for someone as nosy as me.

"I'm thinking about starting a new series of renderings," Parker said. "I'm concentrating on the younger women today. I've been thinking about how the role of women has changed in agriculture in the last few years. The older women are back at the ranch house cooking our food, while you young women are out here gathering cattle. That's liberation, for sure, but the question is, who's going to feed everyone when this older generation passes away? Anyway, I've got my trusty old Minolta and a ton of black-and-white film. But you know me, I don't really know what I want until I see it, so just act natural."

"Oh, great," I said. "In other words, you and Shelby both will be attempting to catch me in my most awkward, embarrassing moments."

A quiet, understated laugh came from the back of her throat. Her watery brown eyes had lashes so pale they reminded me of a rabbit, as did her quick, tentative movements. Mimicking her watercolor paintings, Parker almost always dressed in browns, tans, or soft golds. Perfect camouflage for the honey-colored hills surrounding us.

"I'm concentrating on the men, as usual," Olivia said with a wink. "I'll be riding shotgun in the truck with Bobby all day."

Olivia and my dad's ranch hand had apparently established a close friendship in the last few months. It had been speculated among the artists that their relationship had become more than professional. The age difference between Bobby and Olivia was at least fifteen years, but no one batted an eyelash among the artists. These days relationships between younger men and older women were almost a cliché.

"I'll be interested in seeing what all of you come up with after today," I said, mounting Badger.

By noon we had filled the pen next to the big barn with about fifty mama cows and their hundred-pound babies, some bearing Daddy's brand, some mine. Not wanting to get any more sweaty and dusty before the barbecue, I sat up on the fence with Shelby, Parker, Olivia, and some of my girl cousins and let the men separate the nervous calves from their protective mamas. Passing a huge bag of peanuts between us, we hollered and rooted for the cows more than the cowboys. Gabe stayed on horseback and let Rebel do the one thing he did well once you could convince him to work—cutting. He was an experienced cow-pony and could almost do it without a rider, and the one thing that kept him working was he knew dinner always followed.

One particularly smart and stubborn mama took a half hour and seven men to separate her from her baby. We cheered her tenacity—''Go, cow. Go, mama''—until the sweating and cursing men on horseback and foot finally separated her from her calf. Her angry call could be heard above all the other cows crowding the fence separating them from their babies.

''That mama definitely deserves a ten,'' Olivia said.

Over the bawling of the calves, the men threw jokes like horseshoes as a couple of them drove each calf down the wooden chute into the Teco cattle squeeze, locked them in the metal cage, and flipped it over to attach the plastic Y-Tex ear tags marked with either my or Daddy's brand. At the same time other men would vaccinate, notch the ear, and castrate if called for, all in perfect synchronization. Cowboy ballet, Dove called it. Sam held the calves heads as they were being done, covering their eyes and talking to them in a low, soothing voice like I'd taught him. Just like Dove and Daddy had taught me. Anyone who worked the Ramsey Ranch was trained right off to treat our cattle with kindness and dignity. We were rewarded by having the calmest cattle in San Celina County.

''Looky this one, Ben,'' Kip called to my dad. ''He's got real nice confirmation. Want to save him for stud?'' He had the ring expander all poised and ready to snap the green rubber castrating ring around the calf's testicles, which would cut off the blood supply and eventually turn the potential bull into a steer. ''Speak now or forever hold your peace.''

My dad gave the bull calf a ten-second consideration, then said, ''Nah.''

It took a few minutes because this calf was determined to stay a bull. He kept retracting his left testicle, causing Kip, after breaking three latex rubber rings, to singe our ears with some colorful and earthy cowboy language.

"You gotta respect the little guy," Kip said, sucking his bruised finger. "I wouldn't give mine up without a fight either." He grinned down the row of us women, making a point to ignore Shelby. " 'Course, they don't make these rubber bands big enough for me."

"Aw, don't listen to him," Bobby drawled as he notched the calf's ear with one swift motion. "They're only big when he's standing up." A roar of men's laughter filled the corral.

"Up yours," Kip answered, then crooned to the struggling calf, "Sorry, little buddy," and released the rubber band.

While we groaned and booed at the men's joking, Shelby slipped down off the fence and started walking toward the house. Kip stopped for a moment and watched her, his sweating face tight with anger. I glanced over at Olivia, who just shrugged and rolled her eyes.

I hopped off the fence and followed Shelby through the backyard, where guests had already started arriving. The picnic tables were filled with foil-covered casserole dishes, and I waved at Elvia and her mother as I tried to catch up with Shelby.

"I'll be right back," I told Elvia.

"Keep him away from me," she replied, setting the long pan of tamales down on a table. I glanced over to where she was looking. Emory hovered near the hot barbecues, watching Elvia with the expression of a lovesick coon hound. Uncle Luke and Uncle Arnie, the official family cooks, were sprinkling the top blocks and tri-tips of beef with their closely guarded secret mixture of salt and chili spices and turning over dozens of chicken breasts. The air smelled sweet and smoky, and my stomach growled in anticipation.

"I'll get back to you," I said, watching Shelby go around the side of the house.

"I mean it," she called after me.

I caught up with Shelby on the front porch of the house. She was sitting on the wooden porch swing, arms crossed, swinging it with a violence that made me glad Daddy had attached it with heavy-duty hooks.

"Whoa, slow down," I said, grabbing the swing. "I'd join you but I get seasick easily."

She stopped the swing with her turquoise cowboy boot and gave me a weak smile. "Sorry, Benni. I guess I shouldn't be taking out my hostilities on an innocent porch swing."

"Better a swing than a human being," I said, sitting down beside her. "Want to talk about it?"

She unfolded her arms and buried her face in her hands. Her shoulders shook with her sobs. I patted her back, letting her cry. I'd forgotten how quickly emotions could turn when a person was only twenty, though I shouldn't have. My relationship with Gabe, middle-aged as it was, had often resembled this hot-cold encounter between Shelby and Kip.

After a few minutes she lifted her head and wiped her eyes with the sleeve of her expensive butter-gold flannel shirt. "I'm sorry," she said. "I don't know why I let that jerk get to me like that."

"Men have a way of doing that to us. But if it makes you feel any better, we do it to them, too."

"It doesn't."

We didn't talk for a moment. I stared out over the front yard to where cars and trucks were parked neatly along our narrow gravel driveway. One of my aunts barreled out the front door, took one look at Shelby's stricken face, and said, "Oops, I'll come back later."

"Oh, great," Shelby said. "Guess I'll be the big topic of conversation now."

"At least until my Uncle Arnie starts sneaking the beer he's smuggled in and Dove finds out. Have you ever seen a grown man get chased by his seventy-six-year-old mother swinging a hand-braided quirt? If he's had more than two beers, she can catch him, too. That should make a great picture.''

She laughed at the image and sniffed wetly.

"Shelby, what's really going on with you and Kip?''

"Same old story you've probably heard a million times. I went out with my friends last night to have a few drinks and listen to some band out at the Frio Saloon. It was one of the few places open on Thanksgiving. Kip told me he was tired, that he was coming back out here to the ranch to go to bed early. He went to bed early all right, but I bet he didn't get much sleep.''

I made a sympathetic noise in my throat, and she continued.

"After we went to the Frio Saloon, we decided to go to that all-night cafe over on Apple Street. You know, the one attached to the Best Western Motel. They've got great chicken-fried steak and mashed potatoes. Anyway, we were sitting at a window table at about two in the morning, and guess who comes waltzing out of Room Twelve with some girl with bleached blond hair out to here.'' She held her hands about six inches from her head. "And a skirt up to her ass. He saw me in the window, but I ran into the bathroom, and my friends got rid of him before I came back out.''

"Shelby, I'm so sorry.'' It was an old story, but that didn't make the pain of it happening any less acute when it happened to you.

"He tried to weasel out of it, but what does he think I am, an idiot? Why are men so incomprehensible? Never mind. It doesn't matter, 'cause he and I are through. Now if I could just convince my heart of that, I'll be fine.'' Her eyes teared up again. "It's so pathetic. I sound like a country-western song, don't I?''

I put my arm around her shoulders and gave her a small squeeze. "That's exactly why so many of them are sold. Let's go get some food before the men scarf it all up. You'll feel better if you eat something. As for why men behave the way they do, I don't have any wise advice in that area 'cause my own husband is snorting like a crazy bull on steroids around my former brother-in-law.''

'''At least he cares enough to be jealous,'' she said.

''A mixed blessing sometimes.''

I stood up, and she caught my arm. ''Benni, there's something else.''

I turned and waited. When I saw the serious look on her face, I sat back down on the swing. ''What is it?''

''Can I ask you a hypothetical question?''

I shrugged. ''Sure.''

''If . . .'' She paused, cleared her throat, and shifted in the swing. ''If a friend of yours was doing something that might be illegal . . .''

I held my hand up. ''Stop right there. Don't forget I'm married to a police officer. Anything you tell me, I'll have to pass on to him.''

Her face fell, and my heart went out to her. She was so far away from her family and any emotional support system she'd managed to build up back home. Knowing I probably shouldn't, I relented and said, ''Look, if a friend of yours is doing something that's against the law, stay away from them. I don't know much about the law, but I do know that being an accessory is not something to mess around with. You're young and very talented. Don't wreck your life because of someone else's stupidity.''

She twirled a piece of her long black hair around a finger. ''Have you ever been in a situation like that?''

I hesitated, not wanting to lie, but sensing that I was getting in deeper than I should. ''Yes.''

''What did you do?''

''Shelby, I don't want to give you advice on this other than get out of it.''

She stubbornly persisted. ''I'm not asking for advice. I just want to know what you did.''

I exhaled sharply. "You have to realize, I wasn't married to Gabe at the time, but I confronted my friend."

"Before you went to the police?"

"I didn't go to the police. My friend did after I talked to him. But that was my experience. Don't take it for yours."

"Don't worry," she said, standing up. "Thanks for listening to me. I think I know what to do now."

Feeling troubled, helpless, and a bit annoyed, I watched her go down the porch steps and turn the corner. I was really trying to take my position as a police chief's wife seriously, but people just kept getting in the way with their problems. Had I done the right thing? Did I give her the right advice? Was I being mean to cut her off? I felt distinctly uncomfortable about telling her about my experience. In my case, he'd been a friend since childhood and a local, well-loved minister—the situation had been complicated. Who was this friend of Shelby's and what had he or she done?

Not your business, a little voice inside my head scolded. *Amen,* I replied and let it go.

Back at the huge steel barbecue, lines had already started forming. Dove was flitting from one place to another shouting orders like a general. I considered offering to help, but with all her daughters and daughters-in-law present, I'd probably get in the way of their precisely timed cowgirl cha-cha, so I grabbed a plastic plate and fell in line behind Shelby, who was doing her best to avoid looking at Kip. From behind the barn came the sounds of men horsing around as they cleaned up at the outside sink.

Emory sidled up and grumbled into my ear, "You said you told Elvia. She won't even talk to me."

I reached up and patted my cousin's smooth cheek. "I did tell her, Emory, honey. That's *why* she's ignoring you."

Wade strolled up, bumped my hip with his, then pushed in front of me. "You don't care if I butt in, do you, blondie? Hey, Emory, long time no see. You had glasses the size of

Coke bottles the last time I saw you." I could smell the liquor on Wade's breath and felt myself stiffen. Wade had always been a nasty drunk, and the only person who'd ever been able to calm him down when he was drinking was Jack.

Shelby giggled. I frowned a warning at her, but her eyes weren't on me. She was mesmerized by Wade. I looked back at him to see what she was staring at, and it suddenly dawned on me that Wade was indeed an attractive man in that rugged, western way that was obviously Shelby's weakness.

Emory stared at him without blinking. "Isn't it amazing what prodigious strides have been accomplished by our fine medical establishment in the treatment of the plebeian and provincial dilemma of acute myopia?"

Wade snorted and winked at Shelby. "Looks like Cousin Emory here is trying to tell us he went to college or something."

"Wade, shut up," I said.

He just laughed and turned to Shelby. "And what did you say your name was, darlin'?"

"Sorry," I said to Emory in a low voice.

He slipped an arm around my shoulder. "No problem, sweetcakes. You know I've been razzed by more macho men than Wade. He always did have a brain whose nearest DNA match was a peach pit."

I hugged him back. "Forget him. Let's tie on the feedbag."

After we filled our plates with the juicy medium-rare beef, smoky chicken, potato salad, thick spicy tamales, garlic bread, corn on the cob, Santa-Maria-style salsa, and pink pinquito beans, we found a table as far away from Wade and Shelby as possible so I wouldn't have to watch Wade make a fool of himself over a girl half his age. But my nosiness got the best of me, and I slipped surreptitious glances at them, watching her feed him a piece of beef, then wipe the salsa off the tip of his mustache with her finger. It wasn't hard to see why Sandra had gotten fed up and left for good.

The next moment I felt my hair lift up and warm lips nibble at my neck. "Hey, save it for later. My husband's around here somewhere." I turned to face my scroungy-looking husband and grinned. "Oh, it's you. Better get in line, Friday, before all the tamales are gone."

"I'm not worried. Señora Aragon hid some for me," he said, grabbing a piece of my garlic bread. He smirked at Emory and straddled the bench next to me. "She loves me. All women do. And who can blame them? I'm irresistible."

Emory gave an amused chuckle. To my amazement, Gabe and Emory had hit it off the first moment they met last night. But I guess I shouldn't have been surprised. As an experienced cop and a quiet observer of human nature, Gabe was adept at seeing through people's manufactured personas to their true characters.

I groaned dramatically. "You are the most arrogant man I have ever met. She probably saved them because she felt such overwhelming pity for someone so incredibly delusional." I reached for my garlic bread. "Get your own food."

"She adores me," he insisted, popping the rest of my garlic bread in his mouth and standing up. "Save me a seat, *mi corazon*, since you're making me fix my own plate."

He was halfway to the food line when the argument broke out. The loud voices could be heard even over the noisy crowd, and everyone in the yard turned and looked toward the commotion. Closing my eyes briefly, I made a fist, wanting to rush across the yard and use it. When Wade and Shelby started fawning over each other, I suspected something like this would happen.

"Back off, boy," Wade drawled to a red-faced Kip. Kip stood in his dusty chaps at the end of the picnic table where Wade and Shelby were sitting. "She said she doesn't feel

like talkin' to you.'' Shelby's face had the self-satisfied look
of a spoiled child who'd gotten her way. A flicker of anger
ignited in me. I knew she was young and just wanted to get
back at Kip, but didn't she care about anyone else but herself? This would ruin the barbecue for everyone. I fought
the urge to go over and shake her by the shoulders.

"Get out of my way, asshole," Kip said. "I don't care
what she feels. She's going to talk to me . . ."

I jumped up and started toward them. Gabe came up
behind me and caught my upper arm. "Benni, let me take
care of this."

I tried to shake free. "I can do it, Gabe."

He ignored my words, pushed me behind him, and
calmly walked toward Kip and Wade. I started to follow,
but Emory grabbed my shoulder.

"Let him," Emory said in a quiet voice.

"He hates Wade," I said, pulling against his hand.

"He does this for a living, Benni. Let him handle it."

Kip gripped the edge of the table, his scarred knuckles
white. I pictured him upending it like in a movie scene.

Wade stood up with deliberate slowness, blocking Shelby
from Kip's view. "I said move along, boy, before I have to
make you."

Kip snatched up a full can of Coke off the table and
threw it against the trunk of the oak tree. Brown fizz exploded across the table. Shelby shrieked and looked down
at her splattered shirt. A couple of my male cousins started
moving in closer.

"Get out of my way!" Kip yelled, pulling a buck knife
from his side, brandishing it with a shaky hand.

Shelby jumped up, her face pale and frightened. "Kip,
you idiot, put that away!"

Wade took a step back. In seconds, Gabe grabbed a piece
of wood from a nearby woodpile, came up behind Kip, and
slammed it down on Kip's wrist. Kip yelped and dropped
the knife, then bent over and gripped his wrist. Gabe moved

in, picked up the knife, and tucked it in the back of his jeans. Then he grabbed Kip by the upper arm.

"Let's go have a talk, son," Gabe said, pushing Kip in front of him.

"You broke it," he whined, clutching his wrist.

Gabe talked low in Kip's ear while walking him toward my dad's office inside the barn. Daddy and Uncle Clarence followed, shutting the door behind them.

I turned and faced the gathered crowd. "Okay, everyone, show's over. Better get back to the food before it's all gone."

After a few minutes of nervous laughter, everyone went back to what they were doing. Wade grinned at me. I walked over to him, frowning.

"Wade Harper, I ought to kick your butt off this ranch," I said.

"Now, blondie, it was just a little ole fight between cowboys over a lady. Ain't the first one you've seen. Doubt it'll be the last."

I gave Shelby a severe look. She had the decency to flush with embarrassment. "Shelby, Wade and I need a few minutes of privacy."

"No problem," she said.

After she left, I really let Wade have it. He had known me long enough to know it was better not to interrupt until I'd said my piece.

"I can't believe you," I said for the fourth time.

"I reckon you said that a few times already," he said. "You're building a mansion out of a rat's nest, blondie."

"Quit calling me that," I snapped.

He pushed the rim of his Stetson up to see me better. "Benni, I'm sorry if I pissed you off, but Shelby's a grown woman—"

"She's twenty years old. Half your age."

"A *grown woman* over eighteen," he repeated. "And she's got a right to talk to who she wants." He squinted his brown eyes, eyes that reminded me so much of Jack's I had to push down the sentimental feeling welling up in me. He pulled a piece of gum out of his pocket, carefully unwrapped it, threw the red paper on the ground, and stuck the gum in his mouth. "What business do you have with it anyway?"

Before I could answer, his face stiffened, and he took a small step away from me. I turned and saw Gabe walking toward us, his jaw looking like it was made of steel piping.

"Got the young pup calmed down?" Wade asked.

"Harper, keep your nose clean while you're in my county. I'm only going to tell you that once."

"Yes, sir, Chief, *sir*," he said, moving his gum from one side of his mouth to the other. "But, you know, it don't appear to me that I've broken any laws. I wasn't the one who pulled a knife, now was I?"

Gabe just looked at him a long moment, then turned to me. "Let's go finish eating."

"Try and behave," I said to Wade.

He just grinned and unwrapped another piece of gum.

We'd only gone a few steps when Wade called out, "Hey, Ortiz."

Gabe stopped and slowly turned around.

"Just remember one thing." Wade looked at me for a long ten seconds, then back at Gabe. "She might be livin' in your stable now, but don't you *ever* forget—it was my brother who greenbroke her."

Color drained from Gabe's cheeks, and he sprang at Wade. I threw myself in front of Gabe and pushed on his chest with all my strength. One hundred and ten desperate pounds against one hundred and eighty pissed-off ones is not an equal contest.

I talked as fast as I could, "Gabe, forget it. He's just trying to provoke you. He's full of crap, and you know it. Don't let him get to you."

I yelled over my shoulder, "Wade, get out of here.

Now!" Wade just chuckled when I grabbed Gabe's upper arms and dug my nails into his skin.

"Please, Gabe," I said. "He's a jerk. You know someone here will leak it to the papers. You're playing right into his hands. Don't let him do that to your reputation."

Gabe stopped and looked down at me, a cold, unrelenting look on his face. In that moment I caught a glimpse of the man who'd worked undercover narcotics so successfully in East L.A.

"Gabe, please," I pleaded softly.

I felt his body relax under my hands, which told me that, for now, he'd back off.

"I'm starved," Wade said, walking past us, spitting his gum on the ground next to Gabe's foot. "Guess I'll go see if there's any chow left. Nice talking to you."

Gabe stiffened again, and I gripped his arm tighter until Wade had melted into the crowd around the barbecue across the yard. I glanced around at the people who'd observed their altercation. Greer and Parker gave me sympathetic looks. Olivia whispered something to Bobby, who laughed. Emory winked at me and scratched behind his left ear, knowing that could make me smile even under these circumstances. It was our childhood method of nonverbal language. The summer we'd spent together we'd devised a whole series of hand signs that enabled us to communicate without anyone else knowing. It worked especially well in those long revival meetings at church, though we were always getting whispered admonitions from Dove to quit our fidgeting.

A scratch behind the left ear meant, *Hang loose, we'll talk about this later.*

I tugged on my right earlobe. *Thanks.*

"I should have beat the shit out of him for talking about you like that," Gabe said.

I pulled him toward the kitchen where I assumed Dove, the aunts, and Señora Aragon were still working. "And have it spread across every newspaper in the county? That's just what he's hoping. The best thing to do with Wade is ignore him. What happened with Kip?''

"His wrist is pretty bruised, but I don't think it's broken. Your dad's taking him to the clinic in town to get it X-rayed.''

"Will there be any trouble for you for hitting him?''

"I could still arrest him for brandishing that knife, so I imagine he'll keep his mouth shut.''

"Let's forget both of them and get you something to eat.''

Gabe allowed me to lead him toward the kitchen. Inside, as I'd suspected, Dove held court along with my aunts. The kitchen was warm and meaty smelling with the scent of Señora Aragon cooking refried beans in a huge iron skillet. Elvia, obviously hiding from Emory, was unwrapping some foil-covered cakes and pies.

"Got a man here who needs to be fed,'' I called, pushing him toward a stool. I sent a silent message to Dove with my eyes. Somehow, with what we'd always called her seventh sense, she'd already heard about the ruckus between Gabe and Wade and went into action. Nothing tames an ornery male beast, she'd often said, like a plateful of food. Within minutes the ladies were fussing over Gabe, filling a plate with barbecued chicken, the tamales that Señora Aragon had indeed set aside for him, salad, rolls, and a huge serving of refried beans smothered with Jack cheese. My aunts would keep his irritated male ego occupied for a while. He fell right into it, joking and talking, the fight with Wade temporarily shelved. His quick switch of focus made me remember Dove's unwavering assertion that most men's attention spans were as long as the average two-year-old's.

"What happened out there?'' Elvia whispered as she unwrapped a chocolate cake sprinkled with coconut.

"I'll fill you in later. I need to talk to someone.''

Leaving Gabe to the ministrations of his fan club, I went

out to the front porch and scanned the crowded front yard
for Shelby. Someone needed to tell her just what kind of
trouble she was heading for by getting involved with Wade,
and it appeared that privilege would be mine. Not seeing
her, I went looking behind the barn.

A large group of people had gathered by the big corral
where some of my girl cousins had set up three metal trash
barrels and were timing themselves in barrel racing. There
were probably some great picture opportunities, so I was
guessing that Shelby was somewhere in the crowd. Sure
enough, I found her with Greer, Parker, and Olivia sitting
on the wooden corral watching the young cowboys try to
beat the women's times. Next to them was Roland Bennett,
the owner of Bennett's Gallery of Western Art downtown.

"Roland, you made it!" I said.

"Have you ever known Rolly to miss a free meal?"
Greer said with her deep, contralto laugh.

"Now, Greer, I haven't even inspected the food yet," he
protested, his well-fed face assuring us it wouldn't be long
before he did. He was dressed in new black Wranglers, a
black silk cowboy shirt, and a suede vest decorated with
intricate Native American beading that probably cost five
hundred dollars. A paunchy little man with round copper-
colored glasses and a thin filigree of blond hair covering his
oval head, he wore his clothes awkwardly, as if they were
a costume. Which, I guessed, in a way they were. Getting
to know him the last few months, I could imagine him leaving the western art world when it was no longer the hot
thing and putting on a double-breasted navy jacket and cap-
tain's yachting cap or a three-piece suit and antique pocket
watch if that were the dress of his favored customers. But
costume or not, he knew how to do one thing, and he did
it well—and that was match artist up with collector. That
knowledge could sometimes make or break an artist's career.

"Don't worry, Roland," I said. "There's plenty of chow

left. No one ever goes away from a Ramsey barbecue hungry.''

I turned to Shelby, who was fiddling with a filter on her camera. "Shelby, can I talk to you a minute?"

"Sure, go ahead," she replied, not looking up from her camera.

"In private."

She glanced around at the rest of the group. They all gave embarrassed downward looks. She shrugged and said, "Sure, why not?"

"Let's go over to the garden," I said. Though it would probably get crowded later when the women were done in the kitchen and Dove wanted to show off her one acre flower, fruit, and vegetable garden, right now it was empty. "There's a bench underneath the walnut tree."

"Whatever." She bit the word off with a petulant tone. I had a distinct feeling this talk wasn't going to go well.

I was right.

"Chill out, Benni, I'm not going to marry the guy," she said after hearing my warning about getting mixed up with Wade.

"That's good, since he *is* already married," I replied.

She peered through the viewfinder of her camera, focusing it on something across the garden. My eyes followed the camera's lens. A rabbit sat among Dove's winter squash. He froze when Shelby's shutter clicked, then disappeared with two hops into the undergrowth.

"You know one of the first things I learned when I started studying photography?" she asked.

I didn't answer, not wanting the conversation to veer away from the subject at hand—her flirting with Wade.

"It was a quote by Dorthea Lange. She said 'One should really use the camera as though tomorrow you'd be stricken blind.' I've never forgotten that. It's also how I try to live all my life." She fiddled with the camera in her lap, ignoring me with an adolescent deliberateness. A pollen-fat bee hovered above us, then darted up into the cloudless sky like a tiny helicopter.

An impatient sound gurgled in my throat. Only someone who was so young and immature could take a quote like that and twist it around to justify doing whatever felt good at the moment—no matter who it hurt. "I'm pretty sure she didn't mean her words to be used as a justification to live thoughtlessly."

"Benni, I consider you a friend and I appreciate your concern, but I've lived on my own since I was seventeen and I really have managed to survive quite well. If I want to hang out with Wade or anyone else, I will, and I don't think it's any of your business one way or the other." She stood up, slung her camera over her shoulder, and walked through Dove's apple trees without a backward glance.

Irritated, I sat there for a moment, knowing she was right about one thing. It wasn't any of my business. But I couldn't help feeling like a big sister wanting to warn her that the trail she was riding down was most likely washed out around the corner and she was heading for a nasty fall. I sighed and stood up, also knowing there was nothing else I could do. Like all of us, she had to make her own mistakes. She just had no idea how big a mistake Wade Harper could be.

My only other chance to head this potential wreck off at the pass was to talk to Wade, an exercise in futility I didn't relish and certainly didn't want Gabe to see me do. I had to try, though, for Shelby's sake and for Wade and Sandra's. If there was any chance of saving his marriage, he had to haul his tail back to Texas as soon as possible.

I walked from crowd to crowd in the waning November sunlight looking for Wade, but couldn't find him anywhere. I didn't ask anyone as I was getting enough curious looks as it was. Finally I gave up and decided that someone upstairs was trying to tell me to let the situation go—at least for now. Inside the ranch house, the sofas and chairs in the living room had already been pushed to one end, and I found my husband, along with various members of my family, sitting around five card tables, the first round of the annual poker game just starting. Dove was wearing her lucky dog-pee-yellow "I Ain't Old, I'm Sundried" cap. That meant the serious playing had commenced.

"Going to join us, honeybun?" Dove asked, shuffling the cards like a Vegas pro. She dealt them swiftly, then picked hers up and frowned.

"This isn't a hand," she said. "It's a foot."

Not that her comment meant anything. I'd once seen her bluff her way into winning a fifty-dollar pot of quarters. My uncles and aunts and various cousins had settled in with huge mugs of Folger's coffee, bowls of M & M's, and salted cashews. That meant the games would be going until way after midnight, the men being granted special dispensation from the ten o'clock curfew. They'd started early this year— 4:00 P.M. rather than when the sun went down—probably because Dove was feeling lucky.

Gabe scooted over to make room for me at one of the tables. I shook my head no.

"No, thanks, I'm too tired. You all would get my money in two minutes. I think I'll get some cake and go in the bedroom. Has anyone seen Elvia?" I wanted to run the whole Wade-Shelby-Gabe thing by her.

"She went home," Dove said, slapping a card down and picking up another. "One of Sofia's grandbabies was feeling kinda puny, so Elvia drove her over to see him."

"I'll call her, then."

I went into my old bedroom, full now with sleeping bags, overnight bags, and the various paraphernalia of traveling women. I pushed aside a bunch of heavy sheepskin jackets and wool-lined Levi jackets and rested my back back against the maple headboard. I dialed Elvia's number and was surprised when she answered.

"How's the baby?" I asked.

"Fine. It's Maria's first, so she's nervous. It was just a bit of colic."

"I'm going to kill him if I can ever find him," I said, lapsing straight into my whining. That's one of the advantages to having a friend who's known you since childhood. You don't need to go into a lot of background detail.

"What did Wade do to Gabe to make him so mad?" she asked.

I told her.

"Greenbroke you? That sounds like Wade, crude and pathetic. And to think he still has the ability to procreate."

"The thing between him and Gabe I can handle. I'll just keep them apart while Wade is here. It's Shelby I'm worried about. She's young and angry and . . ."

"Stupid," Elvia finished.

"I was going to say stubborn, but stupid works. She thinks she has everything all figured out, but I'm afraid she's getting in chin deep pitting Kip and Wade against each other. They both have hair-trigger tempers and enough sense between them to buy half a cup of store-brand coffee. Someone's going to get hurt before this is through."

If my words had been a poker hand, they would have worn crowns.

3

AFTER A LONG conversation with Elvia, I turned on the miniature television sitting on the dresser and promptly fell asleep in the middle of a thrilling, edge-of-your-seat movie about a malevolent tornado. I woke up at ten o'clock surrounded by tiny sleeping cousins. Trying not to wake them, I eased out of bed and headed for the living room, where the poker games were still going full force. After refusing another invitation to join, I went outside to attempt once more to find Wade. Never mind the situation between him, Kip, and Shelby—we still had some unfinished business with that foul-mouthed crack he made about me. The yards around the house and barn were quieter now with most of the younger children bedded down for the night in the haphazard array of trailers, campers, and tents. Only a few dozen adults and teenagers were still wandering around. Somewhere a guitar played, and someone sang an old cowboy ballad I remembered from my childhood, used to settle down restless cattle and cranky children. Nostalgia like a thin icicle stabbed my heart. It seemed only months ago that I was one of those sleepy kids, my legs and arms tangled with my equally exhausted cousins, warm and secure in the knowledge that the adults were there protecting us and making sure everything would be okay until we woke in the morning to the smells of toasty campfire coffee and honey-cured bacon.

I walked over to the corral behind the barn to watch the horses settle in for the night, letting the sounds of their wet nickering and hooves pawing the dirt soothe me. A few minutes later I overheard voices inside the barn. Loud, angry voices.

I ran around the corner in time to see the door fly open and Shelby stomp out, pulling hay from her tangled hair, her face dark with fury.

"Shelby, what's going on?" I asked. "Are you okay?"

She glared at me and didn't answer. I stared after her retreating figure, turning around when I heard someone come up behind me.

"Shelby . . . darlin' . . . wait . . ." Wade sputtered.

"Wade, what did you do?" I demanded.

His face twisted into a frown. "I didn't do nothing, Benni. I was just giving her what she's been asking for all evening, and then she gets weird on me. Shit. Women."

The toxic scent of alcohol caused me to step back. "Wade, you jerk! How much have you had to drink? Did you try to force yourself on her?"

"I didn't force anything. She just chickened out when we were getting down to business. She told me it was over between her and that other guy."

I pressed my fingers to my temples. "She's just a kid, and you were taking advantage of a fight between her and her boyfriend. Can't you see how despicable that is?"

"She knew what she was doing. She was using me, too."

I took a deep breath. "Look, just go back to the bunk-house and get some sleep. And stay away from Shelby Johnson. That's an order."

"No problem. That woman is crazy, *loco*. She and that twerp deserve each other." He shoved his hands deep into his jean pockets and walked off.

I considered following him to make sure he went straight back to the bunkhouse, then decided that I'd had enough of his and Shelby's love triangle and chose instead to go back around to the corral, climb back up on the railing, and think about how much easier life was when I was ten years old. A few minutes later, Emory's voice came out of the darkness.

"Hey, sweetcakes, you seemed out of sorts this evening. Are you feelin' okay?"

"Just tired."

He walked over to me and leaned against the railing. "Sick and tired of the trials and tribulations of your fellow human beings?"

From my perch on the railing, I smiled at him. Emory always knew how to get right to the heart of what was bothering me. "No kidding. Let me tell you the latest."

Wade and Shelby's sordid tale only took about five minutes, but Emory listened without interrupting, his eyes shadowed in the moonless night.

He grabbed my knee and shook it gently. "There's not much you can do about folks who are determined to screw up their lives, Benni."

"I know, but don't they realize how their stupid sexual games can hurt so many people? For what? I just don't get it, Emory. Why mess up their lives for such a little thing?"

He leaned back against the railing and looked out into the dark field beyond us. "Because it isn't a little thing. Sex is a very, very big thing. Of course, our society has chosen to trivialize it by using it to sell everything from toothpaste to family vans. I'll wager if you quizzed your husband he'd tell you that a good percentage of the crimes committed in your fair county involve sex in some way. It is by no means a little thing. There's nothing bigger or as all encompassing in our lives except for death."

"Why, Emory Delano Littleton," I exclaimed. Behind me the horses stirred, nervous and snorting. "It sounds like you've been involved in some deep philosophical contemplation. Are you getting serious on me in your old age?''

His soft laugh rumbled through the cold air. ''Keep that under your cute little Stetson, dear cousin of mine. Don't want to ruin this decadent southern Lothario image I've worked so hard to create.''

I laughed in return, hopped down off the railing, and hugged him.

''Emory,'' Gabe said, coming around the corner, ''if I caught my wife like this with any other man but you, he'd be *carne asada*.''

''Is the poker game over?'' I asked. ''Did you win?''

Grinning, he pulled out a small wad of bills. ''Arnie was royally pissed at my royal flush.''

Emory *tsked* under his breath. ''Chief Ortiz, I could report you for illegal gambling.''

Gabe winked at me. ''Brave words from a man just caught behind the barn in the arms of another man's wife.''

''And on that note, I'll leave you two to your good night ritual. See you in the bunkhouse, Cousin Gabe.''

I watched Emory walk around the corner. ''I'm so glad he's here. I've missed him.''

''I can tell.'' Gabe pulled me to him, and I inhaled his musky, gingery scent. ''And I'm going to miss your warm body tonight. I think you might have become a habit with me.''

I nuzzled his neck. ''More addictive than jogging?''

''No contest, *querida*.''

We kissed until it was too tempting to continue, then started back toward the main buildings. Just as we reached the bunkhouse, the pine door flew open, and two male bodies fell to the ground, swinging fists and cursing. Sam, Bobby, and Emory followed. It only took a moment in the light from the open bunkhouse door to figure out it was Wade and Kip rolling in the dirt.

''Sam, Bobby, grab Kip. Now!'' Gabe yelled, jumping

into the fight. He wrapped an arm around Wade's neck and hauled him backwards. Sam grabbed the tail of Kip's shirt while Bobby tried to capture his friend's flailing arms. Emory stood back, watching the fray, an amused half smile on his face.

Wade struggled against Gabe's hold until Gabe tightened his forearm enough to show Wade he meant business.

"All right, all right," he croaked to Gabe. "Let me go."

"Then cool down," Gabe snapped and released him with a small shove. He planted himself between the two panting men. "I'm only going to say this once. If this happens again, I'll escort you both off the ranch myself. If you two want to beat the crap out of each other over some woman, that's your business, but it's not going to happen here. There are kids and ladies here, and they don't need to be subjected to this. Are we clear on this?"

Neither answered.

Gabe's voice dropped an octave. "Are we *clear* on this?"

They both nodded, their eyes fixed on the ground. Uncle Luke and Daddy stepped out of the camper parked next to the bunkhouse.

"C'mon, Wade," Daddy said, shaking his head in annoyance at his disturbed sleep. "We've got a spare bunk in the camper here. You 'n' Kip just need a bit of distance between you." Uncle Luke grinned and winked at me. He and Daddy were old hands at diverting the attentions of squabbling cowboys.

Wade shot Kip another angry look before following Daddy and Luke into the camper.

Gabe walked me back to the house where the living room lights were still blazing. Though it was past midnight, I knew the women in my family; they'd be up until the early morning hours gabbing.

"I hope Wade isn't planning on staying long," Gabe said when we reached the front steps.

"I'm sure he won't," I said. "He's got a ranch to run."

"He'd better watch himself. I'd just as soon lock him up as look at him, to be truthful."

"You've spent too long playing poker with Dove. You're beginning to sound like her."

He looked down at me, his irritation gone for the moment. "I think your whole family is starting to rub off on me."

"And this is a bad thing?" I laughed softly, put my arms around his waist, and slipped my hands in the back pockets of his Levi's, pulling him against me.

He groaned under his breath. "Woman, you are killing me."

"Just wanted to make sure you dream about me tonight."

"Guaranteed," he said.

Inside the house I was forced to replay the latest in the Kip and Wade war. I purposely left out the part about seeing Wade and Shelby come out of the barn together, realizing I'd forgotten to tell Gabe about it. My guess was that somehow Kip had found out about Wade and Shelby's tryst, and that's what set off the latest fight.

"You tell them for me," Dove said, wiping off the counter, "that any more of their shenanigans, and I'll be driving 'em into the chute and rubberbanding them myself. That oughta calm them down some."

"She'd do it, too," Aunt Kate said, sipping a mug of hot cocoa.

We spent the next half hour poking fun at the general stupidity brought about by testosterone, getting settled down to sleep at about one A.M. Stepping over the minefield of sleeping bodies, I crawled into my childhood bed next to two of my cousin's little girls. I fell asleep, my last thoughts before unconsciousness being about the huge country breakfast we'd all enjoy the next morning.

The one we'd eventually get around to making when all the crime scene personnel had left.

4

"HONEYBUN," DOVE WHISPERED. "Wake up now."

I jerked up, disoriented for a moment. "Jack!"

A flash of memory mixed with troubling dreams about my late husband and his brother washed over me, and for a moment it felt like a dam broke in my chest. Dove's voice had awakened me in the same way it had on that early morning Wade had come to the ranch to tell us Jack had been killed.

Two of my small cousins stirred next to me, turned, and groaned in their sleep. Their soap-sweet little-girl scents eased me back to reality.

Dove squeezed my arm. "Wake up, honeybun. I need you."

I crawled out of bed and pulled my jeans over my long cotton waffle underwear. She handed me my sheepskin jacket and old mooseskin moccasins, motioning me to follow her. In the living room we stepped over bodies cuddled in sleeping bags and blankets. On the front porch, my aunt Lollie waited, her thin, reddish face contracted with worry.

"What's going on?" I asked in a low voice. My breath blew like white smoke in front of me. The sun was just under the horizon, the cloudless sky bleached the color of wood ash. The air was damp and cold, the morning birds silent.

"We need Gabriel," Dove said. "Try not to wake anyone else up."

"Where?" There would only be one reason why she'd want me to arouse Gabe this early.

"Up in the field behind the barn. Past the corral," Aunt Lollie said, hugging herself in the cold morning air. "Lordy, I wish Clarence hadn't convinced me to quit smoking. I need a cigarette."

Dove pushed me gently between the shoulder blades. "We figured it would look less suspicious if you fetched Gabe. We'll wait up at the corral."

I ran across the yard and eased open the pine bunkhouse door. The room was warm and tart with the robust scent of men. I tiptoed across the wooden floor to the bottom bunk where Gabe slept. Sam snored above him, curled up like a huge dog under his dark wool blanket. I bent down and before I could touch Gabe's bare shoulder, his eyes snapped open, his expression alert as a guard dog's. It was a habit, he told me once, that he'd acquired in Vietnam and never lost.

"*Querida*, what's wrong?" He swung his legs over the side of the bed, reaching for his Levi's and flannel shirt.

"I'll tell you outside," I whispered. In a couple of minutes he joined me, sitting on the outside steps to pull on his socks and hiking boots.

"I think Dove and Aunt Lollie have found a body," I said.

"You *think*?" His voice was sharp as he quickly tied his boots.

"Well, I'm pretty sure. It's in the pasture behind the barn."

"Who is it?" He walked across the front yard in a long, determined stride. I skipped to keep up with him.

Blinking the sleep out of my eyes, I shook my head. "I

don't know. They didn't say." My thoughts turned to Wade and Kip and I wondered if they'd fought again after everyone had gone to bed. "Was Kip in the bunkhouse?"

His eyebrows moved toward each other in a scowl. "He was when we turned out the light."

We found Dove and Aunt Lollie standing next to an oak tree in the corner of the pasture behind the main corral. Next to them lay a human body. When we got close enough to see who it was, I gave an unbelieving gasp.

Shelby Johnson stared up at the sky, but she wasn't seeing anything. Not anymore. Gabe stooped down and placed his fingers on her neck.

I turned back and looked at my gramma and my aunt. Aunt Lollie had her arm around Dove.

"Who found her?" I asked.

"I was taking a walk up the hill to watch the sunrise," Aunt Lollie said, "and I saw something lying under this here tree. Some crows were circling around. From a distance I thought it was a calf who died or had been killed by a coyote. When I came closer . . ." She swallowed hard. "I ran as fast as I could and woke Dove."

Gabe stood up and turned to us. "Did you touch anything?"

Both women shook their heads.

"How did she die?" I asked.

"There's no overt evidence of violence," he said. "Looks like she might have fallen and hit the back of her head."

"You can actually die from that?" I asked. "I thought that was strictly TV stuff."

"A blow to the head in the right way has been known to cause immediate death," Gabe said. "But there's a good chance that she might have been shoved. Most people don't fall backwards on flat ground like this without some help. She was just unlucky enough to have a rock right where her head hit."

The anger in Wade's face when Shelby had come out of the barn flashed through my thoughts. Though I didn't want to contemplate the possibility he could be involved, as soon as I could get Gabe alone, I had to tell him about the incident.

"Go back down to the house and bring me my cellular phone from the car," Gabe told me. "This is county land. I need to call the Sheriff's Department. Take Dove and Lollie with you."

"That poor, poor child," Dove said as we hurried back to the house.

"You'd better tell everyone," I told her. "But tell them to stay down here. Gabe's like a she-bear when it comes to crime scenes."

Within the hour the Sheriff's Department had a crime scene crew there stringing the familiar yellow-and-black tape, and taking pictures, and measurements, and searching the area for physical evidence. I knew enough to stay out of Gabe's way when he went into his Sergeant Friday mode, and though this was not his official investigation, professional courtesy was being shown to him by the sheriff's investigation team. The detective on call was a man Gabe had played racquetball with, so there wasn't as much of the mine-is-bigger-than-yours contest that often took place when a crime scene was claimed by two different agencies. I hovered around the edge of the scene with the rest of my family waiting for some news. Dove kept the younger children inside the house watching videos and making sandwiches and cookies for everyone.

Gabe, standing over to the side watching the investigators search the grass around Shelby's body, caught my eye and gestured for me to come to him.

I ducked under the crime scene tape and crossed the wet pasture. "What do they think?" I asked, looking up into his sober face.

He scratched his stubbled jaw with the back of his fingers. "Too early to make any judgments. They weren't real happy when I told them how many people were out here yesterday, and I don't blame them. Is there any way you can give them a list of who was invited to the ranch?"

"They aren't serious? There had to be two hundred people here."

"They are entirely serious. Some people will be obvious suspects, but they're going to have to question everyone they can."

This seemed as good a time as any to tell him what I'd seen take place between Wade and Shelby the night before.

Gabe's face hardened as he listened. "Tell that to the detective who questions you," he said when I was finished.

"I can't believe he'd—" I started, then stopped. I didn't believe Wade would kill Shelby. Not in cold blood, anyway. I could, however, picture him giving her an angry push, her falling back . . .

I chose my words with care. "I really don't believe he'd leave her out here for someone else to find. If . . . and I'm only saying *if*, he did push her, he'd have gone for help. Wade has a temper, but he's not that coldhearted."

Gabe didn't answer, but his expression indicated he didn't believe me for one moment.

"I know him," I insisted.

"Just tell the detective," Gabe answered.

Our conversation was interrupted by the arrival of the sheriff himself. Gabe went over and started talking to him, and I wandered back down to my relatives gathered behind the fence. They crowded around me like cattle to salt mix, asking questions. I held up my hand in protest.

"I don't know anything," I said. "And right now, no one does."

I started walking back toward the house with plans to help Dove when Wade called my name. He strode toward me, his lined face troubled.

"Tell me what they found," he said.

I didn't answer immediately. I was still irritated at him for acting like such a jerk yesterday and for taking advantage of Shelby and Kip's fight. *And,* a little voice inside me said, *because he just might not be as morally upright as you insisted to Gabe.* Would he have left Shelby out in the elements to die? Not the Wade I knew all those years . . . but people change, and Jack's death and losing the ranch might have affected Wade in ways I didn't know.

"As far as I know, they haven't found anything except Shelby's body." I pulled my sheepskin jacket closer around me. The shock of her death was starting to sink in, and I wanted to run into the house, cuddle on the sofa with my little cousins, and get lost in a cartoon world where you bounced right back from being hit in the head with an anvil.

"I can't believe it." He turned his head to spit a long stream of tobacco juice. "Who would do a shitty thing like that? She was a real nice girl."

I was not surprised that it hadn't occurred to him that he'd be a prime suspect. Wade had never been known for being the brightest bulb on the Harper family Christmas tree.

"When did you last see Shelby?" I asked.

He kicked at the dirt with the toe of his worn boots. "When you saw us by the barn. She was pissed at me, but she was fine." His eyes blinked repeatedly, protesting the bright midmorning sun. "Are you sayin' they're going to think I had something to do with it?" When I didn't answer, his face grew worried.

"Benni, I didn't kill her. I swear, the last time I saw her she was fine. As far as I know, she went home. I went to the bunkhouse, and, well, you know the rest. You were there. Then I slept the rest of the night in the camper with Ben and Luke. That boyfriend of hers is probably who done it. He'd smacked her around once in a while, you know."

"Did she tell you that?"

"Yeah."

"You two sure got emotionally intimate fast," I said,

wondering why in the world she never told anyone else about Kip.

He shrugged nonchalantly. "Guess I'm easy to talk to."

"Sure, Wade, you're a regular Johnny Carson. Did you leave the camper anytime during the night?"

"I think I might've gone over to the workshop and used the john once or twice. I don't really remember. I was kinda ripped."

"Well, you'd better remember real quick, 'cause they're going to be questioning you soon."

"That's my story. I never saw her again after our fight."

I glared at him. "This is unbelievable. You've only been here a day and already you've managed to get into two fights, almost cheat on your wife, and become a possible murder suspect. What are you planning on topping that with today? Blowing up the ranch?"

He pulled off his hat and slapped the side of his leg. "That's chickenshit, Benni. I wasn't the only one involved in all that."

"What's chickenshit is a twenty-year-old girl lying dead in a field."

"I didn't kill her, I swear." The angry tilt of his jaw lowered, and his eyes softened in that warp-speed change of mood that was the Harper boys' specialty. It never failed to tug at my heart when I was married to Jack, and now, seeing it reenacted in Wade, my years with Jack tumbled back from the midnight caverns of my subconscious right smack into today.

"I want to believe you, Wade. I really do."

"I know I'm a screwup," he said. "That's why Sandra finally packed up her bedroll and moved on. I don't know what to do. What me and Shelby did yesterday was stupid, I know that. I was lonely, and she was mad. But I swear on my daddy's grave she was fine when I left her."

I didn't answer. My emotions were too on edge at the

moment to discuss his involvement any further. "I need to go help Dove right now. We'll talk later."

He nodded, his face blank, but his brown eyes clouded with worry.

Inside the house, Dove had the kids working in an assembly line making sandwiches and pressing out butter cookies to take out to the crime scene workers. The youngest ones were sitting around her huge television watching a Barney video. I helped myself to some bacon and eggs and sat down at the kitchen counter.

"I purely despise that big purple lizard," Dove said. "He gives me the willies."

"Magenta," I said, sprinkling Tabasco on my eggs.

"What?"

"Barney's magenta, not purple. Elvia told me that. It's a common misconception among Barney amateurs." I bit off a piece of bacon and smiled at her.

"Ain't true. That lizard's as purple as an eggplant."

I shook my head. "Magenta."

"Purple."

I pointed my half-eaten bacon strip at her, punctuating each syllable. "Ma-gen-ta."

Dove's great-grandkids watched our spirited exchange in fascination, not used to seeing someone argue with Dove. Then they starting jumping up and down on the sofa, ready to latch on to any silly thing after being cooped up in the house for hours. "Barney's magenta, gramma Dove. Barney's magenta! Magenta, magenta, *maa-genn-taaa*!" They screamed the last word and collapsed in a fit of giggles.

"Well, thank you very much for your input, Miss Know-It-All-Smarty-Pants," Dove carped as she mixed up egg salad for sandwiches.

Aunt Ruth walked over to the television, peered over the top of her glasses, then laughed. "Why, Dove, I think Benni's right. Barney is definitely magenta."

I smirked at Dove.

She came over and slapped the back of my neck with her hand. "Quit being so sassy and gettin' the grandbabies all riled up. I swear you're as bad as one of them. Now get to work. The folks out there are going to need something to eat, and Pizza Hut don't deliver this far." Everyone laughed, and for a moment the tension surrounding the terrible incident was eased.

The crime scene personnel worked until late afternoon. We were all eventually questioned by one of the five detectives they had working on the case. At the sheriff's detectives' request, the other women and I made a list of everyone we could remember seeing at the barbecue yesterday. When we were finished, it was 187 names long.

Gabe glanced over it before handing it to one of the detectives. "I'm glad I'm not in charge of this investigation," he said.

Later that afternoon, Gabe and I sat on the porch swing and watched the last of the detectives drive away. Once the coroner's van had picked up Shelby's body, Dove allowed the children out of the house, and they'd run whooping and hollering around the yard, trying to release their pent-up energy. The day had turned bright and cool and smelled of damp earth and smoky leaves.

"I told the detective about Wade and Shelby's argument," I said. "He didn't react too much." I watched Gabe's skeptical face, my voice hopeful.

"It certainly doesn't make him look like a class act, but it doesn't necessarily mean he killed her," he conceded.

"Why would he?" I asked. "It doesn't make sense. It makes more sense if Kip killed her."

Gabe pushed the swing back and forth with his foot. "Because, sweetheart, a lot of homicides don't make sense. Usually it just takes a split second of someone losing control. They won't be ruling out anyone this early in the game."

"I know Wade," I said. "He might be a cad, but he's no murderer."

Gabe reached over and tickled me. "A cad? Been watching a little too much PBS, don't you think?"

"Stop it!" I wiggled away from his hands. "You're one to talk, Mr. I-Don't-Read-Anything-But-Literary-Fiction."

"Louis L'Amour lover."

"Book snob."

We were squabbling good-naturedly in an attempt to keep our minds off the rough ending to the family gathering, when Emory walked up.

"Are we heading back to San Celina tonight?" he asked. We'd invited him to stay with us since he'd probably be bored out on the ranch, especially with no vehicle to get into town.

Gabe slipped his arm around my shoulders. "Whatever the *señora* wants."

"To be honest, I'd like to sleep in my own bed tonight," I said. "The gallery opening is tomorrow night, and I want to be rested for it." I laid my head back against the swing. "It's going to be sad. Shelby's photographs are featured along with Greer's paintings. She asked me to take pictures at the opening to send to her family, to prove she'd finally become a success."

A sobering silence enveloped us. We were all old enough to grasp the real tragedy of a life lost so young.

"Who will notify her family?" Emory asked.

"The Sheriff's Department will take care of that," Gabe answered, his deep-set eyes turned down and serious. "I don't envy that assignment. It's something you never get used to doing."

We went inside the house to get my things and say good-bye to Dove and the aunts. "Don't you keep him to yourself the whole time," Dove scolded me, giving Emory a big hug.

"Believe me, I won't," I said. "As soon as I get sick of him, I'll ship him back out here to you."

"Excuse me, ladies," he said, "I *am* in the room."

"Oh, hush," Dove and I said simultaneously, causing everyone to laugh.

Gabe, driving his sky-blue Corvette with his usual disregard for speed limits, beat me and Emory home and was boiling water when we walked in.

"Spaghetti okay with you two?" he asked.

"As long as I don't have to make it," I said. "I made enough sandwiches today to feed a small Latin American country."

After showing Emory to the guest room, I checked the answering machine. Between Gabe and me we had eleven messages. Nine were artists from the co-op wanting me to call them back with details about Shelby's murder, and two were for Gabe—one was Jim Cleary, the other, the sheriff himself. Gabe returned his calls. I didn't. I'd see all of them tomorrow night at the gallery opening and I had no doubt that Shelby would be the biggest topic of conversation that night as well as the remainder of the week. Until I was forced to, I didn't even want to think about it.

During dinner, we deliberately didn't discuss anything of more importance than the activities of the upcoming Heritage Days.

"Cow Plop Contest? Kiss the Pig Contest?" Emory asked toward the end of the meal. "Please explain these peculiar western competitions to this poor, ignorant southern boy."

"Just for the record, it was not my idea," Gabe said, standing up and taking his plate over to the sink to rinse off.

"The Cow Plop Contest benefits the homeless shelter," I answered. "There's a big corral at the rodeo grounds that's painted into square yards. You pay five bucks for a square and hope the recently fed cow does his business there. The winner gets a year's free ice cream from the San Celina Creamery. The losers just get a lot of fun."

Emory grinned. "Yes, but the real question is what does the cow get?"

"Relief," Gabe said.

We groaned, but laughed anyway.

"And the pig kissing?" Emory asked.

Gabe groaned on that one.

"That's one you'd better make sure and see," I said. "The money raised for that is for Corrie's House, a shelter for abused and neglected children. People vote by paying a dollar, and whoever gets the most votes has to kiss a pig on Thursday night at the farmer's market. And guess who's rumored to be winning?" I giggled and jerked my thumb in my husband's direction.

Gabe rolled his eyes and stuck his plate and silverware in the dishwasher.

"We will definitely have to immortalize that on film," Emory said. "Tell me, Chief, will you shave first?"

"Oh, no," I said. "If I have to suffer, so does the pig."

"Just for that remark, you two get to finish kitchen detail," Gabe said.

"I'll take you around town tomorrow," I promised Emory when we all said good night at ten o'clock. "Show you the museum and all the changes."

"The bookstore will be one of our stops, I trust," he said, his eyes lighting up.

"Masochist," Gabe said, shaking his head.

"Aren't we all when it comes to our women?" Emory said, arching one eyebrow in my direction.

"Touché," Gabe replied.

In our bedroom, pulling on one of Gabe's long sleeved tee shirts, I said, "Elvia would not have liked being referred to as Emory's woman." I crawled under our flannel-covered down comforter, snuggling next to his warm body.

"She could do worse."

"You try to convince her."

"No, thanks. That's your department." He pulled me under his arm. "Man, it feels good to be back in our own bed."

I draped my leg over his and curled close, listening to his breathing slow down as we both neared sleep, my thoughts moving back over the incidents of the day.

"Gabe?"

"Hmm . . ."

"Do you think things really are getting worse? I mean, in San Celina this last year or so. The violence. I mean . . ."

His body stiffened slightly, and I knew he'd taken my words in a personal way. He'd only been chief a little over a year and was sensitive to the *Tribune*'s recent assertions that the crime rate had risen since he'd been hired. I rubbed my hand across his bare chest in a slow circle. "I don't mean it's your fault," I said, trying to backpedal. "I mean things are so different than when—" I stopped, realizing I'd gone too far.

"When you were married to Jack."

"No! I mean, maybe, during that time it was . . . less . . . scary. It's just that things now . . ." I inhaled a shuttering breath. "It scared me that Shelby was killed at our ranch. The ranch has always been a place where I felt safe, where it seemed like nothing could hurt me or anyone else."

He didn't answer. I crawled on top of him and looked down into his face, stiff with anger in the dim light. Gingerly, trying to avoid his prickly whiskers, I brushed a kiss across his lips.

"Gabe, don't be upset. I'm sorry if I made you feel bad. I'm not blaming you." I nibbled his unyielding bottom lip. "C'mon, Friday, don't be mad. You're a wonderful chief of police. Absolutely the best I've ever slept with. I'll do anything to make it up to you." His mustache tickled as I felt his lips turn slightly up under mine.

"Anything?" he said, rolling me back over and taking

my face in his big hands. "Not being a man who foolishly passes up any golden opportunity, I'm afraid you just may regret those words, *querida*."

But, of course, I didn't.

5

AFTER EMORY'S FAVORITE breakfast the next morning—jack cheese, green onion and guacamole omelettes—the three of us lazed around trading sections of the Sunday paper. I eagerly read the article about the women's western art show in the Lifestyles section of the *Tribune*. It was titled "Making Art Equal—A Lifetime Journey" and had quotes from many of our artists including Olivia, Greer, and Parker. Emory kept Gabe and me in stitches as he critiqued the paper in a way that only a veteran journalist could. Around noon, we all finally showered and dressed, and Gabe headed down to the sheriff's office to see what was going on with the investigation, while Emory and I drove to the bookstore to update Elvia.

Her tiny MG was parked in front. Though it was her day off, she was there as usual. Her employees one time threatened to pitch in and have a Murphy bed installed in the wall of her office so she'd never have to leave. People laugh, but that was why Blind Harry's was so successful.

"She works too hard," Emory said, already sounding proprietary. "She needs to learn to have a little fun."

"Right, and you're the one to show her how," I replied. "If you're wanting to impress her, cuz, I'd suggest finding a different tactic than criticizing her work habits.''

''That'll change when we get married,'' he said.

I stopped, blocking the front door, and turned to gape at him. ''Pull back on them reins there, honey. You sound like you honestly believe that.''

His face was serene. ''Sweetcakes, I've believed it since I was eleven years old.''

We entered the bookstore, and before I could even reply, something happened that, if it were possible, made it even less likely Elvia would ever exchange wedding vows with my lovesick cousin.

First, I need to explain about Sweet William.

Elvia has never had a pet. A workaholic since she was five years old and operated her first Kool-Aid stand (sugar five cents extra), she never had time for pets. Not that she hates animals. She just never had time in her quest for some ambiguous work-oriented goal to bond with anything but the cyber-fish on her computer's screen saver. To tease her, I often threatened to buy her one of those fancy little dogs who look like mops with eyes.

''Don't you dare,'' she'd said. ''If I need any animal companionship, I'll take one of my brothers to lunch.'' So I didn't. But that didn't keep someone else from doing it.

A longtime customer of hers, an elegant, elderly lady named Evelyn Mullar, loved Elvia so much because of the time she took to talk to her and help her, she left her entire estate to Elvia—twenty thousand dollars in stocks and bonds and a mint-condition '57 Chevy Coupe her brothers were currently fighting over.

And Sweet William. A championship Persian cat the color of undercooked pancakes, he had an attitude that can only be described as Elvia-like—temperamental and definitely high class. And picky about who he deemed worthy of his affection. Of course, he loved Elvia immediately—cats of a feather, so to speak. The rest of us he tolerated. And that was on his good days. All her employees . . . and

I . . . had the thin, white scars on our hands as proof of our sincere intentions and his fickle personality. Elvia ignored our complaints and said she could appreciate his discriminating taste.

Like I said, a match made in Hallmark heaven.

The minute he set his golden eyes on Emory, he adored him.

"What in the world did you do to that cat?" I exclaimed as Sweet William jumped down off his customary perch next to the cash register (we swore he liked the sound of money dropping into the coffers almost as much as his owner) and wrapped his perfectly groomed body around Emory's gray wool slacks, purring like a small expensive Cadillac.

"What a lovely creature," Emory said, bending over and picking Sweet William up. He tucked him under his arm as naturally as if he'd raised him from a kitten. Sweet William's eyes closed, and he hummed in ecstasy.

"Amazing," the spiky-haired clerk behind the counter said, her kohl-darkened eyes wide with surprise. "That cat hates everyone except Elvia."

Emory winked at the clerk, causing her to blush a bright pink. "He's just particular about his friendships. I can 'preciate that."

I just shook my head and laughed. Just then Elvia's office door opened, and she started down the stairs. Her face was in that concentrating work scowl until she got halfway down the stairs and she spotted Emory holding Sweet William. She stopped, looked at me, her expression turning into an I'm-going-to-kill-you-when-I-get-you-alone scowl. Only someone who knew her as well as me could tell the difference. I gave her a big smile, thankful I'd eaten breakfast. At least I'd die with a full stomach.

"Hi, Elvia," I called. "Look how Sweet William just took to Emory right off. Isn't that great?"

She reached the bottom of the stairs and strode across

the floor to us. That is, if a five-foot-one-inch woman can stride. Her tiny heels click-clacked across the glossy wooden floor. I looked up at my cousin's face as he watched her walk across the room. His eyes announced to the world that all he wanted to do was just tuck her Chanel-suited little figure under his other arm and walk off into the sunset. When she reached us, she grabbed Sweet William from Emory and dumped the cat on the counter. Sweet William looked astonished and hurt, having never been treated so unceremoniously. Emory's eyes sparkled with amusement.

"What do you two want?" she snapped.

"I was just giving Emory a tour of the town's hot spots," I said. "How could I pass up Blind Harry's? The most successful bookstore on the Central Coast. Shoot, in California, I bet." I knew the way to Elvia's stubborn heart. "C'mon, give us the fifty-cent tour. Emory hasn't ever seen your bookstore. I've been bragging about it for years."

I was right, and once she started walking us through the store, she temporarily forgot her annoyance at me and her dislike of Emory. Her face lit up as she talked about book trends, the possibilities opening up in CD-ROM, and her eventual plans to buy the used clothing store next door and expand her square footage. Emory listened intently, asking intelligent questions and keeping his lovesick expression hidden. Elvia started to relax when we ended up in the basement coffee house where we sipped lattes at one of the round oak tables scattered about the large room. Vivaldi played softly in the background, Sunday being classical music day at Blind Harry's. Elvia rotated the background music to accommodate all her customers. Wednesdays, featuring bluegrass and country oldies, were my favorite days at the store.

"Any news on Shelby's death?" Elvia asked when Emory excused himself to wander around the coffee house and peruse the book-lined shelves. The only criteria for Elvia's casual lending library of used books was that you replaced a book you borrowed with another, thus always providing an eclectic and changing array of free literature.

I leaned back in one of the heavy oak library chairs. "Not yet, but Gabe was going to the sheriff's office this afternoon, so I'll know more tonight. If there's anything to know. Gabe thinks there might be some foul play involved, but he said she also could have just fallen and hit her head."

Elvia looked as skeptical as I felt. "Backwards?"

"It does sound like a bit of a stretch, but the alternative is to believe that someone at the barbecue left her to die." I couldn't say the word murder. "I find that much less appealing."

She nodded, not verbalizing what we were both thinking. Wade had that kind of temper, though I'd never seen, him manifest it toward a female in all the years we lived at the ranch. He'd been raised by his tough-handed Texan father to believe that a man never beat up on women or kids, or creatures that were weaker or smaller than him. It was an old-fashioned mixture of condescension and respect, and though I had always been a bit uncomfortable with John Harper, Sr.'s beliefs, which also included the assertion that women belonged in the kitchen and kids should be seen, not heard, I respected the fact that he taught his sons to never take advantage of their brute strength. But John Harper had been dead a long time, and people often change over the years, rejecting the things they'd been taught as children. Maybe Wade had stepped over the line his father had drawn for his sons so many years ago.

"May I borrow a book?" Emory asked, walking back up to our table. "Or I'd be happy to purchase it, if that is your preference. This is one of my favorites, and I haven't reread it for a while." Elvia's face was neutral, almost genial, a distinct step up from the annoyed look of an hour ago. My hopes were raised about the date I'd so rashly promised Emory.

When he held up the book for her inspection, two lines

bisected her perfect black eyebrows, and my hopes were trampled under galloping hooves.

"You don't need to buy it," she said, standing up, her voice crisp and businesslike. "Just return it when you're through." She turned to me. "What time is the reception at Roland's gallery tonight?"

"Seven," I said, confused at her sudden change of mood.

"I'll see you there." She walked away, her head held high. Now that she couldn't see him, Emory watched her retreating back with an open expression of adoration.

I turned back to my cousin. "Emory, what book are you borrowing?"

He held the faded used book for me to read the title. Then it all became clear. I couldn't help but laugh.

"Why would *Pride and Prejudice* make her mad?" he asked.

"I don't know how you do it, Emory, but that's her all-time favorite book in the world. I mean, she has parts of it memorized."

Emory just smiled his slow, southern smile.

"Fate," he said.

6

EMORY AND I spent the next few hours driving around San Celina visiting places he remembered from his summer here twenty-five years ago. After a tour of the folk art museum, we stopped off at Liddie's Cafe for lunch.

"Emory Littleton, you've done grown into a movie star!" Nadine Johnson squealed when we walked into Liddie's brown-panelled truckstop foyer. "Come over here and give me a hug right now." Nadine had ruled as head waitress at the cafe whose neon sign made the improbable claim "Open 25 Hours A Day" since before I could read the home-cooked items on the peeling plastic menus. She had a memory as long and sharp as an ice pick, especially if you tickled her or ticked her off. Not surprisingly, Emory fit into the former category.

"You don't be gone so long, you hear," she said, smacking his back with her order pad after leading us to one of the six-person red vinyl booths.

"Yes, ma'am," he said, pulling off his tweed jacket which she snatched from him and carefully hung on the coat rack attached to the booth. We ordered cheeseburgers, onion rings, and chili-cheese fries.

"And a vanilla Coke for Emory," Nadine said triumphantly.

"Lord have mercy, Nadine, I can't believe you remembered," Emory said, laughing.

She smacked him again with her order pad. "I reckon I ain't that old yet, Emory Littleton. And I expect a big tip. If that jacket of yours didn't cost you five hundred dollars, I'll eat my apron."

"I'll make sure Benni gives you at least thirty percent," he said.

"Ha!" she said. "That'll be the day."

"So much has changed," he said after she left. "Thank goodness Liddie's and Nadine haven't."

"The changes aren't as noticeable when you're living here, but I know what you mean. Life seems to be like one of those bullet trains, doesn't it?"

When our food came we reverted to our childhood roles, arguing over who got the biggest onion ring or the juiciest-looking cheeseburger.

"Quit hogging all the chili," I said, jabbing my fork at his over our shared chili-cheese fries.

"You don't need it, Miss Piggy," he replied, clinking his fork against mine. "Cottage cheese thighs will surely turn off that husband of yours." We were in the midst of a spirited fork fight when Greer and Parker walked up.

"Behold our illustrious leader," Greer said, laughing deeply. "Not to mention she's also the wife of a highly esteemed city employee."

"She started it," Emory said, getting in the last jab. Just like he always did as a kid.

I stuck my tongue out at him. "Whiny baby."

"We'd better get in here and referee before they get thrown out of this joint," Greer said to Parker. Parker smiled and slid into the booth next to me.

"Just stay away from my chili," Emory said, scooting over to make room for Greer.

"Are you all ready for tonight?" I asked Greer.

She shook her head no. "I thought being interviewed for that art magazine was nervewracking, but this has it beat by far."

"Have you been down to Roland's gallery this week?" Parker asked.

"No," I said. "I've been so busy getting ready for our exhibit at the museum as well as the things I'm involved with for the Heritage Days that I haven't had time."

"Greer's paintings look spectacular," Parker said, her wide cheeks stained crimson from the cold outside. "I think this will be a real turning point in her career. Major galleries all over the country will be begging to show her after her opening and that article comes out."

"I can't wait to see them," I said, smiling at Greer. Her face held the mixture of pride and dread I'd come to learn was common to artists about to show their work publicly.

"I'm grateful to Roland for the opportunity," she said. She nodded at Parker. "Her time will come soon, I'll venture to say," she said graciously. "And she's a lot younger than me."

Parker blushed and ducked her head. "If I'm lucky."

After their orders of chef's salads arrived, we discussed Greer's reception. Emory and I were sharing a piece of lemon icebox pie when Parker brought up Shelby's photographs in the show.

"It's going to be kind of weird, don't you think?" she said, stirring her melting ice with a red-striped plastic straw. "I mean, seeing her pictures and knowing she's . . . not here anymore."

"Tragic," Emory said, and we all murmured agreeing noises.

"What's Gabe say about it?" Greer asked. "Did they rule it an accident?"

"I guess it's still up in the air. He doesn't know much," I said. "It's not really his investigation since it happened on county land.'' I sighed and rested my chin on my hand. ''I just don't want to believe she was killed on the ranch I grew up on.''

Greer reached over and patted my other hand. Her palm was dry and cool. ''I know what you mean. If that had happened on our ranch, I'd be going bonkers. It's been in my family five generations, and we've been lucky enough to escape any criminal activity.'' She rapped her knuckles on the countertop. ''At least any we know about. Let's just hope they discover it was an accident. For everyone's sake.''

Parker nodded in agreement and pushed aside a piece of boiled egg, a troubled look on her face.

''Let's try and enjoy tonight anyway. I'll see both of you there.'' I nudged Parker so I could slide out of the booth.

At home, Emory claimed the shower first, so I was lying on the sofa, channel cruising, when Gabe walked in. I clicked off the television and turned eager eyes to him.

He held up his hand before I could speak. ''There's nothing to tell, so don't even start.''

I sat up and threw the channel changer at him. He caught it one-handed and grinned.

''Oink, oink,'' I said, smiling back. ''You know, I really do have a vested interest this time, because it happened on my family's ranch. Don't hold back on me, Friday, and don't give me any crap about it being official business 'cause I'll come over there and smack you hard, I swear I will.''

He sat down in his black leather recliner, kicking off his topsiders. ''Sweetheart, I love it when you talk rough to me.'' He pushed back in the chair.

I started to throw a pillow at him, then changed my mind and put it behind my back. ''Seriously, Gabe, what's going on?''

His face sobered, and he stroked his porcupine beard. ''Not much. I imagine it'll be one of those homicides where the only way they'll make any headway is to question and requestion the people at the party.''

"Is anyone from her family coming out?''

He shook his head, his eyes unblinking and hard. "No. They just wanted to know when her body could be shipped back, and her father demanded to talk to the sheriff personally. He threw around the fact that he golfed with a couple of U.S. senators and had some kind of tenuous connection to the White House. I guess that was supposed to insure John's complete cooperation."

"I bet that really endeared him to John." John Quincy Nesbit, San Celina's county sheriff, was a local man who knew San Celina County and its citizens as well as he did the bloodlines of the championship Weimaraner dogs he raised on his ranch north of San Celina. He was the original good ole boy who knew how to play that image to the hilt when it suited his purpose. He rarely let it be known that along with getting a degree in criminology at USC, he also got one in nineteenth-century French literature. He and Gabe loved flaunting the fact that they were the only two top city officials who didn't play golf.

"John can handle a snooty Chicago surgeon," Gabe said. "It's the local people who have him worried."

"Why?''

"He's just taking the same heat I do whenever there's a murder. All you Central Coasters seem to think that even though the rest of the country has major crime, it is somehow more of an insult when it happens here in your little piece of Eden."

I didn't answer, knowing that was a little return jab for the remark I made in bed last night. He was right, in a way. We did have a rather unrealistic sense of entitlement. The last few days I'd heard the same lament from my aunts and uncles about the rural areas where they lived. Crime had certainly become more mobile in our country, and those of us raised in rural and semirural communities were a bit naive in thinking that it wouldn't affect us. We'd often had to do without the services found in big cities so, in compensation, we'd prided ourselves on sacrificing convenience for a safe and clean environment for our families. Now, it seemed, even that was gone.

"No one in her family cared enough to come out," I said, feeling an incredible sadness. Her family was more heartless than she even had managed to convey to me. "If someone in my family had died like that, the whole clan would be out there haranguing the police."

"How well I know," he said with an ironic smile. "Getting involved has never been a problem with your family. But not everyone's like that. I've seen both kinds of reactions in homicide investigations—those who are involved in every little detail and those who just want to bury their dead and get on with it."

"Which do you think is better?"

He shrugged. "For the homicide investigator, it's always easier when you don't have someone dogging your steps. On the other hand, often family and friends can give insight into a victim's background that even the best investigator can't dig up. Six of one, I guess."

"Shower's free," Emory called.

"You go first," I said to Gabe. "I need to contemplate my wardrobe."

I thought about Shelby and the people in her circle here in San Celina as I stood in front of the closet gazing at my clothes. I pulled out the deep rust broomstick cotton skirt I'd bought at a new store downtown called Santa Fe Trails and added a black linen shirt. With my black Tony Lama boots, a hand-carved leather belt and a tiger's eye bolo tie I'd swiped from my dad, that would have to do. I pulled out an Arrow shirt, a slate blue cashmere pullover and a pair of gray wool slacks for Gabe.

We ended up taking two cars, the Corvette and the 1950 Chevy truck, since none of the vehicles we owned rode more than two comfortably except my old Harper pickup, which both Gabe and Emory vetoed. Gabe surprised me when he handed his Corvette keys to Emory and said, "Consider it yours while you're here." My cousin Emory had won over my husband more completely than I'd realized.

It took Gabe and me less time than usual to find a parking space downtown since many of the students were not yet back from their Thanksgiving holidays. It was a cool, pleasant evening, and with Gabe's arm around me as we walked down Lopez Street, I could almost forget the tragedy that had happened less than forty-eight hours earlier.

Roland's Gallery of Western Art was situated next to a restaurant called the Mercedes Cowboy where the cuisine was definitely more decorative than rib-sticking. On the other side of the gallery was a new establishment called Miss Christine's Tea and Sympathy. Teahouses were just starting to catch on in San Celina and were slowly becoming the place where businesswomen congregated, with an atmosphere (and prices) that tended to keep out college students. I'd met Elvia a couple of times at Miss Christine's, but always felt a bit panicky in the knick-knack–crammed rooms, like a clumsy adolescent in the crystal section of Gottchalk's Department Store. Elvia was subtly trying to guide me into my society-wife role. I think she pretty much threw in the towel when she caught me scraping dried mud and manure off the heels of my boots on the curb in front of the tearoom.

Roland's gallery was small but open feeling, with walls panelled in faded red barn siding that he bragged he'd paid some old farmer next to nothing for. That old farmer, a regular customer at the Farm Supply, just chuckled when he told Daddy and his friends that he reckoned getting paid to let a bunch of crazy city folks haul away a load of termite-eaten wood he was going to have to take a day off to burn was okay by him. Roland had used the wood in a clever

way to create a rustic look that set off the western paintings
and sculptures in his gallery to a wonderful advantage. With
simple track lighting, an occasional placing of "naturally
aged" farm and ranch implements on the walls, and his ten-
thousand-dollar mahogany and steer horn desk, he'd created
a gallery that could rival any in Taos or Jackson Hole.

Inside the gallery, people were already crowded shoulder
to shoulder, holding the requisite wineglasses filled with local chardonnays and zinfandels and munching on shrimp-
dotted crackers and seaweed-wrapped California rolls.
Though I saw some familiar faces in the throng of colorfully
dressed people, many of them were strangers to me, probably out-of-town collectors here to check Greer's and
Shelby's work. I looked over at Greer's smiling face as Roland introduced her to a group of matrons dressed in
pseudo–Santa Fe clothes featuring an abundance of
turquoise, howling coyotes, and sequins. She glanced up,
saw me, and gave me the subtlest eye roll. I gave her a
discreet thumbs up and turned back to my husband.

"Want anything from the bar?" he asked.

"Since I doubt that Roland has allowed a lowly Coke at
this shindig, I'll just take club soda. No food. I think I'd
rather go out to eat afterwards."

"Sounds good to me." I watched him move through the
crowd, getting caught twice before he could make it even
halfway to the bar in the back. It would probably be a while
before he returned with my club soda, so I turned to study
Shelby's photographs on the wall next to me, since trying
to actually maneuver in this crowd constituted a serious risk
of smashed toes.

I gazed up at the photographs, remembering the day
Shelby had taken them. Daddy and I were moving cattle
from one pasture to another. She caught me in myriad
ways—chasing through high grass after an itinerant cow,
my legs spread wide in the stirrups; me checking one of
Badger's shoes for a stone, backlit by the morning sun, my

still somewhat stubby braid poking out from under my battered Stetson; me sitting against a tree trunk, teasing Bodie,
my dad's Australian shepherd, with a piece of ham, Daddy
grinning in the background. Her photographs were stark and
strong and real, capturing the life of a ranch woman like
none I'd ever seen.

My favorite was an 11 x 14 of me and Dove sitting on
the porch. Shelby had titled it "Gentling the Calf." I had
taken off my hat and was sitting cross-legged on the ground
in front of Dove's chair. I don't remember what we were
talking about, but we were both smiling. Dove had reached
over to brush something out of my hair. The tender look on
her face caused my throat to clench up.

"She was a very talented young woman," a deep voice
said behind me. "That picture brought tears to my eyes."

I turned and looked up at the huge, snowy-haired man
who, because of the crowd, stood inches from me, close
enough for me to feel his body heat. He had to be at least
six foot four and was as square and solid as a granite building. He wore his hair pulled back in a ponytail and was
dressed in worn Levi's and a gray flannel Pendleton shirt.
His eyes were small, busy, and the color of dark brown
raisins. An intricate turquoise cross earring swung from one
ear. His tanned face was criss-crossed with deep lines like
cracks in old adobe. I would have guessed his age at seventy
or so. There was something familiar about him, as if we'd
met before, but I couldn't put my finger on where or when.

"Yes," I agreed. "Shelby was very talented."

He gestured at the photograph with his half-empty glass
of wine. "Is she a relative of yours?"

I hesitated, not sure if he meant Shelby or Dove.

"The extremely lovely older lady," he said, his rumbling
voice sounding just short of laughing at me. Was he being
sarcastic about Dove's looks?

I hesitated again, feeling a strange urge to walk away
from this man's intense gaze. I mentally shook myself. What

was wrong with me? This nice older man was just trying to make casual conversation. Why was I putting all sorts of innuendo to it? "She's my paternal grandmother," I said, keeping my voice neutral.

"Is she married?"

"Widowed."

"Does she live around here?"

"Yes."

"Are you close?"

"Very."

He gave me a long, speculative look. "Does she have a name?"

I looked directly into his ferret eyes, tired of his bold questions. "Yes."

He sipped his wine, amusement softening his wrinkles. "If I give you a dollar, will you tell it to me?"

"No." I glanced around the room, looking for someone I knew so I could politely escape this irritating man's cross examination.

His laughing voice returned. "Is she wanted by the police or perhaps the IRS?"

"Of course not," I said in a tart voice.

He waited long enough to make me feel foolish.

"Dove," I finally said.

"Dove," he repeated. "Dove." He rolled her name over his tongue in a way that made me distinctly uncomfortable. "What an extraordinary name. Does it fit her?"

I shrugged. "Some people might not think so."

He sipped from his glass again, undeterred by my coolness. He continued studying me in a manner that was definitely agitating. "And what does granddaughter think?"

I forced a polite, close-lipped smile. "I think granddaughter needs to use the ladies' room. Please excuse me."

"Certainly," he said, his smile never wavering. "We'll talk again, I'm sure."

Melting into the crowd, I thought, *not if I can help it,*

buddy, though I still wasn't sure why he made me so uncomfortable. I remembered reading somewhere that people's chemicals actually did react to each other, that some scientists believe that was the secret behind "love at first sight" as well as people disliking someone on the first meeting. In the same article, psychiatrists discounted that theory, stating that all our reactions have roots in our background somewhere. Whatever was true, this man set my teeth on edge and I wanted to stay as far away from him as possible. I wandered over to the portable bar, where Emory was sipping a caramel-colored drink and staring across the room at Elvia. As usual, she was surrounded by admiring men. Emory's face looked thoughtful.

"That devious look brings back memories," I said. "What are you plotting and what's in there?" I pointed at his old-fashioned glass.

"Ginger ale. My ulcer can't take any of the mediocre bourbon our host has provided for this shivaree. And I'll have you know I'm not plotting. She's desperately in love with me. She just doesn't know it yet."

I grabbed his glass and took a huge gulp. "You always were a kid prone to fantasy. Far be it from me to try and impose any reality into that beautiful little world you've concocted in your feather-headed southern brain."

He gestured at the bartender for another ginger ale. "Your eyes are wild, sweetcakes. What's wrong?"

I twirled the ice around in my drink. "You know I hate gatherings like this. Everyone trying to outsnob everyone else. Then there's the whole thing with Shelby. Just looking at her pictures made me want to cry. And there was this guy who was kinda weird, asking all sorts of personal questions."

His face grew serious and protective. "Where is he?"

"You can't miss him," I said. "He's about ten feet tall and has a white ponytail."

Emory gazed out over the crowd, his eyes sharp behind

his professor eyeglasses. ''Is the man you're referring to wearing a gray flannel shirt?''

''Yes, and a stupid-looking turquoise earring,'' I said. ''I know I'm overreacting, but he . . .''

Emory gave a small chuckle.

''What's so funny?'' I asked, turning my gaze to the man. At that moment, he looked up from the gaggle of sparkling society matrons surrounding him and spotted us staring at him. He held up his wineglass in a salute. Emory nodded in reply.

''Do you know him?'' I demanded. ''Who is he?''

''Remember that personally signed photograph I sent you for your birthday three years ago?''

It hung in my bedroom next to my vanity, where I saw it every day when I fixed my hair. It was a black-and-white photograph of a woman leading three horses, her head turned slightly so you couldn't see her face. Through the leaves of the oak tree shading the woman, a hint of a child's face peered, like a Cheshire cat, through the foliage. It was a brilliantly whimsical picture that never failed to touch my heart. But it was no wonder because the photographer was the famous Pulitzer Prize–winning Isaac Lyons, a man whom many believed to be more talented than Ansel Adams.

''He took it,'' Emory said.

I looked back over at the man who had since turned his attention back to the fawning ladies. ''That's Isaac Lyons?'' Now I realize why he seemed so familiar. After Emory had sent me the print, I'd seen a book of Isaac Lyons's photographs in Blind Harry's. Though I'd never have spent seventy-five dollars for a book of nothing but pictures, I spent an hour looking at them in the store. It was a book on county fairs. He captured the heart of his subjects in a way that was gripping, touching, and at times almost frightening. It made me think of Indian tribes who feared getting their pictures taken, afraid it would capture their soul. That's exactly what his pictures felt like, so intimate that it seemed he'd stolen pieces of their souls. At the back of the book was a small self-portrait, his shadowed face almost unrecognizable. But he'd turned his ability to capture a person's essence on himself and revealed just enough to make him seem familiar to me.

"What happened between you two?" Emory asked. "I've only met him casually at a few soirees such as this, but he seemed a nice enough fellow."

"I don't know. It was the way he watched my every move. He was just so . . . searching."

"He's a photographer, Benni. That's his profession."

"Something else," I said. "I don't know what. He was way too interested in Shelby's picture of Dove. I wonder what he's doing here in our town. It's not like we're on the A list for art shows here in San Celina."

"That's his MO," Emory said. "He travels around to small towns and stays awhile, looking for subjects. His specialty is common people, if you're familiar with any of his work."

"Well, he can be the King of England, for all I care. He still gives me the creeps."

Emory looked back over in Isaac Lyons's direction. "You might have to get used to him, sweetcakes, 'cause it appears he's moving into your territory. And rumor has it he's quite the ladies man."

I turned back to stare at the man and felt my blood pressure start to rise. During the few minutes I'd been talking to Emory, Dove had arrived, and Mr. Lyons had extricated himself from his admiring throng of art lovers, holding out his bearlike hand and smiling down at her. And darned if Dove wasn't smiling back. Simpering might be a better word.

"Oh, geez," I said.

"Don't overreact," Emory whispered in my ear. "Believe me, I've had experience with my own long-widowed and much sought-after daddy. If they even sense you disapprove, they rebel like teenagers and do exactly the opposite of what you want them to do.''

"Dove's no fool,'' I said, though my words seemed hollow when I saw her touch the photographer's arm in a way that can only be described as flirtatious. ''She'll never fall for his line.'' One of my aunts had obviously done her hair up in a complicated braided bun with a few silvery tendrils trailing down her neck. In her good silk navy dress, wearing silver hoop earrings, she did present an arresting picture. It never occurred to me until that moment that my grandmother had once been, and still was, an attractive woman. One capable of being desired by a man. For some reason, that troubled me—the idea that she could have the same vulnerability that sometimes left me slightly fearful of the sensual power that my own often mystifying husband had over me.

"Um-hm,'' Emory said. ''While you stew, I think I see a slackening in the action around my own fair lady. We'll compare notes later.'' He patted my back and maneuvered through the crowd toward an unsuspecting Elvia with the same determination I'd seen in bulls heading toward unsuspecting heifers.

Tired of the noise and warring smells of women's perfumes, I slipped through a back doorway to the small room behind the gallery where Roland kept his true working office as well as paintings and sculptures waiting to be unwrapped, logged in, and priced. I wandered around, looking at the labels on the boxes, trying to kill time before going back into the crowd. I flipped through some matted but unframed pictures lying against the wall. Some were duplicates of Shelby's show prints except for her missing signature. The alarmed back door was open, and I stuck my head through it into the alley to inhale a breath of fresh air. Greer was leaning against the back wall of the brick building, a lighted cigarette in her fingers. At the end of the alley, through the open door of Sweet Dreams Coffee House, a sweet, mournful blues melody floated down to us.

"I didn't know you smoked," I said, stepping out into the brightly lit alley. She dropped the cigarette on the ground and mashed it with her coffee-colored boot. The smoke she blew out mingled with the cloud caused by the cold night air.

"I quit ten years ago, so I had to bum this off the bartender. Boy, it sure doesn't relax me like it used to."

I leaned next to her against the wall. "Feeling a bit overwhelmed?"

"Absolutely. I mean, I'm thrilled as can be, you know that. There's actually art reporters here from both the *San Francisco Chronicle* and the *L.A. Times*. And at least three-fourths of my works have acquired that blessed little red 'sold' sticker. Roland's a genius, no doubt about it. It's just that after all these years, it's almost a letdown, you know? And there's the thing with Shelby." Greer shook her head, her beaded earrings catching in her hair.

"I know."

"Have you heard anything?"

"No, and I'm not likely to. Like I told you this afternoon, it's not really Gabe's investigation."

"Don't he and the sheriff communicate?"

I shrugged. "Some, but Gabe has enough city crime to worry about. I'm sure he'll keep up on it, but it's not a priority in the sense that it's not his department's responsibility to clear it."

She gave a small chuckle. "My, my, you are learning the rhetoric of the political wife, aren't you?"

I grimaced. "That did sound kinda pompous, didn't it? But I'm here to tell you, this thing has me as spooked as a colt on a windy night. Especially since it happened at our ranch."

"I can imagine. I guess that gives you quite the incentive to get involved . . . again, Miss Marple."

I leaned over and pushed her gently. "Nancy Drew, thank you very much. Or Trixie Belden. Or even Kinsey Millhone. But Miss Marple? Please, I'm not that old. And I'm not going to answer that on the grounds it might get me in trouble with a certain law enforcement official. Besides, I'm too busy this week to play detective. You should know that."

"You and me both," she said, sighing. "This week, I've agreed to teach four workshops, judge an art show, give three talks on women in the arts, and be interviewed by some writer from the *L.A. Times*. Not to mention that Roland wants me to get started on my next series since this one is sold out. This clutching for fame business sure keeps you from doing what it is you really want to do." She gave a mocking smile. "Then again, it's part of the creative arts game these days, right?"

"Just glad it's your game, not mine. By the way," I said as we both started back inside, "you're familiar with the western art world. What do you know about the photographer Isaac Lyons?"

"Honey, he goes beyond western art into just plain *art*. I know he did a book recently on western landscapes and that the West has become his latest interest. I also hear he's a man who really loves the ladies. Did a book on female nudes a few years back that made the bestseller list. Got named in a paternity suit once, but it proved to be a false claim. Not bad for a seventy-nine-year-old man."

"He's seventy-nine?"

"There about. Why the interest in old randy Isaac?"

"I just met him."

"Here? Tonight? Isaac Lyons is at my gallery opening!" Her face flushed pink. "I have to get back in there and meet him. I can't believe it! Isaac Lyons at my gallery opening." She dashed through the doorway and went into the small bathroom next to Roland's office to check her hair.

"I can't believe you didn't see him," I said, following her. "He's pretty hard to miss."

"I took my contacts out because they were causing my eyes to turn a very unattractive shade of vermillion. Everyone except the people right in front of me are a big blur."

"Just look for the gargantuan white-headed blur and you'll have found him." It didn't seem the appropriate time to tell her that I thought he was a jerk who was scoping out my grandmother in a most inappropriate way. Photographing nudes? He'd better not even think it.

If possible, the crowd had become even more tightly packed in the last half hour. The hum of human voices sounded like a convoy of tractors. The two bartenders looked frazzled though their crystal tip jar overflowed with bills, the generosity of the guests being enhanced by the neverending flow of medium-grade wine and champagne. I was searching the crowd for Gabe with the intention of convincing him to sneak away with me when I saw Dove and her new friend head my way.

"Honeybun, I want you to meet someone." Her voice cut through the noisy crowd like a hot knife through butter. With her arm intertwined in his, she pulled him toward me. He towered over her five-foot frame, smiling like a huge, cream-fed cat.

"Isaac, this is my granddaughter, Benni Harper. She runs the folk art museum I was telling you about. Her name should be Ortiz 'cause she's married to our chief of police, and he's the nicest young man you could ever want to meet, but she's balky as an old milk cow and wants to be Miss Liberated-Woman-of-the-World. Makes addressing Christmas cards a big pain in the butt, in my opinion. Benni, say hello to Mr. Isaac Lyons. He takes pictures for a living and he's wanting to take some out at the ranch. I've invited him to stay awhile, though for the life of me I still can't imagine what anyone would want with pictures of our old ranch. I told him about Shelby, poor little child, that she was taking pictures of our place, too, and what happened to her. I said there might be some sorta bad luck swirling about our land, but he says that don't bother him at all, so I said you're welcome to stay as long as you clean up after yourself.''

He smiled down at me, his dark eyes sharp and amused. "How do you do, Ms. Benni Harper, Liberated-Woman-of-the-World.'' He held out a huge cool hand.

"Mr. Lyons." I gave it a short, irritated shake as Dove continued to chatter about his visit, which, apparently, was starting tonight.

"Call me Isaac, please," he murmured.

"We're going to blow this joint and get some coffee and real food," Dove said. "I'll tell your daddy on my way out that Isaac will fetch me home."

"But—" I started, but before I could protest further, she kissed me on the cheek and was leading Isaac toward the door. More than one set of irritated society-matron eyes followed them.

That was more than I could take. She'd just met the guy, for cryin' out loud. She wasn't going anyplace with that man without me. I started to push my way through the crowd after them when I felt a hand clamp down on my shoulder and pull me up as short as a roped calf.

"Whoa, there, Calamity Jane." My husband's voice rumbled in my ear. "I know that look, and whoever it is you're heading for, forget it. I don't want to have to arrest my own wife for assault and battery."

"Let me go," I said, pulling against his grip. "Do you know who that is? Do you know his reputation? Dang it, Gabe, let me go."

He grabbed my hand and pulled me into the gallery's empty back room. The party noise dropped to a soft buzz when he firmly closed the door.

"What in the world are you talking about?" he asked.

I jerked my hand out of his. "Isaac Lyons, the photographer. He's a playboy. He takes pictures of naked women.

And he just left with my grandmother. He's talked her into letting him stay at the ranch. We have to do something.''

Gabe grinned. "I've seen his photographs. He's good. Dove and Isaac Lyons. Bet he's in for a wild time."

I glared at Gabe. "This isn't funny. I think he's up to something."

"Benni, what could he be up to? He's a famous photographer who's taken a shine to your grandmother. He probably wants to photograph her."

"*That's* what I'm afraid of."

"It's art, Benni," he said, ruffling my hair.

I slapped at his hand. "You think so? Maybe I should offer him my services, then."

He lifted my chin and kissed me on the lips. "Over my dead body, *querida*. Your fair limbs are strictly for my perusal."

"Hey, you two, no making out in the back room," Parker said, walking into the room. "You do have the right idea, though. Hide from the maddening crowds. Mispronunciation intended." She sat down on a folding chair and heaved a big sigh. "I'm bushed, and this week's festivities haven't even started yet. Have you had a chance to talk to Greer?"

"Yes," I said. "She's nervous as a barn cat, but holding up fine. Are you ready for your demonstration and talk on women in the western arts tomorrow?"

"As ready as I'll ever be," she said, grimacing. "Trying to explain to people why and how I create is so hard for me. I know how important promotion is these days, but I wish I could just paint and not have to also be a 'character' to sell my work."

"Speaking of characters, did you manage to meet Isaac Lyons?"

"I hovered at the edge of a group of his admirers and listened to him. He's quite a fascinating man with some very definite ideas about what art is and isn't. He was using Shelby's photographs as an example of how artists should put themselves in their art, that each photograph should not only be a story of the subject, but a story of the artist and that if you really studied an artist's lifetime of work, it should reveal the true personality of the artist.''

"Too bad Shelby's lifetime was cut so short," I said.

"Yes," she agreed, her voice soft. "Yes, it was."

I turned to Gabe. "You think we could sneak out without making too much of a dent in the crowd?"

He slipped a warm hand underneath my hair and squeezed my neck. "I think there's a good chance they won't even notice we're gone."

"Go over the wall, kids," Parker said. "If anyone asks, I never saw you escape."

We slipped through the back door into the alley and walked past the bluesy sounds still coming from Sweet Dreams. "I'm glad that Greer's having her time in the sun," I said, tucking my arm through Gabe's, "but Shelby's death put a damper on the night for me." He just murmured in agreement.

"Gabe, what do you think happened?" I asked when we reached the truck.

He opened the passenger door, his hand resting on the small of my back. "I don't want to speculate with so little to go on."

"But you must have an opinion, a feeling of some kind."

"What I feel is irrelevant."

"Not to me. I want to know what you think."

He walked around the front of the truck and climbed in. "Are you going to nag me all night until I answer this?" he asked.

"Probably."

"I suspected as much. Look, this is just speculation, but in the interest of marital harmony and my nervous condition . . ."

"You don't have a nervous condition."

"I'm developing one at a rapid rate being married to you.

I'll just say it looks like she was in a fight with someone who pushed her. She unfortunately fell and hit her head on a rock in a freak accident and died. The person panicked and ran. When he or she gets caught, the charge will most likely be manslaughter. I don't really think it was planned. Does that make you feel any better?''

"But how in the world will they find out who did it?''

"Tedious footwork by detectives. Most likely they'll just keep questioning people and rereading people's statements until something jumps out at an investigator or someone feels guilty and confesses.''

"Does that happen very often?''

"Not often enough, but it happens. Now, can we get something to eat? I'm starving.''

"Let's go to Liddie's. Nadine's been complaining she hasn't seen you in weeks.''

But when we drove past, I changed my mind. There in a window seat, glowing under one of Liddie's yellow globe lights, sat Dove and Isaac. He held her hand across the table. Her head was thrown back in silent laughter.

"Forget Liddie's,'' I grumbled. "Let's get pizza.''

Gabe chuckled under his breath.

"You wouldn't think this was so funny if it was your mother Isaac Lyons was seducing.''

His smile was bright against his dark skin. "*My* mother is too sensible to be seduced by someone like him.''

I opened my mouth to snap an answer, then closed it. Having had more years under the marriage belt than my high-and-mighty husband, I knew that it was treading on shaky ground when spouses started comparing maternal personality quirks.

Unsmiling, I looked directly into his amused eyes. "So tell me why Isaac Lyons would be interested in my grandmother.''

His smile faded at my serious question. "Why shouldn't he be? She's a fascinating woman with an interesting life.

Not to mention a whole lot of fun and nice to look at. Also, there's something about you Ramsey women that's just somehow irresistible.'' He smiled again. "I should know.''

I reluctantly conceded a half smile, still not comforted, but warmed by his audacious flattery. "You know, we've switched places. Usually you're the suspicious one.''

"They say the longer people have been married, the more alike they become.''

"Oh, dear Lord, help me,'' I said.

"Amen to that,'' he replied.

7

"It's for you," Gabe said, answering the phone the next morning. I was still in bed, peeking at the clock at five-minute intervals wondering just how close I could cut it and still make it to the museum by eight forty-five. The first docent tour started at nine, Greer's lecture was at ten o'clock, and Parker's at eleven. We'd sold tickets and promised a continental breakfast as part of the admission price. I still had to go by Stern's Bakery and pick up the mini apricot coffee cakes, almond croissants, and chocolate muffins.

"Who is it?" I mumbled into my pillow.

He tossed the phone onto the bed next to me. "I didn't ask, but they sound frantic." I struggled up and through filmy eyes watched him pull on a white dress shirt. "This is my last shirt, by the way. Are you going by the cleaners today? I would, but I'm in meetings all day."

"I'll put it on my list of about a zillion things to do," I said, picking up the phone. "Hello?"

"It's Parker." Her voice was low and breathless and sounded very far away. "I just thought I'd tell you first thing because I know how you hate not knowing what's going on."

I shook my head, trying to completely wake up, and watched Gabe button his shirt. When he got to the top button, it popped off. He swore softly in Spanish.

"Just a minute, Parker." I put my hand over the receiver. "Gabe, calm down. Get a needle and thread out of my sewing basket and come here."

"Tell me what?" I said into the phone.

"About the trouble at Roland's gallery last night."

"What trouble?"

"It happened right after you left. Kip showed up drunk and on the warpath. He'd heard that Roland had tripled the prices on Shelby's photographs and he accused Roland of killing her just to make himself more money in commission."

"That's ludicrous," I exclaimed. Gabe walked back in the room holding a spool of white thread and a needle. He started taking off his shirt.

I shook my head and gestured for him to sit down on the bed. Cradling the phone on my shoulder, I threaded the needle, bit off the thread, then knotted it. Encircling his waist with my legs to get closer, I started sewing the button back on.

"Hmm," he said and started nibbling my neck.

Stop it, I mouthed, pushed him back, and continued to talk as I sewed. "So, what happened after that?"

"Luckily, the sheriff was there, and he managed, with the help of some other guys, to get Kip outside and calmed down. Then that other guy from your dad's ranch, the one Olivia's hanging out with . . ."

"Bobby Sanchez?"

"That's the one. He came out of The Steerhead Tavern across the street and told the sheriff he'd make sure Kip got home. While all this was happening, Roland locked himself in the bathroom." She giggled softly.

I laughed along with her. "He is such a pathetic excuse

of a man. Frankly, that *was* tacky to raise the prices so quickly. It's disrespectful.''

"That's the art world, Benni. It's an old joke, but a true one—that death makes you a much more valuable commodity.''

"It's still tacky."

"Welcome to the real world. Well, I just wanted you to be up-to-date on all the information. How long's it going to take you to solve this one, Detective Harper?''

I looked straight into the blue eyes of my husband. "Parker, this week I'm a chili judge, a tour guide, a parade entry, and who knows what else. I'm going to leave solving murders up to my brilliant and hard-working husband.''

"If you say so." She giggled again. "See you at the museum.''

"Very well stated, Ms. Harper," my husband said when I hung up the phone. I bent my head down, bit off the remaining thread, and placed a quick kiss on his chest.

He pulled me around so I was straddling his lap. "If I tear off the rest of my buttons, will you sew them all on like this?" He ran his beard up and down my neck.

"Would you quit that?" I said, pushing him away. "My neck is beginning to look like someone scrubbed it with steel wool." I untangled myself from him and stood up. "You're late, Chief, and so am I. Don't forget the auction at the Forum tonight. Dinner has to be quick and easy.''

"I'll try to get home early." He started buttoning his shirt. "You meant what you said on the phone, didn't you?''

"About you being brilliant and hard-working? Of course, dear.''

He gave me one of his unblinking, interrogating cop looks.

"You know that doesn't work on me, Friday," I said, pulling my tee shirt over my head. "I know your tricks. If it makes you feel better, what possible reason could I have to get involved with this? I liked Shelby, and yes, it bothers me that it happened at the ranch, but I'm taking you at your word that it was an accident and that the person responsible will eventually confess.''

"I didn't say that exactly. A confession is what we *hope* for.''

"Nevertheless, I don't think anyone's in any real danger. Frankly, with the way Kip's been acting, I still say he's the prime candidate.'' I told him what happened at the gallery after we left.

"He's certainly *one* of the suspects.'' I watched Gabe's reflection in the long mirror as he straightened his tie, resisting the temptation to ask who else they suspected. The last thing I wanted to do this morning was get into a debate over Wade's innocence or lack thereof.

"Have a good day,'' I said, opening my lingerie drawer.

"Speaking of having a good day, what exactly are you planning to do with yours?''

I turned to face him, arranging my features in what I was sure was an innocent look. "Oh, stuff. You know, museum stuff. Heritage Days stuff.''

"Leave Dove and Mr. Lyons alone,'' he warned. "She's a grown woman and allowed to have her own friends.''

"He's scoping her out! I have to warn her.''

"Benni, let her have a life. Don't you think she deserves that after all the years of being alone?''

I turned back to my drawer and started digging through it. He came over and kissed my bare shoulder. "Think about it,'' he said.

"I will.'' *All the way out to the ranch.*

After he left I finished dressing, putting on new tobacco-brown Wranglers, a tan long-sleeved shirt, and a pair of dangling boot-shaped moonstone and silver earrings I'd bought recently from one of our newest artists—a jewelry designer who was having difficulty maintaining enough product to sell because everyone at the co-op kept buying his new creations.

In the kitchen, Emory, wearing a rich, wine-colored velour robe, was reading the *San Celina Tribune* and drinking
black coffee.

"So, what are you doing today?" I asked, pouring myself a half a cup and filling the rest with milk and two tea-
spoons of sugar.

He looked up from his paper. "Still drinking your coffee
like a child."

"Eat dirt. Want to come help at the museum?"

"I think not. After slumming my way through your bird-
cage liner here, I thought I'd mosey on downtown and see
what the natives are doing."

I took two large gulps, then set the cup down in the sink.
"You know, hovering around Elvia like some kind of weird
stalker is not going to endear her to you."

"Who said anything about Elvia?" he said, giving me
an indifferent look. "I'm going to drop by the newspaper
and say hey to one of the reporters there that I've made an
acquaintance with on-line."

"You've got connections at the *Tribune*?"

He smiled. "Sweetcakes, I've got connections in places
that would straighten that curly hair of yours."

I made a face at him. "By the way, Gabe's stint as auctioneer starts at seven o'clock in the Forum downtown. Gabe
and I are meeting here at five to decide about dinner. We'll
probably go out. You're welcome to join us." I glanced at
my watch. "Geez, I gotta go. A busload of hungry seniors
from Santa Barbara County will be expecting chow, and I've
still got to pick it up."

I pulled into the museum parking lot a mere two minutes
before the chartered bus did. Greeting the senior citizens
cheerfully, I instructed the docent to start the forty-five minute tour while I helped arrange the food and coffee on the
long tables my assistant, D-Daddy, had already set up on
the long porch of the museum. Luckily the weather was

clear and cool today with just enough sun to make the old Sinclair hacienda look its best.

"Running late, eh, *ange*?" D-Daddy said in his French-tinged Cajun accent. He hooked the banquet-sized coffee pot to a thick orange extension cord and set it on the long table.

"D-Daddy, I have a feeling the whole week is going to be like this," I said, picking a few dead flowers out of the twin whiskey-barrel planters on both ends of the porch. We'd planted marigolds and daisies for a change of pace from the native wildflowers we normally rotated according to their blooming schedules.

Wiry white eyebrows bunched over his dark brown eyes. "See the newspaper yet?"

"No, I was in too much of a hurry this morning."

"On your desk," was all he said. By the narrowing of his eyes, I knew that there was most likely an article about Shelby's death. I sighed deeply, trying not to dwell on the fact that times had indeed changed in San Celina County—that, like it or not, violence had become a more frequent occurrence here on the Central Coast.

The tour ended in the co-op's large main studio, once the hacienda's stables, with me giving a short history of the co-op, our goals, and our accomplishments. This last year we'd spent more time in community outreach with artists traveling to schools and retirement homes, giving free classes in everything from doll making to leather carving to watercolor painting. We were most proud of the fact that we'd started donating our artists' time and talents to "Art for Kids"—a summer program, sponsored by our local YMCA, that opened the possibilities of art to underprivileged kids in hopes that it would keep some of them away from gangs, drugs, and alcohol.

While the sixty-some-odd seniors were enjoying their mini-brunch, I helped set up chairs for Greer's lecture on women in western art. Parker was setting up some of Greer's paintings, while Greer perused her notes.

"Do you want a podium?" I asked. "We have one in the storeroom."

"No, I get too nervous standing behind something like that. I'll just pace in front of my paintings here."

"You look great." She was dressed in an elegant black wool jacket with white western-style piping, a pair of starched black jeans, and what I knew had to be four-hundred-dollar boots. "Like the successful artist you are."

"Thanks, but I still feel like an imposter. When I see a group of people gathered together like this waiting to hear me speak, I still have the strongest urge to join them, waiting for the 'great artist' to come out and give us incredible insights into her artistic vision. Then I realize it's me they're coming to hear and I want to head back to my cabin in the hills."

"I guess it's an unavoidable part of the game these days. People who love your work naturally want to meet you, see the person who brought them so much pleasure. You'll dazzle them, and when prints are made of your paintings, they'll fly off the shelves."

"A mixed blessing for an artist," she said ruefully, turning to inspect one of the paintings she had displayed. She straightened her spine and turned back to me. "Better hit the ladies' room before I go on." She headed back down the hall past my office.

"She enjoys it a lot more than she lets on," Parker said softly.

I turned to look at Parker with surprise. I hadn't even heard her walk up behind me. Was there an edge of bitterness in her voice, or was that just my imagination?

"Talking in front of groups is always hard," I said diplomatically. "Especially when the subject is so personal."

Parker shrugged, her brown eyes level and flat. When Greer came back into the room, Parker's face softened into a smile, and I shook my head slightly, not certain about what I saw in her expression a minute ago. She and Greer were good friends . . . or so I thought. Then again, I'd grown to understand how precarious friendships among artists could be. It was a difficult situation, your colleagues also being your competitors, especially in our media-obsessed world where your background and looks, whether they were manufactured or real, seemed to be almost as important as the work itself. Elvia's visiting authors complained about it all the time. Could it be that same phenomenon was happening in the visual arts? If so, there was no doubt that Parker would have a problem with her shyness, her nondescript appearance, and her unexciting background.

After Greer's presentation, which was amusing, lively, and informative, Parker gave a talk on her work. One-on-one, Parker's gentle and sensitive nature was obvious and endearing, but before a crowd, her tone flattened and her enthusiasm became forced and artificial-sounding. It broke my heart when the audience started shuffling their programs and whispering among themselves. When she hurried through her finish, the bulk of the group gathered around Greer while I noticed Parker disappear down the hallway. I followed after her and found her in the back storage room, a small, stuffy enclosure that had only one small window high off the ground. She was leaning against the wall, staring at a stack of blank canvases.

I knocked on the doorframe to keep from startling her. "Are you all right?"

Two spots of powdery blush glared off her pale cheeks. Her eyes were red-rimmed and teary. She took a deep breath and swiped her hand across her left cheek to wipe away nonexistent tears. "I'm fine. Talking in front of groups just scares me. I'm sure I bored them silly."

"No, you didn't. You know people these days, their attention spans are about this long." I held my thumb and forefinger an inch apart.

"Thanks for the try, Benni, but I'm an artist, remember? Visual details are my life. I could see what was happening with those people. I'm just not good at explaining what I do or what I'm trying to do with my art. I've always felt that if I haven't communicated my feelings in my paintings, then I've essentially failed as an artist. Why does the world insist on an artist explaining what she does? You know what Robert Frost told a person once who asked him what one of his poems meant? He said, 'You want me to say it worse?' That's how I feel, that me talking about my art diminishes it somehow. Next to Greer, I look like a stupid thirteen-year-old.'' She put her face in her hands in much the same way I remembered Shelby doing when she was agonizing over Kip's infidelity. Love in its many forms causes the same kind of pain.

She lifted her head and blurted out, ''It's not fair. It's so much easier for Greer. She grew up talking to people like that, learned how to charm them, play the game. And that's what it's become, a game. An idiotic game with the winner being whoever can turn herself into the most interesting personality.''

I shook my head dumbly, surprised at the intensity of Parker's bottled-up anger. She'd kept it well hidden under her gentle exterior.

''Why do you think Greer got that showing?'' she asked. ''Or why she was featured in *Rosettes* magazine? All that great ranch history. So *interesting* to the readers. So authentic.'' She spit out the last word.

''She *is* very talented,'' I said in Greer's defense.

''Yes, she is, but not any more than a lot of artists and less than some. But it's also a lot easier to develop your talent when you don't have to struggle to put boxed macaroni and cheese on the table. Not to mention being able to afford the best paints, brushes, canvases, and framing.'' Her thin mouth bunched at the corners. ''Both the people Roland featured in his gallery had advantages I'll never have. I don't care what anyone says—the best art doesn't always get promoted. And without promotion, it doesn't get seen. And if you don't get seen, your career is dirt.''

I was speechless against her tirade, though a part of me was tempted to point out that, advantages or not, Shelby was dead. Parker certainly couldn't envy that. But, on the other hand, I felt a deep compassion for Parker. It was similar, I guessed, to the way I felt these days when I attended a society event with Gabe. So many of the events involved people who were the upper crust of San Celina society, like Greer—old ranch families who owned spreads that were three times the size of my dad's, in better locations and worth millions more dollars; and lawyers and doctors and politicians all with *Vogue*-perfect wives who had never mucked a stall or peeled a bushel of apples in their manicured lives. I always felt like there might be a clump of cow manure clinging to the heel of my not-often-worn high heels. I sometimes envied how easy life had probably been for many of them, how they didn't have to worry about whether they could afford one more vet bill for a beloved horse whose frequent bouts with colic had cost me five times what I paid for him.

''I'm sorry,'' I said, realizing that there was nothing much else I could say. All I had to offer her was a sympathetic ear.

Her expression suddenly switched, and she became the Parker I'd known before. Or thought I'd known. ''I'm sorry for dumping on you like this, Benni. I know you have more than your own share of problems this week. And I sound like a horrible person, I know, especially when Greer's been so nice to me. She's loaned me money and fed me when I was literally starving. I can't believe I just said what I did.'' Tears welled up in her pale brown eyes.

''It's all right,'' I said. ''You were just frustrated and nervous from having to speak in front of those people. Not everyone has a talent for that. It has nothing to do with your ability to paint, and people know that. Besides, think about it—most of the people who see and enjoy your work will never meet you. An artist's work ultimately has to be judged on its own merit and not on the ability to market it. I truly believe that.''

Her bottom lip quivered as she gave a forced smile. A sheen of tears brightened her eyes. ''You're naive, Benni. You really believe that good will ultimately triumph. But it doesn't always. Take my word.''

A few hours later, while eating lunch with Emory at Froggie's Grill downtown, after swearing him to secrecy, I told him about my conversation with Parker. I took a bite out of my salsa-covered tri-tip sandwich.

''I don't think it's naive believing that good will eventually win,'' I said, taking a french fry and pointing it at him. ''Geez, believing otherwise would make a person feel like killing herself.''

Emory took a bite of his Chinese-chicken salad and went right for the throat of the story as succinctly as the lead in one of his newspaper articles.

''Or someone else,'' he said.

8

"So, what's on the agenda tonight?" Gabe asked, pulling off his jacket when he walked through the door at a little past five o'clock.

"Ask the social chairperson," Emory said, sipping a glass of iced tea.

I pointed at the opened datebook on our oak coffee table. "How quickly you forget. You are playing auctioneer tonight at the Forum. It benefits the Crime Victims' fund. Tomorrow night there's the crowning of Miss San Celina and the blessing of the animals down at the mission. Wednesday night is a dinner honoring our women artists at the mayor's house." I grimaced at that. Another event I'd have to dress up for. "Thursday night is farmer's market, of course, with the chili cookoff and the results of the beard-growing contest."

"Thank goodness," Gabe said. "Then I can shave."

I poked him playfully in the side. "Thursday night is also the night they announce the winner of the 'Kiss the Pig' contest. I hear from Maggie that your officers are even using their beer money to buy tickets."

Emory laughed. "Get that video camera ready."

Gabe replied, "If the police chief is sick, it's customary

for his wife to stand in. I feel a cold coming on.''

"In your dreams, pal," I said. I glanced back down at the datebook. "Friday is the fashion show, which I managed to wiggle my way out of. Elvia's in charge of that. I think you're slated for the 1940s segment."

Gabe nodded. "The clothes were delivered to the station today."

Emory gave me a questioning look.

"It's a fund-raiser for the Historical Society. People will be wearing fashions popular in San Celina County from the mid-1800s to present day. A lot of the clothes are from the collection displayed at the Historical Society. That's the old library you used to go to when you were a kid."

"The Carnegie one?" Emory asked.

"Yep, we'll have to drop by so you can see the museum Dove and her friends run." I glanced back down at the datebook. "On Saturday it's the parade, the fiesta, and all its accompanying hullabaloo as well as the dedication of the new mission bell. The western dance and fiddling contest follows that evening. The cow plop contest happens on Saturday, too." I flopped down on the couch. "And that's just the stuff you're involved with. During the day, I have Heritage walk tours and workshops, and then there's the children's carnival and Heritage costume contest and judging the junior crafts show and . . ."

Gabe held up his hand. "I've heard enough. Just make me a list of where I'm supposed to be at what time, and I'll be there."

I smiled sweetly. "I'm your wife, not your secretary."

"Point taken. I'll tell Maggie to do it."

I groaned. "I'll do it, Friday. Leave the poor woman alone. She has enough to do keeping you organized at work."

He winked at Emory. "Works every time."

"Your arrogance knows no limits," I grumbled.

We all agreed that Chinese food was the easiest way to

go tonight and decided on The Golden Dragon across the street from the Forum.

At the restaurant, Emory brought up his visit at the *Tribune*.

"Not a bad little operation," Emory said, sipping his green tea.

I stirred the ice in my Coke. "What a compliment coming from the star reporter of the world famous Bozwell, Arkansas, *Courier-Tribune*."

"Don't be petty, sweetcakes," he said mildly, then nodded at Gabe. "I tip my hat to any man who can live with her mouth for any length of time."

"Turn blue," I said.

"Okay, you two," Gabe said, taking the Kung Pao Chicken from me. "Settle down or you'll be sent home without seeing the auction."

I grinned at Emory. "He thinks that's a punishment."

"By the way," Emory said, "heard something interesting from the crime beat reporter."

Gabe continued eating, but his eyes grew wary. "That right?"

Emory nodded. "Heard that there's some key evidence that the detectives found that might point toward someone specific."

I stopped eating my Orange Chicken and looked at Gabe. "Is that true?" He didn't answer.

Emory backed off when he saw the annoyance on Gabe's face. "Sorry. Habit. They weren't specific about the rumors, just vague innuendo."

"It's Kip," I said. "I'll bet a hundred bucks it's Kip."

"Not my investigation," Gabe said sharply and glanced at his watch. "I've got to get to the auction. They wanted me there fifteen minutes early." He set his crumpled napkin next to his plate. "This one's on you, Emory."

"My pleasure," Emory murmured, reaching inside his

jacket for his wallet. We silently watched Gabe walk out of the restaurant.

"He's a might peeved," Emory said, pulling out his American Express card.

"Just that old territorial male thing," I said. "I think he forgot that you're a newspaper reporter. They're not his favorite people." I scooted closer to him in the U-shaped booth. "So, what's the evidence?"

"I wasn't lyin' when I said they were vague. They have a snitch in the sheriff's department, but apparently this person is very concerned about keeping his or her job and didn't give enough away to actually print anything."

"I still think it's Kip," I said.

"Thinkin' don't make it so."

"Another piece of wisdom from the Arkansas oracle."

"Just for that, I'm taking your fortune cookie," he said, grabbing it out of my hand.

"Hey! Give that back. It's my favorite part of the meal."

He broke it open and read the fortune inside. His pushed his bottom lip out slightly and wrinkled his brow. "You know, Albenia Louise, these things are written so they can apply to just about anyone, but I believe I'm seein' some divine prophecy here." He handed me the tiny slip of paper.

Someone close to you will need your help.

"Oh, geez," I said, feeling a small pang in my chest.

THE FORUM, A huge Roman-style building with white columns and long windows, was constructed in the eighties, despite the protests from traditionalists whose goal was to keep San Celina true to its mission past. Nevertheless, it became the most popular place in town for civic and private parties simply because its roomy interior was clean, large, and well lit. Inside, almost every chair was taken, and people congregated around the back of the room at the wine-tasting tables set up by local wineries, a rapidly growing industry in San Celina County.

Emory and I stood surveying the boisterous crowd searching for a place to sit. Gabe was already in front, conferring with the Junior League president, a china doll–faced, spa-thin woman named Pamela Howell, who was married to a local physician. She playfully felt my husband's left bicep and stood on tiptoe to whisper something in his ear. The Junior League was cosponsoring this event with the Historical Society, and she'd called our house numerous times to arrange the details with Gabe and inform him of what new item she'd talked a local merchant into donating. In her immaculate designer outfits, she was the epitome of a proper society wife and she somehow, with a word or slight eyebrow movement, always made me feel like a bull-calf in a roomful of stained-glass windows. Which pissed me off. And as usual, my feelings were about as subtle as an Hawaiian sunset.

"Don't worry about her," Emory whispered in my ear. "You could play ice hockey on that face. I bet she can't even close her eyes they've been tucked so many times. She probably beats her servants and makes them eat store-brand peanut butter while she sucks down the gourmet stuff. And I recognize that glassy-eyed look—she's a klepto if I ever saw one. Probably bulimic, too. I could investigate—do an expose."

I laughed. "Her husband's a very respected plastic surgeon, so I imagine she gets facelifts for half price."

"Hope she donated all that excess skin to a worthy cause."

I smiled at him gratefully. Emory gossiped more creatively than most women I knew. "I guess it's small consolation. Her husband smokes cigars that would choke a horse, spits when he talks, and the type who's always trying to body-hug other women. He's kinda disgusting. No, make that *really* disgusting."

"And you're worried about impressing these people? Don't worry. Your police officer knows the difference between caviar and fish eggs."

"Hey, Benni, over here!" Olivia Contreras stood up and gestured at two seats next to her. I went over and laid my jacket over the two seats.

"Thanks, Olivia. I thought we might have to sit on the curb outside."

Emory nodded hello at Olivia. "Y'all want any wine?"

"You buying? I'll take another chardonnay," Olivia said, her voice slurring a bit. I shook my head no and sat down next to her, leaving the aisle seat open for Emory.

"Pretty great turnout, isn't it?" she said. "I've been eyeing that Fence Rail quilt since Evangeline started it two months ago." She pointed to a queen-sized quilt done in a medley of blues and purples.

"It is beautiful. I haven't decided if I'm going to bid on anything yet. Do you have anything in the auction?"

"A couple of signed posters and a numbered seriograph of one of my cowboy portraits. The one I did of Bobby mending fence last year."

"I know that one. It's gorgeous. But then again, he's gorgeous."

She frowned and drained the wineglass in her hand. "Guess I wasn't the only one who thought so."

I widened my eyes in question.

"You haven't heard about the infamous photographs? I'm surprised. With your contacts, I'd have thought you heard right off."

I didn't feel like going into—yet again—how little I knew about Gabe's work so I just said, "Guess this one flew right by me."

"Our friends Shelby and Bobby. Apparently I wasn't the only person he enjoyed posing for."

"So?" Bobby was certainly the consummate cowboy. It

wasn't surprising that Shelby would want to use him in her work.

"So, it would have been nice if he'd been wearing clothes."

I tried to keep the shock off my face in an attempt to at least appear to have a modicum of sophistication. Nudity in art was a very acceptable thing. I tried not to think of Dove and Isaac. "Well . . ." That was about all I could come up with to say.

"Well, it ticks me off, that little cheat. See if he gets any more free meals or clean sheets off this lady."

So the rumors were true. Olivia and Bobby did have more going on in their relationship than strictly artist and model. I fidgeted in my seat, not sure how to answer her. Then again, she brought it up, so I let my curiosity win and asked, "How did you see the photographs?"

"They were in my mail today. They're disgusting. Some are of the two of them together—out in the dunes somewhere. I guess she must have used a timer." She set her glass under her folding chair. It was obvious to me now that, judging by the glassiness in her eyes, she'd been drinking long before coming to the auction. That would explain why she was being so free with such humiliating information.

"Do you have any idea who sent them?" I answered, and wondered if Gabe or the sheriff's detectives knew about them. They might not be anything except what they were—a young photographer's experiment with human form. On the other hand, they could be significant.

Olivia shook her head. "I should have known better than to get hooked up with a man younger than me. He was great in bed, but apparently he has the attention span of a fruit fly."

I made a sympathetic noise in my throat simply because I didn't know what else to say. Before she could continue,

Emory came back with her wine, and we settled in to watch the auction.

It still amazed me, watching Gabe switch into his public persona. In the last year and a half he'd served as chief of police, he'd gotten to know many of the people in the audience, which ran the social gamut of university bigwigs, wealthy old ranching families, and influential people from all colors of the political spectrum. He teased and cajoled them by name into bidding on the donated sculptures, quilts, paintings, weekend-at-San-Celina-Inn packages, golf clubs, leather goods, and sides of custom-cut beef. Next to him, Pamela handed him a card describing each donation, looking as perky as Vanna White. I sighed and stared at the toes of my boots, dreading the party at the mayor's house later on this week.

My attention was diverted when a familiar voice called out a bid over the murmuring crowd.

"Twenty dollars!" Dove's loud voice called out.

I sat up higher in my chair and searched the crowd for her.

"I have twenty dollars for a signed print from Isaac Lyons, Pulitzer Prize–winning photographer," Gabe said into the microphone. "Do I hear thirty?" Immediately, people started shouting out bids.

"Oh, brother," I said out of the side of my mouth to Emory when I finally spotted her. She leaned over and whispered something to Isaac, who put his huge arm around her shoulders and pulled her closer. When the bids reached three hundred, I stood up and scooted past Emory's long legs. "I've seen enough. I'm going home. Would you give Gabe a ride?"

"Sure," Emory said and left it at that.

Outside I stood for a moment, trying to decide if I wanted to go straight to the car or get a cup of coffee first. I nixed Blind Harry's simply because too many people knew me there and I wasn't in the mood to chitchat. Sweet Dreams

was more popular with the college crowd, and though I
didn't always like the music they played, at least the regular
patrons didn't have a clue to my identity and didn't care.
Solitude in a crowd was what I was craving right now as I
tried to organize my jumbled feelings about Dove and her
new friend, Shelby's death and its ramifications, and a mild
depression brought on by watching Pamela, which proved,
yet again, it was obvious that Gabe and I weren't exactly a
perfect fit.

"Looks like I wasn't the only one who needed air," a
deep voice said behind me.

I turned around and looked up into Isaac Lyons's genial
face. He was dressed tonight in black Levi's, a white snap-
button cowboy shirt, and a chunky turquoise bolo tie. I
didn't respond to his words or his smile. My dislike of him
was irrational, immature, and unfair. And I couldn't help it
one bit.

He continued talking as if I hadn't snubbed him. "I still
hate it when my work is on display and I'm being judged.
You'd think after all these years I'd get used to it, but I
haven't. I had this horrible fear that no one would want it.
Bless your grandmother's kind heart—that's why she started
the bidding."

"Excuse me," I said, knowing if I stayed much longer
I'd say something I'd regret, "but I'm not feeling well."

"Hope you feel better," he called to my back.

I walked up the street toward Sweet Dreams feeling like
a real jerk. What was it about that guy that made me so
prickly? Didn't I think that Dove deserved to have someone
in her life? What was I really afraid of?

Her being hurt, I told myself. I saw him as a sophisticated man of the world and was afraid he would just use
her or make fun of her. And I was worried that she didn't
see it—would believe that he really found her attractive.
Face it, my more blunt side said, what you're saying is that

a man like that couldn't possibly be interested in your un-sophisticated grandmother.

Or, the nasty little voice continued, *maybe what's really bothering you is that you're feeling the exact same thing about you and Gabe.*

Stop it, I told myself. *I like who I am. I don't want to change. I don't need to compete with the Pamela Howells of the world. Life was so much easier when I was married to Jack.*

I stopped in the middle of the sidewalk and closed my eyes, not believing I actually thought those words. I loved Gabe—more than I could imagine loving any man. Yet a part of me longed to go back to when the world was safer, when I had more control, when I knew who I was. *When Jack was alive.*

"Whatcha doin', blondie, communing with nature?" Jack said.

My eyes flew open. It wasn't Jack, of course. Wade grinned at me.

"I just left the auction at the Forum," I said. "It was getting too crowded for me, and I needed a cup of coffee." I continued walking and he fell in beside me.

"Want some company?"

I didn't, really. People were exactly what I was trying to escape from at the moment, but the look of loneliness on his face pricked at my raw emotions.

"Sure," I said reluctantly.

We passed by the Mission Newsstand, closed now, and he grabbed my arm when we were in front of The Steerhead Tavern.

"Let's go in here. I want a beer. Coffee'll keep me up all night."

"Wade, that place is a dive." The Steerhead Tavern was the last of the old cowboy/oilfield worker hangouts left in downtown San Celina. Most of the bars now were either upscale yuppie hangouts full of expensive wood, ferns, and mirrors, or buck-a-bottle beer joints, catering to the college students, where the lines were long and the music loud. The Steerhead, squeezed between the Mission Newsstand and a boot and saddle repair shop that had been there for as long as I could remember, had a neon sign with a cowgirl holding a glowing cow skull perched over the front door and the requisite fifties glass brick windows and Coors beer signs. It was dark inside and loud with men's competitive beer-bright voices. I squinted through the smoky haze at the Bud Light flags draped across the wall. "They have decaf at Sweet Dreams."

He took my hand and led me to an open booth in back. "Ah, blondie, loosen up. Just one beer, okay? Then we can go have coffee at one of your frou-frou places."

"Get me a Coke," I called as he went over to the bar. "In a bottle." I wasn't about to trust a glass in this place. I ran my fingers lightly over the knife-carved formica table in front of me, trying to read the Braille-like messages in the dim light. Across the room, two men and their dates shot pool under a long plastic pool table light advertising Miller High Life. From the glowing jukebox came the sounds of Dwight Yoakum and Buck Owens walking the streets of Bakersfield.

"One Coke in a bottle," Wade said, sliding into the seat across from me. I picked it up, wiped off the lip with my sleeve, and took a drink.

"Aren't we Miss Priss tonight?" he mocked lightly, taking a long drag off his foamy mug of beer.

"Wade, you know I hate places like this."

"Just one beer, okay? I just wanted to sit in some place I remember. I heard that Trigger's went under a few months ago."

I nodded. Trigger's was a bar over by the bus station where he and Jack used to meet their friends for a beer whenever they came to town to buy feed or order some part from the Farm Supply. It was also the place where, almost two years ago, Wade had fought with Jack over the running of the Harper ranch and then left him there. Jack had continued drinking and had ended up dead after his old Jeep overturned on a desolate stretch of Highway One. When I'd read in the *Tribune* that Trigger's owners had lost their liquor license and filed for bankruptcy, I gave a silent hallelujah.

"Nothin's the same," Wade said, his mouth turning downward. The song on the jukebox changed to an Alan Jackson song—"Chattahoochee." Its brave and hopeful words about young boys just on the verge of manhood, talkin' about cars and dreamin' about women, made my limbs feel weighted and old.

"Things change, Wade." I ran my fingers up and down the round ridges of my Coke bottle. "People change."

"Yeah, I guess they do. Look at you. Mrs. Chief-of-Police-Society-Lady. Who would have ever thunk it?"

His challenging tone was just this side of picking a fight, so I sipped my Coke and didn't answer his question. A fight was definitely one thing I wasn't looking for tonight. "Who have you seen since you've been here?"

"Your daddy was nice enough to loan me one of his trucks, and I've been dropping in on a few people, but I haven't stayed long. You know how it goes. People don't much like being around someone who failed."

I nodded and didn't reply. I knew exactly what he meant. So many ranches were on the edge of going under these days that seeing one of their own who hadn't made it was an unwelcome reminder of what might lie in their future.

"What are you going to do?" I asked. *Go back to Texas,* I wanted to say. *Beg your wife to take you back.*

He shrugged. "It's kinda hard. I guess you know the police have been hassling me. They're sure I was the one who killed Shelby. I'd like to go back to Texas, but I don't want to leave with people thinkin' I'm running from something I didn't do. I do have some pride left." He stared down into his beer, not meeting my eyes. "But nobody believes I didn't kill that girl. I can see it in their eyes."

I reached over and took his hand, rough and scarred and so much like Jack's that the sweetness of the Coke coating my tongue turned slightly salty. "Wade, I'm sorry. Really, I am."

He looked up at me, his eyes glittering in the bar's umber light. "You think it, too, don't you? It's 'cause of that hardass cop you married. You've changed. *He's* changed you. Shit, Benni, why'd you have to go and do that? How could you do that so soon after Jack died? Didn't you love my brother?"

I jerked my hand out of his. "What a rotten thing to say."

"If the boot fits."

I took a deep breath before answering. "Wade Harper, you know I loved Jack. How dare you imply—"

"Then why'd you jump so fast into the sack with the first man to come sniffing around? And a Mexican on top of it. It makes me want to puke, and it would have Jack, too."

Trembling with anger, I slid out of the booth. "That's where you're wrong. I knew your brother a lot better than you ever did, and he would have wanted me to be happy because unlike you, he really understood what love was. Maybe if you'd listened to him more closely, you not only wouldn't have lost our ranch, but you wouldn't have lost your wife."

I ran out of the bar, ignoring his voice calling my name. Outside, I almost knocked over Tracianne Doyle and her husband, William, a local orthodontist who himself had a slight overbite. Tracianne and Pamela Howell belonged to all the same clubs and lived in the same exclusive neighborhood where their expensive houses sat directly on the golf course—the second and ninth tees respectively.

"Benni Harper!" she exclaimed, her tone surprised and

smug. Smug was her specialty. "Are you all right?"

I stared at her a moment, speechless, my heart flowing like a microwaved Hershey bar into my stomach. The police chief's wife seen fleeing the one cheap bar left in San Celina, her face on the verge of tears, would no doubt be the juiciest topic of conversation with the country club lunch crowd tomorrow.

"Fine," I struggled out, knowing there was no saving the situation now. Tracianne was nicknamed Tell-all Traci for a good reason. I walked away, feeling her eyes on my back until I turned the corner.

When I got home I took a long shower, holding my face under the spray, resisting the urge to break down and sob. Not wanting to face Gabe's questions as to why I left the auction early, I turned out the bedroom lights and crawled in bed, hiding in the cool darkness. Wade's words had struck a nerve deep inside me; he'd voiced a question that I was sure had been on many people's minds and probably had been whispered behind my back. How much had I really loved Jack if I could marry another man so quickly? Had this situation happened to someone else when I was with Jack, I would have been right there with everyone else commenting on the fickle nature of the woman involved. How different things were when it was you. I fell into a troubled sleep, images of Jack and Gabe intermingling in my dreams.

Gabe's and Emory's voices woke me, and I lay in bed listening to them laugh and discuss the bids made at the auction. The shower ran, then went off, and I eventually felt the bed move. I contemplated telling Gabe the whole story now, getting it over with, then decided I just wasn't up to the task. The tears that had been teetering on the edge of my eyelids all night flowed silently down my cheeks.

"Benni," he whispered. I slowed my breathing and pretended to be asleep.

He kissed the back of my head, then touched his lips to

the skin just below my eye. He froze for a moment and I held my breath, bracing myself for his questions.

"*Yo te amo, niña,*" he said in a low voice and curled around me without another word.

9

"I MAY AS well tell you before you hear it on the streets,"
I said to Gabe the next morning while waiting for my bagel
to toast. Emory was in the shower, and though it was a given
that we'd discuss the encounter with Wade in minute detail
later, I wanted to tell Gabe first.

"Tell me what?" Gabe asked. He reached into the refrigerator and pulled out the low-fat cream cheese.

"I saw Wade last night. We stopped off at The Steerhead
Tavern. Tracianne Doyle and her husband, Dr. Doyle, were
walking by when I was leaving. I was . . . kind of in a
hurry."

"That place is a dump," he said mildly, spreading cream
cheese on his plain bagel. He poured a cup of coffee and
sat down.

"It was Wade's idea. He needed to talk and he feels
comfortable there." My bagel popped up. I put it on a plate
and sat down across from him.

His face was expressionless, which could mean anything
from he was extremely pissed or just thinking about whether
to have cereal with his bagel. I wondered if I'd done the
right thing by telling him. He was angry at Wade already,
and this would only make things worse. But he was my

husband, doggone it, and I wanted things to be open between us. It was what I was always ragging on him about, so in all fairness, the situation went both ways. Besides, no doubt he'd hear about it from someone today anyway.

"So, what exactly did he want to talk about?" Gabe asked.

My mouthful of bagel stuck dry and hard in my throat. I sipped my coffee, then said, "You know, stuff. Memories. He's . . . he's kind of having a hard time moving on. Emotionally, that is."

His eyes fixed on me intently. "Is that why you were crying last night?"

"I'm fine." There was no way was I going to tell him word for word what Wade said.

"I ought to run him out of town," he said calmly. "I ought to kick his ass."

I made a noise in my throat that was neither positive nor negative, not wanting to help that smoldering fire along. "I just wanted to tell you because Tell-all Traci will be on the phone first thing this morning, and I was sure it would eventually filter down to you."

He stopped chewing. "Tell-all Traci?"

"Tracianne Doyle. That's what she's called. I'm sure the fact that the police chief's wife was seen running out of The Steerhead Tavern will be a switch from their usual conversation of which designer dress they're going to wear to which social event." I stood up and went over to him, touching his shoulder. "I'm sorry if this causes any problems for you."

He pulled me down onto his lap. "*Querida*, I think we both know that I don't especially like you going there, particularly with Wade Harper, but that has nothing to do with what Mrs. Doyle and the rest of the society matrons in this county think. What they say doesn't bother me in the least, and if my job depends on what these women or their husbands think of my wife's companions"—his eyebrows went up—"as sleazy as they might be, or the way she chooses to spend her evenings, then it's not a job I want or need. What matters, or should matter, is that I do my job policing this city. Frankly, I've only lived here a year and a half. I could leave anytime and start over." His eyes bore into mine. "The real question is, could you?"

"What?"

"Start over somewhere else. Where you didn't know anyone but me." He watched my face, his blue eyes steady and waiting.

I knew what he was asking and, to be truthful, I hadn't ever thought about it. Except for a few fleeting moments right after Jack died, when I wanted to run as far away from San Celina and the Central Coast as I could, I'd never even contemplated living anywhere else.

I was saved from answering by my cousin strolling into the kitchen smelling of Ralph Lauren aftershave.

"What a marvelous picture of domestic bliss," he said, walking over to the coffee pot. "I hope you both act this lovestruck in front of Elvia. Positive reinforcement is always helpful."

"You're hopeless," I said, standing up, not looking at my husband though I sensed his gaze on me.

"Not hopeless, hopeful," Emory countered. "Blissfully hopeful. Eternally hopeful. My faith would move mountains."

"Yes, but will it move one stubborn hundred-pound *señorita*?" Gabe asked. "Pigheadedness is a trait that seems to run in the San Celina female." He turned to me, his face neutral. "Refresh my middle-aged memory. What's on your agenda for today, sweetheart?"

"I've got to pull my shift giving historic house tours—two of them, actually. One to a group of Constance's rich friends from the city. Then I'm going out to the ranch to see Dove. Then it's the blessing of the animals tonight and watching you crown the new Miss San Celina. That's about

it.'' Emory and Gabe looked at each other, then looked back
at me. I started cleaning up the table.

"Benni," Gabe said, "Don't start a fight with Dove
about Mr. Lyons—''

"Gabe," I snapped back, "don't tell *me* what to do with
my family."

He held up his hands. "*Lo siento, mi amor*. Do what you
want. See you tonight."

After he left, Emory sat quietly watching me clean up
the kitchen. "He's right, you know," he finally said. "You
should just leave Dove alone on this one."

I whipped around and shook a paring knife at him.
"Don't you start, too, Emory Littleton. I have to warn her
about this man. My gosh, she's been widowed for almost
forty years. What does she know about men?"

"She only raised a few of them," he answered, leaning
back in his chair. "I think she can take care of herself."

I threw the knife in the sink. "And I think you should
mind your own dang business."

"Sweetcakes, much as I think you're cute as a bug when
you're all riled up, this is gettin' old, real old. I think I'll
mosey on out of here until you buzz back down to earth."
He stood up and started for the living room.

I sailed across the room and encircled his waist with my
arms. "I'm sorry, Emory," I said, burying my face in his
chest. "Don't be mad. But I just feel like I have to talk to
her, that I'd be a rotten granddaughter if I didn't at least
try."

He hugged me tightly. "I know, kiddo. Just don't push
too hard, okay? You can be a might like a foamy-mouthed
pitbull at times, you know?"

I smiled up at him. "I'll be diplomatic."

He tugged at a strand of my curly hair. "And I'm next
in line to marry Princess Di."

The historic homes tour was a project that was a joint
money-making venture between the folk art museum, the

Historical Society, and the local quilt guilds. This week the homes had guild members wearing period costumes while they worked on quilts and other pioneer crafts during the tours. The tour itself consisted of ten houses and adobes within a one-mile radius with a stop at Elvia's bookstore and coffeehouse at the end for refreshments and a talk on the county's history by Mr. Bulfinch, the head of Cal Poly's history department. A shuttle would be available six times a day for a side trip out to the folk art museum should anyone opt to add that to the agenda. There was also art by our women artists displayed at each home, as well as in many of the galleries downtown. We'd had a surprising number of reservations, considering it was the first week after Thanksgiving, but the Christmas frenzy had not entirely taken over the world yet, and people were in just a festive enough mood to travel and perhaps do a little early Christmas shopping, which of course was just what we were hoping.

I finished both tours by one o'clock and decided to grab a quick cup of coffee at Blind Harry's before heading out to the ranch. I hadn't seen Dove all day, but I didn't think her turn guiding tours came until later in the week. As I dumped milk and sugar into my coffee, I couldn't help but wonder what she and Isaac were doing today and hoped it wasn't a day that Daddy decided to fix fence on the other side of the ranch. I looked over the crowded coffee house trying to spot an empty table.

An auburn-haired woman in a yellow and brown calico dress from the Oregon trail days stood up and waved at me over the noisy crowd. I threaded my way through the chairs to the small round table in the back.

"Hey, Benni Louise, set your old self on down here and rest up a spell. We've both done served our time in the support of San Celina history."

"Hey, Amanda Aurora Lucille Landry, I'll do just that."

Amanda Landry, a local attorney with her own private

practice, was named by a romantic and slightly batty southern mother who loved George Sand, mint juleps, and blues musicians—not necessarily in that order. Almost six feet tall with hair the color of cordovan leather, she was a native of the grand state of Alabama, a fact that was obvious the minute she opened her wide, Carly Simon mouth.

"Ah think y'all just have the cutest accents hea-yuh out west," she said the first time we met when she joined the artist's co-op a few months back. She made the most astounding pictorial quilts and vests that she'd been giving away to friends for years. Finally a friend in her quilt guild convinced her to start selling them, and though she told me the thought of going commercial just plumb tuckered her out, she did like the idea of her quilt creations being taken seriously.

"And," she said at our requisite meeting where we discussed the rules of the co-op, "Ah know you'n me are going to get along just fine, 'cause Ah've been following your crime-fighting career in that rag of a daily paper since Ah got here. Not to mention that you tend to be one of the favored topics on the DA grapevine. Ah just told those ole graysuits, 'Hey, if y'all do a better job at keeping them criminals behind bars, then itty-bitty cowgirls wouldn't have to be rounding up the bad guys.' "

I definitely had a fan in Amanda Landry. Her friendly relationship with the DA's office came about before she set up her private practice with a substantial inheritance from her father, whom she cheerfully labeled the crookedest judge in Montgomery County's history; she had worked in San Francisco as a deputy DA in charge of the sexual assault/ child abuse unit. She successfully prosecuted the nastiest bad guys this side of a Hollywood producer's nightmare . . . or dream, depending on their values. She accepted the same job down here in San Celina when she grew tired of big-city politics.

"Small-town politics are so much more petty . . . and

fun," she'd said with her hearty, slap-your-back laugh.

She'd worked in the district attorney's office until even small-town politics got on her nerves . . . about a year. Luckily (according to her), old Judge Landry finally saddled himself a cloud and rode off to that great coon hunt in the sky, and she collected her long-awaited inheritance.

According to Gabe, the DA was sorry to lose her. She'd won cases . . . a lot of them. They'd taken to calling her "Queen of the Sex Team." Now, because of her private income, she could pick and choose her clients.

"So," she asked. "What're you up to? It has to be better than what's back at my office—two wills, a yuppie adoption, and yet another lawsuit against McDonald's. Guy claims they put too much ice in his drink and it cracked a tooth. For this I gave up rapists and wife beaters?"

I told her I was going out to see Dove and, before I knew it, had spilled out the whole story about her and Isaac and my misgivings about him. Then I lapsed into the whole Gabe/Wade thing, my worries about Wade being involved with Shelby's death, what Olivia had said last night, and whether I should tell anyone. She listened intently, her intelligent brown eyes blinking rarely, leading me on with short, direct questions.

"Shoot," I said, pausing to take a breath, a bit embarrassed that I revealed so much. "No wonder the criminals hate you. I'll be telling you my deepest, darkest sex fantasies next."

"Please, save those for Gabe," she said, patting my hand. "You just needed to talk, and I was an understanding ear. That's the thing, you know, about all human beings, including criminals. We all love to talk about ourselves, and that's what cops and prosecuting attorneys count on, that eventually a criminal feels the urge to brag to *someone* about how they pulled one over on all us symbolic parental figures. Bragging trips them up more times than not."

"Well, sorry for bending your ear," I said, standing up "Send me a bill."

"Don't worry about it, girlfriend. It all evens out in the end."

I turned to leave, then stopped and said, "Amanda, I know this is probably a bit premature, but Wade's so certain that they're going to pin this on him . . ."

"Is he a scumbag? I don't defend scumbags. That's one advantage to being semi-independently wealthy with ill-gotten money."

"No. He's a redneck cowboy who deserves to be slapped upside the head about ten times a day, but he's not a scumbag, and I don't think he did it. I really don't."

She nodded and sipped at her hot tea. "Tell you what. You call me if they charge him. I know the sheriff's department, and they surely love to close their files as quick as possible, but I won't let them railroad an innocent man."

"Thanks, Amanda."

Her reassuring words made the drive to the ranch a little less stressful. I didn't realize until I'd talked to her how scared I was for Wade and how alone I felt in defending him.

With all my relatives gone now, the ranch looked strangely and sadly empty when I parked under the white oak that shaded the front yard. Inside Dove's clean, cinnamon-scented kitchen, I threw my sheepskin jacket on a stool and helped myself to some leftover roast beef and mashed potatoes. The microwave *pinged* at the same moment I heard Dove and Isaac's voices on the front porch. I had just taken my first bite when they walked in, pink-cheeked and laughing.

"Well, look what the north wind blew in," Dove said, holding a basket of tiny pale green apples from her three pampered trees. Isaac carried two dusty orange pumpkins. A square black camera hung from a worn leather strap around his neck. "Hope you didn't take all the leftovers. That was going to be our lunch."

I looked straight into her clear blue eyes and said, "Only his part."

A small chuckle erupted from his direction.

Dove pinched her lips together and set the apples down on the white-tiled counter. "Isaac," she said, not taking her gaze from me, "would you excuse me and Miss Smart-mouth for a minute?"

"Sure thing, Dove." Isaac placed the pumpkins carefully on the counter next to the apples and gave me a wink before he left. I glared at him, feeling the strongest urge to bounce one of Dove's hard little apples off his white head.

"All righty, little miss," Dove said, whisking my plate out from under my fork. "We're going to have ourselves a talk."

"Hey!" I said, reaching for my food. "Give that back."

"I'm not going to be a-talkin' to you while you're eating. You're just like your Daddy and won't hear a word if you got your mouth full."

"Speaking of Daddy, what's he think about you inviting a stranger to stay at the ranch?"

"Your daddy is a heap smarter than his daughter. I own one third of this ranch and I've got the right to invite anyone I want to stay here."

"Gramma," I said, "be reasonable. You don't even know this man. He's . . . he's . . . ." I threw up my hands in exasperation.

She narrowed one blue eye at me. "He's my guest, young lady, and I'll expect you to treat him with respect. What *is* your problem? Where in the world did you ever get the idea that what I do and who I see is any concern of yours? I'm a grown woman, and you need to keep out of my business." She threw my plate full of food into the sink, spraying brown gravy across her clean counter.

"Me keep out of *your* business? Me!" I sputtered. "You, the queen of interfering—"

She picked up an empty iron frying pan and slammed it down on the stove's burner, causing a clang that rattled the whole stove. "Don't you take that tone with me or I'll—"

The door opened and the source of our argument walked back in. We turned to look at him as he strolled calmly across the carpeted living room and cupped his monstrous hand underneath my elbow.

"I think we need to take a walk before you both say things you'll most likely regret."

I jerked my elbow away. "Leave us alone, Mr. Lyons. This is none of your business."

He clamped his hand on my shoulder. "Ms. Harper, I wasn't asking."

I jerked away again and looked to Dove, waiting for her to jump down his throat, to tell him that no one manhandled one of her grandkids like that.

She just glared at me. "Do what he says."

Openmouthed, I turned around and ran out the door, so mad I could spit nails. I kept going through the backyard, the orchard, around the barn, and through the back pasture until I reached the path to the creek that meandered like a snake through the ranch. The cold autumn air cut deep into my lungs, but I couldn't stop running. Underneath my feet, the dried leaves and grass crunched like toast. When I reached the creek bank I slowed down, picking my way carefully down the steep path to the water. I sat down on a large stone and watched the water bugs skim across the surface as my pounding heart slowed back to normal.

The sound of the trickling water gradually soothed my raw nerves, and rational thought began to return. Why was I acting like such a spoiled brat? What was it about this man that set me so much on edge? Was I really afraid of Dove being hurt or was it that I didn't want to share my grandmother with anyone? As I trailed a stick through the water, the chilled air caused me to shiver underneath my cotton shirt. How was I going to go back and somehow make amends for my childish behavior? I still didn't like or trust Isaac Lyons, but Dove and everyone else was right. It wasn't my place to dictate who she should see no matter how sincere my concern was.

Behind me, the sound of breaking twigs and crackling leaves told me I wasn't alone anymore. By the heaviness of the footfalls and the sound of his breathing, I didn't have to turn around to see who it was.

"Got a spare rock?" Isaac said, coming up beside me.

I shrugged and didn't answer, my noble and mature intentions of a moment ago shattered. It irritated me that he was again pushing his way in before I was ready to concede.

He sat down beside me with a small groan, his overwhelming body filling the spot by the creek that had been my hiding place since I was a little girl. I resented his presence and wondered how he'd found me.

"Dove told me where you'd probably be."

I ignored him and continued studying the trickling water. Above us, a Phoebe flycatcher flitted from branch to branch, scolding us like a cranky old aunt. I shivered again and in the next moment felt the heavy warmth of his fleece-lined leather jacket around my shoulders. I considered pushing it off, then decided that I might be stubborn and unyielding, but I wasn't stupid.

Finally he said, "Benni, I'm not going to hurt your grandmother. That's a promise."

I looked at him out of the corner of my eye. The camera still hung around his thick neck. Did he ever go anywhere without it?

"How do I know that?" I asked. "I don't know anything about you."

He pointed to his camera and asked, "May I?"

I shrugged. He slipped the lens cap into his shirt pocket and brought the camera up to his eye. The shutter's clicking was so soft, a deer could walk by unstartled. He didn't ask me to smile, and I didn't. He stood up and circled me, talking continuously as he snapped pictures.

"You know, a good picture takes a strong subject as well as a strong composition. All the equipment and filters and talent in the world can't make a subject interesting if there isn't something substantial there to begin with." His voice came from behind me, cajoling and demanding at once. "Look at me, Benni." I twisted around and looked over my shoulder. He clicked a picture. "What a photographer leaves out is just as important as what he includes. Only then does the real picture, the real truth, emerge."

I frowned. He snapped a couple of pictures. "The truth as the photographer sees it," I said.

He lowered his camera and smiled at me. "Very good, Ms. Harper. I suspect you would have been an excellent student of photography."

I didn't react to his flattery, still not trusting him, still waiting to see where this was leading.

"I'll tell you a secret," he said, stepping with his long legs across the narrow creek. "No one really knows where good pictures come from." I followed him with my eyes. He clicked another three or four shots and murmured, "Beautiful." He looked at me over the camera. "How to find them is to always reach for the unsafe thing, the unexpected image. You have to disarm your subject as coldly as a soldier in battle. And after all that, sometimes they are just, pure and simple, a gift from God." He lifted the camera back up to his eye. "Think of me in ballerina tights and toe shoes."

"What?" I said and laughed when the picture compulsively drew itself in my mind.

He snapped off a quick rat-tat-tat, then grinned. "Gotcha." He stepped back over the creek and sat down beside me. "Now, you're angry at me even though you don't know me. What can I do to change that?" The soft whir of the camera rewinding film sounded like a small frantic animal.

"I think you're using Dove," I blurted out.

He contemplated me silently. The camera stopped rewinding. Without taking his eyes from my face, he opened the back of the camera, removed the film, and put it in his pocket. "You think so? Is it so hard to believe I would be attracted to your grandmother?"

Before I could answer, he continued.

"Your grandmother is a remarkable woman and an excellent photographic subject. Very natural. My project on California western women is not entirely a sham. It'll sell well, no doubt about it."

"But you're not here just to take pictures of women roping cattle and canning peaches."

He smiled and fitted the lens cap back on his camera. "Dove said you were a sharp one, that it would be, to quote her, pretty near impossible to pull one over on you."

I pressed my lips together, determined not to let his compliment affect my goal. "So why are you here?"

"I don't have any children," he said, locking his thick fingers around one knee. "And I've been married five times. Sounds impossible, I know, but somehow with each one it was either too early or too late or some other crazy reason why we didn't have a family." He looked past me to the water spilling into a miniature waterfall formed by a dam Emory and I had tried to build the summer he stayed here. Moss had grown furry and green over the rocks we'd hauled from the lower creek with overly enthusiastic plans for a swimming hole. "A part of me regrets it now that I'm old. Especially when I see the family surrounding your grandmother. I envy the love that would cause a granddaughter to forge in and butt heads with someone just because she thinks he's going to hurt her grandmother."

I bit the inside of my cheek, fighting the empathy I was starting to feel toward this man.

"We childless people are a special group, whether it's

by choice or not. We love intensely because when we do we can focus on one person. But we at times can also feel an incredible loneliness that no one with children will ever truly understand.''

I swallowed hard, knowing exactly how it felt. I stared down into the clear, running water, wanting to scoop some up and cool my burning face. ''Why are you telling me this?'' I asked in a low voice.

''My fourth wife, Catherine, was the love of my life. She was . . .'' He paused for a moment, remembering. ''She was the photograph I'd been searching for my whole life. It was her second marriage. Her first husband was an aviator, a career Navy man. Their daughter, Gina, was twelve when he died. An experimental plane he was flying went down at Edwards Air Force Base. When Catherine and I married, Gina was thirty-five and already had three sons. They were close to their teens and didn't pay much attention to the old man with a camera around his neck who married their grandmother. Then Gina got pregnant one last time, and my whole life changed.'' He looked down at me and smiled. ''She looked just like pictures of her grandmother at that age. To me, she looked just like what I'd always pictured my own daughter, or granddaughter, looking like. And she was fascinated by cameras from the time she was a baby.''

My eyes widened. ''Shelby,'' I said. ''She's your granddaughter.''

He nodded. ''Catherine died four years ago from a heart attack. Happened just like that.'' He snapped his fingers softly. ''I married again, but it didn't work out. I should have known better, but I was looking for what I had with Catherine and I know I'll never find that again. Shelby and I were close from the very start. She truly accepted me as her grandfather even though I technically wasn't. She called me Papa Lyons.'' His voice caught. ''It was me who encouraged her to go away to college here in the West. I told her if she wanted to be a true artist she needed to first discover who she was and I knew that would be impossible while she lived in Chicago.''

"You're here to find out who killed her."

His brown eyes grew glassy and hard as creek stones. "Gina and Marcus—Shelby's father—just wanted her body shipped back, and that's that. Gina said it didn't matter what happened, that it wouldn't bring Shelby back."

"But it does matter to you." I looked at him steadily.

"Whoever did this will be punished. It won't bring her back, but I need to have justice. For her . . . and for myself. Otherwise, I won't be able to let her go."

A cool breeze blew through the thick trees. I hugged my knees and burrowed deeper into his jacket. It smelled of Polo cologne, the aftershave Gabe wore, and a sharp, metallic scent I couldn't name. "I know," is all I answered.

He held my gaze for an uncomfortable minute. "I know you do. Dove told me about Jack."

"His brother, Wade, is a suspect."

Isaac nodded.

"I don't think he did it."

"Dove doesn't think so either. She said he was raised good. That his mother was an honest, hardworking woman."

"She was," I said, remembering my former mother-in-law, who had been warm and loving to me and her sons the whole time I lived on the ranch. "She is." What Dove didn't know was Wade's little foray into delivering drugs last year when he was trying to save the Harper ranch.

Isaac's camera-trained eyes narrowed; the deep crevices in his face seemed to fold inward. "But you're not entirely sure of him."

I didn't answer.

"It appears, Ms. Benni Harper, that we're both after the same thing, but the question is, are you willing to take a chance on finding out the truth?"

"Do I have much of a choice?"

"I suppose not." He pushed himself up from his rock and held out his hand. "So, partners?"

I hesitated for a moment, then stood up and took it. We shook solemnly, like two horse traders sealing a deal. His hand was cold and uncalloused and completely enveloped mine.

"Partners," I said.

10

BACK AT THE ranch Dove had ham and cheese sandwiches and freshly baked cinnamon rolls waiting for us. She looked from my face to Isaac's, appraising us like a couple of yearlings she was about to buy. "So, you two get your fence lines all sorted out?"

Isaac smiled at me. I gave him a small smile back.

"Yes, ma'am," he said. "I believe we have."

She nodded her head in approval and pointed to the breakfast counter. "Then y'all better get some food in you. Hot coffee, too. It's a cold day."

I went over to her and slipped my arms around her neck, burying my face in her sweet, almond-scented skin. "I'm sorry, Gramma, for being such a brat. Will you forgive me?"

She lightly slapped my shoulder. "Get along and eat, honeybun. You're so mean flies wouldn't light on you, but I reckon I'll keep you since I'm so used to you."

I turned to Isaac, who was already at the counter putting mustard on his sandwich. "That's about as close as she gets to saying 'I love you.' "

"But she does make a mean ham sandwich," he said, grinning.

• • • •

IT WAS FOUR o'clock when I arrived home. One message flashed on the answering machine.

"I have some paperwork to clear up," Gabe's voice said, "so I'll meet you in front of the mission at six o'clock."

Tonight was the blessing of the animals, the dedication of the new mission bell, and the crowning of the new Miss San Celina, which Gabe had been talked into doing. After the ceremonies, Parker and Olivia were giving an hour-long painting class to children twelve and under at the San Celina Art Center across the creek from the mission.

When I arrived, the children were already lined up with their pets, ready to stroll past Father Martinez for the blessing. I threaded my way through a line of squirming, captive kittens, puppies, hamsters, tiny greenish-yellow finches, squawking chickens, and even a snake in a homemade cage belonging to a grinning freckle-faced boy with glasses. He wore a tee shirt that said, "Jesus walked on water. Imagine how He could surf!"

"His name is Rodney D.," he said when he saw me look at his treasured pet with apprehension. " 'Cause he don't get no respect."

Gabe waited on the top steps by the mission's double-wide church doors. Against the whitewashed walls, he surveyed the crowd with searching eyes. I stopped, waiting for that moment his eyes picked me out of the crowd. He spotted me, and his face lit up. We met halfway up the steps.

"*Hola, preciosa*," he said, dropping a kiss on top of my head. "How'd it go at the ranch?"

"Fine. Isaac and I have an . . . understanding. Sort of."

"Good." He slipped an arm around my shoulders, and we walked down the steps toward the stage that was set up for the coronation and dedication. A rooster flew in front of us chased by a young girl wearing pink gardening gloves. A saucer-pawed yellow Labrador puppy wiggled out of his young master's arms and started chasing the rooster, which had flown over the railing and was splashing around in San Celina Creek. The puppy stood at the railing and barked hysterically. The rooster girl's mother dashed in front of us.

"We'll all need to go to confession after this blessing ceremony," she said wryly as she hopped over an escaped rabbit and headed for the steps down to the creek. The puppy, claimed by a young Latino boy with braces and Clark Gable ears, continued to bark as the boy carried him past us, the puppy's back paws bouncing against the boy's knees.

"He's not mean," the boy assured us.

Gabe smiled down at him. "*Perro que ladra no muerde.*"

The boy grinned and maneuvered back in line. "My dad always says that."

"What'd you say?" I asked.

"Barking dogs seldom bite." He put a warm hand on the back of my neck. "So, what do you have planned after this? I'm starved."

"After I watch you crown the queen, I'm going over to the Art Center to help Parker and Olivia set up for their painting class. I should be home after that. I haven't even thought about dinner."

He looked up at the stage where the mayor was tapping his finger on the microphone. "Guess I'd better get to my post. I'll see you at home." He brushed a kiss across my lips and sidestepped a baby goat being pulled by a teenage girl.

I watched part of the ceremony, then wandered over to the Art Center where I found Olivia, Parker, and Greer laying white butcher paper down on the long, foldout tables.

"You're missing the crowning of San Celina's newest queen," I said, picking up a bunch of paint brushes.

"Beauty pageants," Olivia said, scowling. "Haven't we women made any progress in the last thirty years?"

I shrugged, understanding her frustration, but not feeling

as virulent about the subject. "They're all over eighteen," I said. "To each her own."

Olivia scowled deeper at my bland response. "Sorry, Benni, but I think this overriding infatuation with youth and good looks, which beauty pageants are distinctly promoting, preserves the myth that women's only contribution to society is decorating some man's arm and making babies— nice-looking babies. And we all buy into it. Women are the worst perpetrators. We are our own worst enemies."

Parker stopped unrolling the white paper, looked up, and nodded. "She's right, Benni. If you're a homely woman in this society, you'd better be ready to work twice as hard as a pretty one because there's not anyone there paving the way for you." Greer continued picking through a red coffee can of old paintbrushes, a concentrated frown on her face.

"You're right," I conceded. "But that's not really what we're arguing here. We're discussing what feminism really is. Don't you think that the whole point of feminism is allowing women to do whatever they want whether we agree with it or not?"

"Not," Olivia said, "if it sustains this adoration of youth and good looks. What about experience, wisdom . . . talent?"

"Those things count," I said. "Maybe not in beauty pageants, but in—"

"The arts?" Parker said. Sharp points of color dotted her cheekbones. "Don't bet on it, Benni. You like country music. Take that as an example. Have you listened to who's being played on the radio these days? When was the last time a new Willie Nelson or Loretta Lynn song was played? The song that was number one for the last three weeks was sung by a thirteen-year-old. A *thirteen-year-old*! And a very pretty one, I might add."

"There's always Tony Bennett. He's old and he's not that pretty and look how popular he's become . . . again."

"But he's a man . . ." Olivia started.

"Lord, have mercy," Greer interrupted, giving a dramatic sigh. She picked up a plastic container of red tempura paint and held it up as if making a toast. "For us old broads, may there always be Tony Bennett. And Paul Newman. And Clint Eastwood."

"And don't forget Tom Selleck," Parker said. "He's getting up there in age, too." We all laughed.

"Do you all need any more help here?" I asked, using Greer's joking as a way to change the subject. The whole youth versus talent topic seemed an impossible problem to solve, and Olivia especially needed to chill out before attempting to teach the joy of painting to young children.

"We're fine," Parker said, giving me a sympathetic look. "Sorry we're so snappish, Benni. We artists always get a bit testy when we're around people too much. We do much better staying in our little holes inhaling turpentine and linseed oil."

A sheepish expression smoothed out Olivia's face. "I guess I did get on my soapbox there for a minute. *Lo siento, mi amiga.* I'm just more sensitive than usual these days about age. I've been working as a bartender to support my painting for fifteen years and I don't know how much longer I can do it. Sometimes I feel like my time has come and gone."

"No way," I said. "Think of all the artists still producing in their eighties and nineties. I know our society has gone youth crazy, but I've said this before and I really do believe it. Good art will eventually triumph. Not every time, but enough times. Don't get discouraged. Think of Harriet Doerr. Or Georgia O'Keeffe. Think of Isaac Lyons."

Olivia walked over to the closet and pulled out a paint-splattered smock. "Easier said, my friend, easier said." The agitation of a moment ago was replaced with resignation.

Unable to think of anything else to say to appease her, I just said, "See you all later," and started for the door.

"Where are you headed?" Greer asked.

"Thought I'd go on home and think good thoughts about dinner. Maybe something will appear by the time Gabe gets home."

"Maybe a stop off at the market might be smarter," she said, laughing.

"Or Nick's Pizza."

"I'll walk a few blocks with you," she said. "My car's parked downtown, and I left my smock in the back seat. With this group, I'm sure I'll need it."

"Are Parker and Olivia doing okay?" I asked as we walked down Lopez Street. "I'm worried about them." Their attitudes troubled me, though they didn't come as a complete surprise. I had no idea until I became so directly involved with the arts how complicated life became as an artist climbed higher up the public scale. Like most people, I idealized the artist's life, assuming that their lives were somehow fuller, happier, and less conflicted because they were able to work at something they loved. I was beginning to realize that very few things in life were as simple as they looked.

"They're just letting off steam," she said. "It's really difficult in the arts these days. For everyone, no matter what your age or talent. Takes a tough nut to hang in there for the long haul."

"Do you think what they say is true? Does youth matter that much? More than talent?"

She pondered my question a moment, then brushed a strand of white hair from her tanned face. "Not youth only, though that's certainly something that a company investing in your future thinks of, if nothing else but for the sheer economics of it. It's more like—to steal a Cajun word— *lagniappe*."

"D-Daddy uses that word. It means a little something extra. Sort of unexpected."

"Right. Like that artist Bev Dolittle."

"I know her. Her paintings are everywhere."

"Back in ninteen seventy-nine she painted that water-color—'Pintos'—and it was issued in prints by the Greenwich Workshop for sixty-five dollars. The public took a fancy to her work . . . and her . . . and ten years later those same prints were selling for ten thousand dollars. Her original works go for as much as a hundred and fifty thousand dollars now, and there isn't one of her limited edition prints that doesn't sell out on release." She glanced sideways at me, her blue eyes clear and determined. "You know, they've started calling that the 'Dolittle Phenomenon.' The fact that one painting can change an artist's life. Though most artists would rather die than admit it—a lot of us hope that will happen to us. But it doesn't to very many, and some artists—good ones, ones even better than Bev Dolittle, give up."

"That doesn't seem fair," I said.

Greer laughed and slapped me lightly on the back. "Honey, as my dear old granddad used to tell us kids, 'Fair is something you pay to ride the bus.' "

I laughed with her. "Sounds like Dove. The art world sounds so . . . so calculating."

"And what isn't in this grand world of ours, dear girl?"

We passed by Roland's gallery, where he was directing a young man in the replacement of Greer's paintings with more of Shelby's photographs.

"What the . . . ?" Greer said and burst through the front door.

Inside Roland's harsh voice echoed in the small gallery. "Be careful, you idiot! That's a signed photograph."

The young man gave Roland a bland look and set down the wooden frame. He ran his hand over his freshly shaved head as if to nervously stroke hair that was no longer there. "Gotta hit the john, man," he said, hitching up his loose khaki pants.

"I simply despise hiring college kids," Roland said,

watching the boy walk away. "But I don't have any choice
in this town."

"What's going on here?" Greer asked, her voice shaking
with anger. I looked down at Shelby's signed photograph.
It was one of me, though I wasn't easily recognized. The
shot showed me in the distance chasing an uncooperative
cow, the San Celina hills cut stark and black against the
gray afternoon sky. Nipping at the heifer's heels was Repeat,
the daughter of one of Daddy's best Australian shepards. I
glanced at the discreet white tag in the corner. Roland had
indeed tripled the price, just like Parker told me earlier.

"Now, don't get mad, Greer—" he started.

"Mad! I'm triple-time pissed off, Roland Bennett. What
in Sam Hill do you think you're doing with my paintings?"

He shook his head, arranging his face in a sad expression,
but the light in his eyes revealed his true feelings. "You
know people, Greer. They grab on to something whenever
there's a scandal. I'm trying to do right by Shelby and get
the most I can for her work. The money all goes to her
estate, of course."

"At my expense?" she said, her complexion white with
anger.

"Now, I'm putting your paintings right here so people
can see them just as they walk in . . ."

"Not good enough, Roland. You put those back in the
front window, or I'll pull them out of your gallery alto-
gether."

He gave a slimy little smile. "Not possible, Greer. You
signed a contract."

"Well, I'll unsign it!"

"Not possible."

"I'll go to a lawyer. I'll sue your fat little butt. I'll . . ."

I grabbed Greer's arm. "Let's go outside for a moment.
We can deal with this later." I knew Greer, and if she got
going she'd end up saying things she'd regret later. I didn't
know how much influence Roland had in the western art

field, but I did know it was never good to burn a bridge until you decided whether you'd ever need it to get over that particular river again. If Greer acted rash, he might be able to ruin her career permanently. I tugged at her arm. "C'mon, Greer. Let's come back later."

She shook off my arm and pushed through the door. I gave Roland's smirking face a disgusted look and followed her.

"That jerk. That lowdown, miserable jerk . . ." She pounded her leg in frustration as I followed her down the street. In front of Sweet Dreams, I grabbed her arm and stopped her.

"Greer," I said firmly, pulling her inside the warm, steamy coffeehouse. "We're getting something to drink. You have to calm down."

I finally got her seated in the outdoor garden patio in back with a cup of hot herb tea and got her vehement words and declarations down to an occasional "shit." Above us, the sky turned the dusky lavender of early evening. A green finch sang in a cage just inside the back door.

"I could kill him," she said.

"What he's doing is despicable, no doubt about it," I agreed. "But don't you think you're making too big a deal about it? His little gallery is nothing in the larger scheme of things."

She stared at me over her steaming tea. "To you it's a small thing, Benni, but sometimes the small things are all we can control. I fully expect to be treated like a second-class citizen when I eventually start rubbing elbows with the biggies, but I'd like to have some respect in my local area."

"And you do," I insisted. "He's just trying to make as much from Shelby as he can while her death is still an item of curiosity. It's despicable and certainly straddles the fence of professional integrity, but I still don't think what he does in his little gallery is going to affect you long term."

She took a long drink of her tea. "It better not. It's just

that a lot of important people are going to be looking at his gallery this whole week and him moving me out of the window is humiliating. I guess young and pretty isn't enough these days. You gotta be dead, too.''

Her words shocked me silent. Before I could think of an answer, she stood up. "I have to go," she said. "Parker and Olivia need my help.''

"Are you going to be all right?" I asked, following her out to the street. We stood under the flickering old-fashioned street lamp. They were decorated this week with twisted silk poppies and ivy interspersed with small wooden cutouts of the mission, covered wagons, and Chumash Indian symbols.

"I'm fine. Thanks for trying to help, but this is just as much a part of being an artist as figuring out what shade of blue to use. I'll deal with Roland. In my own time and in my own way.''

"Just don't do anything rash. Remember, you have more important things to think about than Roland Bennett and his puny little gallery.''

"I know." She nodded sharply and started walking back toward the Mission Plaza. I watched her straight back until she turned the corner.

I headed back toward my car thinking about all that just took place in the last hour and a half—Parker's and Olivia's comments on looks and youth, Roland's greedy brazenness, Greer's understandable anger and humiliation. Maybe I should ask Emory to look into Roland's background. What did we really know about Roland? He'd only been on the Central Coast for a couple of years. He could be anyone, with any sort of sordid background. He breezes into town, opens up a gallery, and immediately talks two of our most talented artists into signing a contract with him. And I had no idea how many other artists had signed contracts with him. His was the only gallery in town that specialized in western art, so it might be more than I realized.

Could the utterly fantastic accusation of Parker's be

true—could Roland be involved with Shelby's death just so her photographs would be worth more? Wouldn't that be self-defeating in the long run? She hadn't become big enough yet for her work to be worth much. Then again, she was Isaac Lyons's granddaughter. Could Roland have found out Shelby's connection to Isaac? Would that have made her work more valuable to collectors? Would Shelby have told Roland something like that to convince him to represent her work? Shelby had been ambitious and probably would use what she could, but she was also so youthfully idealistic about her art. I knew that from long days spent with her as she photographed me at the ranch, listening to her ramble and enthuse about art as compared to what she disdainfully called "commercial dreck." I think a part of her really did want to succeed on her own without help from either her socially connected parents or her famous step-grandfather.

I turned the truck toward home, knowing I should drop by the museum to see how things went today, but it was already past seven o'clock and I was tired of being a problem solver and sympathetic ear. Besides, I was hungry. Really hungry. Gabe and I hadn't made any plans, so I decided to wait at home and see if he called. The phone was ringing when I unlocked the door.

"Glad I caught you," Gabe said. "My duties are completed. What did you have in mind for dinner?"

"I was contemplating that very subject as I walked in the door. Nick's Pizza has a strong lead in the race. How does that sound?"

He hesitated. "Dean asked me to join them at that new Cajun restaurant over by the college. May's going to be there." Dean Pendleton was the district attorney, a greyhound-thin man who was an avid windsurfer and strong supporter of the Special Olympics. I liked his wife, May, a Chinese-American mathematics professor at Cal Poly whose family had lived in San Celina County for five generations. She and I shared a common passion for oral history and were always exchanging books on the subject. I thought for a moment. Usually I enjoyed going out with May and Dean, but I didn't know if I was up to social chitchat at this particular moment.

"No pressure," Gabe said. "He and I are going to be talking business mostly. She was only going to come if you did."

"I'm really tired," I confessed, knowing how long Gabe and Dean's conversations could sometimes run. "Can you ask her for a raincheck?"

"No problem. I'll be home whenever."

Since I had no idea where Emory was or what his dinner plans were, I decided to go with my original craving and order a pizza. Since I didn't have to consider Gabe, I ordered a sausage, pepperoni, and double cheese. After totally gorging myself, I lay back on the sofa and cruised the TV channels until I settled on a PBS rerun of *Pride and Prejudice*. I promptly fell asleep and was awakened by a shrilling phone. Disoriented, I stumbled over to it.

"Hello?" I peered through the dark room at the clock on the wall. In the shadows it seemed to read ten-thirty.

"Benni?" a familiar male voice answered. I searched my addled brain for a connection.

"Yes?"

"You better get yourself down here real quick before someone gets hurt bad."

"Who is this?" I demanded.

11

"It's Tony."

Tony, I thought. My still sleep-groggy brain zipped around like a lightning bug. Tony? Oh, *Tony*. He was one of the artists at the co-op, a metal sculptor who worked part time as a welder and sometimes, like Olivia, as a bartender. Was he the artist overseer of the week? My heart started pounding. Had something happened at the museum?

"What's wrong?" I said. "The museum . . ."

"It's not that. Everything's copacetic. Greer's the overseer this week. No, I just thought I'd better call you before things get out of hand."

"What do you mean?" I clicked off the TV set, which was now showing some type of show about the dangers of dust mites in our beds. They looked like huge Godzilla-like fleas, and I shivered at the thought.

"I'm working at the Frio Saloon tonight, and we've been having a problem with your brother-in-law. Thought you might want to come down here and talk him into leaving before he gets himself into trouble."

"Shoot, how drunk is he?" I asked.

"He's had eight beers and three shooters of tequila," Tony said. "Not that I'm counting."

"Oh, great." I sat down on the sofa, clutching the phone to my ear. "Has he gotten into any fights yet?"

"Not yet, but his attitude's gettin' uglier with each drink. The only reason I'm calling you is I know he's already kinda in hot water over that thing with Shelby. I figured it would probably be better for him to keep kind of a lower-type profile. You get my drift?"

"Yes, I get it." How to accomplish it—*that* was the problem. "Look, try to stall serving him any more booze. Water it down if you have to. I'll be there as soon as I can. Forty-five minutes, tops."

"I'll do my best, Benni. Just thought you'd want to know."

"Thanks, Tony. I owe you one."

I grabbed my purse and started out the door, then stopped. Gabe would probably be home any minute and wonder where I'd gone. I dashed off a quick note saying I had to help a friend and would be back in a couple of hours. I didn't dare add any details. The Frio Saloon at night was a rowdy, anything-goes kind of place full of oil-field workers, cowboys, bikers, and a few brave yuppies looking to temporarily rub elbows with the working class for stories of bravery around their office's Braun coffeemakers the next morning.

Santa Flora had long rolled up her sidewalks by eleven o'clock. Ten miles out of San Celina, one mile off the free-way, the small country town consisted of a Moose lodge, a post office, the Rainbow Hut cafe, a liquor store, a volunteer fire department, and a large feed supply building that glowed huge and silver in my truck's headlights. At the far end of Main Street was the almost imperceptible turnoff for the town of Frio, whose own claim to fame was a U.S. Department of Forestry station and the Frio Saloon. The trip to it would entail twenty miles on a two-lane snake-twist highway where a large share of cars and pickups piloted by tipsy Frio patrons ended up plowed into hillsides or nose-driven into weedy ditches. It wasn't the first time I'd made a trip to the Frio Saloon to pick up a drunk and disorderly Wade, but it was the first time I'd done it alone.

As I pulled the truck over the bumpy railroad tracks and headed down the narrow road toward Frio, Jack's presence seemed to permeate the truck's cab. His face, lost to my conscious memory in the last few months, suddenly flared up again, burning itself into the passing landscape. I saw his hands in the jagged ink spots of oak trees dotting the moon-lit hills, his eyes in the blurry stars dotting the cobalt sky, his laugh in the engine's rumble coursing through the thick, chilled air. I passed small ranches and farms, their windows glowing yellow and welcoming, the road rough and bumpy beneath my tires; my kidneys felt bruised and beaten, and the undulating road caused a sour, sick feeling in my stomach. When the road started to climb, the truck wheezed and I downshifted. I'd forgotten this hilly part of the drive. I struggled with the truck, urging it silently in the misty night, encouraging it and myself, talking to the engine, to Jack, to God.

C'mon now, don't conk out on me. Oh, Jack, I'd like to kill your brother. Lord, please make all this okay. Protect Wade, protect me through this terrible night.

Twice I saved "suicide squirrels" when I caught their bright, panicked eyes in my headlights, swerving and re-adjusting as they scampered through the maze of my moving tires. At the bridge crossing Frio Creek, I slowed down reluctantly, wanting to flee, knowing I couldn't. The square, dark green ranger station was locked tight, a lone amber light shining over the solid door. Across the road, the Frio Saloon peeked out of the haze, damp air staining its red clapboard walls dark with spots the color of old blood. The dirt parking lot was packed with dusty, ten- and twenty-year-old ranch trucks with an occasional new Jeep Cherokee or Toyota Landcruiser decorating the mixture like rainbow sprinkles on chocolate icing.

Inside, the blaring music, cigarette smoke, and malty smell of spilled beer assaulted me like an invisible fist. My arrival didn't cause a ripple in the sea of human flesh. People stood squeezed together, elbow to elbow, skin touching damp skin. I searched the crowd with dismay, looking over the throng of humans choking the ten-table restaurant. The large square room to the left held two ancient pool tables, a wall full of antlers, and a scroungy local band perched on a homemade plywood stage playing Willie Nelson's "Faded Love." The lead singer wore a black shirt with purple cut-outs of the naked women you see on diesel truck mud flaps. His silver hat band caught the overhead track lighting and sparkled like new aluminum.

Tony wasn't working the front bar or at the semicircle bar next to the pool tables. I walked through the double-wide back door onto the patio where the smoky smell of cooking ribs warmed the night air. Scanning the constantly milling crowd, I clenched my fists in irritation. I'd never find Wade.

Tony's voice called out over the buzz, "Benni, over here!"

I looked toward his voice. He was selling bottled beer and wine coolers out of a tub of ice next to the barbecue pit. I pushed through people until I was standing in front of him.

"Tony, where's Wade? I can't find him." A cold wind whipped through the patio, and I pulled my sheepskin jacket close around me. The heat from the barbecue warmed my face, but my back stayed cold.

He shook his head in disgust. "Who knows in this crowd? Did you check the head?" He reached into the aluminum tub and pulled out a couple of long-neck beers and handed them to a bearded man wearing a red-and-black-checked hunting shirt.

"You askin' bout Wade Harper?" the man said.

I nodded.

"He and some guy started throwin' words back and forth, and we told them to take it off the premises. They was walkin', if you want to call it that, out thataways last I saw." He pointed to a stand of eucalyptus and oak trees a couple of hundred yards past Frio's fenced-in back patio.

I closed my eyes briefly and wished on a nonexistent falling star that Wade had never come back to San Celina. When I opened them, Tony and the bearded man were staring at me, their faces apprehensive.

"How long ago was that?" I asked.

The man cocked his head and thought. " 'Bout half hour, forty-five minutes. I think I saw Wade come back kinda bloody-nosed heading towards the john."

"You okay?" Tony asked me. He handed out another beer, then shook ice off his fingers.

"I will be once I get Wade out of here. Can you check the bathroom for me and help me herd him out to my truck?"

The apprehensive look returned. I couldn't blame him. A drunk Wade was not someone to be reckoned with lightly. The bearded man just shook his head, took a long drag of beer and wandered back into the crowd.

"Please, Tony." I tried not to sound as desperate as I felt.

His face relented. "All right, Benni. Heaven knows, you've gone far beyond the call of duty more than once for us artists for your lousy seven bucks an hour. Just running interference with Constance so the co-op can keep going makes us all indebted to you for life. I'd have killed myself long ago if I didn't have my sculpting to look forward to. Let's go find your brother-in-law."

I gave him a grateful look and didn't answer, afraid that if I said one word at this point I'd start crying. Despite the constant bickering and often childishly competitive spirit among the co-op members, there was also a streak of loy-

alty, a sense of family that showed itself at unexpected times
like this.

I followed him down the hallway to the bathrooms. As
usual, the line to the ladies room was ten deep while the
door to the men's room was more revolving. I stood looking
at the rough, wooden floor while Tony searched the bathroom. A few minutes later he came out, pushing a staggering
Wade in front of him. Dried blood had congealed under
Wade's thick ginger mustache. A stupid smile lit up his face
when he saw me.

"Benni-girl," he said, his words slurring. "Kicked some
ass, I did. Kicked some smart little ass." Behind him, some
girls giggled. He turned and gave them a sloppy grin, attempting a bow. Tony and I caught him before he toppled
over. The girls giggled again.

"Time to go home, Wade," I said, grabbing one arm and
pulling him up. Tony rolled his eyes at me and grabbed the
other.

"Kicked some cowboy ass," Wade repeated.

Somehow we maneuvered him through the crowd and
out to my truck. Thank goodness Tony was there to help.
Getting Wade stuffed into the cab without Tony's strength
would have been close to impossible for me.

"Is his bill all settled up?" I asked.

Tony laid a warm hand on my shoulder. "Don't worry
about that right now. I'll let you know. Just get him out of
here before he and Kip tangle again."

"How bad was Kip beat up?" I asked, wondering if we
had an assault and battery problem to contend with.

"I have no idea. I didn't see the fight. Like Lyle said,
they took it off the premises. I'm guessing he doesn't look
any worse . . . or any better."

"What a mess. A big stupid mess."

"Don't get too riled up. I see this all the time. Two guys
duke it out, mostly throwing air punches, connecting enough
times to draw a little blood. Once that happens, they both

tend to back off. I just wanted you to get Wade away before it got bad enough that someone brought out a knife or a gun.''

From inside the cab, Wade groaned and shifted. His bare head hit the window with a hollow thump.

''Ouch,'' Tony said, smiling. ''He's going to feel that tomorrow.''

''That's not all he'll feel, I'm sure,'' I said. ''Where's his hat?''

''Who knows? When we close at two, we reconnoiter the rooms and patio and take all the crap people have left and put it in a big cardboard box next to the stage. It'll show up eventually, unless someone takes it.''

''Thanks. For that . . . and everything.'' I held out my hand.

He shook it. ''Hang in there, boss. See you at the parade on Saturday.''

''I hope so,'' I said. ''If Gabe doesn't kill me first for bringing home my drunk and bloody ex-brother-in-law.''

He grinned. ''We all got our burdens. I'll trade you my ex-wife for your problems any day.''

''No, thanks,'' I said, laughing. His ex-wife, a speed freak, had gone after him with an ice pick, connecting four times before the police arrived. She was eventually incarcerated for attempted murder. ''Guess I'll just count my blessings while I drive home.''

During the ride home, I counted all right, but it wasn't my blessings.

''Twenty million times,'' I ranted to a snoring Wade. ''That's how many times I feel like I've had to do this. Have you ever heard of Alcoholics Anonymous? Don't you care about anyone but yourself? You jerk, I'm not even related to you anymore. Why should I care if you get the crap beat out of you? You jerk, you big, stupid, dumb jerk. I ought to just dump you on the side of the road right now.''

He snorted in his sleep and turned his head. Drool pooled

at the edge of his mouth. I turned my head in disgust and concentrated on the flashing white lines in the middle of the black road. Tule fog had moved in, and my old truck's headlights barely broke through the soupy mist. I flipped on my high beams.

''Do you realize what kind of trouble I'm going to be in when I get home? Gabe is going to burst a blood vessel. I ought to drive us both in a ditch right now and save us the agony . . . no, save *me* the agony of his lecture. Have you ever been lectured by Gabriel Ortiz? That man can cut melons with just his verbs. We're in deep, deep crap, buddy, and it's all your fault. Why in the world I care about saving your worthless butt is beyond me.''

His eyes fluttered, then he heaved a deep sigh. I wondered briefly if being drunk was like being in a coma. Could the person sometimes actually hear, comprehend in some deep metaphysical way, what you were saying?

I don't care, I thought. I cracked my window to clear the truck's cab of his alcoholic stench. The scent of wet earth and goats floated in. An improvement, but not much.

The drive back on the desolate highway seemed to take only seconds, and soon I was through Santa Flora and heading up the on-ramp to the freeway. I glanced at my watch. It was almost one A.M. I slowed the truck to fifty-five, trying to articulate a plausible explanation as to why I would rescue someone who technically wasn't any more related to me than the man in the moon and had acted like the king of the morons since he'd arrived. My brain felt positively burnt. Not even Spielberg could come up with a good story for this one.

Our front porch light was a single bright beacon when I turned the corner onto our dark street. When I pulled up to the front curb, I was tempted to keep going, and would have had my copilot not been a smelly, passed-out drunk.

Gabe stood on the porch, arms crossed and stony-faced. Scary, but expected.

But Emory, my good buddy, my childhood comrade, my erstwhile partner in crime, stood next to him, his posture eerily similar, his face frozen into an expression I'd never, ever seen on him. Emory pissed. Now there was a new adventure.

They were down the porch steps and across the yard standing next to the truck when I opened my door. Wade picked that particular moment to wake up from his stupor and bellow out, "Where's my hat?"

Noticing him for the first time, Gabe and Emory stared at Wade, speechless. Then they both started talking at once. Gabe placed a hand on Emory's shoulder.

"Excuse me, but she's my wife," he said. "I get to yell at her first."

"By all means, sir," he said, holding out his palm while giving me a severe look.

After the last three unbearable hours, their condescending attitudes were just what I needed to eliminate any vestige of fear and replace it with a barely containable anger— mostly at the entire male sex. Before Gabe could bark out a complete sentence, I held up my hand. "Nobody's yelling at anybody. Not now. Not later. What you are going to do is help me get Wade to bed, and then we'll talk. Sensibly. Without yelling. Like *adults*."

Gabe opened his mouth to speak.

"Don't even think about it," I said, narrowing my eyes.

The look on my face or my tone or something must have really impressed them, because they glanced at each other and without another word went around the side of the truck and roughly pulled Wade out. While they half dragged him across the yard, I went into the guest room and spread Gabe's new sleeping bag down on the floor next to Emory's bed. When I informed them of the sleeping arrangements, Emory's stiff expression relayed what he thought of sharing a room with Wade, but he didn't verbalize it.

Wise move, dear cousin of mine.

After Wade had been taken care of, I went into the kitchen to get a glass of milk for my burning stomach. Was this what an ulcer felt like? Gabe and Emory followed me silently, watching me pour the milk into a mug, add almond extract and sugar, and stick it in the microwave. Then I faced them.

"Okay, before you two even start, I'm telling you I didn't have a choice. I got a call from Tony at the Frio Saloon. Wade was causing some problems there and needed to be picked up. There was no one else he could call, and neither of you were here to come with me. I know it was probably not the smartest thing to do, but I did it and that's that. As it is, he got into a tussle with Kip before I arrived, but at least I hustled him out before anything serious could happen." The microwave *pinged*, and I took out my mug of milk, testing it with my forefinger before taking a sip. "Any questions, or can I go to bed now?"

Emory spoke first. "Sweetcakes, much as I'd love to bless you out good for bein' so contrary and foolish, I know enough not to mess with you when your fur's all standin' on end, so I'll be going on to bed and talk with you tomorrow." He turned to Gabe. "My deepest sympathies, Chief."

"Suck eggs," I called to his retreating back.

"I love you, too," he answered.

"I'm going to take a shower," I informed Gabe.

His nostrils flared slightly, but he didn't answer. Not a good sign. I took my warm milk into the bathroom and lathered my hair twice trying to wash away the acrid smell of cigarette smoke.

The light was out in our bedroom, so I felt my way to the bed and crawled in. The bedside clock said two A.M. The warmth from Gabe's body tempted me, but I plumped my pillow and turned on my side away from him. I spoke to the pale moonlight coming through our bedroom window.

"I know you're mad because I went to get Wade without

calling you and I know it's because you're scared that I could have gotten hurt. But I honestly didn't feel I had a choice and I really don't want to fight about it."

"All right." His voice was cool, neutral.

His noncombative response surprised me. For a split second, I almost asked him what he was thinking, then decided to let well enough alone.

A few minutes passed, and I lay there stiff and wide awake. The milk and shower hadn't relaxed me as much as I'd hoped. Outside, a mourning dove started its soft, rhythmic cooing. The sound caused a heavy, sad feeling of nostalgia for an unknown something to rise up and fill my chest. Gabe shifted next to me, then reached over and pulled me into his arms. I pressed myself as close as I could, burying my face in his scratchy neck.

"*Querida, querida*," he said, pressing his strong hands into my back I could feel the heat from them through my thin tee shirt. "Don't you think I understand about *la familia*?"

I drew in a shuddering breath, trying not to give in to the tears pooling at the corners of my eyes. "But he's not," I whispered. "Not anymore."

He touched my forehead gently with his lips. "Not in the law, perhaps, but in *tu corazon*. That is a different animal. No one knows better than me that the human heart is a law unto itself."

"I'm sorry I scared you and Emory," I said.

"I'm almost getting used to it," he said, his voice wry. "Now, your cousin—he might have a few words for you tomorrow. He's never experienced one of your escapades firsthand. I think he was a little annoyed because I wouldn't use my authority and put out an all-points-bulletin."

"I'll talk to him. Grovel a bit and promise I'll never do it again."

"Groveling wouldn't be bad, but if I were you I'd try to refrain from breaking one of the ten commandments."

I slapped his chest lightly. "Hey . . ." Then I thought about it. "Well, maybe you're right." I lay my head back down on his shoulder. "I think I might actually be able to sleep now."

"Me, too. One last thing though."

"Mmm?"

"Just so we're clear on this. As mature and understanding as I am being about why you feel obligated to help your ex-brother-in-law, given the opportunity, I'm still going to kick his sorry ass."

"Yes, dear," I said, laughing softly in the darkness, knowing he was just letting off steam.

Or so I thought.

12

IN MY DREAMS there were bells. Shrilling, screaming bells.
I woke with a start when I felt Gabe fumble over me and
reach for the phone.

"Why isn't that stupid thing on your side of the bed?"
I asked, his warm chest smothering me in not an unpleasant
way.

"Ortiz," he said into the phone.

I struggled out from under him and glanced at the clock.
Ten after six. The alarm would have gone off in twenty
minutes anyway. It seemed we'd fallen asleep just seconds
ago. I pulled the edge of my pillow over my head and tried
to go back to sleep. Gabe's terse, angry voice cut through
the down feathers and caused me to bolt up and listen.

"He's here," he said, then was silent. "No, I'll bring
him down. Give us an hour." He slammed the receiver back
on the phone.

"What's going on?" I asked, pulling our thick quilt up
around my chilled arms. I knew enough from his side of the
conversation that it most likely involved Wade and that it
wasn't good. Just how badly had he beaten Kip?

"Kip Waterman's body was found this morning behind
the Frio Saloon. The Sheriff's Department wants to talk to

Wade." He threw back the covers and pulled on a pair of white boxer shorts. He flung our bedroom door open, letting it hit the wall with a deep, wood-chunking thump. Pulling on my robe, I scrambled after him.

He was already dragging Wade up out of the sleeping bag when I reached the guest room doorway. A bleary-eyed Emory sat up in the queen-size bed.

"What the . . . ?" Wade sputtered as Gabe shoved him down on the bed.

"Get your boots on, Harper," Gabe said. "I'm taking you down to the sheriff's office."

Wade sat on the edge of the bed looking up at Gabe with confused, bloodshot eyes. The cloying old-liquor smell of him filled the room.

"Maybe he should take a shower first," I said.

Gabe frowned at me. "He's going now."

"What's going on?" Emory asked, reaching for his velour robe.

"Kip Waterman's dead." Gabe spit the words out. "The person last seen fighting with him was Wade."

"What?" Wade stood up, wobbled, then abruptly sat back down. "How . . ." His chapped lips parted in surprise.

"I'm getting dressed," Gabe said. "Be ready to leave in ten minutes."

"Think I'll start a pot of coffee," Emory said, laying a hand briefly on my shoulder as he passed. "Looks like we'll be needin' it."

Wade looked up at me, his face a mixture of confusion and resignation. "We threw a few punches, blondie, but he wasn't dead when I went to the john. He was laying next to the creek a-bellyachin' about Shelby. I only connected twice." He balled up his right fist and looked at it. Blood stained the crevices brown.

"Go wash your face and comb your hair," I said, trying to buy myself some time while I thought about what to do. Again, I felt torn between my husband and someone who'd been a part of my life for a good deal longer than Gabe. Just how much did I owe Wade because of our past connection?

The benefit of the doubt, at least, a small voice said.

"There's a new toothbrush in the medicine cabinet in the bathroom," I said. "And don't say anything until I can get Amanda down there."

He stood up, grabbing on to the brass bed post for support. "Who's Amanda?"

"Your attorney," I said grimly.

I went into the bedroom, closing the door behind me. Gabe was bent down, combing his hair in front of my vanity table mirror. He was already dressed in jeans and a navy cable-knit sweater.

"I'm going with you," I said.

He slipped his comb into the back pocket of his Levi's. "No, you're not."

"You're going to railroad him." I tore off my robe and reached for my jeans.

He came over and took both my shoulders in his hands. They were warm and familiar and, at this moment, not one bit comforting. His thumbs lightly caressed my collar bone. "*Querida*, I'm not doing anything. I'm merely making it less embarrassing for everyone by taking him down to the sheriff's department myself."

"How did Kip die?"

"He was apparently knocked out with some blunt object. Then someone held his head down in that creek out behind the saloon. Preliminary call by the coroner is death by drowning, though until they do an autopsy they won't be completely sure if it was the blow that killed him or the water."

I pulled away from his hands. "I'm calling Amanda."

A sharp, disgusted sound came from Gabe's throat.

I pulled on my jeans and zipped them up. "He deserves to have someone on his side."

"If he's innocent, he doesn't have anything to worry about."

"Right. No innocent person has ever been convicted in our wonderful legal system." I looked over at my angry husband. "Please, Gabe, just give him a fair chance."

He ran a hand across his face in exasperation. "It's not me you have to convince. I probably won't even sit in on the questioning. The homicide happened on county land. Again, it's up to the Sheriff's Department."

I walked over and lay my hand on his chest. "But they respect you. They'll listen to you."

"I'm sorry," he said. "I would do anything for you, you know that. But this time . . ." He cupped my chin in his hand. "This time, I think you've called it wrong."

I touched his hand briefly with my fingertips, then pulled my chin away, though not in anger. His eyes turned down in sadness.

"We have to go. *Yo te amo.*"

"I love you, too, Friday."

After he'd left with a cleaned-up and subdued Wade, I dialed Amanda's home number. In the background, Bonnie Raitt was giving the whole world something to talk about.

"Hey, Benni Harper, how's tricks?" she asked, breathing hard.

"I'm sorry to bother you so early . . ."

"Don't sweat it, girlfriend. I was just doing some serious bonding with my treadmill. Hold on a minute . . ." In a few seconds, the background went silent. "So, is this your before-coffee morning voice or is something wrong?"

I quickly told her the situation. As I talked I sensed more than heard her mental switching from good ole girl to experienced attorney.

"How long ago did they leave?" she asked, her voice all business.

"About five minutes ago."

"That doesn't give me much time with the way that husband of yours drives. You said the victim was found behind the Frio Saloon?''

''Yes.''

''Then it's the sheriff's baby, all right. I'll get down there as quick as I can. You said you told him not to say a thing until I got there?''

''Yes, but I don't know if he'll listen to me.''

I heard her inhale deeply and I could picture her shaking her auburn head. ''You'd better hope he does, my friend. Meet me there.'' She hung up without saying good-bye.

Feeling that I'd done as much as I could for now, I finished dressing and went into the kitchen. Emory had a cup of coffee waiting.

''So, what's the story?'' he asked, handing me the warm blue mug.

I added cream and sugar, explaining as much as I knew at this point. ''I called Amanda Landry, that attorney I told you about who belongs to the co-op. She's going to meet me there. Then I guess we'll see just what they have on Wade.''

''And how about you and the chief?''

I sipped my coffee. ''We're fine, considering the impossible circumstances. I think we're actually starting to form something that supersedes his job and my relationships in this town.''

''I think they call it a marriage,'' Emory said, pulling the tie on his robe tighter.

''Ha, ha,'' I countered halfheartedly.

''Is there anything I can do, sweetcakes?''

I looked at him a moment. ''Unless you can find someone who might want both Kip and Shelby dead so that my ex-brother-in-law can get off the hook and back to Texas . . . not much.''

He looked back at me, his green eyes steady. ''Not ever bein' one to mince words with you . . . what if he's the one?''

"He's not."

"You sound certain. At the risk of getting my head bit off, why is this so doggone important to you one way or the other?"

I stared down at my scuffed boots. "I'm not sure. Maybe it's one last thing I can do for Jack. Next to me, he loved Wade more than anyone in the world. Gabe called it *la familia* last night. It's like that. One last thing for Jack, because his family meant everything to him."

Emory held out his arms, and I went to him, feeling warmed by the touch of someone whose blood carried the same genetic codes as mine. *La familia.* That of the blood and that of the heart. Both were important. Who could say which affected us more deeply?

"Bad stuff going down, honey," the receptionist at the sheriff's office said when I walked in. She was a woman I'd met and talked to at length about our common interest in antique conversation print fabric at a sheriff and city police picnic last summer. Mary Agnes was a tough, no-nonsense lady who looked like Hollywood's version of the perfect grandmother—all lace-collared dresses and a halo of pink-white hair. She'd driven a school bus for fifteen years until she decided to, as she put it, pursue a safer job path working for the sheriff's department. She ran the busy office as efficiently as a seasoned drill sergeant, leaving in her wake a sometimes cowering, but always grateful, group of detectives and lab technicians. At Christmas she received more gifts and cards of gushing adoration than the sheriff himself. Those detectives knew which side of the bread to butter.

I rested my elbows on the high wooden counter. "So, what's the scoop?"

"Your handsome husband's gulping coffee in John's office, your hungover ex-brother-in-law's being grilled by the county's finest, and I sent that smart-mouthed attorney friend of yours down to the break room to cool her heels and nasty tongue with a soft drink." She peered at me over her half-moon tortoiseshell glasses. "You tell her to watch her mouth, or I'll make sure she'll regret it."

"I humbly apologize on her behalf, Miss Mary," I said, borrowing the title dubbed by her students. "She's from Alabama," I added as a bone to appease her, feeling like a turncoat. *Sorry, Amanda*, I said silently, *but we need Miss Mary on our side.*

"Figured as much," she said with a flip of her wrist. Mary Agnes was a transplanted Bostonian—according to her, a Yankee-in-exile even after forty-two years. "You tell her I wouldn't take attitude like that from the Pope himself, even if I was still Catholic."

"I'll tell her. How long have they had Wade?"

"About half hour or so. He went in voluntarily, you know. And they have to stop any time he asks for an attorney. He apparently hasn't asked yet." She stamped a stack of papers—bam, bam, bam—then looked up at me. "Nice-looking boy, but he's about a half bubble off plumb, isn't he?"

"Sometimes, Miss Mary, I think more than a half."

In the break room, Amanda was pacing in front of the drink machine like a caged badger. A half empty paper cup of Seven-Up sat on the round table next to her. She was dressed in a navy pinstriped power suit with matching pumps. With her three-inch heels, she'd stand an inch taller than Gabe. I was impressed. I hoped the detectives would be . . . when they finally saw her.

"Benni!" She pulled an unlit cigarette out of her mouth. "You said you told your brother-in-law not to talk to anyone before I got here."

"I also told you he often doesn't listen to me. I didn't know you smoked."

She pulled the cigarette out of her mouth and looked at it irritably. "I haven't for years. It was either this or a Twinkie." She tossed it in the large green trash can and picked up her Seven-Up. "Where did they get toad-lady? She could have given Margaret Hamilton a run for her money for the Wicked Witch of the West role."

"She was real impressed with you, too," I said, sitting down at one of the unwashed tables. A dusting of sugar dotted its brown surface. Amanda sat across from me. "What did you say to piss her off so quickly?"

"Nothing, I swear! She just took an instant disliking to me."

I nodded and didn't press it. Amanda's demeanor, especially when she was caught unprepared, could get a bit snippy. And Miss Mary Agnes did not tolerate snippy. All those years driving school buses, I guessed.

"Forget her," Amanda said, reaching down for her black leather briefcase. "I'm going crazy out here imagining what stupid things your brother-in-law might be sayin' to make things harder for me than they already are."

"I'm sorry, Amanda. Can't you just tell them to tell him you're here so he'll stop talking?"

"It doesn't work like that. Since he's agreed to talk to them, they don't even have to tell him I'm here."

"Are they going to arrest him?" I asked, mentally rehearsing what I would tell his mother back in Texas.

"If they have probable cause they could," she said, digging through her briefcase. "Depends. I don't know what they have on him."

"As far as I know, it's only that he got in a fight with Kip and was the last one seen with him."

Her wide mouth set in a grim line. "And that they'd fought before over a woman whose own death is highly suspicious and with whom they'd both had a romantic relationship."

"I wouldn't call what Shelby and Wade had a relationship . . ."

Before we could talk any further, a short, balding man wearing a short-sleeved white shirt and striped blue-and-red tie came into the room. He looked straight at Amanda.

"You Wade Harper's lawyer?"

"Yes, and I'd like to see my client now."

He held out his hand. "Be my guest. He stopped talking about ten minutes ago. Third door on the left."

Her face contracted in a frown. "When did he ask for me?"

He sighed dramatically and ignored her question. "Third door on the left, counselor."

She brushed past him and called out to me over her shoulder. "Wait for us here. This shouldn't take long."

The sheriff's detective looked at me curiously, then turned to contemplate his candy choices. I walked out of the break room and down the hall to John's office. Someone had taped a black-and-white glossy of Sheriff John, the children's television host from the fifties, above John's name.

I knocked on his door and heard his deep voice call out, "Come on in."

Inside, Gabe sat across from him in a mahogany and black leather office chair, drinking a cup of coffee. Considering the circumstances, they both looked entirely too relaxed and cheerful.

"Benni!" John said, standing up. "Come have a cup of coffee. Just got my shipment of Peet's in from Berkeley. Best coffee in the universe." He reached for a cup on the credenza behind him. "You take cream and sugar?"

"Why did you start questioning Wade before his attorney could get here?" I demanded, not looking at my husband.

Gabe said, "Benni . . ."

John turned back around and gestured at Gabe that it was okay. He handed me a mug of coffee. The heavy beige mugs had bucking broncos on them. "I'll answer her question. We asked him if he wanted to talk to us about what happened last night, and he agreed. When he asked for his attorney, we stopped questioning him. Everything's by the book. He wasn't forced to do anything at any time." His brown eyes studied me with a steady gaze.

I held his gaze. "Why did he ask for a lawyer?"

He glanced over at Gabe, who nodded at him. "Benni, all we did was ask him if he minded emptying his pockets. Then we confronted him with some physical evidence that had been collected at the Johnson homicide. The interview ended at that point."

"What physical evidence?"

"Some chewed gum. A very unusual brand . . ."

"Clove," I said softly.

He nodded. "He had a pack in his pocket. We'd sent the chewed gum down to the lab in Santa Barbara. They were beginning to start tests for DNA and trying to figure out the brand when one of their techs recognized the smell when it was cut open. It's not been conclusively proven to be that brand, but it doesn't look good."

"That's pretty flimsy," I said. "A lot of people were at the barbecue. He was always spitting gum out all over the place. Someone could have planted it. And he could have been up in that pasture before Shelby was killed and spit out some gum and . . ."

"Yes, it is a long shot," he interrupted, "and rest assured, he's only one of our suspects."

"Who else?" I demanded

He smiled slightly. "I'm sorry, but that's not information we're releasing to the public yet."

"I'm not the public!"

"Sorry." He held up his hands in apology. "Considering your relationship with Wade Harper, I shouldn't even be discussing the case with you. It's an awkward situation for all of us."

"Benni . . ." Gabe started again. Ignoring him, I whipped around and left John's office. I was sitting outside on a bench under an oak tree when Gabe found me.

He sat down beside me without saying a word. I kicked

at the damp dirt with the heel of my boot, biting my lip until it felt bruised and swollen.

Gabe laid his hand on my knee. "You know, you aren't responsible for Wade Harper."

"What about what you said last night about *la familia*? Was that just all a bunch of sentimental bullshit?"

He gripped my knee tightly. "No, it wasn't bullshit, but maybe I was being a bit sentimental. That's easy to do late at night. I just don't want you feeling responsibility where you shouldn't."

I stood up and dusted off the back of my jeans. "I can't help it. Right now, I'm all he has and I'm not going to desert him. There's a lot about Wade you don't know. He might seem like a redneck jerk to you, but I know that if I called him anywhere, anytime and told him I needed him, he'd drop what he was doing and be there. How can I do less for him?"

When he didn't answer, I started walking back toward the sheriff's office. Through the window, I could see Amanda's head and then Wade's. I saw them move toward the door. I turned and faced Gabe, who was still sitting on the bench. His black hair ruffled in the cool morning breeze.

"Don't worry, I'll pay Amanda's fees out of my own money. I'll sell some of my cattle if necessary. It won't come out of our joint account."

He jumped up and in a flash was standing in front of me, his hands gripping my upper arms. "Do you think I care about that, you crazy woman? I just can't stand seeing it tear you up like this."

I trembled slightly under his hands. "I can't let them pin this on Wade. I don't think he killed either Shelby or Kip. I have to . . ." My voice trailed off, but we both knew what I'd almost said, that I'd have to find out who did. "Gabe, I don't know how to make you understand that the Wade you see isn't the only one there. For so many years, when we all lived together at the Harper ranch, he always put everyone else first. He served himself last at every meal I ever remember us eating. When there wasn't enough to go around, he ate less even though he worked the hardest. When somebody needed to borrow money, he was always there to lend it without interest or without a time limit to pay it back. Wade was barely twenty when their dad died and the whole responsibility of the ranch fell on his shoulders. To keep the ranch going and to support Jack and their mom, he hired himself out to other ranchers and then came home after ten- or twelve-hour days and worked the Harper ranch until midnight or one in the morning. Jack was still in high school, and Wade made sure he never missed one prom, one party, one school function. And though he complained, he never stopped Jack from going to college, and he could have. Jack would have done anything for Wade. Wade stopped being a young man the day John Harper died, but he still let Jack be one. Until Jack died and everything started falling apart and Wade started doing all those stupid things to save the ranch, he was a good man. I think he still is, somewhere underneath all that hurt. I can't desert him, Gabe, I just can't."

There was so much more to it than that, but the rest included Jack, which I couldn't bear to verbalize to Gabe. Wade was the only one who understood and loved Jack as much as I had. Though I knew Wade and I were destined to drift further and further apart as Jack's life slowly became a distant part of both our personal histories, I sensed that something in this situation was an important part of closure for both of us.

My words didn't seem to faze Gabe. His face grew dark with anger; his grip tightened. "Get out of it, Benni."

Behind me, I could hear Wade's and Amanda's voices as they came out of the front door of the sheriff's office. "Please, let me go," I said softly. "I need to take Wade out to the ranch."

He pulled me into a tight embrace. My head against his

chest, I could feel the captured-animal beating of his heart.

"Please," he said.

"I'm sorry," I whispered. I looked up at his face, now focused on Wade's. Wade glanced at him, then abruptly ducked his head.

I stood on tiptoe and lightly kissed Gabe's stiff jaw. "I'll be home soon." I felt his gaze on my back as I walked toward Wade and Amanda.

When I reached them, I swallowed before speaking, trying to clear the salty taste in the back of my throat. "So, what happened?"

"He's not charged with anything," Amanda said. "Yet. But I sure would have preferred him calling me *before* he so graciously told his whole life story to the police."

"I said I was sorry, Miz Landry," he said, giving me a "who put a stick up her butt?" look.

"Sorry doesn't feed the bulldog, my dear boy," she said. "Or keep the cops from going what appears to be the easiest route and pin this on you." She turned to me. "He needs to keep a low profile. Is he staying with you?"

I shook my head, still aware of Gabe's gaze on us. "No, I'm taking him out to my dad's ranch."

"Good idea. I don't think they have anything but circumstantial evidence. For now, anyway. DNA testing takes time even if they decide to spend the money on it. Gum at the murder scene, even if they prove it's his, is pretty flimsy evidence. And apparently they do have other suspects."

"That's what the sheriff said, but he wouldn't tell me who. Do you know?"

"Not yet, but I'll find out."

"It's probably that hand of Ben's. Bobby somethin'. Mexican guy," Wade said.

"Sanchez," I filled in. "Bobby Sanchez."

Amanda frowned at him, glanced over at Gabe, and took Wade's arm. "Let's walk toward our cars." Once we got out of listening distance, she asked, "Why would you say that?"

"Him and Kip were punching on each other last night, too."

"Before or after your fight with him?"

"Before."

"Did Sanchez leave?"

Wade shrugged. "It was crowded there. He could have. I didn't really notice. It wasn't one of my top priorities, so to speak."

We reached my truck, and Wade leaned against the passenger door.

"So, what happens now?" he asked Amanda.

She pointed a manicured finger at him. "What happens now is you stay on the ranch, keep your head down and your nose clean. At this point, you don't want to do one more thing that will bring attention to yourself. I'll get my investigator to poke around and see if she can dig up anything."

Wade glanced over at me, his face pulled tight with worry. "That sounds like it might take some money."

"Don't worry about it," Amanda said.

Wade straightened his spine, visibly inflating his chest. "I don't take charity . . ."

Amanda rolled her eyes and started, "Look, my red-necked buddy, you don't have a choice."

"Don't worry about it, Wade," I said. "Get in the truck." I gestured at Amanda to follow me around to the driver's side. She was a great lawyer, and I was lucky she'd agreed to help us, but I knew that Wade was definitely not her favorite kind of man and that she was doing this as a favor to me. Yet another person I'd somehow have to convince that Wade wasn't as bad as he seemed. "I'll keep an eye on him. Let me know if you find anything."

She nodded. "Girlfriend, I'm going on your instincts here because my own says he just as well could have done it as not. Hope you're not just blowing sincere but hot air.''

"I'm not," I said, holding out my hand. "Thanks for coming down here so quickly and for taking Wade's case. Don't worry about the bill. You know I'm good for it.''

"Oh, forget that," she said, pushing my hand away and enveloping me in a Obsession-scented hug. "You're the friend I'd sure as shucks want on my side if I was accused of a murder. I'll talk to you tonight. You're invited to the mayor's soiree for the artists, aren't you?''

I grimaced. "Oh, geez, I'd completely forgotten about that. Some kind of food tasting or something, isn't it?''

"Caviar. *Flavored* caviar, yet. Quite the rage back east, I'm told.''

I stuck my finger down my throat. "Sounds yummy.''

She laughed. "This from a woman who eats baby bull's balls.''

"And that's an exit line if I ever heard one. See you tonight.''

On the drive to the ranch, Wade was quiet, staring out the window, his head hung low, like a whipped dog. Without his Stetson, he looked younger and more vulnerable, which made me feel sad for him. I made a note to call the Frio Saloon to see if they'd found his hat.

When we pulled up in front of the ranch house, he jumped out of the truck before I turned off the ignition. I sat in the driver's seat and watched him walk out to the barn, the one place he always felt comfortable. Dove came out onto the porch, wiping her hands on an embroidered tea towel. She met me at the top step.

"Sheriff called this morning," she said. "Your daddy's pretty tore up about Kip. Been on the phone to Kip's daddy in Montana a couple of times already this morning.''

I sat down on the porch swing. She draped the towel over her shoulder and sat next to me. I leaned my head against her soft shoulder and stared out over the front yard grass.

Dew still sparkled in the morning sunlight like little pieces of melting ice.

"I didn't know where else to bring Wade," I said. "I was there at the Frio last night. Everything's such a big mess."

"Best you tell me about it so we know what we're up against."

When I'd almost finished, the wooden screen door opened, and Isaac came out. He carried two mugs of hot chocolate topped with whipped cream.

"Kind of chilly out here," he said, handing them to us.

"Thank you, Isaac," Dove said, smiling up at him. The glow on her face froze my heart for a second, and I turned away, cupping my hands around the warm mug and inhaling its steamy sweetness. It worried me to watch her allow herself to become so vulnerable. She had to know Isaac would leave after he found out who killed his granddaughter.

As I sipped my hot chocolate, Dove filled Isaac in on what I'd told her. He glanced at me every so often, his big, creased face solemn and emotionless. When she finished, he asked me, "What is your opinion on it, Benni?"

I looked at him over my mug. "I don't think Wade did it. He certainly could win awards for being a stupid jerk, but he's not a killer."

"I agree," Dove said. "I've known that boy since he was too small to spit. He wouldn't attack a helpless man."

Isaac nodded, satisfied. "Then we have to find out who did it."

"I know," I said.

"Just you be careful," Dove said to me, setting down her mug. "The good Lord has surely protected you before, but he might be gettin' a bit weary of pulling you out of scrapes."

"I'll watch out for her, Dove," Isaac said.

"I'll hold you to that promise," Dove said. "Don't think I won't."

"Excuse me," I said. "I'm perfectly capable of looking out for myself." My comment set both of them to chuckling.

"I am!" I protested.

We were haggling that point when we were interrupted by the arrival of Gabe driving his dad's old Chevy pickup. He came up the steps, his face in his professional cop mask. He nodded at Isaac and bent down and kissed Dove on the cheek.

"*Buenos dias, abuelita. Cómo estas?*"

"Ain't pushing up daisies yet, grandson. You're looking a bit thin. Isn't my granddaughter feeding you right?" She turned and wagged a finger at me. I smiled weakly, knowing what she was trying to do, bring a bit of lightness to the tension between Gabe and me.

"Don't blame her," Gabe said, glancing over at me. "I'm a big boy and could follow a recipe if I wanted to."

The front door opened, and Wade stepped out, his raspy voice saying, "Hey, Dove, there any way I can sweet talk you into fixing some bacon and eggs for a hungry cowboy who would sure appreciate—" He stopped when he saw Gabe.

"I'll see what I can do," Dove said, standing up.

"No, *abuelita*," Gabe said, laying a hand on her shoulder, pushing her back down gently. "After what Mr. Harper has put everyone through in the last twenty-four hours, it wouldn't hurt him to miss a meal. He can just wait until you fix lunch for the rest of the help."

Wade sucked on the toothpick in his mouth, his eyes narrowing. The white scar under his left ear started turning pink. I stood up, recognizing the sign that he was about to explode.

"I'll fix you something to eat, Wade," I said, trying to avert a fight and realizing the minute the words were out of my mouth that they would only make things worse.

"No, you won't." Gabe said the words slowly and deliberately.

Wade spit out his toothpick and grinned slowly at me. "You letting him get away with that, blondie? Shoot, it's bad enough you're sleeping with Pancho here. You gonna let him tell you when you can take a piss, too?"

A strangled sound came from Gabe's diaphragm, and before any of us could react, Gabe grabbed Wade by the shirt-front and pulled him off the porch. He landed two punches before Wade recouped and swung back, connecting just below Gabe's left eye.

"Stop it!" I screamed, running down the porch steps toward them.

Dove grabbed a broom and followed me. She poked at the two men rolling on the ground.

"You boys quit it now!" she yelled, sticking them with the bristles.

Afraid she'd get hurt, I pulled her back and commanded, "Go get Daddy!" As she scurried toward the barn, I edged closer to the men, thinking if I could somehow get between them, they'd come to their senses and stop. Gabe knocked Wade to the ground and landed a kick in his stomach. Wade grunted, rolled in a ball, and laid still a moment.

"C'mon, *pendejo*, c'mon," Gabe taunted him. "You've been wanting this. Let's go."

Wade bounded up with a roar.

I saw my chance. For a split second, there were about three feet between them, and I started to dart between them. Abruptly I felt my feet lose connection with solid ground. A strong arm locked itself around my waist, and I felt myself moving backward.

"No use both you and Gabe sporting a shiner," Isaac's voice rumbled in my ear. "Better let the boys haggle this one out."

"Lemme go," I said, swinging my feet in the air, feeling ridiculous. "I've got to stop them before someone gets hurt."

He set me down on the top step of the porch, keeping a

firm hand around my upper arm to hold me back. "Benni, I haven't been here long, but even I can see this has been brewing for a while. Let them get it out of their systems."

Involuntarily I flinched every time a fist connected with skin. The minutes felt like an hour before Daddy and a couple of his friends came running from the barn. It took another few minutes before they pried the panting and cursing men apart.

"Land sake's alive," Dove said, taking charge. She glared at both of them. "I ought to whip your butts for acting the fools that you are. You!" She pointed at Wade, who looked at the ground like a dog caught peeing on the carpet, wiping his bleeding mouth with the sleeve of his shirt. "Already in enough trouble to drown ten bulls and you're bucking for more. Ben, take him out to the barn and clean him up."

She turned to Gabe. "And you!" Gabe attempted a smile, his face trying to form itself into his charming, little-boy-caught-playing-hooky look. His already blackening eye, swollen lip, and torn sweater kind of blew the charming part. She wasn't buying that scam anyway. "You!" she repeated. "The chief of police fighting like a common hood. You should be ashamed. What kind of example is this for all those young police officers? What would the citizens of San Celina think?" Then she stepped up to him, looked into his bright blue eyes, and shot the clincher. "What would your *mother* think?"

Before he could answer, she said, "Get into the kitchen, and we'll get you cleaned up. I ought to make you pull weeds in the garden for the rest of the day like I used to my boys when they fought, but I reckon that they'll be needing you down at the police station, though heaven knows how you can be takin' care of the crime in a city when you can't even keep your own fists to yourself." He followed her meekly, not answering any of her scolding.

I watched the screen door slam behind them. "I guess I

don't need to lecture him on this particular incident."

Isaac laughed heartily. "No, I'd say your grandmother pretty well has that covered."

I sat down on the top step. With a groan, he joined me.

I picked at the toe of my boot. "I don't know what I'm going to do with them. They're acting like a couple of teenagers. Wade I can understand. He's never been able to control himself, but Gabe should know better. What in the world is he going to gain out of fighting Wade?"

Isaac answered in a soft voice, "Benni, honey, Wade wasn't the man he was fighting."

I looked over at him, surprised silent. "Oh," I finally said.

"So, what are your plans for today, partner?" he asked, wisely changing the subject.

"I have to get down to the museum to check on things, that's for sure. I've been neglecting my job big time. I suspect, though, that some of the people in the co-op are involved somehow, so maybe I can find out if any of them were at the Frio last night and saw anything significant. But first I think I'll go by the Frio and see if the people working there know anything. I'll use the excuse of looking for Wade's hat. He said he lost it sometime last night."

Isaac nodded. "I've been meaning to tell you that the police finally released the key to Shelby's apartment to me. I'm going over today to look around. Maybe something will turn up there."

"Need any help?" I touched his hand lightly with my fingertips. Seeing her things had to be hard for him.

"Not right now," he said, his expression growing distant. "Perhaps later."

I didn't answer, and we sat in a companionable silence for a few minutes. Deep inside the house, we could still hear Dove's voice wrangling at Gabe, tender then scolding, then tender again. She had a real soft spot for my husband, but he wouldn't be hearing the end of this one for a long time.

"Want to rendezvous later on, then?" Isaac asked. "Compare notes?"

"Sure. How about Blind Harry's at five o'clock?"

"I'll be there."

I left without confronting Gabe or my ex-brother-in-law again, not because I was mad, but because I was just plain tired of the intense emotions surrounding both of them. I wanted to tackle the problem of finding out who killed Shelby and Kip, and emotions only made logical thinking harder. There had to be a connection between those two, more than just the fact that they were sleeping together. Though jealousy had certainly been a motive more times than not in murders, this time it just didn't feel like that to me. I was so deep into trying to find a connection between them that I almost missed the turnoff to Santa Flora. Wade's hat. And a chance to question any of the workers.

The drive to the Frio Saloon was much more pleasant in the late-morning sunshine. The air was clear and cool, tempting me to roll down my window to inhale its dusky, wet earth smell and catch the last hint of early morning fires from the small ranches along the twisting road. I stopped at a tiny local grocery store at the fork to Lake Santa Flora to get a cup of coffee. A rusty cowbell announced my entry. I was pleasantly surprised to find Greer sipping from a paper cup and shooting the breeze with a tough-looking biker chick arranging a shipment of cigarettes behind the counter.

"Benni Harper!" Greer said. "What in tarnation are you doing here?"

"Hi, Greer," I said and walked over to the serve-yourself coffee machine. "I'm fortifying myself before going out to the Frio to look for Wade's hat." I finished doctoring up my coffee and walked over to them. "It just occurred to me I probably should have called first. Do you happen to know if they're open this early?"

She glanced down at her man-sized watch. "It's past eleven, so I'd say you're safe. Someone will probably be there. They're open Wednesday through Sunday now for lunch.'' She sipped her coffee. ''Why are you getting Wade's hat?''

''Were you at the Frio last night?'' I knew that Greer, living only a few miles away, sometimes dropped in at the saloon. A lot of the artists who lived around Santa Flora, known for its cheap house rentals, frequented the Frio since it was the only place in the area that stayed open past nine o'clock. Many artists lived on odd time schedules that didn't conform to Santa Flora's Mayberry-like customs.

''Yes, for a little while,'' she said, twirling her drink in her cup. ''But I must have left before Wade got there. I heard what happened to that young hand of your dad's, though. Sorry to hear it.''

''Yeah.'' I sipped my coffee. It tasted thick and sludgy with a bitter aftertaste. It hit my empty stomach like a hard, warm baseball. ''They questioned Wade and, from what I hear, Bobby Sanchez, too. I guess he was there last night.''

Greer nodded. ''I did see the fight between Bobby and Kip, if you want to call what they did fighting. More yelling than fists. Me and Olivia and Parker had a good laugh over it. Didn't see the one with your brother-in-law.''

So both Parker and Olivia were there last night. I hadn't seen them, but with that crowd, that was understandable. ''What were Bobby and Kip fighting about?''

She turned her palms up and rolled her eyes heavenward. ''Don't know, but I'm assuming it had something to do with those pictures Shelby took of Bobby.''

''You know about those?''

''*Everyone* knows about them. At least, everyone at the co-op. Olivia's not one to suffer in silence.''

I looked back down into the dark coffee. My stomach gurgled a warning, and I knew I'd better not drink anything stronger than water before I could get some food into me. I tossed the almost-full cup into the trash and paid the biker chick fifty cents. ''Well, I have a million things to do today.

I guess I'll see you at the mayor's house tonight.''

Greer winked at me. "Wouldn't miss Mrs. Mayor's flavored fish eggs for anything in the world. I'm thinking about smuggling some out and going fishing up at Lake Santa Flora the next day.''

I smiled. "I heard some of that stuff cost twenty-four dollars an ounce. At that price you'd better hook a solid gold trout.''

At the Frio Saloon I had to pound on the door for a few minutes before someone answered.

"We don't open till eleven-thirty," the buck-toothed, gray-haired woman said. She pointed with a chipped crimson nail to a hand-printed sign next to the door.

"I just need to look through the lost and found box for a hat," I said.

She gave me a hesitant look, then said, "Well, come on, then.''

Wade's hat was sitting on top of the almost full pasteboard box next to the bandstand. It was smashed a bit on the crown, but otherwise in pretty good shape. Out of curiosity, I idly poked through the rest of the items—sunglasses; jewelry; hats, cheap plastic wallets; a red, fuzzy stuffed bear, a harmonica. There was even a single black patent leather boot whose story I wasn't sure I wanted—or needed—to know.

"Find what you was looking for?" the woman asked. She was filling the dimestore salt and pepper shakers from huge, restaurant supply–size containers. Her white bar towel apron was clean, but stained pink and pale gold in front.

I held up Wade's hat. "Yeah, thanks." I started to walk out, then turned back to the woman. "Were you working last night?"

She picked up a salt shaker, studied it with the slow, careful movements of a person with a hangover or too little sleep. "Why?"

I walked back over to her. "I was just wondering if you saw the fight last night?"

"Which one?"

Good question. "Uh, both, I guess."

She set the salt shaker down and parked her hands on her bony hips. "Look, I know who you are. Tony told me the whole story about your brother-in-law, and I saw you come get him last night. Like I told the cops this morning, all I saw was that guy you was dragging outta here argue with the young cowboy who got himself killed. A couple of the regulars told them to take it outside, and they did. Then you came and picked the older cowboy up. That's all I know." She wiped the backs of her hands on her towel-apron. "That's all I want to know."

"What about the first fight?"

"Between the guy that got killed and the Mexican guy?"

"Yes."

She shrugged and picked up the blue container of Morton salt. "There was some yelling, and one of the bouncers told *them* to take it outside. I never saw any blows inside here. The blond cowboy came back 'bout a half hour later, but I never saw the Mexican the rest of the night." She looked at me with bulbous, bloodshot eyes. " 'Course, that don't mean he didn't come back or that he wasn't waiting for the blond dude outside somewhere. Seen it happen before. Reckon I'll see it again."

"Well, thanks," I said, not knowing what else I could ask her that could possibly help Wade. All I had so far was that Parker and Olivia had been here and that possibly Bobby could have ambushed Kip later. I wondered if the bar lady had told the police the same thing she told me.

I started to walk toward the door when the lady called, "Wait." She motioned at me to come back. "I have a question for you. You know that girl who was killed? The one who took pictures?"

I nodded.

"She was a real nice girl. She used to come here all the time when she was out taking pictures. Sometimes that cowboy who was killed was with her. Sometimes she was alone. She always left a good tip and always asked after my dogs. I have three dachshunds." The woman stared down at her chipped nails. "I told the police everything I knew. Everything I just told you, but if your brother-in-law did it, I hope they put him away for good. Electric chair good."

"He didn't," I said coldly and turned my back on her.

"For good," she called after me.

It took a few minutes for the sick feeling in my stomach to subside before I started the truck. Though, next to Gabe, he was the last person I felt like seeing right then, I decided to take Wade his hat. He'd probably be working outside with Daddy all day and need the protection. *But,* I firmly told myself, *if Gabe is still there, you are driving right on by.* I wasn't ready to talk about what happened between him and Wade. There was no doubt that Wade had provoked Gabe, and it would have taken a saint not to have reacted. There was also no doubt that before I handed Wade his hat, he was going to get a large piece of my mind. What I had to say to Gabe would take a little more contemplation.

Fortunately Gabe's truck was gone, and the front yard was empty and quiet. I walked around to the back of the house and headed straight for the barn. Wade was alone inside, cleaning tack—something Daddy always made me, my Uncle Arnie, and many of his young ranch hands do to make us contemplate the sin of thoughtless anger. The Ramsey Ranch was known for having the cleanest tack in the county. In the background, KCOW played softly on an old red plastic radio—Terry Clark crooned "Poor, poor, pitiful me."

"Here's your hat, cowboy." I tossed it on the table in front of him.

He picked it up and settled it on his head without looking up. "Thanks."

"I don't know why I bothered," I said. "I oughta let you fry out in the sun. Maybe it would bake some brains into that empty head of yours."

He stopped scrubbing on the leather and looked up. His eyes were still webbed with red lines, and his lip was cut and swollen under his long, sandy mustache. A bruise the size of a small plum bloomed on his cheek. One eye was almost swollen shut. "Look, Benni, I know I acted like the biggest asshole this side of Texas. I'm sorry."

"It's not just me you should be apologizing to."

He lay the old blackened hackamore down on the wooden table in front of him. "I didn't mean to make small of you. You know how much I care about you."

"I know, but . . ."

"He just grates on my nerves, you know? He's always lookin' at me like I'm a piece of shit caught on his boot heel."

I smiled, thinking that was pretty much what Gabe felt Wade thought about him. "He's jealous, Wade. You can understand that, can't you? Whenever he sees you, he's reminded of Jack. I loved your brother so much that it's hard for Gabe. He always feels second best. Think about being in his shoes for a moment. How would you like that feeling?"

He turned his head and didn't answer. I watched his head slowly drop, and in a few minutes his shoulders started shaking.

His sobs gradually became audible, and I went to him, placing my hand on his broad back. I rubbed a slow circle as he bent over the buttery-smelling tack and cried for his brother. Eventually hot tears rolled down my own face, though this time they weren't for my sorrow.

"You have to let him go, Wade," I said.

"No!" He slammed his fist on the table. The tack hopped

and trembled in front of him. In the cool, sun-speckled barn, birds fluttered and chirped, startled by his voice. They darted out through the dovecote at the top of the barn.

"You have to." I continued to rub his back, like you would a frightened child, until his crying stopped. He wiped his eyes with his shirt sleeve, then stood up, hunching over and flinching as he did. Dirt from Gabe's hiking boot stained the front of his shirt.

"I'm sorry," he said, his voice thick and wet.

"For feeling sad because you miss your brother? C'mon, Wade."

"Now I'm not just a jerk. I'm a wimp, too."

I sighed. Men. No wonder they died of heart attacks and hypertension. Maybe they should teach crying classes to high school boys and save us all some grief later on. "I accept your apology. Just no more cracks about me and Gabe, okay?"

He nodded. "I'll apologize to your . . ." He cleared his throat, unable to say it. ". . . Ortiz the next time I see him. Okay?"

I gave him a careful hug. "That would be great. I gotta go now. I'm so behind in my work that this may be my last exhibit if I'm not careful."

He walked with me over to the double barn doors, trying to disguise his limp. "What do you think's going to happen with that guy's murder? Do you really think I'm going to take the fall for it?"

"Not if I can help it," I said. "I'm working on it now. I'll let you know if I find anything out. In the meantime, do whatever Amanda says and please, don't leave the ranch."

"I don't intend to. I just hope this gets wound up soon. Didn't think I'd ever say it, but I'm starting to miss Texas. And I for sure miss my kids."

"We're working on getting you back there as quick as possible." I started out the door into the sunlight.

"Hey, Benni."

I turned around and squinted in the sunlight at the darkened outline of Wade in the barn. His features were undecipherable, and for a moment I had an eerie sensation of seeing Jack again. But for the first time since Jack died, it was something I didn't want to experience, this acute physical memory of him. Though a part of me would always love Jack, that time of my life was over.

"Yes?" I waited in the warm sunlight.

He touched two fingers to his Stetson. "Thanks."

I lifted a hand in acknowledgment, feeling something give in my heart, like a guitar string breaking. "No problem, Wade. What are friends for?"

13

ON THE RIDE to town, I contemplated my next move. After everything that had taken place in the last twenty-four hours, I decided what I needed was to speak with someone sane, sensible, and not ruled by their emotions.

"She's in her office," the clerk at Blind Harry's said. "But she's not alone."

"Who's in there?" I asked.

She pointed to the steep wooden stairs, and I saw my cousin descending, wearing a smile that would light up Little Rock and all its surrounding communities. I met him at the bottom step.

"Either you just won the lottery, or Elvia was nice to you this morning," I commented.

"Saturday night's the night," he said. "And she even offered me a cup of coffee."

"Wow," I said. "She must be melting. She only does that to every sales rep and Tom, Dick, and Harry who crosses her doorstep."

"Don't be such a negative Nellie," he said. "Just because your own sweet life is in tattered shambles, don't be rainin' on my parade."

"You're right," I said, holding my hand to my heart and

laughing for the first time this morning. "I'm being a snot. Congratulations on your success. I wish you a double-wide trailer full of luck on your upcoming date." I stood on my tiptoes and kissed his cheek, whispering in his ear, " 'Cause you're going to need it."

"Just you wait. You're going to be forced to gobble up those words someday. How'd it go this morning, by the way?"

"Don't ask," I said with a groan. "And try not to comment on Gabe's black eye and fat lip when you see them."

A head popped up from behind the paperback mystery section.

"Black eye!" Sam said, his voice jubilant. "Fat lip!" He apparently had pulled an early shift at Blind Harry's today. That explained why he wasn't out at the ranch to enjoy his father's adolescent skirmish with Wade.

"What happened?" Emory asked, his green eyes bright.

"Yeah, what happened?" Sam echoed. His quarter-moon grin was entirely too enthusiastic.

I shook a finger at both of them. "Look, I'm warning you both. Gabe is in no mood to be teased about this. If you want to stay among the living, I'd suggest you just ignore his injuries."

"What happened?" Sam whined.

I told them the condensed version, trying not to laugh at Sam's obvious enjoyment at hearing how his father lost control.

"This is so cool," Sam said. "I would have never thought Dad would get so amped at someone that he'd hit him! Man, I'm going to rag on him about this for months." His face lit up. "Years!"

I jerked my thumb over at his piles of books. "Right now you'd better get back to work or you're going to get bugged by one tiny but powerful little Latina lady."

His dark eyes sparkled with laughter. "She'll cut me slack. I sell too many books."

"You are getting almost as arrogant as that father of yours."

"Walk me out to my car," Emory said. When we reached the Corvette, which he'd miraculously managed to park directly in front of Blind Harry's, he asked, "So, where does Wade stand legally at this point?"

I told him about the gum, what Amanda had said, and the questions I'd asked the bartender at the Frio. "Amanda's going to get her investigator working on it, too," I added.

"You're too involved in this," he said, sticking his hands deep into the pockets of his dark wool slacks. "That worries me to no end." His pearl gray cashmere sweater looked warm and soft in the weak noon sunlight.

"Like I said last night, Emory, I don't have a choice. I'm not going to put myself in danger. Not if I can help it, anyway."

He studied me silently, green eyes troubled. For the first time, I noticed fine age lines radiating from them, and a part of me desperately hoped that my best friend could see how wonderful this man was, how lucky she'd be to have him in her life.

"Don't worry, Emory. I'll be very discreet with my questions."

"I'll see what I can find out with my contacts at the paper. I think you're right that the person who did this is, unfortunately, one of the people closest to her." He reached into the car and pulled out a small leather day planner. "Give me the names of the people who might be involved again, and I'll see what I can dig up."

"Bobby . . . uh, Robert Sanchez. Grew up here in San Celina. Parker Williams . . . her professional name is P.L. Williams. She's originally from Bakersfield. Olivia Contreras. Another native San Celinan. Roland Bennett . . . he's the one who owns the gallery. He lived in San Francisco before coming here, that's all I know. And Greer Shannon. Her family's been here five generations. I guess that's it."

"And Isaac Lyons," he added.

"What? You erase his name right now. He wouldn't kill his own granddaughter."

"Stepgranddaughter," he corrected. "Benni, you've been married to a cop long enough to know that nothing is too outlandish when it comes to homicide." He closed the day planner and threw it back down on the passenger seat. "His name stays . . . for the time being."

I scowled at him but didn't argue. Deep down, I knew he was right, but that possibility was something I didn't want to contemplate.

"We'll have to talk tonight. I didn't even get to hear the details of how you finally convinced Elvia to go out with you."

"Now, you know she wouldn't be able to resist my charming self for much longer."

"You drugged her," I concluded. "That is against the law, you know."

"Get something to eat, sweetcakes, you're getting pissy."

"You are crazy, no doubt about it."

"Now you know that's nothin' if not true. I come from a long, proud line of crazy fools. You know us southern men have to be either plumb insane or drunk on homemade bourbon to have voted on goin' to war without a single cannon factory among us."

"Then you are a credit to your heritage. Call me at the museum if you find anything out. After I talk to Elvia and grab something to eat, I'll be there the rest of the day."

Upstairs, Elvia poured me a cup of coffee and said, "Tell me about this morning's rumble between the cowboy and the cop."

"Sam tattled, didn't he?" I asked. "Couldn't he wait thirty seconds? Geez, he's a worse gossip than Dove and all her old cronies."

"He didn't have details, so give."

I filled her in on everything that had happened in the last twenty-four hours. I was on my second cup of coffee before I finished.

"What a mess," Elvia said. "But I'm not surprised they finally tangled. This has been brewing since Wade arrived."

"I know. Now that some of the steam's been let out of the pressure cooker, maybe we can all get down to business and find out who really killed Shelby and Kip."

She shook her head. "I knew you'd end up getting involved. It's too bad you're too old to join the police academy. I think you missed your true calling in life."

I grinned. "One cop in the family is enough. I've got Emory looking into the backgrounds of those closest to Shelby. Specifically the ones who attended the barbecue. Don't worry, I'll be very careful about who I question. I've learned my lesson. Two head injuries in less than a year are certainly enough for this cowgirl."

"Right." Elvia's expression said she didn't buy my statement for one minute. "But, to help in the cause of keeping you so busy you can't get into trouble, I have a request of you."

I sat up, instantly suspicious at the sweetly conniving tone of her voice. "No," I said instinctively.

"You haven't even heard what it is yet," Elvia said, irritated.

"Whatever it is, I already know it's something I don't want to do."

"I'm desperate. You're my last hope."

"No."

She sat up, straight and authoritative, in her rose-colored executive chair. "Maribelle D'Angelo just had emergency appendectomy surgery."

"My heartfelt sympathy," I said, standing up, preparing to flee. I had no idea what Maribelle D'Angelo's job was, but I was certain of one thing . . . I didn't want it.

She ran her words together so fast I almost didn't catch

them. "She's the cornerstone for the fashion show tomorrow night, and you're the only person I know who's the same size." The fashion show, a fund-raiser for the Historical Society and Fine Arts Guild, was called "San Celina—A Century of Fashion." Elvia was the chairperson this year.

"Fashion show!" I squealed. "No way, José. Not in this lifetime. Prancing in front of all of San Celina like a steer being auctioned off? Not this puppy. Get someone else."

Elvia stood up, an evil smile on her face, and said the words I knew in my heart were coming. "*Mi amiga*, you owe me. Big time. Remember?"

I froze. "Dang it."

Elvia handed me a piece of paper. "This is the place where you'll be fitted, and they'll give you your outfit. I made an appointment for you today at four o'clock. You and Maribelle are the same size, so there shouldn't be much alteration. On the day of the show, be at the Elks Club two hours early so the makeup and hair people can work their magic. *You* might want to think about getting there three hours early so they have extra time."

I stuck my tongue out at her for that comment.

She ignored me and continued. "The show starts at seven-thirty. We're hoping for a big crowd. We've already sold two hundred and fifteen tickets."

"Two hundred and fifteen?" I echoed weakly. "What exactly am I wearing?"

She nodded at the paper. "You're number forty-five— the last one."

I looked down at the paper: *Peacock blue ball gown circa 1884 (bone corset and bustle included).*

"A corset." I moaned. "A bustle?"

Elvia just laughed.

14

"WHERE HAVE YOU been?" my head docent cried when I walked through the museum's front door. "I've left a million messages for you."

"I'm here now," I said in my most soothing voice. "What's wrong?"

"We have two busloads of schoolkids due in at one o'clock, and two of my people have called in sick. I can't give a tour to a hundred children alone."

I resolved it by begging two quilters working in the co-op studios to fill in so that each person would only have about thirty or so charges. I also called the school to make sure that plenty of adults were coming with the kids. When they arrived, I decided to take a group myself, breaking the number per tour guide down even further, and managed to coordinate it so none of us was in the same room at the same time. So it was past three o'clock before I actually went into my office to check my mail and messages. I hadn't been there in a couple of days, and my answering machine had seven flashing messages. I settled back in my chair with my wooden letter opener and started slitting open envelopes while I listened to my messages. The first two were artists requesting information about joining our co-op. The third was a sales rep for a wholesale framing company. I was reading a colorful, crayoned letter of thanks from our last set of schoolkids when Kip's voice caused me to drop the letter and sit upright in my chair.

"Benni? Uh . . . this is Kip. I . . . uh . . . can you meet me at the Frio Saloon tonight? 'Bout eight o'clock? There's . . . I tried to take care of something . . . about . . . you know. I tried to do it for her, not like for money or anything, but it's not working. I'm kinda nervous. They . . . uh . . . Benni, I don't know what to do. Shelby . . . uh . . . she trusted you. You gotta help me decide what to do." A truck rumbled in the background telling me that his call had most likely been made from an outside pay phone. "Please," he said, then hung up.

The machine beeped. I rewound it and listened to it three more times. Even then I couldn't figure out what he was trying to tell me. I hit the top of my desk in frustration. If only I'd come by the museum yesterday afternoon and listened to my messages, Kip might still be alive, and we'd know who killed Shelby. I pulled the tape out of the machine and grabbed my purse.

"I'll be at the police station," I told the lady working behind the counter at the museum's small gift shop.

Gabe was tied up in a meeting, so I waited in his secretary's office. Maggie pressed me for details about his ravaged face.

"I tried for a little levity and told him his face would scare a bulldog off a meat truck. He didn't laugh." She winked at me. Out of all the police department employees, I was willing to bet only Maggie had been brave enough to mention his condition. She knew she had job security.

"I'll tell you," I said. "But you *didn't* hear this from me."

"Ranchwoman's honor," she said, flashing a palm. By the time I finished the story, her creamy brown cheeks were flushed dark rose, and she was laughing so hard tears sparkled in her eyes. "Oh, I wish I could have been there. I wish I had pictures for the department scrapbook."

She managed to bring herself under control by the time Gabe's meeting ended, and she announced my presence with a calm, normal voice. Only the glint in her black eyes as she nodded at me to go on in gave away her true feelings. She closed the door softly behind me.

Gabe was dressed in a dark gray Brooks Brothers suit, requisite white shirt, chic print tie. Very responsible looking. Very . . . police chief–like.

Unfortunately the half-grown-out beard, swollen bottom lip, small white bandage on his left cheek, and rainbow shiner under his right eye sort of knocked the legs, so to speak, out from under his suit's authority. Should I just ignore what happened and get right down to telling him about Kip's message?

"Hi," I said, sitting down on the visitor chair in front of his desk. Then, deciding that ignoring his condition would be ludicrous, I added, "How are you feeling?"

"Fine." He leaned back in his chair. "What's up?"

Okay, I thought. *I can take a hint as well as the next person. We're pretending like it didn't happen.* "Did you eat lunch?" I asked, trying to lighten the room's tense atmosphere.

"Yes."

"Tomato soup through a straw?" I inquired with a smile, trying to get a laugh.

He didn't return it. "Benni, I know you think this is funny, but I personally find it humiliating. I'm very busy. Why are you here?"

"Sorry," I said contritely, thinking I certainly deserved to have my nose bitten off when I couldn't even take my own advice to Sam and Emory. "I've discovered something important about Shelby's and Kip's murders."

"What?"

I opened my purse and set the miniature cassette tape on

his desk. "He called yesterday, but I didn't listen to my messages until about an hour ago."

He pulled a small tape recorder from his desk and listened to Kip's words. I shifted in my seat, feeling helpless and angry again that I hadn't been able to help Kip. After listening to it five times, Gabe leaned back in his chair and rested his chin in his palm.

"What do you think?" I asked.

"I'll send it over to John," he said. "Kip hasn't really given us much to go on. Sounds like Shelby might have seen something . . . a crime perhaps. Or possibly found out about some illegal activity."

"Maybe she tried to blackmail someone!" I added eagerly, "And they killed her to keep her quiet. She must have let Kip in on it, and they got him, too. Did you notice he used the word 'they'? That must mean there's more than one, right?" I scooted forward in my chair.

He came around the desk. "I don't know what it means, and it's not my case anyway. Or yours, I might add, though I know that's a waste of time."

"Hey," I said, standing up and poking him in the chest. "The minute I heard this, I scurried right over here like a good little citizen. Six months ago I wouldn't have told you for days."

Taking my finger and shaking it, he laughed, grimacing at the pain. "Yes, sweetheart, I know, and I'm very proud of you."

I sighed deeply. "If only I'd listened to my messages sooner . . ."

"Stop it," he said. "I don't want you feeling guilty over something that wasn't your fault. Frankly, I'm glad you weren't able to meet him."

"I'm not. I might have kept him from getting killed."

He smoothed down the top of my hair. "Or gotten killed yourself."

"Well, I just want credit for bringing this right to your desk with no sidetracking."

"Credit given. What are you doing the rest of the afternoon?"

This time I grimaced. "Elvia finally extracted her revenge on me. Apparently one of the ladies in the fashion show tomorrow night is in the hospital, and I have to take her place. I'm going by the costume shop downtown for a fitting."

"You're in the fashion show!" He laughed out loud. "Good for Elvia. What decade are you?" Gabe had managed to finagle wearing a classic forties suit and hat. Not a huge departure from his normal mode of dress. He'd threatened Elvia with a boycott if she made him wear a seventies leisure suit.

"Eighteen eighties," I grumbled. "They have me wearing a peacock blue ball gown. I haven't actually seen it yet."

He grinned. "Didn't women wear corsets back then? And bustles?"

"Very funny," I said, holding up a fist to him. "I could give you matching eyes, you know."

He bent over and kissed my fist, wincing as he did. "I'll see you tonight."

"Don't forget, we have the fish egg–eating party at the mayor's tonight. Seven o'clock."

"And you can practice having some class right now. It's called caviar."

"Ha! Etiquette lessons from a man who brawls before brunch."

"Get lost," he said good-naturedly.

I felt better about his sunnier mood as I drove downtown to be fitted for my dress. Maybe the fight cleared everything out of his and Wade's testosterone-filled systems, and we could concentrate now on the real problem—who killed Shelby and Kip? I wondered if Isaac found anything helpful at Shelby's apartment. I glanced at my watch after I parked

the truck in the five-story parking structure. Five minutes
past four. I had to meet Isaac in less than an hour, and the
only new information I had for him was about Kip's missed
phone call. The bartender at the Frio Saloon hadn't shed any
new light on the subject except to say that possibly Bobby
could have ambushed Kip later. I headed for the costume
shop downtown, where the Historical Society was storing
all the clothes for the fashion show. After giving my name
to the female clerk sporting three nose rings, I was directed
to the back fitting room where Helen Berrymore, fund-
raising chairman for the Historical Society, was flipping
through hanging clothing bags and marking off things on a
dark brown clipboard. Helen and Dove were longtime
friends who had a once-a-year date to put up pickles together.

"Hi, Helen. Sorry I'm late," I said, immediately sneezing twice. The room was warm and smelled of mothballs
and Helen's White Shoulders perfume.

"My goodness. God bless you, Benni." She blinked her
round, pale blue eyes rapidly, patting me on the back as if
I were choking, not sneezing.

"I think I'm supposed to get fitted for something." I
rubbed my nose and sat down on a stool next to a full set
of armor.

She flipped through her clipboard. "That's right, Maribelle's appendix burst on her. Looks like you'll be the belle
of the ball tomorrow night."

"Oh, lucky me," I said. "So where's my costume?"

She turned and unzipped a wine-colored clothing bag
hanging behind her. The dress seemed impossibly small, and
a distant ray of hope started to glow within me.

"I couldn't possibly fit in that dress," I said cheerfully,
slipping down off the stool. "Too many tri-tip sandwiches
and moonpies. Guess you all will have to find someone
else."

She peered at me over her Ben Franklin spectacles. "Albenia Harper, you are a size seven, am I not correct?''

"Well . . ." I hedged. "I honestly haven't bought any clothes for a long time. I'm sure I'm much heavier. You know how getting married puts the weight on you." I pouched out my stomach slightly and patted it.

She scanned me with a critical eye. "Take off those jeans, young lady, and we'll just see. Elvia called before you came and said you'd try to wiggle out of this. Where's your community spirit? For heaven's sake, you'd think I was asking you to strip naked and do the frug."

That picture certainly shut my mouth. "The frug?" I managed to say after a few seconds.

"A dance from the sixties," she said, taking the dress off the padded satin hanger. "Been learning all sorts of useless trivia since I agreed to be in charge of the costumes and write the program."

Resigned to my fate, I stood in my bra and underwear and held out my hand for the ballgown.

"This first," she said and handed me the corset. "Otherwise that wide waist of yours will never fit in this dress. I swear, Benni Harper, you are as straight up and down as a boy."

I held the underwear contraption in front of me. "How do I work this thing?"

She turned me around and within a few minutes, after some enthusiastic pulling on her part, I was being punished for every bad thought and deed I'd ever done or would do in the next ten years. "Oh, man," I moaned. "I'm going to kill you, Elvia."

"She's the toastmistress," Helen said as she strapped the basketlike bustle around my waist.

"Good. That'll give me a clear shot at her up there on the podium. Tell me, does this come with a matching pearl-handled revolver?"

She gestured at me to bend over as she slipped the dress over my head. With the help of the torturous undergarments squeezing my insides into Brunswick Stew, it fit perfectly.

"Turn around and let me button you up," Helen said.

Since there were about two million buttons, it gave us time to catch up on local news.

"Heard on the radio this morning about that hand of yours getting killed out at the Frio Saloon last night," she said. "Suck in some air, honey. I'm having trouble with these middle ones."

I breathed in and wondered briefly how in the world women survived in the 1880s. No wonder they were fainting all the time. They never got a clear lungful of oxygen. "Yeah, people are a bit upset out at the ranch."

"They're thinking Wade did it, I heard."

"He didn't. I don't know who did, but he sure as heck didn't."

I heard her cluck under her breath. "Now there I agree with you, Benni. I've known that boy a long time. He's no killer." She turned me around and nodded her head in approval. "Why, you look like a fairy tale princess. There's a little torn place on the hem there, so as long as I got you here, I'll sew it up. Step up on this box here. So, you going to find out who killed those two kids and prove your brother-in-law's innocence?"

"My former brother-in-law," I said, avoiding her question so I wouldn't be forced to lie.

"What's this world coming to? We have certainly had our fair share of murders these last few years."

I made a sympathetic noise in my throat and decided to change the subject before Gabe's name worked its way into the conversation. "So, who else has been in here getting fitted?" Since I hadn't been involved in the fashion show and not gone to any rehearsals, I had no idea who was in it.

Helen rattled on about who was wearing what and what they felt about it, people's scars and stretch marks, who caused her a headache with having to alter their costumes because of weight gains, and how shocking she found that new thong underwear. "Why, we used to throw out panties that rode up like that!"

I let my mind wander as she talked, thinking about what exactly my next move should be in at least steering the suspicion of Shelby's and Kip's deaths away from Wade. The mention of Greer's name brought me back to Helen's conversation.

"What was that about Greer?" I asked.

"Wake up, missy. I was just saying that when Greer came in here the other day to be fitted for her costume—she's wearing a 1930s rose-colored tea dress with the prettiest lace inserts—she was talking on one of those fancy phones people carry now."

"A cellular phone."

"That's it. Bob wants me to get one and I told him that, thank you very much, there isn't anybody in this world I need to talk to so badly they can't wait till I get home. She didn't know I was in that room over there." She pointed to a small alcove behind the racks of costumes that contained a sewing machine and a wall-to-ceiling shelf filled with various tailoring tools. "She was really giving someone the riot act, if you know what I mean. Said she didn't care one whit about Shelby Johnson, that she was alive and she wanted what was due her. That's what she said, wanted what was due her." Helen's voice sharpened in disapproval. "I was surprised at her, to tell you the truth. Sounded a bit cold to me. Not at all what I expected from Greer. Why, her mother was head volunteer at the Red Cross for years before her arthritis crippled her up. But I didn't let on I heard a thing." She patted my shoulder. "All done now. The shoes and such are in that bag there. Now you be careful with that dress. It's a genuine antique."

Her words about Greer echoed in my head as I carried the dress to my truck. I couldn't help but agree with Helen's disapproval of Greer's attitude. Actually, all the artists were starting to get on my nerves—Olivia's anger at the pictures Shelby took of Bobby, Parker's obsession with her public persona, Roland's determination to make as much money off this tragedy as possible, and now Greer's insistence on her so-called "rights" as a featured artist. Everyone seemed to have forgotten—or didn't care—that a young woman and a young man were dead. I was disappointed in their self-centered attitudes and in the calculating and uncaring commercial side of the art world.

I had about five minutes to get to Blind Harry's to meet Isaac. I wished I had more than Kip's phone call to tell him. Maybe he found some clue in her apartment that the police missed.

He was sitting at a back table and had a cafe mocha waiting for me. He stood up and pulled out my chair for me.

"Thanks. How did it go?"

He smiled, but it didn't reach his dark eyes. A strand of white hair had escaped his ponytail and hung next to his weathered cheek. "Fine. I think I might have found something."

I swiped a finger across the mound of whipped cream topping my drink and stuck it in my mouth. "What?"

He pushed a black three-ring notebook across the table to me. I pushed my drink aside and opened it. It held about fifty or sixty plastic pages holding strips of negatives. I glanced back up at him. "I don't get it. Did you find some incriminating pictures or something?"

"No, nothing that obvious, which is why the police probably missed it. It occurred to me that if she was killed because of something she saw, she most likely took a picture of it."

"That seems logical. I never saw her go anywhere without her camera."

His smile was wistful. "I know. It's hard to believe we weren't genetically related."

"So, what did you find that the police missed?"

"I'm sure they looked through her negatives and took any that contained people. But it occurred to me that maybe what she saw didn't have anything to do with people, that there was something else she photographed that caused someone to kill her."

I lifted my drink and took a sip. "And?"

"Look at this." He pointed at a strip of negatives. I opened the binder and took them out, holding them up to the overhead lighting in the coffee house. They were of a barbed-wire fence in the woods somewhere, some oak trees, the edge of a wooden building—a barn or shed maybe.

I lowered the strip and shrugged. "I don't recognize where that is. It could be anywhere in the county."

"Look at this one." He tapped his big finger on the strip in the section below the one I'd pulled out. I held up that one. More trees, a hawk, the edge of a metal corral, another corner of a building.

I looked at him in question, still not getting what he was trying to convey.

"Look at the numbering on the side of the strips."

I peered down at the almost indecipherable numbers. The first strip was numbered one through four. The second, nine through twelve. I looked up at him. "A strip is missing!"

"Exactly. Remember what I said—that what you leave out of a photograph is almost as important as what you allow in? The police were looking for something that was there, not for something that wasn't."

"So, what do you think was on this strip? And more important, where do you think it is?"

"Good questions, and I have no idea about the answers to either. You know this area. I was hoping you'd be able to tell me."

I studied the negatives again. They looked vaguely familiar but they could have been any of ten or twenty places I knew. "Can you have these made into prints?" I asked.

"Maybe I'll see something I recognize then."

"Absolutely. I'll have them done this afternoon and give them to you at the party tonight." He leaned back in his chair. A deep weariness seemed to flood his broad, lined features, and he looked every minute of his seventy-nine years.

"This is hard for you," I said softly.

"Yes, it is."

We were both silent for a moment. The buoyant laughter and conversation of the surrounding tables seemed loud and almost unbearable.

"I only have a couple of things." I quickly told him about the message Kip left on my answering machine at the museum and what little I'd learned from the lady at the Frio Saloon. "It does fit into your theory that they knew something. Something someone felt was important enough to kill for."

"Something Shelby most likely photographed. What could she photograph out in the woods that would be worth killing her over?"

I shrugged. "Could be anything these days. Drugs, cattle rustling, toxic waste dumping, smuggling. There's not a ranch in San Celina County that hasn't experienced all of those things to one degree or another."

"Cattle rustling?" He smiled, slightly amused. "Maybe we should round up a posse."

"Hey, it still happens and it's very sophisticated now. There was one group of rustlers they caught a few years ago who had the inside of an RV gutted and made into a small rendering operation. It would pull up to a fence that borders a side road—or sometimes even a main one if it was late at night—shoot the steer, and drag it into the pseudo-RV. In less than a half hour that steer would be steaks and roasts that they'd drive up the coast and sell black market to different restaurants. Daddy and I have unexplained cattle losses every year, and they aren't all to coyotes and mountain lions.''

He leaned forward and rested his forearms on the oak table. ''Do you think she might have taken a picture of that?''

I sighed. ''I don't know, Isaac. Like I said, there's also drug labs, toxic waste dumping. I even read recently that they caught some people smuggling counterfeit CDs on a fishing boat in Morro Bay. And I'm sure the Sheriff's Department could tell you even more illegal things that take place out in the boonies. One time Daddy and I were riding fence and way at the back of our property found some rusty leg irons locked to a tree with one old tennis shoe nearby and a bunch of empty pork-and-bean cans. It still makes me shudder to think about what that might have been about.''

Isaac shook his head. ''Makes a person think twice about traipsing off in the wilderness by themselves, doesn't it?''

''No kidding. Did you go through everything in her apartment? Maybe she hid them somewhere.''

''Checked every place I could think of.''

''No indication of a safety deposit box or anything?''

''No.''

I finished my drink and stood up. ''I'll think on it and try to come up with something. Maybe seeing those pictures will help.''

''I'll do the whole roll. Looks like there were twenty-four of them. You'll have them tonight.''

At home I found the shower occupied and Gabe lying on our bed reading the newspaper. His hair was damp, so apparently he'd showered already.

''The party starts in an hour and a half,'' he said, not looking up.

''Oh, goody,'' I replied, opening our closet doors and contemplating my clothes, wondering if I could get away with wearing black Wranglers one more time. I compromised by choosing cocoa-brown, narrow-legged wool slacks and a beige cashmere pullover—part of the new wardrobe Elvia had picked out for me. For familiarity, I pulled on my glossy brown Lucchese boots. Society could have everything tonight . . . except my feet.

When Emory finally emerged from the bathroom, it took me all of forty-five minutes to shower, dry my hair, and slap on some mascara and blush. By the time I finished, Gabe was dressed in a tweedy sports jacket, blue chambray shirt, and black Levi's.

When Gabe was in the other room hunting his eyeglasses, I asked Emory, "Did you find out anything?"

"Still got my feelers out," he said, pulling on his Armani sports coat. "Should have something by tomorrow."

ARTHUR CROSSMAN, OUR current mayor, and his wife, Rianna, lived in an exclusive neighborhood out past San Celina's miniature airport. The houses were big and custom built for entertaining with lots of glass and huge backyards bordering a pristine, man-made lake. He was a retired insurance executive and she an ex–Miss California who owned a successful interior decorating business based in Santa Barbara. Arthur and Rianna made the society pages of the *Tribune* on a regular basis with parties that more often than not were fund-raisers for some worthy and newsworthy cause. Tonight's was a combination of honoring our local women artists and Isaac Lyons, whose work Rianna had collected for years.

"Gabe, Benni, I'm so glad you could come," Arthur said when we were shown into the crowded living room already rumbling with the murmur of cocktail chatter. His eyes flickered when he saw Gabe's ravished face, but as an experienced politician, he covered it quickly with a wide smile. "Come in and help yourselves to the caviar and champagne."

He led us through the living room to an elegant dining area where a cherrywood table was covered with silver and crystal dishes. The rooms were decorated in jewel tones of blues, greens, and reds and had a Kentucky country-home feel to them with rich wood trimming and paisley-print wall-paper. At the long dining table, Rianna was directing a woman wearing a black-and-white maid's outfit.

She smiled when she saw us. "Have some caviar, you two. It's quite the rage, you know. We have fourteen flavors of Carolyn Collins's best caviar and some very amusing wines and champagnes to accompany them. The caviar arrived from Chicago today. We can't let Isaac Lyons think we're a bunch of country bumpkins, now can we?"

"We *certainly* can't," I murmured. I felt Gabe's hand squeeze my upper arm as Rianna looked beyond us to greet another group of people.

"Geez Louise," I said in a low voice. "Fourteen flavors of fish eggs. What's this world coming to?" I read the place cards, which were written in fancy calligraphy and placed in front of each crystal dish. "Ginger, orange, Grande Passion, Black Tobikko."

"Here's one you might like," Gabe said. "Lone Star caviar. Smoked with mesquite and heated up with jalapeno and serrano chiles and Absolut Peppar vodka for that distinctive, truly Texan taste."

"Gee, wrap some up to go," I said. "The only fish eggs I've ever experienced have been the kind you put on the end of your hook to catch a trout, and I'm happy to keep it that way."

He handed me a small china plate holding some caviar. "It wouldn't hurt you to try something new. You might like it. Like many things, it's an acquired taste."

I took the plate and looked down at the jellylike eggs. "Anything someone says you have to acquire a taste for instantly makes me suspicious. Makes me think of the emperor's new clothes. My theory is no one really likes this stuff, but nobody has the nerve to be the first one to say, 'For cryin' out loud, does anyone realize we are eating dead fish embryos?' "

He grinned and dumped another spoonful on my plate. "Frankly, I love it. Take some more before this crowd inhales it."

Holding my plate, I made small talk with people until I couldn't think of one more thing to say, then wandered out to the backyard, where the trees sparkled with tiny white lights that made me think of Disneyland more than fireflies. I pictured Snow White and her seven cohorts skulking about the perfectly trimmed bushes and trees. The lake, a short walk down some flagstone steps, shimmered in the moonlight and looked beautiful in an artificial, theme-park sort of way that fit with this whole plastic milieu. I gazed out over the lake, watching the small ripples made by the wind, and couldn't help but think about how, by all rights, Shelby should have been here with the rest of the up-and-coming artists, how this would have been such a special night for her, the first of many in her life.

"Are you enjoying your caviar?" Isaac said behind me.

I turned around and held up my still overflowing plate. "My third helping," I replied. "And if you believe that, I've got some oceanfront property in Elko, Nevada, I'm sure you'd be interested in."

He laughed and came over next to me. "Actually, it is quite delicious, you know. It is . . ."

"I know, I know, an acquired taste. So I've been told." I studied his face. Though his expression was jovial, his eyes were sad. "Are you okay?"

He sighed. "These things get harder and harder."

"Don't I know it. And I'm sure you've done a hundred thousand more than me."

"This one's been especially difficult, trying to laugh and make small talk when all I want to do is shake every person I meet until their teeth rattle and scream that my granddaughter is dead.'' He gazed out over the calm lake. ''By the way, just so you don't think I'm being a snob, I invited your grandmother to be my guest tonight, but much like her granddaughter, she felt that fish eggs were something better left to those who are enamored with hooks and sinkers.'' He smiled at me. ''She also said she met her quota for dressing up this month. And since she wouldn't accompany me, I chose to come alone.''

I smiled back, liking this man better each time we met. Then glancing around to make sure I wasn't seen, I tipped my plate and dumped the caviar into the lake. ''Umm, umm, good.''

He gave a small chuckle. ''If this lake is stocked, there are going to be some very happy fish tonight.''

''Or some very confused ones. I mean, mesquite smoked? So, did you enlarge the photographs?''

''They're in my car. I'll give them to you before you leave. They don't appear like much to me, of course, but you know the land around here better than I do. Perhaps they'll strike a familiar chord in you. I still think the missing film strip is the key to who murdered her. And her boyfriend.''

''You're probably right, but that doesn't do us much good unless we find it. By the way, I do have someone else working on this. My cousin Emory is using his nefarious journalistic contacts to investigate the backgrounds of the people closest to Shelby. Hopefully he'll come up with something—a good solid 'why' someone wanted her dead. What would cause any of these people to go to that desperate extreme.'' I looked up at him. ''Since so many of the people we're suspecting are artists, tell me, if you were an artist . . .'' I stopped and laughed at my words, my face heating up slightly. ''I'm sorry, that didn't come out the way I meant it. You are an artist.''

He patted my shoulder gently. ''I know what you're try-

ing to say. What would cause an artist to want to kill someone?''

''Right. What's the worst thing someone could do to an
artist?''

He thought for a moment, absently rubbing a thumb over
his hulking knuckles. ''I would have to say it would be
stealing from them.''

''Stealing? You mean, like their ideas? Their style?''

''Plagiarism is hard to prove, of course, in any type of
creative art. There's no law against copying someone's
style. But to copy a painting, including the signature of the
artist, and to sell it as an original—that would be the worst
thing that could happen to an artist short of all his or her
originals being destroyed in some way.''

''So, does that happen much in photography?'' I asked,
trying to figure out how that would work into why Shelby
was killed.

''Sometimes, but not often. It's really more a problem in
the fine arts. There's a lot of money to be made in forgeries.
Especially in the western art field. It's become very popular
in Japan and Germany and other foreign countries, and
many collectors are too trusting. They accept a fancy-
looking document claiming a bronze sculpture or an oil
painting is an authentic Remington or Russell without
checking either the background of the art dealer or where
the original might actually reside—usually in a museum
somewhere.''

A cold breeze came up, causing the ripples on the lake
to speed up to escalator-like regularity. I shivered and said,
''Maybe she took photographs of something to do with forgeries.''

''Let's walk back up to the house and get some coffee,''
Isaac said, taking the china plate from my hands and cupping a warm palm underneath my elbow.

''Then we'll just have to look deeper into all those

things," I said as we followed the flagstone steps back up to the party. "It has to be one of them."

"Or something else we haven't thought of," he said, his voice weary. We reached the large patio where the mayor, spying Isaac, came over and grabbed his arm.

"Isaac, we've been looking for you everywhere. I want to propose a toast. There is so much to celebrate tonight." A cloud of pain swept briefly over Isaac's face and then was gone, replaced by his public smile. I slipped away to the back of the room.

"What're you doing hiding back here, cowgirl?" Olivia said, coming up beside me. Greer came up a few seconds later, holding a glass of wine.

"They say the people in the back rows are always the smartest," Greer said, sipping her wine.

"Who said that?" I asked.

"The people in the back rows," Olivia said with a laugh.

We listened to the mayor's speech, his toast to Isaac and the women artists of our community, then moved back outside on the patio.

"Is Roland here?" I asked. "I haven't seen him."

"You are kidding," Greer said. "He's been fluttering around like a bee in a honeysuckle patch. I bet by the end of the night he's worth at least a quarter of a million dollars more."

"As long as it's some of my work he sells, more power to him," Olivia said, bringing a caviar-covered cracker up to her mouth.

Greer's eyebrows shot up. "Yeah, well, you'd better watch him. Roland has a way of manipulating things so that he always comes out on top."

Olivia shrugged. "My cousin's a lawyer. If he screws me, he's going to be sorry."

Greer thoughtfully twirled her almost-empty wineglass. "I was around a lot of men like him when I lived in San

Francisco. My ex-husband *is* a man like him. You really need to approach them like you would a mad coyote—with great caution and preferably a loaded shotgun.''

Olivia frowned at Greer. ''That's the difference between you and me. Someone messes with me, caution is a word *they* need to worry about.''

Greer set her glass down on a glass-topped table, her face tightening. ''Just trying to warn you, Olivia.''

''Warning heard and ignored,'' Olivia said flippantly. Greer scowled and opened her mouth to reply.

Trying to sidestep the potential argument, I interrupted. ''Weren't both of you at the Frio the other night when Kip was killed?''

''Can you believe it?'' Olivia said. ''I heard that they're really hassling Bobby about it. Ha. That's what he gets, the little twerp.''

I watched their faces carefully. ''So, what do you all think?''

''That little *hombre* did it,'' Olivia said. ''Bobby's such a chickenshit coward I could picture him holding an unconscious man's head under water.''

Greer gave me a half grin. ''Think she might be a tad prejudiced?''

I lifted my eyebrows. ''Maybe just a little. What do you think, Greer? About what happened to Kip, that is?''

''It doesn't answer the connection with Shelby. Why would Bobby kill Shelby?''

Olivia snorted.

Greer shook her head. ''I can't imagine that those stupid nude pictures she took of him would cause him to kill her.''

''That's because you don't understand how bad it is to shame your family in our culture,'' Olivia said. ''His mama is a very strict Catholic—head of the altar society at St. Celine's—and his papa is a deacon. One of his sisters is a novitiate. They raised their kids *muy* Catholic. Nude pictures of him showing up in a gallery here in town would humiliate *la familia* and cause them to lose face in our community. If he asked her for them back and she refused . . .''

''I wonder if he signed a model release?'' I said.

Olivia said, ''Take it from someone who knows not only Bobby's low level of sophistication, but also his very active sex drive. If she tempted him with sex, he probably signed on the dotted line quicker than he could shed his tight little Wranglers.''

''So, are you close to getting this one solved?'' Greer asked me.

''I'm not trying to solve anything,'' I said, twitching inward slightly at the lie. ''Just curious more than anything else.''

''And I bet I know why. I hear they arrested your brother-in-law this morning,'' Olivia said.

Luckily, before I could answer, Gabe moved into our circle.

''Ready to go?'' He put his arm around my shoulders. ''It's been a long day for me, and I'm tired.'' His black eye had darkened and spread, giving him a one-eyed raccoon look. His bottom lip appeared less swollen, though. Olivia and Greer looked at his face curiously, but kept their comments to themselves.

I leaned against his familiar bulk and sighed. ''Yes, but I need to get something from Isaac first.''

''What's that?'' He frowned, wincing slightly as he did.

''Some prints he made for me. I'll see if I can break through his crowd of adoring fans.'' I turned to Olivia and Greer. ''I guess I'll be seeing you two tomorrow. Are either of you in the fashion show?''

''Yes,'' they said in unison.

I grimaced. ''You might as well hear it from me first. Maribelle D'Angelo had the nerve to rupture her appendix, and I'm taking her place.''

Olivia let out a whoop. ''*Caramba!* She was the one

wearing that huge eighteen eighties ball gown with the corset and the bustle.''

"I'm bringing my camera for this," Greer said, joining
Olivia's laughter.

"I'll sue," I said.

"It'll be worth every penny," she called after me.

I finally managed to squeeze through the women surrounding Isaac, getting a few irritated looks when he excused himself and followed me to his rented car in the street.
He handed me a stiff yellow 8 1/2 X 11 envelope. ''Call
me tomorrow. I'll be out at the ranch or at the Historical
Museum with Dove—around two, I think. I agreed to talk
to them about old photographs.''

"Okay. If we don't hook up before then, I'm sure I'll
see you at the fashion show. It's at the Elks Club at seven
o'clock. Dove's in it, so I'm sure you'll be there.''

He walked back toward the mayor's house where Roland
met him halfway up the flagstone path. Emory's suspicious
voice echoed in the back of my head—what about Isaac? I
shook my head, refusing to go there. If Isaac was involved
with the killing of his own granddaughter, then I was going
to give up on humankind once and for all.

On the drive home, Gabe kept glancing over at me perusing the photographs. There were twenty of them—various scenery shots of oak trees, rolling hills, a hawk darting
down to catch something on the ground. Four of them
showed the corner of a building—a barn perhaps. Even with
the enlargements, there was nothing on them that looked
particularly familiar to me.

"Whatever she saw," I said, putting them back in the
envelope, "has to be on the missing negative strip.''

"I'm not happy about this," he said when we pulled into
the driveway.

"I know.''

"But I've also learned that there's nothing I can say or

do that will keep you from sticking your nose in where it doesn't belong.''

I turned to him in the dark cab. The streetlight across the street shaded his battered face in a stark, spooky way. "I'm being careful. I have learned something in the last year, you know."

He pulled the keys out of the ignition. "Not enough, apparently. You haven't learned to let the police do their job. The job they are *trained* to do."

I laid my hand on his arm. "I don't want to argue."

"I don't either, *querida*, but I had to say it. It's the only protection you'll allow me to give."

"I promise, I'll be very careful. Isaac and I are just trying to look at the things that the police might not think about. Like these photographs. No one but Isaac would have thought to look at the numbers on the negatives to see if any were missing."

"At least not for a while," Gabe said. "Most detectives aren't stupid. Eventually one of them would probably have thought of that angle."

"So all we're doing is speeding up the process."

He shook his head, unconvinced, but didn't argue.

"There's got to be something on them that got Shelby killed."

Once inside the house, he pulled off his jacket and started unbuttoning his shirt. "Tell Isaac not to be surprised if the sheriff's detectives want to go through her apartment again."

"He said he looked everywhere."

"He's not a trained detective."

THE NEXT DAY the cold front that had hovered over San Celina for the last week moved, and the temperatures soared to a pleasant seventy-five degrees. On the way out the door,

I opted for my plain Levi's jacket rather than my fleece-lined one.

"So, want to have lunch today?" Gabe asked, gulping down a glass of grapefruit juice. "I've got a pretty free schedule for a change."

"I wish I could, but we've got more schoolkids coming in for tours, so I'll probably hang out at the museum all day helping out where I can. I need to check the exhibit again, make sure it's holding up all right. I'm always nervous when we've borrowed from another folk art museum. I picture some kid throwing one of those boxes of red punch at one in a fit of temper."

"And, of course," Emory said, walking into the kitchen, "don't forget your royal appearance at the fashion show. I can't wait to see you in all your corseted glory."

"You'll probably have to have the paramedics give me oxygen if I wear it longer than thirty minutes," I grumbled.

At the museum, I walked through the exhibit to make sure all the Oregon Trail quilts were still undamaged. As with the first time I'd studied the pictures of them in the catalog book the Oregon museum had sent with them for inventory control, I was amazed at the movement and energy of the patterns chosen by these women who had left their homes back East and started out on a journey that almost certainly would, in the four to nine months it took the wagon trains to get to Oregon, gift them with both exhilarating and tragic experiences. The patterns nonverbally reflected their feelings and their impressions of the things seen along the arduous journey—the visual forward movement of a Double Irish Chain, the busy windmill-like feeling of a Flying Star that emphasized the excitement of migration, a Wheel of Fortune made with obvious optimism and hope, and a multicolored album quilt with the names of family members embroidered in the center of each ten-inch block. The wedding quilts especially touched me. Many of the women bravely made the long, dangerous journey to join their fiancés or new husbands. Their quilts were often stitched with intersecting circles and perfect little hearts, the hearts representing love and the circles representing divine guidance.

I couldn't help but think how, even as far back as the middle 1800s when these quilts were made, women were seeking to express their feelings through their art. It made me recall the comment Parker had made a couple of days ago about having to explain your art, that the art itself whether a quilt, a painting, a story, or a photograph, should be self-explanatory, and that if it wasn't, the artist had essentially failed. Then again, it might just be that people were too impatient, wanted things spelled out for them too quickly, without any work on their part. That was the problem these days; people wanted ideas and themes given to them in thirty-second sound bites—or a two hour movie—without understanding there was so much more to be gained by the slow personal discovery of what the artist was trying to say.

"Looks like you're contemplating the mysteries of the universe," Greer said behind me. I turned and smiled at her and Olivia.

"Or," Olivia said, "the overthrow of the government."

"Neither," I countered. "I was just thinking about something Parker said a few days back about hating to try and explain her art to people, that it should speak for itself."

Olivia nodded, but Greer shook her head in irritation. "She's young and idealistic. She hasn't figured out yet that not everyone has the time or the intelligence to study art and figure out the difference between a good picture and a mediocre one. Every time I give a talk, I figure I'm helping to educate a few more people about what good art is."

"That's commendable of you," I said, thinking, not for the first time, how unpredictable people are. Here was Greer, from a somewhat privileged background with a college degree in art and time spent in the city around a very sophis-

ticated crowd, being more tolerant about people's lack of
education and opportunities than Parker, who actually lived
it. "You're right," I said. "She is young. But then, we all
were at one time."

"I'll drink to that," Olivia said.

"You'll drink to anything," Greer teased.

Olivia grinned. "Especially if someone else is buying."

"I didn't see her at the party last night," I said. "Did I
miss her in the crowd? There must have been a hundred
people there."

"She didn't go," Greer said.

"Why?'

Greer lifted her shoulders, unconcerned. "I have no idea.
I saw her yesterday, and she just said she wasn't going."

EVEN THOUGH IT was Thursday, it ended up being one of
our busiest days at the museum. The weekend tourists had
already started arriving for the Heritage Days celebration
and were looking to be entertained. Elvia called at three
o'clock to make sure I remembered my hair and makeup
appointment and to crow about the prepaid attendance to the
fashion show.

"Three hundred twenty-seven," she said, her voice glee-
ful. "And we've even been promised a thirty-second spot
on the local news tonight."

"That's great," I said. "Just make sure it's not the thirty
seconds I'm stumbling around on stage."

"Did you get fitted?" she asked.

"Why are you asking me that when I know darn well
you probably called the costume shop and checked on me
after I left?"

"You're going to look beautiful," she said, sidestepping
my accusation.

"So when's the date with Emory?" I asked in return.

"Saturday," she snapped. "Then he'd just better get on that midnight train to Little Rock."

I just laughed softly, suspecting she wouldn't get rid of him that easily. "See you tonight, pal o' mine."

I decided to stop off at home briefly to check the mail and grab a bite to eat. Our neighborhood was quiet and empty, as it usually was during the day in the middle of a work week, but today not even Mr. Treton's old Chrysler was parked in his driveway. He was probably down at the VFW Hall giving his quarter's worth of opinion on the float he'd be riding on Saturday. In front of the door sat a gold Blind Harry's bag, stapled shut.

I smiled. Elvia was feeling guilty about forcing me into this ridiculous fashion show. Good. A little bit of deserved guilt never hurt anyone. I opened the bag and found a large gold box of Godiva's chocolates.

"Great!" I said, prying it open eagerly.

Then, with a small scream, I dropped it.

15

THE GRAYING COW'S tongue had obviously been purchased at a local supermarket. I looked around to see if anyone had witnessed my dramatic and somewhat embarrassing reaction. Using the lid, I scooped the tongue back into the candy box and quickly went inside, locking the door behind me. I stuck the box back into the bag and set it on the kitchen counter. Grabbing a Coke out of the refrigerator, I sat down on a wooden chair, contemplating who had done this. The why was pretty obvious. Apparently someone had found out I was looking into Shelby's and Kip's deaths and that someone wasn't happy about it.

That someone was also very clever. He or she knew I'd be suspicious of just about anything that showed up on my doorstep except something that appeared to be from Elvia. I held the icy Coke can against my temple, willing my heart to stop thumping so hard in my chest. It did make me nervous, thinking about someone who was obviously a killer coming that close to where I lived.

But it also pissed me off.

If that person thought playing a juvenile trick like leaving grocery store animal parts on my doorstep was going to stop me from doing what I could to see that Shelby's and Kip's killer was caught, he or she obviously didn't know me very well.

I immediately dialed Gabe's number. Maggie told me that he was out of the office for the rest of the afternoon, but that he'd be at the Elks Club in time to go on in his costume.

"Do you want me to beep him?" she asked.

"No," I said. There was nothing he could do at the moment. "It can wait."

I picked up the bag by its handle and carried it out to the garage where I hoped by the time Gabe saw it tonight, it wouldn't smell too ripe. But there was no way I was keeping this thing in my refrigerator. I locked the garage and walked out to the truck, nervously glancing into the long afternoon tree shadows, more nervous than I would ever admit to anyone.

This person had the advantage of knowing where I lived, knowing my movements, and being able to observe the habits of my neighborhood. I was willing to bet that this delivery took place when Mr. Treton, our only neighbor who was consistently home during the day, was gone. That meant someone was watching where I lived. And watching me.

I locked the doors of the truck before putting it in drive, slowing down and looking carefully at the few parked cars on the street as I passed them. They were empty, of course. Whoever left my macabre little present was long gone. The question was, what else did they have planned . . . and when? The thought of me walking out on a stage was nerve-wracking enough, but now it was even worse. If I'd wanted a reason to back out of the fashion show, here it was. There was no way Gabe or Elvia would want me to strut down that runway after this incident.

Which was exactly why I now decided I wasn't going to tell them about it until after the fashion show. I was sick and tired of cowardly criminals manipulating the lives of their victims. Judging by the juvenile method of intimidation, I surmised that this person wasn't very experienced at terrorizing victims. This was strictly amateur hour, and I wasn't about to let this person think I was spooked, which is exactly what it would look like if I pulled out of the fashion show. I was raised to meet cowardice like this straight on without blinking. I'd walk down that runway with my head held high.

A little voice argued with my bravado as I drove downtown. *Amateurs are the most unpredictable criminals, because they don't have the sense to know when to quit.*

I pulled into the spacious parking lot of the San Celina Elks Club. Elvia decided to hold the fashion show here rather than at the Forum so the large crowd she so optimistically expected would have no trouble finding parking spaces. The low-roofed, 1950s buildings sprawled across the street from the cemetery where my mother and Jack were buried. I gazed over at the green lawn of the darkening cemetery and wondered briefly if Wade had visited Jack's grave. I slung the heavy garment bag over my shoulder and hiked across the already half-full parking lot.

Handmade signs with florescent orange arrows directed me through the maze of back rooms of the Elks Club to a large, airy room that had been turned into a surprisingly efficient beauty parlor. Almost before I could get my name out, my dress was whisked out of my hands and I was being primped and coiffed for my one-minute performance. In less than a half hour, they'd twisted my hair into a complicated nineteenth-century upswept hairstyle. The woman who layered on my thick makeup worked at the college as a fashion design instructor and apparently did a term paper once on late nineteenth-century clothing styles.

"You know, technically the ball gown you've got there is from eighteen eighty-five. Shirtwaists were a big fashion item for women in the nineties. Did you know that?" she asked, slapping thick pancake makeup on my face. I shook my head slightly.

"Yep," she continued. "They were as hot as bellbottoms in the sixties. They didn't have many mannequins then so they used to display them in store windows stuffed with paper. They looked sturdy, but actually weren't. People used to say they were as flimsy as a pompous man's opinions. That's where we get the term 'stuffed shirt' from."

"I know some people that would fit," I said, picturing Roland in late nineteenth-century clothes.

"Me, too." She stroked deep brown eye shadow across my lids.

When she was done she directed me toward the dressing rooms, where it took a girl of great youth and strength to squeeze me into my boned corset.

"I read somewhere that the average waist in the late eighteen hundreds was twenty-two inches," she said, breathing hard as she yanked the ties. "Pull your stomach in."

I held on to a table edge and squeaked, "It's already touching my backbone."

She finally got it tied and strapped on the basketlike contraption that supported my dress's bustle. She slipped the bright blue satin gown over my head and started the long, arduous task of buttoning me up.

When she was through and I was struggling into my pointy-toed shoes, she nodded toward a double door. "That's the designated green room," she said. "There's water and fruit juice and cookies provided by the Historical Society."

"Thanks," I said, picking up my hem and tiptoeing painfully across the carpet. "But if I drink anything, I'll have to pee, and I'm not sure how I'd do that in this dress."

She laughed. "If you absolutely have to, there's a handicapped bathroom across the parking lot in building five. It's quite a walk though. It's supposed to be open just for folks like you."

"Handicapped is exactly how I feel. How long until I go on?"

She checked her pink plastic watch. "You're the last model, so I'd say about two hours."

"I'll definitely keep it in mind, then."

Over in the green room, I found Greer dressed in her 1930s lacy tea dress and Parker wearing a gray business-woman's suit from the forties. Both were sipping paper cups of orange juice. They burst into laughter when they saw me.

"Turn blue," I grumbled and looked over the spread the Historical Society had provided. My mouth suddenly felt dry and my head a little light from not eating. Against my better judgement, I poured myself a glass of orange juice so I wouldn't pass out in front of three hundred twenty-seven–odd people.

"Did you see Olivia?" Parker said with a giggle. I was glad to see that her spirits were a little lighter tonight.

"She couldn't look any worse than me," I said.

"A black Spanish mourning dress," Greer said, grinning. "Circa eighteen sixty."

"My sympathies," I moaned.

As I suspected, about a half hour later, the orange juice I'd drank had worked its way down, and I knew I was going to have to make that trip to the ladies room. I left the group in the green room, which had grown to about fifty people in the last half hour, and started across the parking lot. It was crowded now with people arriving for the fashion show, so I didn't feel nervous about going to the bathroom by myself, though the memory of the package I'd found on my doorstep was still fresh in my mind. Was it a veiled threat? Maybe. Then again, maybe it was just a neighborhood kid's practical joke for the police chief. Where Gabe and I lived was certainly no secret in this town, and our house had been egged before.

Building five was open, as my makeup person promised, and it took a little hunting before I finally found the hand-icapped bathroom. It was apparently once a closet or some-thing that they'd converted because it had double doors that provided a large enough entryway for wheelchairs even with the metal post in the middle. It took me almost five minutes to wrangle around my clothes so that I could use the facilities. I couldn't help but wonder about what women did during the nineteenth-century—not drink at all? I was busy trying to put everything back in place when the lights went out.

I froze, listening. The eerie silence was almost worse than hearing any sound. If the person's intent was to startle me, it worked. My mind raced with possibilities—was someone waiting outside for me? Should I go? Stay? Scream my head off? I groped around the bathroom, searching for something I could use as a weapon. The trash can? I felt around for it. Shoot—it was big one with a flapping lid. Too big for me to pick up and hurl at someone, especially confined in this dress.

"Dang it all," I said softly. There was nothing in this bathroom I could use to protect myself. Remembering the self-defense class I'd taken one time, the element of surprise was all I had going for me. That and a real big voice.

I reached for the door with the plan to scream as loud as I could and hopefully surprise whoever was silently waiting for me on the other side.

It opened before I touched the handle, and a hand in a dark glove appeared. It pointed something at me.

I screamed and ducked.

But not quick enough.

What felt like thousand bees stung my eyes, and I screamed again. I stumbled backwards, clawing at my eyes.

Water, my mind commanded. *Find water.*

I felt my way to the sink, grasping the cold porcelain while I searched for the faucet. I scooped up handfuls and kept washing my eyes over and over, aware of my vulnerable position, but also knowing I couldn't fight at all if I couldn't see. Gradually the sting lessened, and I felt my way over to the door. My eyesight was still blurry from what I guessed was pepper spray, but I had to get to where there were people. I was more of a sitting duck in here. I inhaled as deeply as my corset would allow, preparing to scream and make a run for it. I pulled sharply on the door handle.

It didn't budge.

I pulled again. Nothing.

I felt along the cool tile wall next to the door for the light switch and flipped it up.

Nothing.

I tried the door again. It was as if someone had nailed it shut.

I should have been scared. Instead I was pissed.

"Hey!" I yelled, pounding a fist on the door. "Hey, let me out!"

My voice bounced back and echoed slightly in the dark bathroom.

"Hey, somebody!" I pushed again, then kicked the door with my foot.

I kept up the pounding and yelling for ten minutes or so until I realized that unless someone was forced to use the handicapped restroom like I had, I was stuck here. The fact that the person had obviously taken off and I wasn't going to be attacked as I walked out the door was a small comfort.

My eyes still streaming from the pepper spray, I hiked up my dress and sat down on the cold floor. Like the Victorian lady who had probably first worn this dress, I was feeling a bit faint. Luckily, I was wearing a bustle that, my makeup lady had informed me, had been designed by Lillie Langtry. When you sat down, its metal bands pivoted up so at least I didn't have to stand in the high-top button shoes that were already killing my feet. Every few minutes I'd yell out, hoping a passerby would hear me. Someone certainly had to come looking for me after two hours, I reasoned, if nothing else but on Elvia's command to kill me for missing my cue. Just my luck that I was the last person on the program and not the first.

There's something about sitting in a pitch-black room against your will that makes you look at life in a whole different way. It was the kind of darkness that your eyes never got used to since the door was so well made that not even a strip of light shone out from the bottom. Not that I'd be able to see anything clearly out of my still-streaming eyes.

Well, I told myself firmly, after what I'd calculated was an hour, though I couldn't be sure, *at least you won't die of thirst. And you do have a place to pee. Could be worse. You could have been pushed into a closet with a full bladder.*

I do try to look at life's little problems optimistically.

Especially when I felt myself teetering on the edge of hysteria. I knew someone would come eventually. I would be missed. Eventually.

That word *eventually* was the kicker.

After I'd run out of soothing hymns from my childhood, all the Bible verses I could remember, nursery rhymes, and my extensive repertoire of Patsy Cline hits, I moved on to singing under my breath—''The bear went over the mountain to see what he could see.'' After that I'd be stuck with ''A hundred bottles of beer on the wall,'' and by the time anyone found me, I'd be stark raving mad. Maybe now would be a good time to start talking to the Big Guy. *And, pray tell, why is that always your last resort?* I heard a voice not dissimilar to Dove's in my head.

Then I heard voices in the hallway. I struggled to my feet, screaming from my diaphragm.

''Help! I'm in here!'' I yelled before it occurred to me that it might not be friendly forces out in that hallway.

At this point, I was willing to fight my captor face-to-face rather than spend one more minute in complete darkness.

Just in case, I was standing there ready to spring when light from the hallway flooded the room and I blinked up at a blurry Clark Kent in his baggy forties suit and neat fedora and a semifull beard.

"Superman?" I stammered.

"Are you okay?" Gabe grabbed me by the shoulders. Behind him was a sea of worried faces, Elvia's in the forefront. I hoped that was worry on her face.

"I can't breathe," I said. My eyes still streaming, I saw blackness at the edge of them and felt my legs start to crumple beneath me.

In a flash I was literally swept off my feet and, feeling a bit silly but incredibly relieved, I relaxed as Gabe carried me through the crowd. He swore softly under his breath in Spanish.

"Out of our way," he said roughly and looked over at Elvia. "We need some privacy. She needs to get out of this dress."

"The business office is just down the hall," someone called out of the crowd.

"Oh, Rhett, please, not in front of the help," I said as he carried me down the hallway.

"Is there any situation where you don't feel compelled to make a smartass remark?" he snapped.

Inside the slightly shabby office, Elvia clucked under her breath as she undid the buttons in back.

Gabe stuck his head out of the office door and yelled. "Somebody get her clothes."

"I know you didn't want to do this, but you didn't have to go to such drastic measures," Elvia murmured, helping me out of my bustle, corset and other nineteenth-century undergarments. A knock on the door and a discreet hand produced my jeans, flannel shirt, socks, and boots.

"What happened?" Gabe asked, his arms crossed over his chest in that stance that raised my hackles as surely as a dog protecting its dinner.

"Someone turned out the light when I was taking a leak and then sprayed me with what I think was pepper spray.

Then when I tried to leave, they somehow locked the door. How'd they do that? I've never seen a bathroom door that locked from the outside.''

"They slipped a metal bar between the double handles," he said. "Did you see or hear anything else?"

"The hand wore a dark glove," I said. "That's all I saw before they sprayed me. I told you they shut out the light when I was peeing. And when I tried to turn it back on, it wouldn't work."

He unfolded his arms, his eyes flickering as his brain processed that information. "They probably shut it off at the main circuit breaker."

Elvia gathered up my dress and shoes and gave me a small hug. For her, that was extremely affectionate, so I knew she must have really been worried when I didn't make my cue.

"I'm sorry, Elvia," I said. "Really, I am."

"Not your fault. I'll take these back to the Historical Society. You just go home and get some rest. Call me tomorrow." She eyed Gabe but didn't say anything. She knew we were about to get into it and she was a wise enough friend to realize it was our battle. When she reached the door, she said over her shoulder, "By the way, your debt's not paid."

I gave a small laugh. "*La Patróna* has spoken."

Gabe didn't crack a smile.

"I guess we can talk about this at home," I said.

"Count on it."

After assuring the people who hung around and helped search for me that I was all right, I found my purse and headed for my truck, my grim-faced bodyguard following me like a loyal Doberman pinscher.

"I'll drive," he said, taking my keys from me. "I'll send a patrolman for my car."

At home, I reluctantly showed him the tongue that I'd found on our doorstep. After looking over the package thor-

oughly, he wrapped the meat in a plastic bag and stuffed it
in our outside trash can. While he changed out of his forties
costume, I fixed his favorite Mexican hot chocolate, hoping
to sweeten the discussion we were about to have. It didn't
work. As usual, he thought I was too involved and I thought
he was overreacting. We were sitting at opposite sides of
the kitchen table, clutching our mugs and glaring at each
other when Emory walked in.

"Whoa, Nellie," he said, looking at Gabe's face, then
mine. "I'll slink off to bed and see you two in the morning."

When we were alone again, Gabe said, his voice tired,
"Is there any crime that happens in this town that you aren't
involved in?"

"That's an exaggeration, and you know it. As for being
involved, you grew up in a small town yourself. You know
what it's like. I can't help knowing as many people as I
do."

"I know," he said, looking down into his still-full mug.
"It's just that you've come close to really getting hurt so
many times, I'm afraid you've used up all your luck."

I reached over and put my hand on his. "Gabe, don't
worry. You know this is strictly college high-jinks crap. I
mean, a cow's tongue? Locking me in a bathroom? Even
pepper spray is something that you can get at any sporting
goods store these days. If they'd been serious they'd have
hit me over the head or something when I came out of the
bathroom."

He looked up at me, his face serious. "They could have.
It was a metal bar they used to jam those doors shut."

"You said yourself Shelby's death was probably a spur-
of-the-moment thing. Kip's, too. So I'll just be extra careful
until the killer is caught."

"And stop asking questions?"

I traced a finger over his knuckles. They were rough and
slightly chapped. Faint black lines still stained their crevices

from his patient and loving work on Sam's car a few nights ago. "I won't lie to you. Both Isaac and I have good reasons why we are investigating, and I know neither of us will stop. I will promise to be careful and not to break any laws."

He took my hand and squeezed it gently. "I would prefer you didn't ride your horse in the parade on Saturday. Not just for your safety, but for others. We don't know how far this person might go."

I started to protest, then stopped. He was right. Putting other people at risk was irresponsible. "All right. I'll watch it from Elvia's office upstairs."

I was rinsing out the cups while Gabe was showering when Emory stuck his head in the doorway. "Everything swingin' low and easy, sweetcakes?"

"Everything's fine, Emory. Come on in. What's up?"

"Been working hard all day on your behalf. There's lots of dirt to report."

I glanced over at the closed bathroom door. Through it I could hear the shower still running. I was glad, for once, that Gabe took long showers. "Quick, tell me what you found out. Gabe's being really cool about this, but I don't want to press my luck." I leaned against the counter and folded my arms.

Emory opened a small leather notebook and frowned, trying to decipher his own cramped notes. "First, Mr. Roland Bennett. Five years ago, he was a bunny's whisker away from being indicted in regards to an appraisal scam he and another dealer were involved with. His specialty was recent widows who needed money quickly or were just too upset over their husbands' deaths to think rationally. Apparently he'd appraise a work low, then his friend, claiming to be new in the business and a bit naive, would sweep in and offer a few thousand over Roland's appraised amount. The widow would, of course, jump on it, and then Roland and his friend would sell it for double or triple the amount and split the profits."

"And they got away with it?"

"Art appraisal is a tricky business, and most of the women and a few men were very prominent citizens who didn't want to press charges because of the personal humiliation of being snookered. He messed with the wrong man, though, when he tried to rip off an old Texas oilman by appraising two Schreyvogel oils in his mama's estate at fifteen and twenty thousand dolllars, respectively. Bennett's dealer jumped in and offered the oilman forty-five thousand for the both of them. But that ole Texas boy, having dealt with many a honey-tongued horse trader in his life, got suspicious and obtained a third opinion from another appraiser. That appraiser, a legitimate one this time, weighed the paintings in at seventy-five and ninety thousand dollars. Quite a difference. And you know Texans—they hate anyone even tryin' to pull one over on them. He went to his attorney, but before anything could happen, the old Texan guy croaked, and Roland and his buddy skedaddled out of the Lone Star state to seek their fortune in California. Roland started the rumor that his friend was the brains behind the deal, thereby saving what little reputation he had left. He's kept his nose clean ever since."

"That we know of," I pointed out.

"Precisely."

"How could that work into Shelby's and Kip's murders?"

"I just report the facts, my dear. You're the brains in this outfit. Next, we have Parker Leona Williams of Bakersfield, California. Story fit for a confession magazine. Father ran off when she was ten. Mother was an on-again, off-again secretary for a number of small manufacturing companies and basically an unrepentant drunk and sleep around. Older sister served some time in state prison for being the driver in a liquor store robbery when she was a mere two days past her eighteenth birthday. Parker was fourteen when her sister went to prison and her mom went on a drunk and ended up in detox in the county jail. She lost custody of Parker, who was then shuffled around to a series of foster homes where she eventually found herself in the home of a Mr. and Mrs. Cal and Blythe Fellows. Mrs. Fellows was an art teacher, so I'm just taking a wild guess here and assuming it was her influence that started Parker down her artistic road.''

"She never mentioned them," I said. "Or her family. But that's not unusual at the co-op. A lot of the people there have things in their pasts that they don't like to talk about.''

Emory's voice was mild, "Who doesn't?" He looked back down at his notebook. "The Fellows were killed outside Tracy, California, in a five-car accident a year ago.''

"How sad," I murmured. "And her sister and mother?''

"As far as my sources could tell, they're still in Bakersfield, but both are of a rather transient nature, so who knows?''

"No wonder she was bitter about Greer," I said. Emory's eyebrows went up, and I told him about her sudden change of personality when she and Greer spoke about their art at the museum. "She's probably not only jealous of Greer's talent and financial situation, but also of her close-knit family.''

"Our Miz Greer and her kinfolk have their problems, too.''

I sat up in my chair. "What?''

"Seems the Shannon ranch isn't doing as well as could be these days.''

"No big news there. Whose is?''

"At least you and Ben are breaking even. Apparently the Shannons are thinking about selling some prime roadside pasture land by Highway One to a group of investors looking to put in a golf course and country club.''

"I know that piece of property. It's been in their family for over a hundred and fifty years! I can't believe they'd sell it to developers. Where'd you find that out? I haven't heard a thing through the rancher's grapevine, and neither has Daddy or Dove or they would have told me.''

"It's very hush-hush at this point. Things like that get people all riled up and sending in letters to the editor. You know, that whole public trust–private ownership thing. It's going to make the Shannons look mighty sour to their long-time friends and neighbors.''

Remembering the furor two months ago about the land surrounding Bishop Peak and the housing development that was still in limbo, I knew he was right. "How did you find out about it?''

He leaned over and tapped a finger on my nose. "It's what I do, sweetcakes. And I do it very well.''

I swatted at his hand. "Keep talking.''

"Actually," he continued, "it wasn't that hard. Most of the transactions so far are on public record—environmental impact reports and such, though it appears that some people might have had their palms softened a bit to keep it quiet. I found out by simply calling real estate agencies, asking about bidding on the Shannon property. The supervising agent at the first four reacted with 'huh?' It was on number five that I received a 'Who's asking?' Bingo.''

I shook my head. "I knew things had been tough the last few years for them, but, shoot, it's been that way for all of us. Cattle prices are ridiculously low, and the government gave price subsidies to the dairy farmers again by buying their old milk cows and flooding the market with cheap, low-quality beef. I knew things were bad, but I didn't think the Shannons were so hard up they'd have to sell prime land.''

"Better a part than the whole, I guess. Apparently there's been some medical expenses also. Their grandmother?''

I nodded. "I knew about that. She's got Alzheimer's, and they've had to put her in a special hospital. If they're anything like us, they probably didn't have any insurance for it, and those places aren't cheap.''

"So they'd need money fast and, like most ranchers, all they have is land."

I sighed. But for the grace of God, I couldn't help but think, *But how would that fit in with murdering Shelby and Kip?*

"What else?" I asked.

"Bobby Sanchez. No great discovery there. His family's very socially prominent in the Hispanic community and very religious. But you knew that. If he had a motive, it had to be those pictures. Which we only know about through Ms. Contreras's statement. Do you think they really exist?"

"I don't know," I said, suddenly frustrated with this whole scenario. "Isaac never found any negatives. Maybe whoever sent them to Olivia has them." It embarrassed me knowing these intimate details about the lives of my friends and colleagues. How would I look them in the face again?

Hearing the shower shut off, I said, "Hurry, anyone else?"

"Olivia Contreras herself. A few parking tickets. A bust for being part of a sit-in during her sophomore year at Berkeley. She never graduated. Has worked a series of odd jobs since coming back to San Celina. Needs money, but then all of them do."

"So why is she driving a new truck?" I asked.

He shrugged. "Leased maybe? I didn't check on that."

I pushed myself out of my chair. "I suppose. Well, we're not any closer to finding out who did this than I was fifteen minutes ago."

"Process it all for a while," he advised, ripping out the sheets of paper and handing them to me. "Something will click."

I lay in bed that night, the stories of each of the suspects swirling about my head, keeping me from sleep. Which of those circumstances would be grave enough to drive a person to kill? What circumstances would drive someone to that extreme? Would I—could I—ever be that desperate? I loved the ranch I grew up on with all my heart—it was a feeling that was hard to explain to someone whose only experience with the land was the small plot of ground in the back of their suburban tract home or condo. But would I kill for it? I know I wouldn't. Human life was more important than rocks and trees. What about a position, a career? I knew of people who'd killed to preserve that. To protect someone I loved from physical harm? That I could imagine doing.

Finally I eased out of bed and stood by the window, watching the shadows in our small front yard change and darken. In the dead of night, problems always seem larger, more impossible to solve—darkness seems to diminish us humans and our feeble attempts at bringing order to a chaotic universe. I thought about Shelby and a life lost so young and wondered if I'd just worded my advice differently, if she'd just not confronted her friend, if I'd just . . . who knows what—she'd still be alive. I thought about Isaac and how successful his life had been professionally, and yet the two people he'd truly loved in his life were gone. I wondered about Kip and the family he'd left back in Montana— did they even think when they'd waved good-bye less than a year ago that they'd never see him again? And I thought of Jack—how in some ways my life with him almost seemed like a dream now. How Wade seemed only half a person without him. Was there anything I could do to help Wade move on?

"*Querida.*" Gabe's voice came gently out of the darkness. "Come back to bed."

I crawled back under the down comforter and fit my body around his.

"Do you want to talk about it?" he asked, putting his arms around me.

"No," I murmured.

"You know the biggest lesson I learned in Vietnam? And later, being a cop? That we don't have control. Over anything. All we can do is the best with the circumstances we're given."

I laughed softly. "This from the man who double-knots everything?"

Echoing my laugh, he kissed my temple. "I said I learned it. I didn't say I practiced it."

"I'm glad we found each other, Friday."

"Likewise, *niña*."

I WAS DRINKING a glass of orange juice the next morning when a clean-shaven Gabe walked into the kitchen.

"Feels much better," I said as he rubbed his smooth, spicy-smelling cheek against mine. "In the excitement, I forgot to ask who won the beard-growing contest."

"One of my sergeants," he said. "The one we call 'ape-man.' "

"What did he win?"

"A case of shaving cream." He poured some orange juice into our blender, added protein powder, a banana, and some kiwi, and turned it on high.

I grinned at him. "And the pig-kissing contest?"

He gave me a level look. "The picture will be in the *Tribune* today. Knock yourself out."

I giggled. "I'll send a copy to your mother and sisters. By the way, I'm going to spend most of the day at the museum, so don't worry. The place will be packed. We're expecting a lot of early-bird tourists."

He poured his breakfast drink into a large glass. "Just be careful."

"That goes without saying."

He looked at me over the edge of his glass, his eyes dark. "Not in your case, it doesn't."

I stuck my tongue out at him. He just shook his head and finished his drink. When he kissed me good-bye, he tasted vaguely like an Orange Julius.

In my office at the museum, I couldn't settle down to do any real work, so instead I read Emory's notes about Roland, Olivia, Greer, Bobby, and Parker over and over. I couldn't help but wonder which one of them was the "friend" that Shelby had approached. In my gut, I knew that had to be the person who'd pushed her and who'd killed Kip because he'd found out. What I couldn't figure out was if Kip had a suspicion about who killed Shelby, why didn't he go to the police immediately? That's what most people would have done. Unless . . .

Unless they'd been involved in something they were trying to hide from the police. That certainly was what Kip's message on my answering machine seemed to imply. But what? What could he have been involved with that would have gotten him killed? What had Shelby been involved with? I couldn't imagine her doing anything illegal. She just didn't seem to have any reason—or be the type. Not that there was a type. I'd been fooled before and was slowly becoming as cynical as my own husband. Unfortunately, people just as often took the low road as the high when it came to getting what they desired. And one thing I knew about Shelby—she desired success.

I read over the notes again and thought about each person's motive. Parker, Olivia, and Greer were all artists striving to become known. Olivia and Greer were closer to breaking out from a mere regional arena into a national arena. If someone interfered with that, would either of them kill? I know their art meant a lot to both of them, but enough to kill another human being? Parker's chance of becoming a commercially successful artist was small, as it was in most arts. For every artist who makes it, there are thousands who remain Sunday painters for the rest of their lives. Though most, deep in their hearts, dreamed of the success that came to so few, they knew and could accept the arbitrariness of fame and lived their lives with joy and gratitude with only an occasional twinge of regret.

Parker Williams had a lot of bad breaks in her life, and bitterness seemed to float across her emotional ocean like a layer of spilled oil. But was she bitter enough to kill? Then there was Bobby. I'd known people who'd killed to save their reputations. He probably wouldn't do it for himself, but I understood the sanctity of the family in a Hispanic household and knew that to save his mother embarrassment, he just might do it if he thought he could get away with it. Then there was Roland, whose motive would be out and out greed—certainly not the first time that had happened. Or Shelby could have found out something that he didn't want known. Perhaps something to do with another foray into forgery? I looked over the slips of paper again. Lust for fame, bitterness, panic, greed, fear of exposure. All believable motives for murder. And they all had opportunity by being at the barbecue. Not to mention it was so crowded at the Frio Saloon that any one of them could have followed Kip and Wade out to the creek and taken advantage of Kip's drunk and battered situation. Motive, opportunity. What about means? Since both were spur of the moment, they all had that, too.

I leaned back in my chair and rubbed my temples with my fingertips. Where to go from here?

Dig deeper and always look for the story behind the story, I remember Emory writing me once in a letter in which he was telling me his thoughts on good journalism. That's where the real meat is—in the facts that aren't so obvious. Get the who, what, when, and where, but never forget that the thing most readers are interested in is why. And the why is often found in the people surrounding the story. Look for the person who doesn't want to talk to you and hound them until they do. *That's* where the good stuff is.

I sat forward and picked up Emory's slips of paper. Look behind the story. Dig deeper. How would I do that? I didn't have the resources of the police, and apparently they hadn't found anything yet . . . at least not anything that would cause them to charge someone.

Dig deeper. I had only one resource that the police and my dear cousin didn't, and that was my long and varied connections in this town. I picked up the slips of paper and stuck them in my purse.

"I'm going to lunch," I told the docent behind the counter. "I'm not sure when I'll be back."

Then I headed to see the only person who knew everything about everyone within a fifty-mile radius of San Celina—Bud the Hot Dog Man. Even the cops were aware of Bud Stumpey's prodigious knowledge of activity, both legal and illegal, and they courted him like a prom queen, hoping to gain a tidbit now and then. He doled out his information sparingly, his criteria in confiding in a person as capricious as the famous Central Coast winds.

His silver hot dog stand ruled the corner of the Save-rite Drugstore parking lot downtown, a spot he'd held for twenty years. His hot dogs were juicy, all beef, kosher paragons of pleasure served in a gently steamed bun that had those little black seeds that dalmatianed your teeth with every bite. With fresh Vidalia onions, French's yellow mustard, and chopped kosher dills, they were worth every cent of their two-dollar price. Soft drinks were a buck, toothpicks a nickel. And he only allowed you one napkin unless you were under six years old.

I parked five blocks up the street, avoiding the parking structures that were bound to be full at this time of day. I needed the exercise anyway. Especially if I was going to get one of Bud's hot dogs, which were certainly not known for their low-calorie healthfulness. Not that he had any intention of changing his menu. When a new San Celina resident, one of the many transplants from Southern California, playfully suggested he stock turkey and tofu franks for those who didn't eat beef or meat, he refused to serve that person for three months. Bud knew his niche and didn't deviate.

He was open 365 days a year and gave away free hot dogs on both Thanksgiving and Christmas to San Celina's burgeoning homeless population.

"Benni Harper!" he exclaimed when I walked up. He wasn't any taller than me, and it was guessed that his age was anywhere from fifty to seventy years old. His hair had been white as a cotton ball since the day he opened up twenty years ago, and the pink caterpillar scar along the edge of his tanned jaw had been a source of speculation and urban myth for years. He lived alone in a small house downtown, his only company his parrot, Six-Gun, who quoted the Bible and cursed like a cop with equal abandon. Bud jumped up from his webbed lawn chair with the attached red-and-white umbrella and opened the hatch to his silver stand. "One extra mustard and onions, no pickles coming up." Bud took pride in knowing the preference of each of his regular customers. I'd been a faithful once-a-week imbiber since my college days. He handed me my hot dog wrapped in a napkin and pulled out a dripping can of Barq's root beer. "What's new in the worlds of folk art, law enforcement, and bovines?" he asked.

I popped the top of my root beer and took a deep drink. "Nothing that I'm sure you don't already know about, Bud. Actually, I'm here to sit at your feet and beg some information." Two college kids came up beside me and started counting the change in their pockets.

He nodded at the patio chair next to his. "Let me get these youngsters taken care of." I sat down gratefully, knowing that his invitation meant he'd talk to me. No one who was smart ever sat down until invited personally by Bud, who reserved it for people he really liked or those who came to him for advice. He had become a sort of surrogate priest, confidant, and grass roots legal expert to San Celina's poor, homeless, and young. He was a walking self-appointed social services expert and probably knew more secrets about the people in this town than all the priests in the county combined.

I watched him fix up two hot dogs for the college students, telling them they were seventy-five cents short and they could pay him later, but that they'd better not forget because he had a memory as big as Alaska. Three more customers came up, and he had a small rush that kept him busy enough for me to finish my hot dog and most of my Barq's.

A lull came, and he sat down next to me. "Enjoy it?" he asked.

I smiled and toasted him with my can. "You have to ask?"

"Good. Now, what is it you need to know?"

"First, has the sheriff's department been to talk to you yet?"

He smirked. "Of course."

"And?"

"I answered their questions."

I waited, knowing he'd tell me everything in his good time.

He tugged at one of his white jaw-length sideburns. "The guy they sent wanted extra onions on his first time."

I *tsked* sympathetically under my breath. Huge faux pas on the detective's part. They must have been really busy and sent a rookie who ignored their instructions on how to treat Bud. All the locals knew you never asked for special treatment the first ten times you bought a hot dog from Bud. That was tantamount to trying to kiss the pope's ring before being asked.

He continued, "He asked me if I'd heard anything about the murders through the grapevine. I told him no."

I sipped my root beer and tilted my head, listening.

His smirk got bigger. "What I heard was directly from the horse's mouth. He really should learn to ask the correct questions."

I laughed and wondered again if the speculations many of us had tossed around were true. That Bud, with his sharp mind and often incredible legal knowledge, was an attorney who left "the life" to run his hot dog stand. He had a good-natured but sometimes wickedly revengeful relationship with law enforcement that certainly acquired its roots somewhere. He just barely forgave me when I married the chief of police.

I sat forward in my lawn chair. "So, you talked to Shelby?"

He nodded. "She was a real sweet little girl. She had money but didn't flaunt it. I like that in a person. She donated two hundred dollars to help buy hot dogs for my Thanksgiving Day feast. Not many kids her age would do that."

"I liked her, too. That's why I'm trying to find out who did this."

He ran a tongue across his teeth, then pursed his lips. It was a gesture he always affected right before he gave advice. "Willing to bet your new husband won't be too happy about that."

I took another sip of my root beer and gave him a little smile. "I only bet on sure things. Seriously, I'm merely working the angles the police have already tried . . . and failed. Besides, it's not Gabe's case."

He chuckled. "You two have been fun to watch, I'll grant you that. Well, I'll tell you what I didn't tell the sheriff's detective because he annoyed me to no end. What were they thinking, sending that greenhorn to talk to me?"

"Had to be crazy," I agreed. "What did Shelby tell you?"

"Saw her early the day after Thanksgiving. I was eating breakfast at Liddie's as usual, and she asked if she could join me. Said she needed to talk to someone impartial, get something off her chest."

"Can you tell me what?"

He sucked on a back tooth and frowned. "Said she saw something the day before that troubled her. Something she thought might be illegal that involved a friend. Asked me what she should do about it."

I drew in a deep breath. "What did you tell her to do?"

"Said if it were me and this person was really my friend, I'd talk to them about it. But that was just me."

I exhaled, feeling a small modicum of relief, or at least shared guilt. "She asked me the same thing right before she was killed. She squeezed me into a corner when I tried to get out of giving her advice and asked me if I'd ever been in a similar situation. I had, and I had to admit I didn't go to the police. She asked me if I'd have done it differently if I had the chance to do it again, and I couldn't lie and say I would, but that it wasn't necessarily the right thing for her to do." I rested my chin on my fist. "I wish now I'd just said nothing. I feel like I contributed to her death."

He leaned back in his lawn chair, his tanned jowls folded over with regret. "I know. This is one time I wished I'd kept my mouth shut. Or told her to go straight to the police. But she didn't give me any details, and, frankly, I didn't want to know any. I stupidly assumed it was something like smoking pot or shoplifting."

We stared at each other soberly, knowing that we'd both carry the guilt for this, deserved or not, for the rest of our lives.

I asked, "Did she give you any hints about who this person might be or what they did?"

"All she said was she had proof. And that it was in a safe place."

"No hint where? Her apartment was searched very thoroughly."

"Only that no one would ever think to look where she hid it. That's all she told me."

I stood up and threw my aluminum can in his recycling bag. "That's not a lot to go by, but thanks anyway."

I was halfway across the parking lot when I heard him yell my name. I turned and waited as he hurried up to me. "One more thing I just remembered. Don't know if you can make heads or tails of it, but she said it was a career buster. That this person would never work again if it were found out. That help any?"

"A career buster," I repeated. "It might. It narrows it down, anyway. Anything else?"

He shook his head. "That's it. Let me know if there's a memorial fund or anything, okay?"

"Sure will, Bud. Thanks."

A career buster, I thought as I walked the five blocks back to my truck. That eliminated one person—Bobby Sanchez. If those pictures of him were released, it would have embarrassed him and his family and he might have been razzed to death, but he'd still be able to cowboy. That left Roland, Greer, Olivia, and Parker. All of them had careers that were certainly worth ruining if they'd been caught doing the wrong thing. But what was that thing? Since all of them were involved in the art world, the only crime I could think of would be forgery. But which of them? And how? And why? The why would almost certainly be money. It appeared that all of them needed that to some degree or another.

I opened my truck door and climbed into the cab, sitting there for a moment tapping my fingers on the cold steering wheel. My speculations seemed ridiculous even to me. Art forgery and the fencing of it was a complicated business. And besides, it didn't make sense with the very slight clue that Isaac and I found—or rather hadn't found—the missing strip of negatives. I was sure that was the proof Shelby was talking about, and the strips numbered before or after it were taken outside, so it seemed a logical progression that the missing strip was, too. What had she taken pictures of? A person transporting forged paintings? Even if she had, the person doing it wouldn't have had the paintings out in the open—they would have been covered up. How would that be proof?

There was no doubt, though, that whatever proof she had and had told this "friend" about was something that scared him or her enough to kill her. Maybe not intentionally, but even if it was an accidental push in a fight, that person had left her out in the elements to die. Maybe she could have been saved had help been called right away. For some reason, until now it hadn't occurred to me how similar the situation was to how Jack had died. He, too, might have been saved if someone had just not walked away.

I suddenly felt a hot-white anger at this person who had cared so little about sacrificing both Shelby's and Kip's young lives.

I leaned my head on the steering wheel. *Let it go,* a voice warned me. *You've been down this path before. Why can't you just let the police do their job?*

Isaac's anguished face burst into my mind. *Because of that,* I answered. Because the police didn't care whether Wade ever made it home to his family. Because, though I knew most of them to be hard working, caring people, it was just a job to them, a file to be cleared off their desks. To Isaac—and to Wade—it might mean their very ability to emotionally survive.

I drove back to the museum determined to investigate deeper into the backgrounds of the four people I still suspected. In my office, I reread Emory's notes and thought about how I could find out more. While I was sitting there, my mind a complete and utter blank as to where to go next, the phone rang.

"I finally caught you. Good." Amanda's honeyed voice flowed through the receiver. "How's our boy doing?"

"Fine, I guess. Lying low like you instructed him. I, on the other hand, am going crazy trying to get a handle on who killed Shelby. Let me tell you what I've found out so far, and you tell me what you think." I ran Emory's and

Bud's information by her and told her how I thought that eliminated Bobby and that art forgery might be the reason why Shelby was killed. "What else could she have seen that would hurt someone's career?"

"Sounds logical enough," Amanda agreed. "Leilani's done a little deeper checking than your cousin and came up with almost similar results."

"Almost? What else did she find?" Leilani Jones, Lei to her friends, was a former San Celina detective who had been an investigator for the DA's office before going to work for Amanda. She was a smooth-skinned, strong-boned Samoan woman with a face as perfect as a beauty queen's. She was always getting pissed off because people talked to her in Spanish, thinking she was Latino. She once showed me how to hide a pistol in your cleavage and button up your blouse so it didn't show. I tried it, and she almost bust a gut laughing. Either her gun was too big, my bra too flimsy, or my cleavage too small. At any rate, she was the best investigator the DA's office had ever had, and they still hadn't forgiven Amanda for stealing her.

"Roland Bennett has a couple of ex-wives."

"So?"

"Three to be exact. It's number two who's so interesting."

"Who was she?"

"A Louella Ebersole."

"Why is she so interesting?"

"She's from Bakersfield."

I waited. "And?" I finally said, trying to keep the impatience out of my voice. Like most Southerners, Amanda dearly loved to draw her stories dramatically out to the enth degree.

"Okay, okay, I'll quit messin' with you. Louella Ebersole is Parker Williams's mother."

"What!"

"My reaction exactly. The plot thickens. They were apparently married for three years from the time that Parker was ten to thirteen. They were divorced citing irreconcilable differences. He moved to San Francisco shortly afterward and resumed his art dealing career. While he lived in Bakersfield—which, by the way, was right after he fled Texas—he didn't hold a job and yet always seemed to have plenty of money. Bakersfield PD records show that officers were dispatched out to their house four times on domestic violence calls. That's it for him.''

''Her ex-stepfather,'' I said, still unbelieving. ''Boy, she certainly pulled one over on us. I would have never guessed. The question is, are they involved in anything illegal together?''

''His record's been clean as the proverbial whistle since he left Bakersfield. Maybe he cleaned up his act.''

''Or maybe he just got better at not getting caught.''

''Touché, my little buddy. Next comes Olivia.''

''That new truck bothers me. I know she doesn't have the money to buy it.''

''You're right. It's leased. That was a cinch to find out.''

''Then I guess that eliminates her.''

''Not necessarily. There's still the jealousy factor because of the possible relationship between the deceased and our Mr. Sanchez.''

''That's pretty lame, though. I mean, killing someone over a man? Ruining your whole career, your whole *life* because some turkey cheated on you? I don't think so.''

''Maybe it's lame to you, but I saw it happen too many times to count when I was a prosecutor. Girl, I've seen women who killed their own babies to try and save a relationship with a man.''

I felt my stomach roil. ''I can't imagine that.''

''Then you need to watch a little more tabloid TV. Or come down and read through the old case files in the DA's office.''

''So Olivia's still a possibility. What about Greer?''

"Now there's an interesting situation. Did you know that her family's ranch was in Chapter eleven?"

"No! I heard they were kind of hard up but I didn't realize it had gone that far. They'd lost a good number of cattle because of some bad feed they bought, though I don't know exactly how many, and they've had some medical expenses for their grandmother that were real high." Then something occurred to me. "What about her personally? Rumor has it for years that she got a huge settlement from her ex-husband. Did she invest that in the ranch?"

"I'm one step ahead of you. I've got a call in to a friend of mine in San Francisco who has connections with a records clerk downtown. I should have her divorce settlement information by the end of the day. Want me to call you at home?"

"Definitely. That's everyone, I guess. We're still not any closer to figuring out which one killed Shelby, are we?"

"Hang in there. This kind of stuff is just like mining. Sometimes it just takes a little more digging. I still have Lei on the job, and we know what a pitbull she can be."

"Tell her hey for me and that Gabe says she can come back to work for him whenever she wants. He says he'll beat whatever you or the DA's office offers."

"Over my dead carcass," Amanda said cheerfully. "Watch your back now."

"Don't worry about that. I'm getting real good at it."

I hung up and dialed the ranch. Dove answered after three rings, laughing uproariously as she said hello.

"What's so funny?" I asked.

"Just Isaac," she said. "I swear that man's gonna make me bust a gut before he leaves with his stories. What's up, honeybun?"

"I need to talk to your . . . uh . . . boyfriend." I stuttered the last word. Their relationship still was a little weird for me.

"What's wrong, got a rock in your gullet?" she asked slyly.

"I'm fine," I said, attempting to be mature. "Is he there?"

A few seconds later he took the phone. "What's up, Benni?"

"I just wanted to tell you what I learned today." I started with the information Emory had found out and went through what Amanda and Lei had discovered. "It makes a good case against all of them except Bobby," I said. "Frankly, we're not any closer than when we found out all this."

"Then we—no, make that I—need to rattle some cages."

"You can keep that *we* in there."

"No, ma'am," he said. "You are going to stay out of this. We heard about your little escapade at the fashion show, so you're going to lie low while I do some questioning. I'm not about to get pummeled by either your grandmother or that formidable husband of yours. Besides, I'm worried about you myself."

"No way am I letting you go this alone, Isaac. We'll meet for breakfast tomorrow and formulate a game plan. Eight o'clock at Blind Harry's. Don't be late or you'll be buying." I hung up before he could protest. Just before I did, though, I heard an almost imperceptible click, and my stomach lurched. The new extension in the co-op's kitchen. I'd forgotten all about it.

I jumped up and sailed down the hallway to the kitchen, but by the time I got there, it was empty. I walked through the studios and across the breezeway to the crowded museum. Surveying the parking lot, I picked out Parker's car, Greer's car, and Olivia's truck.

That narrows it down, I thought. Maybe. I went back to the studios and started opening my stacked-up mail. There wasn't much I could do about it now. If one of them was involved with Shelby's and Kip's deaths, she knew now that

Isaac and I were watching her. At least she didn't know what we had up our sleeves. Our next move was still a secret to her.

Then again, it was to us, too.

16

I SPENT THE rest of the day trying to catch up on the paperwork pile that never seemed to recede. Emory phoned at four o'clock to tell me he wouldn't be home for dinner tonight.

"I'm driving down to Santa Barbara to buy a new suit and test-run a restaurant that was recommended by someone at the *Tribune*. I've already sent flowers and candy. Two dozen long-stemmed blush pink roses and a five-pound box of Godiva chocolates. Had to Federal Express the candy up from Santa Barbara."

I snorted over the phone. "Flowers and candy? If you think you're going to win Elvia's affections with some fancy hothouse roses and expensive imported chocolate, you're barking up the wrong tree, Mr. Hound Dog."

"Who said anything about giving them to Elvia? I sent them to her mama."

I threw back my head and laughed. "Oh, geez, you're good. If Mama Aragon falls in love with you, Elvia's a goner."

"The candy and flowers are just in gratitude for the wonderful tamales she served me for lunch today."

"How in the world did you get an invitation to lunch?"

"Sweetcakes, dear Señora Aragon does remember me from my childhood visits, and I merely did the neighborly thing and stopped by to pay my respects and ask her and Señor Aragon's permission to date their daughter."

I shook my head, still laughing, not at all surprised at his chutzpah. "You realize Elvia's going to kill you if—no, make that when—she finds out."

"I'll tell her on our wedding night."

"Emory, you could give Billy Graham lessons in faith."

"Hallelujah and amen, Sister Albenia. Don't wait up for me."

I arrived home at the same time as Gabe. His angled cheekbones were sharp with fatigue, so I didn't bring up what I'd learned about the suspects in Shelby's and Kip's murders. He certainly didn't look like he was in the mood to argue, and I knew I wasn't. We ordered pizza and spent a quiet night cruising the TV programs.

It was past ten o'clock and we were already in bed when the phone rang. He answered the phone, then handed it to me, an annoyed look on his face.

"Benni, it's Amanda."

I sat upright. "What's up?" I knew she wouldn't call this late unless it was something important.

"Sorry it took so long, but the friend who found out this information for me went to a party and just got home and called me herself. Your buddy Greer's personal financial situation looks very grim indeed."

"How's that?" I asked, ignoring Gabe's low grumbling next to me.

"Apparently she didn't get a very good settlement from her husband and since the divorce has had no other source of income except the ranch. And that's been pretty dicey this last year or so."

"But I heard he was very wealthy and that the divorce was because of his affair with some young girl. No offense

to your profession, but sounds like she got a real lame lawyer.''

"No offense taken, but there's more to the story. There's
a rumor—just a rumor, mind you—that my friend checked
out with a contact on the narcotics squad in San Francisco.
Story goes that Greer was caught selling nose candy to her
fancy artist friends. Hubby is rumored to have kept her on
a short leash money-wise, and she decided to procure her
little ole self a part-time job that didn't take too much time
away from her art. Anyway, one of the so-called artists
turned out to be an undercover cop. Bad luck on her part as
it was just around the time of her separation. Her husband
used his considerable political leverage to have the charges
disappear in exchange for an uncontested divorce with min-
imal financial gain on her part. She agreed, word has it, to
save her reputation and pain to her family. Not to mention
that really good canvas and paintbrushes are difficult to ob-
tain in prison.''

"Wow." I paused for a moment, still shocked. "Wow."

"You already said that. Certainly gives her some reason
to kill someone who found out about it.''

"So, maybe that's the illegal activity that Shelby was
telling me and Bud about. Maybe Greer offered her drugs.''
I felt the bed move. I turned and looked at Gabe, who was
sitting straight up now, frowning slightly at me.''Could be.
Is that it?''

"For now. What's your next step?''

I continued to look at my husband, our quilt covering his
lower torso, his frown now a glare. I considered pulling off
my tee shirt to distract him. "Uh, soothing the savage
beast.''

"I take it he didn't like what he heard?''

"You're taking it right. I'll call you tomorrow.''

She gave a deep chuckle. "Make it fun, girl. Just make
it fun.''

Gabe crossed his arms. "Tell me that wasn't what I thought it was."

I crawled across the covers to him, scooting between his legs. "That wasn't what you thought it was."

"Benni . . ." he warned.

"As you already know, it was Amanda." I quickly told him what she'd found out about Greer, rubbing my hands along his forearms as I talked. My physical cajoling didn't move him. "I'm sorry, but there's just so many reasons why I can't sit on the sidelines with this one."

"Let Wade fry," he said succinctly.

"It's not just Wade," I said sadly and, for the first time, told him about my conversation with Shelby and how responsible I felt for her death. How ashamed I felt for the inept way I'd handled her plea for advice.

"Oh, *niña*," he said, his voice pained, uncrossing his arms. "It's not your fault. She was a grown woman. She made her own choice."

"No, Gabe, she was a young girl, and I foolishly pointed her down a road that led to her death. I can't walk away from this one. Please understand that. I'm being so careful. Really, I am. That's the reason I'm telling you all this, so you can tell the sheriff's detectives. They probably already know a lot of it, but see, I found out something from Bud that they couldn't. Sometimes friends and family can help in a case—you said that yourself."

"You're taking on entirely too much responsibility for the circumstances," he said, taking my face in his hands. "But I've learned one thing. I may as well try to stop an earthquake as try to control you. You are a hard-headed, stubborn, insubordinate woman and you have been since the day we met."

"Insubordinate? This ain't the Marines, Friday."

"And for that you should be thankful. You would have been court-martialed ages ago." He slid under the covers. "Get under the blankets now. It's cold."

I settled down next to him, tracing a finger down his smooth brown upper arm. I touched it briefly with my lips, tasting his skin. "Shelby and Kip were so young and had such long lives ahead of them. I'm never going to understand why someone had to take that away from them for what was probably a stupid reason like money or jealousy."

He lay on his back and stared at the ceiling. "Pascal thinks it's for happiness."

"What? How can killing someone else bring anyone happiness?"

"He says that all men seek happiness. That it is everyone's ultimate goal and that the reason some go to war and some don't is the same desire, but interpreted in two different ways."

"How can going to war—or killing someone—bring anyone happiness?"

"The problem lies in our definition of happiness. It's changed since Aristotle's time. Today it's subjective, a feeling. If you feel happy, then you are happy. Back then, happiness was an objective state, not merely a feeling. The Greek word for happiness literally translates to mean 'good spirit,' or maybe a better interpretation would be 'good soul.' They believed to be happy was to be good. Now the world generally believes to be happy is to *feel* good. And if someone stands in the way of you feeling good, eliminate them. I've seen it a lot. Too much."

"But what kind of people feel good about hurting other people?"

He turned to me, kissing both corners of my mouth gently. "That, *querida*, is a mystery to everyone but God."

The next day, Saturday, I was up and dressed before Gabe had even cracked open an eyelid. For a change.

"What's the rush?" he asked. "You are not, I repeat, *not* riding in the Heritage Days parade." He sat up in bed and watched me attempt to braid my hair in front of my vanity table's mirror. Though a little past my shoulders now, it was still too short to do anything except make a stubby braid. I undid it with a grunt of irritation, bent over, and brushed it hard, not caring if I ended up with hair as big and curly as a Texas beauty queen's.

I flipped my hair back and said, "I heard you the first time you growled your orders yesterday, Sergeant Friday."

He smiled serenely. "Just wanted to clarify. Where are you going?"

"First I'm meeting Isaac at Blind Harry's for breakfast. Then we're going to watch the parade from Elvia's office window. The rest of the day I'll spend at the museum. It's going to be a busy one. We close at five though, so everyone can go to the fiesta. I may take time to go by the rodeo grounds and watch the cow plop contest. I have square number thirteen. Guess that means I won't win."

"I bought two but I don't remember their numbers. I assume someone somewhere has a record of it."

"Probably. What're you doing?"

"Eating a leisurely breakfast. Reading the newspaper. Then I'll just probably wander around downtown and check on things. I'll be wearing my beeper, so call if you need anything."

"How about I meet you for dinner? Six o'clock at the fiesta? In front of Lupe's tamale cart, wherever she decides to park it?"

"Sounds good. Stay alert. Don't go anywhere alone. Don't, I repeat, don't close up the museum by yourself. Maybe I should assign someone to stay at the museum, even though we're stretched to the limit."

"Yes, *sir*. Yes, *sir*. Not on your life, *sir*. Permission to leave, *sir*."

"Woman, your smart mouth will be the ruin of me yet." He threw a pillow at me, which I dodged, laughing at his slow reflexes. I'd already partaken of my morning caffeine.

I blew him a kiss. "*Hasta la vista.*"

Isaac was waiting for me at Blind Harry's, where it was more crowded than usual for a Saturday morning. His face was sober and hard this morning, and I noticed a few people staring at him hesitantly, as if they recognized his face and were working up the courage to approach him. His expression obviously kept them from it, and I wondered if he'd developed that forbidding persona on purpose. It occurred to me for the first time what a burden fame could be, especially when the everyday problems of life made a person desire anonymity so they could suffer without being judged. He clutched a mug of black coffee in his monstrous hand as if he thought someone would snatch it from him. I bought a couple of blueberry muffins, a cup of coffee, and joined him.

"Bad night?" I asked, sitting down across from him.

His eyelids drooped slightly, his voice a hoarse whisper. "It hits me at the oddest times. I've been through this before. You'd think I'd have remembered what it was like."

I nodded in understanding.

He leaned forward, resting his elbows on the wooden table. "So, what are you up to today?"

"My orders from the CEO are to lie low. Gabe's feeling a bit tense about the bathroom incident Thursday night. He thinks we're being just a little too successful about—excuse the pun—flushing out Shelby's killer. He's afraid that next time the person will actually try to hurt one of us."

He rubbed his thumb over the edge of his mug, a thoughtful look in his dark eyes. "He's more concerned about you than me, I'm sure. But he's right. I feel incredibly guilty about getting you so involved. You're physically an easier target than me, and this person is obviously a coward."

"You did not get me involved. I got myself involved. And you have no reason to feel guilty. I would be doing this whether you were here or not. And you called it right when you said this person is a coward. So far all they've done is play silly little tricks. Believe me, I've experienced worse."

He gave a sheepish smile and picked up a muffin, slowly breaking off a piece. "There's something else that impels me to ask you to do what Gabe requests. I received a lecture from your grandmother last night after the fingers of gossip reached out to the ranch with news of your little incident Thursday night."

"And you still have ears?" I asked, laughing.

He touched one ear and smiled. "They're singed, but still functioning. She's nervous because this person has picked you to harass."

I laid my hand on his. "Don't worry. I promised Gabe I'd be careful today and I will keep that promise. But I have a real feeling that this is all going to come to a head soon. If it's any of the people we suspect, they aren't professional killers, and I think their guilty conscience will compel them to show themselves sooner or later."

He shook his head doubtfully. "I've been on this earth a lot longer than you have and I don't share your belief that justice eventually triumphs. Some people just plain don't feel guilty. I'm going to echo your husband now and urge you to be very careful."

"I said I would. Do I need to sign it in blood?" I asked, trying not to sound exasperated.

"No, just your word is sufficient. Dove told me about the last few escapades you'd been involved with, and, to quote her, 'Lord knows she's got a head as hard as a coconut, but even she can't take another head injury.' "

I laughed and stood up, picking up my coffee and muffin. "I'll wear a helmet, okay? I promise, promise, promise that I'll be careful. Now, are you coming with me to watch the parade? I've got a very *safe* bird's-eye view from Elvia's office window."

He shook his head no. "I'll watch it from ground level. Better pictures from there. Then I've got an appointment out at the Wheeler ranch today. They're letting me tag along and snap a few pictures."

"Letting you?" I teased. "You have to know they are probably thrilled out of their minds to be included in your book. Are you going to the fiesta? It's in the field near the rodeo grounds."

"Wouldn't miss it. Dove and I will see you there."

"I'll look for you. A little inside tip. Try Lupe's tamales. They are like manna from heaven."

"I'll make sure to sample one."

I headed upstairs to Elvia's office, where there were already ten or eleven people laughing and eating off the fruit and croissant platter on her credenza. Elvia, as usual, was on the phone, probably tracking down a lost shipment of books.

Emory, who was gone before I was up this morning, was drinking a cup of espresso over by the window. I walked over and tickled his side. "Hey, cuz, you must've rose with the chickens this morning."

He smiled down at me. "I'm trying to give you and the *señor* as much privacy as I can. Besides, I had a lot of things to do to get ready for tonight." He glanced surreptitiously at a sour-faced Elvia. Obviously the person on the other end of the line was not telling her what she wanted to hear.

"She's actually going through with it," I said. "I don't believe it."

He set his tiny espresso cup down on a nearby table. "Ought to smack you for that, sweetcakes. You were selling me goods you never expected to deliver."

I smiled innocently at him. "Just using a technique taught to me by the master manipulator himself. Let's not forget the time twenty-five-some-odd years ago when you promised the two older Shanley boys a new carburetor for their pickup. They showed up at our ranch two hours after you were on your way back to Arkansas."

"That was different. They were going to beat the crap

out of me. I was desperate.'' He grinned at me. ''Worked, though.''

''Don't be too sure,'' I warned. ''Rumor has it that they heard you're back in town and they're hunting you down for payment.''

''Not to worry, Albenia Louise. I have a platinum American Express card. A few beers, a couple of steaks, and they'll be right as rain.''

''And a new carburetor if they're still miffed?''

''Whatever it takes to save my precious hide.''

''Like I said, I learned from the best.''

''Also, I haven't forgotten that you're paying for this.''

''A hundred bucks, that was our deal. Bill me.''

''Don't think I won't.''

We crowded to the window when the strains of San Celina's high school marching band started playing the always popular ''76 Trombones.'' Like all small town parades, the San Celina Heritage Days parade was extremely long on enthusiasm and a bit short on professionalism. Most of the floats consisted of trucks decorated with a mixture of home-grown roses and mums and handmade tissue paper flowers with a few spangly, semiprofessional-looking floats left over and refashioned from San Celina's Mardi Gras parade. There were a lot of costumed people on horseback and every high school marching band in the county as well as accompanying drill teams. When I saw my dad and my uncle Arnie ride by dressed in 1880s western clothes, I hung out the open window and called to them. Daddy turned and waved at me, throwing me a big smile. At the same time, I caught a glimpse of Roland Bennett across the street, watching the parade from the offices above his gallery. The hateful look he gave me froze the words I was getting ready to shout at them. I moved away from the window, more unnerved than I wanted to admit.

When the parade was over, I drifted over to the combination espresso/coffee machine, where a scowling Elvia was holding a small black espresso cup.

"Did you cuss those people out good?" I asked, deciding against the espresso and settling for a plain cup of coffee.

"This is the second time Random House has shipped my order to some horror bookstore in Massachusetts called Black Harry's. They won't do it again."

"I'd hope not. Are you ready for your date tonight?" I was taking my life in my hands by asking, but as usual my curiosity got the better of me.

"He sent flowers and candy to Mama," she said, her voice dripping scorn. "She's already buying bride's magazines."

I sipped my coffee. "You could do worse." Now I was really asking for it.

Her scowl deepened. "One date, *amiga*, and I use that word *friend* loosely. Then I'll drop him off at the train station myself."

I looked at her over my coffee cup. "Don't forget the best part of marrying Emory. You and I would be related. About ten times removed, but cousins nevertheless."

"That's supposed to be an incentive?"

I grinned and wiggled my fingers good-bye. "Have fun."

At the museum I was kept busy helping with tours and answering questions. There wasn't one minute I was alone, which I patiently informed Gabe each of the five times he called.

"Would you quit worrying?" I said the last time he called at about four-thirty. "I'll be closing up in a half hour, and D-Daddy and a bunch of other people are here and will remain here while I close up. I'll see you in front of Lupe's cart at six o'clock."

"Better make it six-thirty," he said. "I'm having a quick briefing with my field sergeants at five-thirty, and it may run longer than I anticipate."

"Okay. By the way, I didn't get away to the cow plop contest. Did you see it?"

"Number fourteen won, though it was debatable for a moment with a slight overlap problem. The judge actually had to measure length and width."

"Just my luck. Oh, well. See you at the fiesta."

I was locking up, with D-Daddy fiddling with something on his little Toyota pickup, when Olivia and Bobby drove up. Surprised that they were back together, I watched Bobby step down from the high cab and walk toward me. Involuntarily I stiffened when he reached the hacienda's long porch. It was dark already, and the lone, yellowish porch light hardened his angry face.

"I've got something to say to you," he said.

I looked over at D-Daddy. Frowning, he reached into his tool chest and picked up his Sears Craftsman hammer. I held up my hand, assuring him things were under control.

"What's that, Bobby?" I asked.

"You've been asking questions about me and Olivia."

I didn't answer, but couldn't help wondering what they'd heard. And from whom.

His voice shook slightly. "That stupid little rich girl did nothing but cause trouble since she came. Maybe we're all better off without her, so why can't you just let things be?"

I gave him a steady look. "Because, Bobby, someone murdered her, and that's wrong."

He touched his Stetson nervously. "There's no proof it's murder. She could've just fell. That's what everyone's saying."

"And what about Kip? He just fell with his head in the creek?"

He let out a string of Spanish curse words that were very familiar to me, having grown up around Elvia's brothers and being married to Gabe.

"Watch your mouth, Bobby," I said when I recognized

the Spanish word for whore. "I don't take that kind of abuse in English or Spanish."

He glared at me. "You're just harassing us 'cause we're Mexican. You're assuming if there's violence involved, it must be us hotheaded *Mexicanos*. You're just like that *pendejo* brother-in-law of yours."

"And you are full of crap, Bobby Sanchez. First, Wade isn't my brother-in-law, and second, in case you missed it, I am married to a man who's half Mexican. And, believe me, I know better than anyone that violence comes in all races, creeds, and colors so you can take that attitude and—"

D-Daddy interrupted my tirade. "You okay, *ange*?" He caressed the heavy hammer in his calloused hands. Bobby frowned at him. Through all of this, Olivia stared blank-faced at me through the truck window.

"I'm fine, D-Daddy," I said. "Bobby was just leaving. Right?"

He spit on the ground and whipped around, saying something inaudible to Olivia when he climbed in the passenger side of the truck. They peeled out of the parking lot, kicking up gravel and dirt.

"You been snooping again, eh, *ange*?" D-Daddy said, shaking his head.

"No . . . yes . . . well, sort of. You know the cops suspect Wade. I'm just trying to get him back home to his wife and kids and make sure whoever did this to Shelby pays." I didn't want to go into how I felt partially responsible for her death.

"The mister, he's not likin' it, no, sir, I bet."

"You'd win that bet for sure, D-Daddy. Thanks for your help."

He stuck his hammer in his leather tool belt. "Don't need no gun, me. Craftsman upside the head do just fine."

I laughed and patted his arm. "Thank goodness it didn't come to that."

The rodeo grounds were only a mile or so up the road

from the folk art museum. By the time I arrived, the dirt and gravel parking lot was so crowded with people that I didn't worry for one moment about being alone. Miguel, one of Elvia's brothers, and a young blond female officer I knew slightly, Bliss Girard, were stationed at the opening of the parking lot.

I rolled down my window, nodded at Bliss, and asked Miguel, "Where's the action, Officer?"

"Lupe's run out of tamales once already, so you'd better hotfoot it over there if you want any," he said, resting his forearms on the window edge and leaning into the cab. "*El Patrón* is around somewhere."

"I'll find him. Have fun."

"I will as soon as my shift ends at . . ." He checked his large black watch. "Eight o'clock."

I stood outside the rodeo ring, studying the list of evening events—the trick riding show, the pig races, dancing by native Chumash Indians, and then a concert by a local band, The San Celina Range Riders. I wandered over to the carnival grounds where the smell of cotton candy; hot dogs; fried tacos; and barbecued tri-tip, a San Celina staple, seduced my tastebuds. The flashing lights of the concession booths, the cajoling shout of the carnival barkers urging me to win a faded stuffed animal with "one thin dime," and the exhilarating screams from the people riding the neon-lit Tilt-a-Whirl and Haunted House rides brought back fond memories of when I was one of those teenagers grasping the worn metal bars, Jack next to me, laughing in my ear.

But the memories didn't ache the way they would have six months ago. I glanced at my watch—five-thirty. In an hour I'd meet my husband at the tamale stand and sweet talk him into riding the giant Ferris Wheel with me where we could kiss when our bucket reached the top.

I was eating a corn dog and watching a couple of teenage boys try to win stuffed tigers for their girlfriends when Isaac and Dove walked up. She had her arm looped through his, something I was *almost* getting used to.

"How're they doing?" Isaac asked, watching the boys toss the ping-pong balls into the fishing bowls.

I laughed. "So far all they've won is five goldfish."

"Which will be dead by next week," Dove said wryly. "I know. I've officiated at many a goldfish funeral myself."

I grinned. "Hey, it was the only carnival game I could win. What're you two up to?"

"Just taking in the sights," Isaac said. "Anything new on the investigative front?" His face was anxious in the flashing carnival lights.

I hesitated, then decided not to tell him about the incident between me and Bobby or about Roland's look. Telling them would serve no purpose, and I didn't want to ruin their evening. "I think we're at the point where we just have to wait for someone to show their hand. Gabe says sometimes it's like that."

"Then let's just have some fun," Dove said, glancing up at Isaac's troubled face, then giving me a subtle look that said change the subject. "C'mon, honeybun. We'll make Isaac win us one of them useless stuffed animals. I want that polar bear there. Kinda reminds me of someone I know." She smiled at Isaac and pointed to the prizes at one of the basketball toss games. "how good are you at shooting hoops?"

He laughed and shook his head. "Horrible. Let's try something else." He held out his other arm to me, and I slipped mine through it. "Better yet, How about I buy you a churro and a lemonade instead?"

We strolled over to the churro stand and while we were waiting in line, I glanced over to a Heritage Days history display set up on some portable walls. "Get me a churro, but no lemonade," I told Isaac. "I'll be back in a minute."

I walked over to a poster tacked up on one of the portable walls. The joint efforts of the Cal Poly history and art departments had produced an eight-foot-by-eight-foot poster using india ink and bright acrylic paint. It showed the mission plaza during the mid-1800s with burros and Franciscan fathers and Chumash Indians and Spanish women grinding corn for tortillas and hundreds of other people doing things common in San Celina County's varied, multicultural history. To add some fun to the project and to encourage people to really study their work, a large banner was tacked across the top of the paper mural—*¿Donde esta Waldo?*—where's Waldo?

I laughed and searched for the skinny cartoon man in his striped shirt, spit-curled hair, and funny hat. I was still searching when Isaac and Dove walked over with my churro.

"Thanks," I said, taking the long, doughnut-like Mexican pastry from him. I licked the brown sugar that fell on my hand. "Isn't this great?" I nodded over at the mural. "I haven't found him yet. These things drive me crazy because he's always right there in front of my face, and I never see him even though I look over the spot a million times."

Then it hit me. Something so obvious that I could have kicked myself for not thinking of it before. The best way to hide anything. *In plain sight.*

I grasped Isaac's arm. "I know where the negatives are."

17

HE THREW HIS churro on the ground. "Where?"

"Back at the museum. At least I think they might be." I tossed my churro in a nearby trash can. "I'm going to go see."

"Not alone, you're not," Dove said.

I glanced at my watch. "Shoot. I told Gabe I'd meet him at Lupe's tamale cart at six-thirty, but I have to go see if I'm right." I turned to Dove. "Look, Isaac can go with me to the museum to see if what I think is right. Would you go meet Gabe and tell him I'm going to be a few minutes late? I don't want him to worry."

"And what am I supposed to tell him about where you're at?"

"Just tell him I had to go get something at the museum and that Isaac went with me. That shouldn't worry him."

She crossed her arms. "Only if you tell me what it is you're going to get since I'm missing all the fun."

I took a deep breath. "I might be shooting blanks here, but I think, I'm hoping, that Shelby hid the negatives in the photo album she gave me the day before Thanksgiving. What better place to hide the evidence of something illegal than with the police chief's wife?"

Isaac nodded. "It's exactly how Shelby would think. She loved reading Nancy Drew mysteries and watching *Murder, She Wrote* on TV." He grabbed my hand. "Let's go."

"Y'all be careful," Dove said.

"We will. If anyone follows us, we'll come right back and get Gabe. I promise."

Isaac kept a close eye on the passenger side mirror during the half-mile drive to the museum. "No one's behind us," he said, his voice tense.

"I didn't think there would be, but it doesn't hurt to be safe."

The museum parking lot was dimly lit by a single security light. I fumbled with the keys in the cold night air and finally opened the front door. Once inside, I quickly locked it behind us. "The album's in my office."

Inside my office, I opened the bottom desk drawer and pulled out the handmade leather photo album.

"Just a minute," Isaac said, taking it out of my hand. He stared at the album, running his hand over the soft leather, fingering the bones and feathers she'd carefully fashioned. He traced the lines of my brand. "She made this?"

I nodded silently.

He swallowed hard, then tightened his jaw. "Let's see what's in here."

There were twenty-five pages with a photograph on each page. She'd mounted them in the old-fashioned way with those tiny triangular picture holders that filled all Dove's photo albums.

We pulled out each photo, and on the twenty-second one we hit pay dirt. On the back of the photo was taped a strip of four negatives in a plastic holder. Isaac held them up to the light in my office, his gray eyes squinting.

"What do you see?" I asked eagerly.

He scanned the negatives. "One is looking through a window—it appears to be of a person painting. Looks like

she took them with a telephoto. One's of just some trees
and bushes—nothing distinct. And one's of a license plate.
The last one of two people with some cows.'' He shook his
head and handed them to me. ''My eyes aren't as good as
they once were, and I don't have a magnifying loop to see
them better. You take a look.''

I peered at the strips, but couldn't make out any more
details than he could. ''I guess we'll have to get some pictures printed.''

''I can do it if I have the right equipment. At least I can
make a contact sheet. That would show more detail.''

I slipped the negatives back into the holder and leaned
against my desk. ''Probably I should just give them to Gabe
to hand over to the Sheriff's Department. If only I could be
sure what was on them.''

Isaac looked at me soberly. ''Are you afraid one of the
people might be Wade?''

I bit my bottom lip, not wanting to answer. ''I just want
to know what it is we're handing over to the police.''

''I want her killer caught,'' Isaac said, his voice sharp.

''I know.'' I looked at the strip again. The three people
in one picture all wore Stetsons, but their faces were indis-
tinct. ''Too bad she couldn't have gone that extra step and
made prints for us.'' I started putting the pages back into
the album. Then an idea came to me, inspired by something
Isaac had said about Shelby. Maybe it was just juvenile and
silly enough to be right. I picked at the edges of the leather
cover.

''What are you doing?'' Isaac asked.

''You said she loved reading Nancy Drew books, right?''

''Yes. So?''

''So, I think she did make things easy for us. I think
there are prints . . .'' I peeled back the leather cover. ''And
here they are!'' Wrapped in protective plastic were four
5 x 7 black-and-white photographs. He crowded next to me,
and we looked at the pictures.

Greer was the person painting. Shelby had apparently been taking photographs around Greer's cabin and saw the opportunity to capture an artist working unawares. I peered closer at the paintings, thoughts of forgery dancing in my head. Was that how she was making the money to support herself, to keep her family's ranch going?

But the paintings weren't copies of Remington or Russell. They seemed to be her own original oils of ranch life. I looked intently at the picture of the license plate. It was a Montana plate—muddy and old—attached to what appeared to be an RV.

The third picture said it all.

"Oh, no," I said, staring at the picture of Kip and Greer loading cattle onto a truck. "This is why Shelby was killed. Greer did it when Shelby told her about this picture."

Isaac gave me a confused look. "Why? She's just loading cattle onto a truck. She's a rancher. Seems natural enough."

I pointed to the side of one of the cows—a Hereford-Angus mix. "Sure, if the brand wasn't mine."

He looked up at me, shocked. "Cattle rustling? My granddaughter was killed for a bunch of cows?"

"Appears so," I said, feeling a sadness at how life can spiral out of control. "Greer was stealing from her friends. That would certainly be worth killing someone over, because not only would it ruin her art career, she'd go to prison and humiliate her family in front of the whole ranching community."

"Do you think her family knew?"

"No, they didn't," Greer answered from the doorway.

Isaac and I jumped at the sound of her voice. When we saw the .45 revolver in her hand, Isaac put his arm in front of me much the same way Dove used to when I was a child and she had to stop the truck quickly.

"How'd you get in?" I demanded.

"Benni, grow up. Keys to this place float around here

like pollen.'' She walked over and grabbed the photos out of my hands, looking down at the handmade photo album. ''So that's where she hid them. I didn't even know she'd given you that album. Smart girl.'' She nodded her approval of Shelby's cleverness. ''But not smart enough to keep what she saw to herself.''

I saw Isaac's face start to redden and I touched his arm and said in a low voice, ''Don't.''

Greer calmly studied Isaac's angry face, pointing the gun at his chest. ''Listen to her, Mr. Lyons. I grew up using guns and I'll shoot you, I swear I will.'' Her voice trembled slightly.

Stay calm, I told myself. *Words are all you have at this point.*

''Greer,'' I said softly, ''why would you steal from your friends?'' *Keep her talking*, I thought, *and pray that Gabe gets annoyed enough to track us down after Dove tells him where we went and why.*

Framed in the doorway, dressed in old jeans and a brown Carhartt working jacket, standing straight and proud, her white hair a halo around her head, she looked like a figure in one of her own western paintings. Her lined face clouded with sorrow. ''I had to, Benni. Bradley left me with nothing, and the ranch is going down fast. It hasn't really made enough money to support any of us in years. I couldn't expect my brothers to take care of me and I had to live. I had to buy paint supplies. Look, I didn't steal from just one person—I spread it around. And I only took from the people who could afford the losses.'' She explained it to us in a reasonable voice, not giving any indication that she comprehended how serious her actions were.

''Why didn't you just get a job?'' I blurted out, quickly regretting the words once they were spoken. What if it set her off?

''Doing what?'' she asked in a calm, rational voice. ''I'm fifty-four years old, Benni. Working on the ranch and being an executive's wife—that's all I can do. Besides, I want to paint. That's *all* I've ever wanted. What could I do? I didn't have a choice.''

"Please, Greer," I said. "Let Isaac and me help you. You're in too far now. You'll never get away with it if you hurt us."

Her face stiffened, then as suddenly as it did, it fell again. Her mood changes made my heart beat furiously in fear. "I'm so tired, Benni. So tired of trying to figure all of this out. All I want to do is paint. I wish Shelby had minded her own business. I wish you'd left this alone. I was only going to do it for a few more months. Once we sold the land on the highway and I made my name as an artist, I wouldn't be forced to do it anymore. Timing—it was all just bad timing.''

"Greer, please give me the gun. Let us help you."

"Shelby was an accident," she said, her voice a hoarse whisper. "And Kip—he sort of was, too. I didn't want to kill him. He'd been in on it, but he panicked when Shelby found out. And then she died, and I couldn't take the chance he'd crack." She rocked backwards on the heels of her boots. "I'm so tired."

I felt Isaac shift next to me, dropping the arm he'd been holding in front of me.

"Don't try anything stupid," she said, shifting from one foot to the other.

"Greer, you need help." I kept my voice low and even. "We can get you help. Just give me the gun and then you can rest."

She looked up at me, her eyes glazed with tears. "I could be famous. I'm good. I'm a good artist."

"Yes," I said soothingly, "you're a good artist. One of the best."

She looked at me sadly. "Turn around, Benni."

I stared back at her, feeling my knees tremble slightly, thinking, *this is it.* I swallowed over the hard knot in my throat and took one last chance. "No, Greer, I won't. If you're going to shoot me, you'll have to look me in the eyes while you're doing it." I prayed that she wasn't so far gone emotionally that she'd accept my challenge.

"Turn around or I'll shoot Isaac in the heart," she said, her voice calm. I turned and looked at Isaac.

He nodded. "Do as she says, Benni."

"No," I said. "She's going to kill us anyway. I want her to look at me when she does."

"I'm not going to kill you," Greer said, her voice weary. She stepped back out of the doorway into the narrow hallway. "Just turn around. I'm going to lock you in this room and take Isaac with me as a hostage so I can make a better deal with the DA. I know I can't get away with this, Benni. I'm not stupid. You're the police chief's wife. How would I get away with killing you?"

Her voice sounded so calm and reasonable that I reluctantly did as she asked.

"Okay, Isaac," she said. I could hear her labored breathing in the quiet room. "*Your* granddaughter ruined my life, so here's a picture for *you* to take to your grave."

The gun exploded.

I screamed and started to turn around.

Isaac grabbed me and shoved my face into his chest.

"Don't look, honey," he said, the words catching in his throat. "It was her last act of friendship to you. Accept it."

18

THREE DAYS LATER they buried Greer. Her funeral was huge; mourners overflowed the Methodist church she'd attended her whole life. It was a literal sea of tan and black cowboy hats and shiny boots. I arrived right before it started and slipped into a back pew. The minister read the twenty-third Psalm and spent a good part of the sermon talking about God's great and tender mercies. I said a prayer for her family and for Isaac and left Greer's, Shelby's, and Kip's fates up to the God I believed was the author of both perfect love and perfect justice. Then I cried at the waste and sadness of it all.

I left as quickly as I could after the service. In the parking lot next to my truck, Buck, one of Greer's two older brothers, saw me as he leaned against a Shannon ranch truck, inhaling quick desperate puffs from his cigarette. His eyes were shadowed by his gray dress Stetson. After a few seconds, he gave the slightest of nods, acknowledging that the family didn't hold me to blame. A great weight lifted off my shoulders.

The day after the funeral, I drove out to the ranch to take Wade to the airport. Isaac and Dove were sitting on the front porch when I drove up, Isaac's travel-scarred leather suitcases sitting next to him. I walked up the steps and leaned against the porch railing, facing them.

"You going somewhere?" I asked Isaac.

"I have work back in Chicago," he said, "things I've put off that can't be postponed any longer. But I'll be back. When the book comes out."

"You're actually going to do a book?" I asked. "When in the world did you find time to take enough pictures?"

He handed me a stack of eight-by-ten photographs. "It's what I did to keep from going crazy while all this was being played out. I'm calling it *Riding Light—California Ranch Women.* It'll contain both my and Shelby's photographs so she'll get her book. I only wish she was here to see it."

Dove put her hand over his and patted it gently. I sat down cross-legged on the porch in front of them and flipped through the photographs. Many of them I recognized from Shelby's months following me around the ranch—some were from the album she'd hidden the negative in. One of Isaac's was of me sitting next to the creek wrapped up in his leather and fleece coat. He'd caught in me a wary, watching expression somewhere between smiling and frowning. One hand was bunched in a fist, the other laying on my thigh, palm open and vulnerable. His photograph did what all the best ones do—tell a story. In that split second, he captured all the feelings I'd experienced in the last two years.

"That one's called 'A Woman Torn,' " he said.

I nodded and kept going through the photographs of friends at local ranches, pausing at one of Dove looking out of a side window at the Historical Museum. Her gaze was wistful and longing, looking beyond the photographer's lens; she leaned out slightly, her arms resting on the ledge, holding her battered Stetson in one hand. Behind her it was dark, but the sun lit up her face, and in her eyes you could see the young girl she once was.

"I love this one," I said. "I want a copy."

"Certainly. I'm calling it 'Dove in the Window,' " he said. "And you'll both get copies of the book as soon as they roll off the presses."

"That's a quilt pattern," I said, surprised.

He smiled. "I know. Dove suggested it to me."

"Well, now, honeybun," Dove said, speaking for the first time. "Looks like we're all saying good-bye to people today." She nodded at the side of the house where Wade had turned the corner and was walking toward us. He carried a dark blue duffel bag. The bruise on his cheek was already starting to turn lavender around the edges.

I'd called Wade a few hours after the incident at the museum on Saturday night. His heavy sigh had been audible over the phone.

"I can go home now," he said, his voice catching.

"Yes," I answered, feeling sad, but also relieved. "You can go home now."

"I'm going to try to get Sandra back. But if I can't, I'm going to be a good daddy to my kids. That much I can do."

"Yes, Wade, that much you can do."

I stood up, handed the photographs back to Isaac, and went down the steps to meet Wade.

"Ready to go?" I asked.

He nodded. "My plane leaves at noon. I can't believe I'll be back in Texas by suppertime."

Just then, Gabe drove up in his Corvette. He stepped out and walked over to Wade and me. They nodded at each other but didn't speak.

"You got your car back!" I said. "What's Emory doing for wheels?"

Gabe smiled down at me. "He bought a car this morning and said he wouldn't be needing mine anymore."

"He bought a car! What kind? Why in the world would he do that? Is he planning on driving back to Arkansas?"

"It's a brand-new Cadillac Seville. And I'm not supposed to tell you this, but for once I'm going to be the one who lets the cat out of the bag. Goaded on by his, in my opinion, questionably victorious date with Elvia, he's decided not to go back to Arkansas, but to stay here in San Celina to wine and woo her. Apparently he's talked himself into a job at the *Tribune* and is having all his worldly possessions shipped out. He was perusing the real estate ads in the paper after you left this morning.''

"He didn't tell me!" I said. "That little twerp. He's moving out here! Oh, geez, the *Tribune*!" I turned to Dove and gave her an accusing look. "Did you know about this?"

She smiled secretively. "I reckon I'd heard a little something about it. But you know me—unlike some people, I don't have a leaky mouth."

I brought a palm up to my cheek. "Elvia! Has anyone told her yet?"

Gabe laughed and ruffled my hair. "Emory said that he was leaving that for you to do."

"Oh, man, she's going to kill me." I grinned. "Emory living here in San Celina. That makes me real happy."

"I can tell." He turned to Wade. "So, Harper, you're heading back to Texas."

Wade nodded. "Reckon it's time."

Gabe looked at him a moment, then held out a hand. "I hope everything works out for you and your family."

Wade took his hand and shook it, nodding over in my direction. "Thanks, Ortiz. You take good care of her now. She deserves it."

"I know," Gabe said.

Wade touched the brim of his hat, then turned to me. "I'll wait for you in the truck."

"I'll be there in a minute," I said.

Dove and Isaac came down from the porch and joined me and Gabe on the front lawn. I looked up at this giant snowy-haired man who, in the short time I'd known him, had managed to steal a tiny piece of my heart.

"I'm going to miss you," I said to him, "I think."

"That's probably the nicest thing she's ever said to me," he said, winking at Dove.

"So, you really will come back and visit?" I asked. "That's not just words?"

"You bet, Benni Harper." He looked down at Dove, his face soft. "I have relationships here now. I'll be back." Then he reached down and pulled me up into a big hug. It felt like being squeezed by a huge polar bear. "Now, you'd better turn your back," he said after releasing me.

"Why's that?"

" 'Cause I'm going to kiss your grandmother good-bye, and I don't want you coming after me with a shotgun."

Then he did. Full on the mouth. And she kissed him back. With a little more fervor than made me comfortable.

Gabe looked at me and grinned.

"Well," I said with resignation, "I just hope we're still that enthusiastic when we're their age."

"Count on it, *querida*," Gabe replied. "I'll go say hi to your dad and give them some privacy. See you at home."

I climbed into the truck and drove down our long drive to the highway.

"Man, there is a lot of memories wrapped up in this truck, isn't there?" Wade said as we pulled onto the empty road.

"Yes, there are."

He leaned back in the duct-taped vinyl seat. "Isn't nothing left of Harper's Herefords anymore except for memories." He stared out the window at the passing bare fields. "I'm going to miss San Celina, but you know, that part of my life is over. It's time to move on."

"Yes, I think it is." We rode silently for about a half mile or so.

"Benni," he said, breaking the quiet, "I just . . . I just want to say thanks again. For believing in me when no one else did. For getting that lawyer when I needed her. For . . . everything. I don't know how I can ever repay you."

"Your debt was paid a long ways back, bro," I said, using Jack's old nickname for him. "Don't even think about it."

Then it occurred to me. What I had to do. I hit the brakes and stopped the truck in the middle of the empty road. "Get out," I said.

"What?" He stared at me like I was crazy.

I climbed out of the cab, taking my Levi's jacket with me. He came around the truck, his face confused.

"What's wrong?" he asked.

I held out the truck keys. "Take it. It's time for me to move on, too."

He stared at the keys, his face crumpling a little.

"I mean it, Wade. Have you got enough gas money to get home?"

He nodded and slowly took them. As they left my hand, I felt my heart give a little dip.

"Are you sure you want to do this?" he asked.

I nodded. "Whatever I need to sign for you to take ownership, you send it to me and I will."

He looked back down the road toward the ranch. "Do you need a ride back home . . . or to town?"

I shook my head. "It's only a mile or so back to the ranch. I'll walk. I need to do some thinking anyway."

He pulled me into a tight hug. I deeply inhaled the scent of him—the smell of clove gum, leather, and Old Spice. The same aftershave Jack always wore. "Good-bye," I whispered.

"Blondie," he said, his voice muffled in my hair, "you take care now. You be happy."

"I am, Wade," I said, tears coming to my eyes. "I already am."

I watched him drive away until all that was left was the faint sound of the muffler that would need replacing soon.

I started walking back toward the ranch and, halfway

there, Gabe appeared in the Corvette. He pulled over and climbed out.

"Looks like you lost your wheels," he said, leaning against the side of the car juggling his keys from one hand to the other.

"Didn't lose them. Gave them away."

"I thought you might."

I made a face at him. "You did not. You think you know me so well."

"Better than you realize." His face grew sober. "Are you all right?"

I smiled and nodded. "Never been better."

"Looks like I'm your ride."

"Appears so."

"Actually, it doesn't look like you have much of a choice."

"Friday, we always have choices."

He studied me for a moment. "So, what's yours?"

"It might depend on where you're headed."

He looked down the road toward the ranch, then the opposite way toward town. "Does it really matter?"

I thought about it for a moment, then answered, "Not as long as I can drive halfway."

He gave a delighted laugh and tossed me the keys.